HONOR BOUND

HONOR BOUND

EDWARD GRANT RIES

TATE PUBLISHING
AND ENTERPRISES, LLC

Honor Bound
Copyright © 2015 by Edward Grant Ries. All rights reserved.

No part of this publication may be reproduced, stored in a retrieval system or transmitted in any way by any means, electronic, mechanical, photocopy, recording or otherwise without the prior permission of the author except as provided by USA copyright law.

This novel is a work of fiction. Names, descriptions, entities, and incidents included in the story are products of the author's imagination. Any resemblance to actual persons, events, and entities is entirely coincidental.

The opinions expressed by the author are not necessarily those of Tate Publishing, LLC.

Published by Tate Publishing & Enterprises, LLC
127 E. Trade Center Terrace | Mustang, Oklahoma 73064 USA
1.888.361.9473 | www.tatepublishing.com

Tate Publishing is committed to excellence in the publishing industry. The company reflects the philosophy established by the founders, based on Psalm 68:11,
"The Lord gave the word and great was the company of those who published it."

Book design copyright © 2015 by Tate Publishing, LLC. All rights reserved.
Cover design by Bill Francis Peralta
Interior design by Gram Telen

Published in the United States of America

ISBN: 978-1-68118-736-5
1. Fiction / Historical
2. Fiction / Action & Adventure
15.08.24

ACKNOWLEDGEMENTS

W. James Nethery for being my prepublication reviewer.
Angela Avancena (editor)

> One hour of life,
> Crowded to the full with glorious action,
> And filled with noble risks,
> Is worth whole years of those mean observances of paltry decorum,
> In which men steal through existence,
> Like sluggish waters through a marsh,
> Without either honor or observation.
>
> —Sir Walter Scott, *Count Robert of Paris* (1832)

1

The heavy iron-bound door closed with a rusty shriek. Fading footsteps echoed, followed by silence. Jamie Drummond lay sprawled on the stones, enveloped in blinding pain inflicted by the kicks of the Spanish guards. For many minutes, he was scarcely aware of his surroundings, consumed in fighting the pain that throbbed throughout his body. At last, sheer will prevailed. He raised his right hand and ran the fingers of his left over the manacle. He pulled carefully on the collar tightly encircling his wrist. It was firmly locked, with no sign of weakness. He felt every iron link in the chain connecting his wrists, searching for gaps or imperfections that he could exploit. There were none.

In the dim light, he extended the chain between his hands to its limit—about two feet. Pulling steadily, he felt every link until he reached the end of the chain, where it was fastened into a heavy metal ring sunk into the stone wall—a length of about five feet. The chain was smooth and felt new. Forcing down the pain that seemed to emanate from every joint and muscle in his body, Jamie rose to his knees and began exploring the rapidly darkening cell. He had been captured in late afternoon, with the brilliant sun sinking toward the horizon and shadows lengthening. Glancing upward to the high transom above his head, Jamie estimated that he had perhaps half an hour before total darkness enveloped him.

Although he realized that escape was impossible as long as his wrists were confined in the iron manacles and the ringbolt in the wall was secure, he was determined to know the potential weaknesses of his prison cell. Feeling his way and prying with his fingers, he tested every pavement stone within the five foot semicircle around the anchoring bolt. While there were pits in the grouting, none of the stones felt loose. His scrabbling fingers found the reeking half-full bucket that would serve as his chamber pot. He shifted its position carefully to avoid upsetting it in his search. He found his meager water supply—a clay pot. He sniffed it, gratified that it did not smell excessively. He lifted and sipped apprehensively. The water was brackish and warm. Not knowing how many hours or days he would have to wait for replenishment, in spite of his parched throat, he put the pot in a safe place. He also discovered a rolled-up straw mat clearly intended to serve as his bed.

Finished with the pavement, Jamie repeated his search of the rough stones of the two walls within his straining reach. He found several on which knocking sounded hollow, indicating that the stones could possibly be knocked loose, but none that could be moved with his hands. Resigned that escape through the walls was impossible, Jamie unrolled the straw mat. In spite of the fetid heat of the cell, he shivered, for his salt-damp trousers and shirt chilled his flesh.

Faintly, he heard sounds that he dreaded—the chittering of rats. In the darkness, he could not be certain if they were the huge native Cuban rats or the smaller wily variety that infested ships. While he could find no egress from the cell, they had found a way inside, probably through chinks between the walls and ceiling. He quaked with disgust, for he had encountered such pests years before in the noisome confines of the courtyard at Newgate Prison. He had seen the bloody damage that their razor-sharp teeth could inflict on a sleeping man's toes. He pulled his sodden shirt from his trousers. He ripped long strips of the linen fabric and wrapped them around his bare feet. He thrust his clenched fists into the waistband of his trousers to protect his fingers while he slept. Twice during the night, Jamie felt a furtive tugging at his cloth-wrapped toes. He lashed out viciously and heard the scurrying as the rats fled. In the dim morning light, he discovered the half-eaten corpse of a brown rat. His wild kicking must have killed the creature, which was set upon by its mates.

A boom sounded distantly and then another. Seconds later, the stone walls shook, and dust sifted down. He coughed spasmodically, unable to avoid inhaling. The British had resumed the bombardment. Jamie counted seconds and estimated that the guns were firing at the rate of more than one a minute, hitting the citadel on about half the shots. An amusing thought intruded, and he chuckled at the incongruity of his circumstances. Perhaps his fate was to be obliterated under the collapsed rubble when his own countrymen succeeded in destroying his prison.

The walls vibrated, and dust flew with every hit, but only occasionally were there crashing sounds signifying real damage. Between the bombardment and his rumbling empty stomach, he was convinced that he would never sleep, but exhaustion is a seductive inducement. He drifted into a troubled sleep filled with horrific dreams of starvation, destruction, and death.

Jamie jerked awake to the rasping of the cell door opening. The light was murky, but daylight had fully come. He sat up jerkily as two shadows moved along the wall toward him.

"En sus pies, cerdos miserables! Rápido!"

Jamie rose to his feet, certain that the barked command required it. With apprehension, he eyed the two uniformed men facing him. One was a guard, short and stocky, holding a bayonet-tipped musket. The other was the officer who had directed his capture the day before. He stood slapping his rattan cane against his palm. Both stood well outside the reach of the chain binding Jamie to the wall of the narrow cell.

The officer spoke, "I am Lieutenant Javier Molina, commander of this prison. While you do not understand our language, Scotsman, I see that you have become sufficiently obedient to stand in the presence of an officer. I do not regret ordering my men to beat you nearly senseless, for you are responsible for their injuries during your capture. I assure you that if you strike any of my men again, senor, I will inflict the bastinado." His mustache twitched as he smirked.

"You will be bound to a table and your bare feet lashed with a cane like this until the soles bleed. The pain is…exquisite." He spoke the word with relish. "I assure you that you will not walk without pain for many days. Repeated punishment can cripple a man for life. I admonish you to not do anything to incur my wrath, senor." He stepped forward as the soldier lowered his weapon and pointed it at Jamie's belly. Drawing back his arm, the officer lashed Jamie across the face. Recoiling, Jamie sought escape from the repeated blows until he fell against the stone wall, lacerating the scabbed wound on the back of his head.

Flinching from the stinging pain in his cheek and scalp, Jamie fought for control. His breath hissed out. The officer stepped back, smirking. "Those strokes are for the hostility I see in your eyes, senor. You will look down and not up whenever any member of my guard addresses you. Do you understand?"

In bare feet, Jamie towered over the slight Spanish officer. With a weapon in his hand, he would have made short work of his tormentor. Furious over the injustice he was forced to endure, he cast down his eyes and muttered, "Aye, sir."

"Once you are sufficiently docile, I will see that you are put with the other prisoners. For now, you will remain confined here, alone, on a diet of bread and water." Lieutenant Molina turned on his heel, followed by the silent guard. Hours later, another guard pushed open the door far enough to slide in a tin plate holding a meager stack of dry biscuit and another clay pot of tepid water.

The half-eaten rat had disappeared, bones and all. His nocturnal encounters with the vermin declined, for Jamie slept uneasily, thrashing his wrapped feet and flailing his arms at every close approach. He took to sleeping during the day, when the rats refused to come out in the faint light.

Victorious against the rats, Jamie fought a losing battle with the lice, which quickly infested his clothing and hair. Although manacled, he managed to strip his clothing enough to pick many of the creatures from his hair and body, crushing them between his fingernails. After every lice-killing session, Jamie watched a trail of ants march in resolutely to carry away the dead. He chuckled as he thought of what would happen if he were to die in this cell. How long would it be before the ants carried away his dead flesh and only whitened bones remained as a mute testimony that he had once lived?

He bore the hunger and confinement in the fetid and noisome cell stoically, but thirst began to inflict its torture. His dreams were vivid. Once more, he was a boy riding with Jock McRae across fields of yellow gorse behind the castle at Strathallan, the muscles of the big bay gelding flexing under his thighs and his yellow hair whipping in the wind. He fought the horse to a stop, dismounted, waded into Machany Water, knelt, and drank deeply of its cold refreshment.

Waking, he licked his cracked lips and then drifted back into a fitful sleep. Bundled against the intense cold, he still shivered as he trudged with his cousins Peter and David through drifted snow to the banks of the Dee. The iced-over stream was frozen solid, glittering blue in the intense sunlight.

He followed the strains of harp music to a canopy where a lovely woman sat plucking the strings, her clear soprano voice soaring over the quiet crowd. The ancient Highland melody brought comfort to his soul. Later, she whispered a prophecy to him that came true years later during the long voyage to Canada and the fierce battles at Louisburg and on the Plains of

Abraham. His mind drifted to Maggie McRae's second prophecy concerning his future, which was unfulfilled.

He woke with a start. Still unfulfilled! In the slow, still hours before dawn, he pondered Maggie's prophetic words, which he had committed to memory from her letter.

> I canna see yer future clearly, fer the Sight dinna respond tae my wishes, but comes when it will and in what words it chooses. I can only tell ye that yer future will lead ye elsewhere than where ye think it should. Neither yer wishes nor those o' yer family count fer aught, fer ye hae a lang and torturous path tae follow, wi' muckle trials before ye find true happiness. Ye should nae be sad at these words, fer eventually all ye wish tae hae in life will be yers, mair than ye are able tae comprehend.

Wishing to live a life guided by reason and not old superstitions, he had refused to believe until reminded of the prophecy's importance by Flora MacDonald during the visit he and Jock McRae had made to her home in Flodigarry, on the isle of Skye.

The prison walls shook once more, for the British batteries had begun their predawn bombardment. Certainly, incarcerated and tortured by hunger and thirst in a solitary cell in the depths of El Morro, with cannon working to bring down the citadel on his head, he was enduring "muckle trials." He could only wonder where he was on the "lang and torturous path" that Maggie had prophesied.

Days and nights slid past in a monotonous procession. After every bombardment, Jamie felt the walls of his cell for cracks, only to discover that they were only hairline. He kept track of days by surreptitiously scratching marks on the wall with a fingernail. The British bombardment continued through all daylight hours and much of the night. Jamie learned to sleep in the brief intervals between bombardments, but his dreams continuously replayed the last voyage of HMS *Stirling Castle*— her heavily wedged cannon firing upward to attack the Spanish guns on the citadel's high parapet, the rapidly shallowing water, her hull slamming onto the submerged rocky shelf that had flung Jamie and many others into the water, the frantic battle to divest himself of his weapons and fight his way to the surface, his futile attempt to hide from enemy sentinels when, unconscious he had drifted ashore below the citadel, and his capture and savage beating at the hands of Lieutenant Molina's guards.

There were occasional crashes denoting structural damage deep in the bowels of the citadel, but in his cell, there was only the vibrating walls and choking dust. Jamie felt a perverse pleasure when the shaking dislodged a stone from the ceiling, and it narrowly missed his head.

His untended head wound healed slowly while the bruises that mottled his body and legs changed from deep purple to an unsightly green to yellow. He thought that it was fortunate that there was no one to see him. He felt his newly scabbed pate, where a falling object had knocked him senseless after his fall from the deck of *Stirling Castle*. The blow had left a deep gouge, abraded further by his fall against the wall. The pain had subsided, but a ridge of swollen and scabbed tissue was a nagging reminder.

Wary of being cut off from food, Jamie tried to hoard meager pieces of biscuit in the remnants of his shirt. To his chagrin, he found that they quickly turned moldy in the stifling humidity. With a shrug, he bolted down the bluish-tinged fragments and tried not to think of what his stomach would make of the spoiling food.

With nothing to occupy his mind, it drifted to reminiscences and scenarios of what his family would make of news of his capture. He could not be certain when his mother would receive the news, for many weeks might elapse before any news at all would arrive in Scotland. The long delay in news could cause the ludicrous situation where he might be rescued and his family still think him a captive of the Spanish. Jamie could not think of any outcome except a British victory, for Havana was surrounded by a navy and army that vastly outnumbered the defenders. While he had a prophecy about his destiny to sustain his spirits, he knew that his own survival from the attack on El Morro was far less certain.

To buoy his spirits in his isolation, he took to sitting cross-legged, with the chains in his hands, tapping out rhythms on the links and singing old tunes in the Scots and Gaelic languages of his childhood.

Sixteen days had passed when the door creaked open to disclose a surprising scene. Facing him were the guard, Lieutenant Molina, and a tall senior officer holding a soiled and rumpled red jacket. Jamie rose swiftly and, in obedience to Molina's instructions, stood with downcast eyes. The senior officer held up the jacket, much stained and torn, in both hands and spoke in slightly accented English.

"Prisoner! I am Captain Luis Vicente de Velasco, comandante of El Morro. This is the uniform jacket of a British officer. Do you recognize it?"

Jamie raised his eyes and gaped. Although tattered, rumpled, and ripped, it was recognizable. The high collar and epaulets marked its wearer as a royal marine captain.

Not sure of the officer's intentions, Jamie dropped his eyes and said, "Aye, sir. I believe that it may be the jacket I lost when *Stirling Castle* grounded and I was flung in the water."

Lieutenant Molina, the guard commander, sneered. "I doubt that."

Captain Velasco said mildly, "Permit the man to try the jacket, Lieutenant."

Molina growled, "Remove your filthy rag of a shirt and try it for fit, prisoner. I still do not believe it is yours."

Jamie said, "I hae lost much weight frae my prison fare o' biscuit and water, and the woolen garment may hae shrunk, but I will attempt it."

Jamie held up his manacles, signaling the impossibility of obeying Velasco's request with his hands chained.

Molina snarled an order in Spanish. The guard stood his musket against the door and fumbled with his keys. A minute later, the manacles were off, and Jamie stood buttoning the bedraggled jacket, which was an obvious fit across his muscular shoulders. In spite of its being soiled and stained from long exposure to salt water and tropical sun, the uniform seemed to transform Jamie. He stood ramrod straight and stared boldly at the officers. The stocky guard took a step backward, awed by the transformation.

Lieutenant Molina said, "As I told you, Comandante, he has hostile eyes and a challenging manner, even after the soldiers beat him."

Captain Velasco smiled. "I would have expected that, for Scots have a reputation of behaving as if they were hidalgos, even among the common mercenary soldiers I have met. I believe that there is no doubt any longer. The man and the uniform belong to each other. Although a prisoner, he is an officer and should be treated as such."

Molina scowled. "I must object. He is an enemy and dangerous. He might attempt an escape and injure many men. It took nearly a dozen to subdue him when we brought him to the prison."

Jamie, incensed at the guard officer's misrepresentation, responded, "I willingly allowed my hands tae be bound on the beach and only fought after I fell on the steps and was beaten."

Velasco turned to Molina. "Is that true, Lieutenant?"

The guard officer dropped his eyes and hesitated before responding, "He fell, but it appeared to be a ruse to enable his escape, which my men prevented."

Velasco persisted, "Did he give you his word not to attempt an escape?"

Molina shook his head. "Of course not. There was no point in asking for it. The word of a common soldier or sailor cannot be trusted. There was no reason to believe his story of being an officer as he claimed."

Velasco pursed his lips. Silence hung heavy in the cell. At last, he spoke, "Conditions have changed since an observant sentry caught a ragamuffin boy wearing the jacket outside the citadel this morning. The boy admitted finding the garment floating in the water below the parapet of the Twelve Apostles. Now we see that this prisoner was truthful concerning his status." He turned to Jamie.

"I believe that I am correct in addressing you as Captain James Drummond, for that is the name by which you were incarcerated in this cell. Will you give me your word as an officer and gentleman not to attempt an escape by your own hand nor injure any of my men in return for parole within this citadel which I command?"

Jamie faced the Spanish commander. "Sir, I willingly give my word nae tae attempt tae escape, but must question how I will maintain myself, fer I came ashore penniless wi' only the barest clothing."

Velasco smiled. "We are under siege, senor, and must share what we can have. You will receive neither more nor less than any officer of my command. Neither will you be safe from injury or death at the hands of your comrades, who persist in their pointless attacks." He turned to the guard commander.

"Lieutenant Molina, see that Captain Drummond is given an opportunity to bathe and shave. Find him shoes and a suit of clothing that will fit that tall frame. Send him to my offices in one hour. I wish to question him."

"Si, mi comandante." Molina nodded, his face impassive, but fury evident in his eyes. The walls shook from a direct hit. The morning's British barrage had begun. Velasco batted away the dust. "Your countrymen have rebuilt the breastworks that we partially destroyed during a counterattack last week." He sighed. "They persist in wasting ammunition, for El Morro's walls are too strong for their guns and the moat too deep to be bridged without horrific losses. I will send a message to Lord Albemarle that we have you as a captive. Since the British have not captured any of our officers to permit an exchange, I expect that you will be our guest for many more days, Captain Drummond."

An hour later, Jamie was seated in a comfortable chair in Captain Velasco's office. Although the air in the room was stifling, there was a small fire crackling behind a black wire screen. The Spanish commander pushed aside a pile of papers to regard Jamie appraisingly. He passed him a goblet of sherry and sipped from his own.

"Shaved, bathed, and dressed in decent clothing, you no longer look like the wild man who seems to obsess Lieutenant Molina. I see no reason to treat you inhumanely while you are our prisoner here in El Morro. I admit that our treatment of common prisoners may seem harsh to you, but I assure you that the Spanish reputation for brutality to prisoners is a product of an earlier age. The French, Italians, Austrians, and British can be equally cruel to their captives. Count yourself lucky to not fall victim to the native peoples of this continent, for many of them could teach lessons in cruelty to the inquisitors."

Velasco templed his long fingers. "While I will not have you tortured for information, Captain Drummond, I do wish to hear what you know concerning Lord Albemarle's plans and capabilities."

Jamie drew a breath, considering his words. "I am a junior officer on a warship o' the invading fleet, Captain Velasco, and nae privileged tae sit in the councils o' war wi' senior commanders. I hae ne'er met the Earl of Albemarle nor glimpsed Vice Admiral Pocock but a single time. I canna tell ye any details aboot the invasion plans or strength o' forces save my ain ship." He paused. "Neither would I tell aught if I was privy tae such secrets, sir. 'Tis a point o' honor."

Captain Velasco smiled. "I expected that answer, and I agree. It is a point of honor. However, I can now tell my own commander when asked if I have interrogated you concerning them. Is there anything that you would tell me?"

Jamie rubbed his chin. "Aye, sir. *Stirling Castle* was ane o' the vanguard o' four ships that received the order tae bombard the citadel at dawn as part o' an attack frae the sea as weel as land tae silence as many guns as possible. Ye see the results yersel—a ship grounded and capsized and fearsome damage tae the others, although I dinna ken how many killed or wounded, fer we were in the van o' the attacking force. Since I came ashore, I ken naething aboot the remainder o' the campaign."

Velasco sat for a while in silence, staring into the fire. He said softly, "I understand that there is a Scottish engineer, MacKellar by name, directing their siege operations. He cannot successfully tunnel in rocky ground, so he builds fortifications above it. The British breastworks advance, and there are daily sorties to reach the walls, which we beat back. Albemarle is stubborn. He lacks enough men to successfully assault El Morro and needs reinforcements from the British forces in Canada and New York. Yet they have not come. If they do not arrive soon, then he must withdraw, for there is yellow fever and other sickness in his army. Its ability to fight is diminishing daily."

He glanced at Jamie. "Do you know why the British reinforcements are so late in coming?" Before Jamie could reply, Velasco shook his head. "Of course you do not, for you are here and not where the reinforcements are located." He sighed. "The knowledge matters little, for I must defend this citadel and the city of Havana, which is the jewel of Spanish possessions in the New World. The conquistadores sailed from here to create the Spanish empire. From here, the treasure galleons sailed to Spain to fuel imperial ambition and glory. We have no choice but to defend it to the death, and so we shall. Just as your comrades will fight to fulfill the orders given them to conquer. It is why we are here, is it not, Scotsman? We are honor bound. Only God knows to whom he will grant the victory."

Velasco was soon called away, but before leaving, he invited Jamie to borrow the only books in the citadel written in English, which he had borrowed from the University of Havana. There were texts on naval architecture and navigation, geography, and the history of Spanish America. There were the familiar books by Richard Hakluyt and, surprisingly, a number of the plays of Shakespeare. Restricted to the citadel, admonished to stay out of the way of the defending garrison, and subject to daily and nightly bombardment, Jamie remained in the room assigned him, except for meals and meetings with Captain Velasco. The books were a welcome diversion while he waited for an outcome to the battle for El Morro.

Jamie sat at the small desk in the room assigned to him halfway up the leftmost bastion. Even at midday, the filtered light from the narrow slit in the thick stone wall was dim. In order to read, he had to light a cotton wick floating in a bowl of whale oil. Immersed in Captain Velasco's stack of books, he missed the tentative rap on the heavy wooden door. The rap came again, much louder.

He pushed the books aside and went to the door. Two visitors stood in the hall. Cowled, belted, and carrying leather satchels, they were clearly not soldiers. One was a tall man with a broad face, youthful and bearded. His companion was much older but of indeterminate age. His lean hawkish face was that of a man of middling years, but his white hair, deep-set eyes, and stooped posture marked him as far older.

The tall man threw back his cowl. "I am Tomas Gomez, and my companion, who speaks no English and has no surname, is known simply as Balthazar. Comandante Velasco has sent us. May we enter?"

Jamie nodded, although he was puzzled. Captain Velasco had not mentioned visitors. There was only the single chair in the small room. Jamie offered it, but the men chose to sit on the narrow bed together. Jamie moved the chair so that he could sit facing them.

Tomas Gomez nodded to his companion, who opened his leather satchel and began taking out surgical instruments and an assortment of small vials and jars. He talked as Balthazar laid out the medications, wrappings, and tools.

"I am a physician, senor, in partnership with my father, Jose Antonio Gomez, known among the populace as Pepe Antonio. Until the British came, he was a physician and councilman in our neighborhood of Guanabacoa. Last year, the government, fearing that Spain's entry into the war on the side of the Bourbon French would bring down the British on our island, sent Juan de Prado as the new captain general to fortify the city and harbor. They also sent Admiral Gutierre de Hevia y Valdéz, head of the Spanish Marine Corps, with seven large ships of the line and two infantry regiments. While the admiral cut a magnificent figure and threw much energy into the project, he failed to fortify La Cabaña Ridge, although ordered to do so. The British attacked that weakness, and that is the reason why El Morro is now under siege and will almost certainly fall. Mi padre mustered the town's militia, which bravely opposed the invaders who landed on the beaches a month ago. The militia were untrained but heroic. They inflicted many casualties on the surprised British but were forced to flee, for our admiral failed to send reinforcements." Tomas Gomez sighed.

"He rewarded Pepe Antonio by making him mayor of Havana and commander of the militia defending the entire city. He is a brave man, senor, for he believes in defending his home and family but expects to die when the British forces overwhelm the Spanish regulars and his ill-trained militia. Juan Salazar, the citadel's physician, was killed in the bombardment a week ago, so Captain Velasco asked my father for my help." He sighed, and his eyes grew distant.

"With Balthazar's help, I have done what I can for the soldiers of the garrison and others here in the citadel. Lieutenant Molina did not tell me that you were wounded in the head when you were captured, or I would have insisted on seeing you immediately. Our nations are at war, but decency requires that we ease whatever suffering we can, even if we were the cause of it." His broad face split in a grin. "You appear to have survived without our help. Now you are here, and we are here. Let us see if there is anything further that we can do. He rose, gestured Jamie to move closer to the window, and brought the oil lamp closer.

Gomez picked up a cotton-tipped stick and inserted it into a bottle. He rubbed it against the ridge of scar tissue on the back of Jamie's head and clucked his tongue sympathetically. "Barbaric negligence. To ease your concern, the substance I placed on the cotton is alcohol, which is wonderful for cleansing and mildly cauterizing wounds. Your wound is closed, or I would already have heard a howl of dismay, for alcohol can be painful on damaged flesh. The jagged scar is perhaps three fingers long and half a finger wide. With your permission, I wish to surgically remove this raised scar tissue. The wound will reopen, but with stitches, it will heal smoothly, which will make the back of your scalp more comely. Balthazar has some efficacious herbs that will ease the pain that you will experience and promote healing. He is wonderfully adept at pharmacology, having learned its mysteries from the Arabs in Morocco. He was captured from a merchant ship as a young man, made a slave to a physician, which, of course, is far better than being made a eunuch. He managed to escape aboard a Dutch ship docked in Tangier. He made his way to Amsterdam, then to Recife in Brazil, and at last to Havana and the employment of my father. I do not know his origin, but I believe that he is a Jew. Here in the domain of His Most Catholic Majesty, he does not talk about his religion, and we do not ask. We accept him for what he is, a marvelous healer. It is enough."

Jamie stared at Balthazar. "I hae ne'er met a Jew. They are very scarce and reclusive in my hameland. I hae heard legends o' their prowess in business, philosophy, and the medical arts. I feel fortunate tae place myself in his hands. I ken that there must be pain before proper healing. Hew awa' and dinna listen tae my protests." Tomas Gomez chuckled at Jamie's bravado, and even Balthazar smiled.

The British bombardment grew from day to day, with more shots fired with a higher degree of accuracy. The Spanish response faded as British cannonading systematically destroyed the guns and their emplacements on the landward side of the citadel. Jamie did not see the damage, for he was denied access to the gun emplacements. Captain Velasco and Tomas Gomez brought daily reports that were dispiriting to the Spanish cause. MacKellar and his engineers had begun to mine, but the Spanish did not know to what purpose.

However, the news was not altogether heartening for the British. The reinforcements from North America did not arrive. The siege operations were nearly at a standstill, with few men working to dump debris into the vast chasm before the walls of the citadel. Yellow fever was rampant in the camps. It was impossible to hide the burials from Spanish eyes on the ramparts. Spies reported that many British regiments were down to half strength. For Velasco, it was no longer a question of which side would prevail by force of arms. It was a matter of whether either army would have weapons and men left to fight.

By July 17th, Gomez confided to Jamie that the Spanish had only two guns in the citadel that were still serviceable. The Spanish soldiers were not able to repair or replace them. Ammunition was running low as magazines were emptied. Jamie was not surprised, for his experienced ears had noted a marked decline in the Spanish firing rate. Without artillery, the Spanish would not be able to keep the British engineers from mining or filling in the ditch. It had become a race against time. Without reinforcements, could the British breach the walls and launch an attack in force before raging disease rendered the attacking force impotent?

Five days later, the sounds of a furious infantry attack and artillery counterattack woke Jamie before dawn. He knelt with his eye to the narrow slit that served as a window. Musket fire winked along the ridge below the British breastworks, with bright flares marking explosions of canister and grape. The confused fighting surged forward in the darkness. Musket fire advanced up the ridge and then abruptly reversed course. A few minutes later saw a repeat of the forward surge, followed by another retreat downslope.

First light through the slit confirmed that the predawn assault had been disastrous for the Spanish, with hundreds of bodies and abandoned weapons littering the slope up to the British siege works. Without a glass, Jamie could not be certain, but to the naked eye, it appeared that the Spanish had failed to penetrate the British position at any point.

Jamie waited for Captain Velasco to appear, but he did not. At midday, there was a knock on the door. Jamie leaped up to admit a disheveled Tomas Gomez, who slumped into a chair, his voice quavering.

"Madre de Dios! Such slaughter! Out of thirteen hundred, less than half came back. So many too injured to survive treatment. Many lay dying, and we could not save them. Velasco is the bravest man I have ever seen, but he will not listen. He has what we Spanish call duende. He is filled with an irrational force, awareness of the inevitability of his own death, and a dash of the diabolical. He will never surrender, even to save his men and people of this city. With that man in command, we will all die here, senor."

Jamie shook his head. "Aye, I saw it in General James Wolfe at Quebec. He apparently wished for a glorious death but gained it only after leading his troops to victory."

The doctor muttered bitterly, "Victory? We have lost at least thirty men a day during this bombardment. Velasco draws more men from the militia to replace them, as if the British cannot see the losses. I have begged Captain Velasco to evacuate the noncombatants and laborers from the citadel, to no avail. El Morro is doomed, and we must rely on La Punta to defend the approaches to the city."

Shortly after dawn on July 24th, the British guns fell quiet. Jamie watched from the slit window halfway up the right tower of El Morro. Four officers, with a soldier carrying a white flag, slowly approached the citadel. They were met by a contingent of Spanish officers near a narrow stone bridge over the deep gorge that stretched across the front of El Morro. British soldiers sat or stood at various places on the looming and now-complete British breastworks that confronted the citadel on the far side.

The British officers and their Spanish counterparts talked for a few minutes, and an officer ran back to the citadel. Nearly an hour passed before he returned with Captain Velasco. There was more conversation, but the meeting ended abruptly, with a loud stream of Spanish and a vehement shaking of the head from Velasco, who spun on his heel and stalked back to the citadel. The British officers recrossed the narrow stone bridge, and the Spanish followed their commander inside the walls of El Morro. Without understanding the words, it was clear to Jamie that negotiations had failed.

It was nearly noon when a dispirited Tomas Gomez knocked on Jamie's door. He collapsed in the chair and drank a cup of water from the carafe before speaking. "It seems that our comandante has rejected an invitation to surrender the citadel. The Earl of Albemarle"—he hesitated—"I believe that is the title by which he is addressed, invited Velasco to write his own terms of capitulation, but it was rudely rejected. I find Velasco's stubborn resistance incomprehensible, for it is clear that the British have successfully driven a tunnel under the right bastion directly under where we sit and will soon mine it with explosives. They intend to invade through the gap when the bastion collapses. Velasco believes that he can dislodge them with an attack by water and thus remove the threat. He will consider surrender on no terms whatever."

Jamie said, "Tae endure bombardment is a tolerable risk, but tae remain in a tower that would surely collapse when the mines explode is certain death."

The doctor nodded.

"I have sent a note to the comandante requesting permission for you to move to the left bastion, although he may send you back to the dungeon for your own safety."

Jamie choked out a reply. "He would send me back tae the clutches o' Lieutenant Molina fer my ain safety?"

Tomas Gomez spread his hands in resignation. "We are in desperate circumstances, my Scottish friend. He will not release you, and you must remain in our custody."

Jamie's reply shocked the doctor. "I will nae return tae the dungeon wi'oot resisting."

"So you are determined to die. I do not wish to be a bystander to such a calamity."

"Then give me a weapon."

Gomez recoiled. "You would take your own life?" He quickly crossed himself.

Jamie smiled. "Nay. I may die at the hands of others, but only after sending my persecutors tae the hell they deserve."

The doctor sat staring at Jamie. At length, he said, "A sword or dagger would be impossible to conceal and invite instant attack. A pistol is too bulky as well and good for only a single shot." He reached for his valise, opened it, and extracted a scalpel. "Here is a fearsome weapon, easily concealed in a pocket, waistband, or shirt. The blade is as sharp as a razor and protected with a wooden guard. They would never expect a prisoner to have one."

He handed it to Jamie, who removed the guard and examined the handle and glittering blade.

"It will rust quickly in this moist air." Gomez handed him a small glass vial. "You must be very secretive, but find a way daily to coat the blade with this oil."

Jamie nodded and slid both objects into his waistband. "Unless I am disrobed, I should be able tae conceal them. I will return tae the dungeon and Lieutenant Molina's tender mercies if required, but weel armed."

Jamie's fears were not realized. By dusk, a taciturn servant arrived, with instructions to move immediately with his change of clothing and stack of books to a room in the far bastion, also with a slit window looking out on the esplanade at the front of the citadel.

Six days passed with a greatly reduced British bombardment. Tomas Gomez brought daily reports on the progress of the British engineers on the mining operation. The Spanish were stauchly resisting their slow efforts. However, on the night of July 30, at two in the morning, cannon and musket fire exploded, and the sky was lit by bright flashes. Jamie jumped out of bed and peered through the slit. He could see nothing but silhouettes of running men. The action lasted less than an hour and then stopped.

Tomas Gomez arrived in midmorning to tell another tale of Spanish failure. Two schooners had stealthily approached the wall of El Morro from the harborside to attack the British engineers working on mining the wall. After emptying their magazines in futile bombardment that apparently inflicted few casualties on the miners, who huddled in the protection of their tunnel, the ships withdrew.

At noon, a servant brought a meager tray of boiled meat, hard cheese, and a small melon. He rushed off, ignoring all questions. Jamie resigned himself to wait until Tomas Gomez returned in the afternoon with news. He had just taken the last bite of the cheese and prepared to attack the melon. The air shivered, the door pulled from the hinges, and chunks of masonry flew from the walls. There was a terrific explosion of sound, and then Jamie could hear nothing, though objects continued to shake and masonry showered his bed, collapsing the legs.

Jamie wiped blood from his nose and rose to his knees. One look through the slit showed billowing clouds of dust and smoke from where the right bastion had once stood. "They have exploded the mine!" he shouted but could not hear his own voice. He crawled through the shattered frame where the door had once stood while the floor continued to shake.

When the floor stopped heaving, he crawled into the corridor. Musket-wielding soldiers rushed past, ignoring him. He rose and stumbled to the spiraling staircase, stepping over fallen blocks, stones, and pieces of broken timber. He descended, thankful that the staircase had not collapsed, and then made his way onto the esplanade. He ducked back, for through the smoke, he saw columns of red- and blue-coated soldiers exchanging fusillades of shots. He fought his way back past the Spanish troops toward the outer doors on the western side of the citadel. After many minutes and false turns, he found a way outside just as his hearing returned.

When he reached the sunlit western parapet, he emerged into noisy, bloody chaos. Bleeding men lay on the ground, groaning piteously. Others, addled by the mighty explosion, wandered aimlessly through the drifting smoke and dust. Jamie caught a glimpse of Tomas Gomez and Balthazar working frantically in a clot of injured men. He moved in that direction. Just before he reached them, he was bumped by a shuffling line of chained prisoners. He quickly turned away, only to feel the cold steel of a pistol barrel pressed into his belly. Jamie's chest constricted as he stumbled back and stared into the black eyes of Lieutenant Javier Molina.

"Another prisoner, Sergeant Sanchez. Chain him swiftly. The boat is waiting for us. I do not intend to see this one escape."

Jamie objected hoarsely, "But I hae Captain Velasco's parole."

"Captain Velasco is no longer in command of this citadel. He was wounded, perhaps mortally, in the hand-to-hand fighting with the British, who stormed across the debris in the breach and gained a foothold on the bastion. My mission is to transfer all prisoners to La Punta across the channel, for El Morro has fallen."

Jamie sagged in defeat and held out his wrists. Molina smiled broadly as the guards snapped the shackles in place. Stumbling to keep his place in the coffle of prisoners, Jamie lurched down the cliff face to the waiting boats.

2

The journey down the winding path was a blur of pain. Every fall yanked the chain, sending men to their knees on the gravel, only to be battered upright by rifle butts and whips. Jamie flinched as Lieutenant Molina barreled past to where a prisoner lay groveling and weeping. Pulled upright by the guards, the man's legs buckled, and he fell facedown.

Molina stood regarding the prisoner, who lay thrashing weakly under blows from the guards. He snarled, "Abrir las esposas! Siga los barcos con los demás!"

The guards looked confused. Molina loudly repeated the order and drew his pistol. Hurriedly, a guard bent to unlock the manacles. The felled man did not stir as the chained prisoners moved away down the path.

There was a sharp crack that echoed off the cliff. Jamie looked back to see Molina reholstering his pistol while the guards rolled the prisoner's dead body into the brush at the side of the trail. A rifle butt bounced painfully off Jamie's shoulder.

"Ojos hacia adelante, o su destino será tuyo!"

Molina, moving past, said, "You would be more obedient, senor, if you understood his command. 'Eyes front! Do not look back if you wish to avoid his fate.' Although, it might be better for you to die here on the trail than to be my prisoner again when we reach La Punta."

There was pandemonium at the bottom of the trail. Soldiers escaping from the citadel huddled under the cliff face to avoid the British sniping from above. Molina screamed orders to guards holding the boats at the tiny wooden pier and at those chivvying prisoners across the shingle. The frantic guards shoved all seventeen men, still chained, into one boat, where they fell over each other. Soldiers huddled under the cliff raced to board the remaining boats. Many threw away weapons and flung themselves into the water, gripping the gunwales of the departing boats. Rowers and guards in the boats beat them off as they struggled to escape the shore. Those who could swim or were so galvanized by fear that they thought they could struck out for the La Punta shore. Others turned back to cower under the cliff face.

Jamie lay under two Cuban prisoners, who wailed their fear in incoherent Spanish. Thrashing furiously, Jamie managed to look back. Red-coated soldiers and marines fired down from El Morro's western parapet. Others streamed down the trail toward the beach. With horror, Jamie saw crews pushing two small cannon into place at the cliff top. While musket fire was ineffective, the boats would come under fire from the guns before they could make the far side of the channel.

A prisoner lying across his legs flailed until he could raise himself on one elbow. Jamie tugged at his sleeve and roared, "Get down, ye fool!"

The Cuban stiffened and fell back, blood bubbling from where he had been shot in the face. A shudder ran through the chained prisoners, who shrank downward. Men crossed themselves, repeatedly muttering prayers as balls whined overhead or thudded into the boat's timbers.

Jamie lay listening to the creaking oarlocks, as frantic rowers sobbed with exertion. After long minutes, the shots faded, replaced by the roar of the light field pieces on the cliff. Spouts of water gouted around them, but no shots hit their boat. Men moaned in relief as the bottom grated on shingle. Guards leaped out and struggled to untangle the chained prisoners. Battered and bleeding from many blows, the coffle was reassembled less the man who had died in the boat.

Jamie chanced a look backward. The channel was littered with floating and half-submerged bodies and wrecked boats. While the British now had the range, two guns could inflict only negligible damage. Lieutenant Molina ordered the prisoners toward the gray stone walls of San Salvador de la Punta. Within minutes, the prisoners were marched inside the black iron gates, across the keep lined with yellow-painted artillery pieces, through a low archway, along a torch-lit corridor, and down two levels into the dank dungeon.

For two days, the prisoners sat chained to rings in a single room. Except for the silent guards who accompanied servants who brought food and water, there were no visitors. Jamie went through the same fruitless routine he had conducted in El Morro's dungeon. He tested every link and chink in the rough stone floor and walls. His only comfort was that guards had not detected the steel scalpel concealed in his waistband or the vial of oil to keep it free of rust. He chuckled to himself. "Aye, 'tis nae a proper *sgian-achlais* fer it is nae a dagger. It must be my *sgain dubh*, fer it hae a single blade and must be hidden frae sight." He never touched it during the day, taking it out for oiling only when he was certain that the other prisoners were asleep.

Without knowledge of Spanish, he could not respond to the occasional questions of the Cuban prisoners or engage in their muttered conversations. On an impulse, he launched a question to the group in French. One prisoner spoke laboriously in fractured but intelligible words. He said that his name was Eduardo Sanchez. He had served some years as a sailor on a French privateer. Raiding in Spanish Caribbean waters had proved their undoing. While the privateer escaped, Sanchez had been in a yawl ashore. While the other crew members died in the fight, he was the sole survivor. He had been a prisoner in El Morro for three years, unable to comprehend why he had not been hanged outright or sent to serve in one of the Spanish warships in the harbor. At last, he had come to realize why he had been allowed to live.

Sanchez held up his hands to show Jamie his mangled and often-broken fingers. He muttered one bitter word—"Molina." He turned to speak to the other Cuban prisoners whom he said mostly lived in Guanabacoa. Many held out hands and feet to show wounds and scars from the torture ordered by the sadistic captain of the guard.

Jamie had faith that the British would soon bring heavy artillery forward to bombard La Punta and the city of Havana from the heights of the captured El Morro. However, his confidence waned with the long delay in launching the attack. Except for an occasional ranging shot, the harbor was silent. He wondered if Lord Albemarle was negotiating with the Spanish and how long that process might take.

The prisoners languished in their common cell for a week. Lieutenant Molina arrived one morning accompanied by half a dozen guards. He gazed at Jamie speculatively. Jamie stared back unflinchingly. Molina turned to examine the Cuban prisoners, who had hastily risen to their feet. He selected two and ordered them removed from their manacles and taken downstairs. When the entourage had gone, Gomez whispered to Jamie. "Et il commence. Je crois que quelqu'un a insulté cet homme de l'ego monstrueux. Maintenant, il doit exercer des représailles contre l'impuissance."

Jamie sighed, for he knew that Gomez was at least partially correct in what drove Molina's cruelty. The privateer had said, "It has begun and will not stop until some of us are dead. He is a man of monstrous ego who inflicts cruelty on the helpless. I pity these poor men who have suffered for years." Jamie's mind flooded with barbaric ways in which he could make Molina suffer, but he realized that such an attack would cost him his own life, for the guards would surely kill him. His mind whirled with possibilities whereby he could exact vengeance and yet escape.

After two hours, the prisoners returned, beaten and bruised, and collapsed on the floor, Two more were selected for maltreatment. It was nearly dark when four guards surrounded Jamie. A smiling Molina confronted him as the guards unlocked his chain. "So, senor of the hostile eyes and lack of civility, I will have my men inflict the punishment you have avoided for so long. Last week, your erstwhile friend and benefactor Captain Velasco died of his wounds. Your British friends have not launched an attack, for they are riddled by yellow fever, dysentery, and other loathsome diseases and are too weak. It is true that their reinforcements arrived from North America, but they are also falling victim to disease. Soon there will not be enough of them to take this city, and they will sail away, leaving you here along with thousands dead."

Jamie glared down at the shorter officer. "If ye wish tae kill me, then proceed. It is entirely in yer hands tae accomplish yer aim."

Molina showed his teeth. "Death would bring an end. I would rather see you suffer as the price for your arrogance." He turned to the guards. "Bring him below. I wish to see how he withstands the bastinado."

The flickering light of the torches in wall sconces in the lower dungeon revealed a low fireplace, racks of grotesque tools, rings hanging from the low ceiling, and a long table with heavy leg stocks and leather straps designed to hold a prisoner firmly on his back with legs extended. A barrel-chested man with a broad oily face supervised the guards, who threw the struggling Jamie flat on his back on the table and pinioned his legs. He spoke in Spanish, and Molina translated.

"He is Gaspar Ortega and has performed the office of the bastinado and other exquisite tortures for seventeen years. He is particularly adept at these practices, which cause great pain without inflicting death or outward marking of the body."

Jamie grimaced as the guards locked his legs into the stocks and began removing his shoes and stockings. "If ye wish me tae tell secrets aboot the British invasion force or beg for mercy…"

Molina leaned over Jamie, leering. "I do not expect you to tell me anything useful to our defense of Havana. My only purpose is to make you suffer, for you humiliated me before the comandante. Only your suffering will suffice. Mercy is the province of God, senor. I advise you to direct your pleas to Him."

The sweating Gaspar Ortega was meticulous in laying out his instruments on a table in Jamie's view. Molina described the punishment with relish. "Bastinado is effective due to the clustering of nerve endings in the feet and their numerous small bones and tendons. The bruises inflicted are particularly painful and take a long time to heal. The punishment is most effective if begun slowly, almost gently, so the inflamed flesh and joints can repeatedly be whipped, raising the level of pain to an unendurable level over many days. Today's session is only for a few minutes to condition your mind and body, but tomorrow's and all succeeding sessions will be longer and more intense."

Jamie stared in dread at the instruments— rattan canes of various thicknesses, a flat wooden paddle, a short-handled whip with leather thongs, and a flexible bat of India rubber.

Ortega took his time, picking up and flourishing each before selecting a thin rattan cane of medium length. Jamie tensed as the torturer used the tip of the cane to probe at his feet, feeling out the bone and joint structures. Molina pulled up a chair to watch.

The torture began with almost gentle raps with the cane on the heels and balls of the feet. Jamie clamped his jaws, determined to not cry out. Ortega changed tools and applied more force. Pain grew until Jamie felt that his feet were on fire. His vision swam. Gasps and hisses of breath became deep groans and roaring as he shouted curses at the smiling Molina. Ortega held up the black rubber bat with a questioning look. The lieutenant shook his head. The first session was over. Jamie lay trembling, soaked with sweat from his ordeal.

Molina rose, rubbing his hands vigorously. "No weeping? No pleading for mercy, senor? Of course not, for you are a battle-hardened warrior. Fifteen minutes of bastinado will not reduce you. Perhaps an hour or two is required, hmm? Very well, tomorrow, Ortega will wear out his arm for an hour. We will see whether you can withstand that much bastinado without screaming for mercy. If not, then two hours on the next day and the next." Turning to the guards, he said, "Release him and take him upstairs."

Jamie was shocked at the condition of his feet, which were rapidly swelling to a club-like shape. He tried to stand, but collapsed against the table, the chain rattling down around his neck. The guards yanked him to his feet and, half-carrying him, got him up the stairs to his place against the dungeon wall and reshackled him to his ring. The silent Cuban prisoners regarded him with pity as the guards departed.

Sleep refused to come, and he could not eat. Pain pounded through his feet and legs so intensely that it induced nausea. Jamie spent the whole of that next day counting his racing pulse, hoping forlornly that somehow Molina would forget to come. Twice, he rose to his knees as guards banged open the door, but they ignored Jamie, seized other prisoners, and led them to the torture chamber. At twilight, they came for him.

Jamie never knew that he had such fortitude as he exhibited during that long hour with Gaspar Ortega and Javier Molina. He groaned, roared, and broke down in deep, inarticulate sobs as knives of pain shot through his feet. Molina rose and leaned over Jamie's face, shouting at him to beg for mercy. The lieutenant was infuriated, for what he got in return were vehement shakes of the head and sprays of sweat. At the end of the hour, Ortega reminded the guard officer of his promise to limit the session.

"Tomorrow!" Molina screamed. "Tomorrow it will be for two hours!"

The guards carried the nearly unconscious Jamie up the stairs, for he was unable to walk.

At dawn on August 11, the British heavy guns opened up on the citadel of La Punta. The walls of the dungeon shook, dust sifted down, and small pieces of masonry spalled from the walls and ceiling under the intense vibration, clattering to the stone floor. Exterior walls and porticos collapsed under the fusillade, windows blew out, and the watchtower fell in a shower of stones. The pounding of the Spanish guns was equally intense. However, in the dungeon, the prisoners knew nothing of the progress of the bombardment. They were occupied with dodging falling masonry and withstanding the nearly constant impacts. After three hours, it was obvious that all of La Punta's artillery had been silenced, and the British rate of fire slowed.

Two guards pushed open the door of the dungeon. Tomas Gomez stood in the entrance. He strode into the center of the room. First, he spoke in rapid-fire Spanish to the Cuban prisoners, who weakly raised a cheer. He rushed to Jamie's side. "Ah, my friend. Your fate at the hands of Javier Molina has been a sad one. No one at El Morro seemed to know where you had gone. Some thought that you had escaped, but when we took Captain Velasco to the British surgeons before he died, the officers attending knew nothing of your whereabouts."

He looked at Jamie's bruised swollen feet with sympathy. "After the bastinado, can you walk at all?"

Jamie replied dully, "To what purpose?"

Gomez leaned close and whispered, "The commander of La Punta has issued the order for the garrison to abandon the citadel and withdraw to the city, which is nearly defenseless with most of the guns on the city walls out of action. Now is the time for you to escape and hide from the vengeance of Molina until your countrymen capture the fortress."

Jamie spoke in a hoarse whisper. "I can walk a little but wi' great pain. The hope o' escape deadens pain, and I can crawl quite weel. But how tae get loose?"

Surreptitiously, Gomez opened his hand, revealing a key. He whispered breathlessly, "There is no time to lose, amigo. I bribed the guards, and they are leaving. I will free you from this chain and help you from the dungeon. There are empty storerooms on this level where you may hide from Molina, for he will not leave La Punta without killing you." The key slid easily into the manacle on Jamie's right hand, and the lock clicked open. Jamie stretched out his arm and flexed his fingers while Tomas fumbled with the left manacle.

The dungeon door burst open. One of the Cuban prisoners shouted, "¡Cuidado! Molina ha llegado!" The guard lieutenant stood in the entrance, hair dishevelled and saber in hand.

He raised the blade and started running toward where Jamie and the Cuban doctor were squatting. "Voy a matar a los dos!"

Startled, Gomez dropped the key and raised his hands to protect his face. Molina swung wildly. The saber ripped open the doctor's waistcoat and scored a deep gash in his side. Bent nearly doublé, Gomez scrabbled away, trailing blood. Molina turned to confront Jamie, who had risen to his swollen feet, fighting the pain by bracing himself against the wall. His right hand was free, but his left was still manacled to the chain mounted into a ring in the floor. Molina slashed, but Jamie twisted away. Breathing heavily, the officer retreated warily, shifting his gaze between Jamie and the wounded doctor.

Molina chuckled. "So no more opportunities for torture, Scotsman. Ortega was killed in the collapse of the wall tower. A pity, for he was a master at his trade. Now you will die, for I am the master of my trade."

Jamie sneered. "A master o' yer trade? A warrior fights fer honor, nae fer lust or tae inflict unnecessary suffering. Tell me, what is yer trade? Master butcher?"

Molina hesitated, confused by the question. Jamie reached stealthily to free the concealed scalpel in his waistband. Seeing the movement, Molina lunged. Jamie twisted away, but the tip of the blade slashed his grimy shirt and sliced the flesh underneath. Molina spun, but Jamie whipped the loose chain in his left hand around Molina's throat and jerked it tight, slamming the Spanish officer against the wall with his greater height and body weight.

They struggled, with Molina attempting to slither free and Jamie trying to reach the scalpel. At last, his fingers closed on the handle. He yanked the blade free of his waistband, but with horror, saw that the wooden guard was still attached. The combatants surged back and forth, scraping the wall and aggravating the burning in Jamie's feet. Raising the blade to his lips, he gripped the wooden guard in his teeth and pulled it free. Molina's body thrashed, forcing Jamie's hand with the scalpel to the right, slashing his own lip. Blood poured down his chin.

Molina managed to turn himself in Jamie's grip so they were face-to-face. The saber was wedged uselessly between their bodies. The lieutenant licked his lips and spat blood into Jamie's eyes. He blinked rapidly to clear his vision, the stink of the Spaniard's breath rancid in his nostrils. Tightening his grip on the chain in his left hand, he brought up his right holding the glittering scalpel. With fear dilating his eyes, Molina saw the danger. He brought up his right hand and locked it on Jamie's wrist. The two combatants surged back and forth, slamming against the wall repeatedly.

Weakened by near starvation and his injuries, Jamie called on every reserve of strength to raise the scalpel to Molina's chin. The guard officer's eyes widened impossibly as the blade pressed against his throat. One hard lunge and it was over. Breath sighed out of Molina with a long-drawn-out "Nooo!" and then his body collapsed in Jamie's grip. Gasping for breath, Jamie sank to his knees, with Molina's body sagging limply to the floor.

Tomas Gomez helped push the body away. "It was an ingenious stroke, amigo. You may not realize it, but you severed his carotid artery. That is why he died so quickly. It is amazing, is it not, how much blood there is in the human body? We are sitting here in a puddle of mine, yours, and his, commingled as if we were blood brothers."

Jamie muttered, "I take nae pleasure frae inflicting death, nae matter how weel deserved. I would welcome ye as a brother, my guid physician, but nae this human trash. It is a pity that he died sae easily. And now we must think o' our ain escape frae destruction, fer the citadel may nae stand many more direct hits wi'out collapsing."

"I have a medicine bag, and both of us have injuries to tend." He gestured at the wide-eyed Cuban prisoners. "I suggest unlocking your manacle and then helping these poor unfortunates to escape, for Molina would have slain them all."

Jamie took the key from Tomas after he was freed and crawled to Eduardo Sanchez, for the fight with Molina had cost him the ability to stand. Sanchez said, "Vous nous avez sauvés par tuer ce salaud Molina. Allez, cacher, je vais libérer les autres. Nous dirons la garnison espagnole que vous êtes mort."

Jamie translated for Gomez. "He says that it is good that Molina is dead and that we are trying to free the prisoners. I told him that we will hide until the British come but urged him to flee to their homes in Guanabacoa."

Jamie embraced Eduardo Sanchez, waved to the departing prisoners, and then helped Tomas Gomez crawl two hundred feet to the most distant storeroom. He returned to fetch the doctor's bag. Without anesthetics, it was intensely painful, but they stitched each other's wounds and bound them tightly. Gomez had a little willow bark extract, which they carefully rationed to ease their pain, for they did not know how long they must hide in the abandoned fortress.

While they waited, Tomas Gomez told Jamie the story of the British assault on Havana and his own father's heroic defense. He explained that he had been delayed in seeking to find Jamie by his father's untimely death a week earlier. The exertions of the defense of the town of Guanabacoa had sapped the old man's strength, and his heart had failed him.

By July 31st, Albemarle completed a siege line running along the entire land front of Havana and erected batteries on the shore from El Morro to La Cabana. That morning, a bombardment began against La Punta and the city walls by mortars, howitzers, and guns. Before the attack, Albemarle sent an officer to ask Don Prado to surrender, but the governor refused, in spite of Tio Antonio's dying plea to save the city from the certain destruction that bombardment would bring. Tomas shook his head. "It seems that our governor has been infected by the spirit of duende as well as Velasco." They sat back to wait, hungry, but not in shape to brave the upper levels of the citadel to find food. By two in the afternoon, bombardment against the city stopped, indicating that parley was underway, for there was no other reason for the cessation.

Twilight came on. At last they could bear the hunger no longer. The doctor volunteered to make the first search. It was well after dark when he crawled back, dragging a sack of bread, cheese, and a leather-wrapped bottle of wine. "I found a larder with enough to sustain us for several days. I must caution you that we are not utterly alone in the citadel. There are several dead men in the corridors above, but no one living. However, we must not strike a spark or set a fire where it can be seen, for it may make some gunner restless to fire a shot."

Jamie grimaced. "I dislike disturbing the dead, but the dead will soon disturb us by decomposing in this heat. I suggest that we return at first light tae retrieve what victuals we can find. Although we are confined down here, the air will prove fresher than higher levels."

Gomez grinned. "You have forgotten the dead lieutenant that you sped to hell this morning."

Jamie laughed. "Aye, weel, smelling his rotting corpse may enliven my spirits, fer his death offers me a chance tae live."

A day passed uneventfully, and another night. The stench of Javier Molina's body became intolerable. On the second morning, stiff and sore from his wound, Tomas Gomez persuaded Jamie to stay hidden while he ventured out to discover what was happening. He returned breathless less than an hour later to report that the British had established a line less than three hundred yards from La Punta, with massive artillery emplacements facing the town walls.

Tomas said, "I would have approached the British ramparts, but there were Spanish sentries on the town walls."

Jamie shook his head. "It would be foolhardy by day and equally dangerous at night. It is better for us to wait for the end of what appears to be negotiations for surrender. We will certainly be found by the troops sent to occupy La Punta."

The doctor frowned. "Unless there is a bombardment. The British must have an unlimited supply of guns and ammunition."

Jamie replied, "They have the reinforcements frae North America and are anxious tae end this battle quickly. Let us remain in hiding another day or twa." They had adequate food, but after another day, their supply of water ran low. Tomas left to find the well that had to exist within La Punta's precincts. Jamie dozed.

He woke to the ruffle of drums and tread of marching feet. Tomas had not returned. From the floor above came the sound of hammering, followed by deep booms loud enough to be caused by a battering ram working on the massive doors. The Spanish garrison, which had abandoned La Punta, must have left them barred and bolted. Wrenching shrieks and popping signaled brackets and bolts giving way. The walls shook when the heavy doors of the citadel collapsed. Above his head came the thudding of boots and shouts as troops raced inside. Jamie struggled erect and abruptly sat, for his swollen feet refused to support his weight.

The door of the storeroom opened and then shut as Tomas Gomez slipped inside. He clutched his wounded side and gasped for air. "Our governor, Don Prado, has surrendered Havana with full honors after the British threatened to destroy the city. They are even now at the city gates."

Jamie smiled. "If ye listen, ye would realize that they are now inside the fortress. They will search every room and cranny until they are satisfied that there are nae armed enemy aboot.

Tae avoid being shot, I advise ye tae take off the saber and pistol ye took frae Molina's body."

Gomez hurriedly complied, placing the weapons on the floor. They did not have long to wait. The latch lifted, and the door creaked open. A musket barrel protruded through the crack.

Jamie called out huskily, "I am Captain James Drummond of His Majesty's Royal Marines, lately a prisoner in this dungeon." As the door swung wide to reveal the red-coated uniforms of two armed marines, he added, "And ane civilian physician, Tomas Gomez, wha came tae rescue me. Treat him as a friend."

The marines at the door stepped aside as a rough voice ordered, "Stand back!" With a basket-hilted broadsword at the ready, Major Jock Armstrong shouldered his way into the room. He turned and barked an order, "All secure here! Continue tae search this level and get that stinking body wrapped in a shroud and ta'en ootside!"

Jock showed his teeth in a wide smile. "Waes me, Jamie! Yer a swankie lad, but I see that ye hae ta'en a terrible skaithin'. Yet ye requited yersel' weel. I saw the dead guard lieutenant in the dungeon, and all the prisoners fled. That must hae been yer doin'."

Jamie took a step, stumbled, and fell. Armstrong and two marines rushed to raise him. Jamie put an arm around the major's broad shoulder. "Aye, I am forfoughten and weary, Jock, frae the whangin' they gie me. I dinna recommend the bastinado fer entertainment, e'en wi' candlelight and soft music."

The jest was typical of the warrior spirit of marines, and everyone present roared with laughter, Jock loudest of all. Marines laid down their weapons to shake Jamie's hand and clap him on the back. Jamie introduced Tomas Gomez, who received warm praise for his brave actions and a promise of good treatment by British doctors, followed by safe passage to his father's house in Guanabacoa.

3

Surgeon Elbridge Pomeroy rose from a kneeling position. "You may put on your stockings and shoes, Captain Drummond. It appears that daily warm soaks with salts for the past two weeks and frequent palpation of your feet has reduced the swelling and bruising from the bastinado. You say that you feel little pain. Let me see you walk without support."

Jamie pulled on his shoes and then pushed up from the bench in the sick bay to a standing position. He took a deep breath and bit down on his lip to mask the dull ache in his right foot. He wanted nothing more than to receive a clearance from HMS *Dragon's* surgeon that he was fit to return to duty. If he had to conceal a pain or two, he was prepared to endure them.

Stretcher bearers had conveyed Jamie and Tomas Gomez to the British Army field hospital behind the artillery batteries confronting the city walls. He bade farewell to the Spanish doctor who had saved his life in La Punta's dungeon. The stitches that Jamie had clumsily inserted in the deep cut in Tomas's chest had festered. An army surgeon had replaced them. He predicted that Gomez faced a bout with fever and sent him to convalesce on the hospital ship floating outside the channel.

Jock Armstrong had maneuvered to have Jamie sent to his own ship, the *Dragon*, where he whiled away the time reading, eating everything he could wheedle from the cooks, and doggedly enduring the surgeon's prescribed soaks and massages. To his great surprise and pleasure, a salvage team had recovered his uniforms and precious Andrea Ferrara rapier from the capsized *Stirling Castle*. That unfortunate ship had been successfully patched and floated off the underwater shelf where she had wrecked on the reef under El Morro's walls. At dinner one evening, Jock related the news that it was unlikely the ship could be repaired sufficiently to make the trans-Atlantic journey to Portsmouth dockyard. Stripping and scuttling were her probable fate.

"Now turn and walk to the far bulkhead."

Jamie dutifully turned and retraced his steps under the watchful eye of the surgeon. Before he reached the end, Jock Armstrong entered. He stood stooped under the low overhead, then slipped into a nearby chair to watch as Jamie made several more turns in response to the surgeon's orders.

"That is quite enough walking." Pomeroy tapped the paper he was holding. "Captain Drummond, you are highly motivated to return to duty, although it is obvious to me that your feet are not completely healed. It may be some months before the effects are completely gone. I recognize suppressed pain when I see it. Your throat and jaw muscles betray you. However, the fleet desires your services. Have you been told where you are bound and when?"

Before Jamie could answer, Jock Armstrong spoke, "He dinna ken his next assignment, fer I hae his orders in my hand." He passed a sheaf of papers to Jamie.

Jamie read for a minute and then looked up. "I am to command the marine contingent aboard *Marlborough*. I understand that she was knocked aboot some on that day we attacked El Morro and I was captured."

Jock responded, "Ye will replace Henry Littlefield, wha was the sole ship's officer killed during that action. *Marlborough* is the auld *St. Michael*, launched at Chatham nearly a hundred years ago. She spent seven years undergoing rebuild and was cut doon frae a ninety tae a sixty-eight. She hae been in many battles, leaks mair than maist, but her timbers are still sound. Her new captain, Thomas Burnett, assumed command in April. He is a very capable mariner."

Jamie nodded. "Being incarcerated and hospitalized since the end o' June, I am nae aware o' what is happening now that the battle fer Havana is o'er. Has the remainder o' the island capitulated? Are we close tae an end tae the war?"

Jock said, "We hae mair than five hundred dead frae battle and untold thousands mair tae disease. 'Tis a mercy that the Spanish are nae contending fer the island. Garrisons are surrendering wi'out a fight or huddling within their inadequate fortifications, praying that British bayonets and artillery dinna seek them oot. Fourteen Spanish ships o' the line hae surrendered as weel, leaving only a few Spanish ships afloat in the Caribbean. The French fleet is maistly bottled up or hiding."

"Then what is there tae accomplish tae secure victory?"

Jock shrugged. "I expect that the fleet will patrol westwards and southwards, seeking tae destroy the last enemy ships until the admiral decides tae send a convoy back tae Portsmouth."

Jock scowled. "In spite o' victory, the talk o' the fleet is all aboot the size o' the treasure. Ye would be astonished at the booty seized frae the Spanish governor's storehouses—eleven million silver pesos, in addition tae untold piles o' stores and the unscathed warships.

"Officers and men alike are in an ugly mood regarding the share that Admiral Pocock confiscated fer himself. I heard it said that he and Albemarle seized a half million pesos each, while soldiers and sailors may get as little as twenty pesos. If our commanders are allowed tae keep their filthy lucre, they will live in retirement like Oriental pashas. Neither was e'er at risk frae Spanish arms. They are greedy and grasping, far different than Admiral Hawke or General Wolfe, wha were brave and maist generous wi' their officers and men. It is unco difficult tae accept or explain tae the men, wha endured unremitting days o' battle and sickness, nae counting those wha died." He cuffed Jamie affectionately. "Perhaps ye will receive a few extra pesos fer enduring the bastinado, but I dinna believe the admiral or general ken or care."

Elbridge Pomeroy interrupted the conversation. "Orders are meaningless, gentlemen. I should have been consulted before they were issued. Mr. Drummond is not yet fit to perform all duties at sea. I would dislike hearing of your burial at sea following a fall from the rigging. I will sign your release only if *Marlborough's* surgeon comes aboard to examine you and accepts responsibility for your continued treatment." He rose. "I will send a note to Jonathan Maxwell to that effect."

Shortly before noon the next day, Jamie stopped his pacing in the waist as the officer of the watch hailed an approaching jolly boat. An officer clambered up, saluted, and announced himself as Lieutenant Maxwell, surgeon of *Marlborough*. Jonathan Maxwell appeared uncommonly young for a ship's surgeon, tall and lean, with sun-darkened features. He returned Jamie's stare boldly and smiled, for he was equally impressed.

He spoke with a Lowland Scots accent. "Sae, Captain Drummond, ye are the celebrated prisoner o' El Morro. I hae heard somewhat o' yer capture, incarceration, and torture. Yer health appears much improved, but let us gae below tae meet with Mr. Pomeroy and conduct the examination he hae requested."

The examination was routine, consisting of palpation, probing, and kneading of joints and muscles. Maxwell asked Jamie to perform various exercises that involved reaching, stretching, mounting a ladder, and jumping down the final few steps. In spite of twinges, Jamie successfully masked the resulting pain. The surgeon impassively eyed Jamie before writing a long passage in his notebook. At length, he laid down his pen and rose. "I wish tae impose a final test. Please remove yer wig, jacket, shoes, and stockings. Come, follow me on deck, Mr. Drummond."

A puzzled Jamie followed the doctor upward. Once they reached the waist, Maxwell spoke in low tones to the officer of the watch, who spoke to the quartermaster, who went below. The mystery was solved when he returned carrying two cutlasses. The doctor accepted the weapons and extended one to a surprised Jamie.

"A convalescing naval officer can easily issue orders aboard ship, but a marine commander is expected tae lead boarding parties and engage the enemy hand tae hand. Show me that ye can, and I will sign Mr. Pomeroy's paper."

Jamie said, "Ho! Can I? Wi'oot opportunity tae practice, I may be rusty, and ye may lay a knap or twa on me, but ye will find me unco brawly!" The grinning officer of the watch waved to a boatswain's mate, who hastily ordered sailors to clear space. Jamie raised the cutlass and crossed Maxwell's weapon in the en garde position.

Blades rang as the two officers battled up and down the deck while sailors, marines, and officers gathered around cheered. The Scottish surgeon was very fit and clearly intent on forcing Jamie to move up and down the deck many times. Jamie's skill was greater, but inactivity and the humid heat swiftly sapped his energy. Within five minutes, both officers were sweating profusely. Jamie could feel his bare feet swelling, but caught up in the exultation of his favorite sport, he was not impaired.

Jamie executed a pretty combination of low- and high-line attacks, and the surgeon's weapon flew from his grip. He raised his hands in defeat, and Jamie lowered his point. The spectators cheered noisily. Maxwell retrieved his cutlass and handed it to Jamie, who passed both weapons to the quartermaster.

Once they were back in the sickbay, the surgeon reexamined Jamie's feet and clucked sympathetically. "Ye are a skilled swordsman and easily bested me. I ken that ye prolonged the combat because ye love the sport. Howe'er, ye canna hide this swelling. We hae nae ice in this tropical heat, although it would be maist helpful. I prescribe salts and cool water at every opportunity." He sat back and chewed his lower lip.

"Tae tell ye truly, ye are nae yet fit fer all shipboard duties. Ye hae great courage and are quite adept at concealing the hurts that ye received. I am o' half a mind tae join Mr. Pomeroy in recommending ye as unfit fer service. Yer records show that ye hae been at sea or in land combat fer the entirety o' this war. I advise ye tae gae hame, Jamie Drummond."

Jamie stared intently at the two surgeons. "I must confess that I am sair tempted tae accept. I yearn fer peace as much as any man, but years frae now I dinna wish tae remember that I ended my service in that manner. Let me stay."

Elbridge Pomeroy exchanged glances with Jonathan Maxwell before scratching the nape of his neck. "It is difficult not to question the sanity of a man who has been through so much yet refuses an opportunity to escape the war."

Maxwell shook his head. "'Tis a matter o' honor and nae subject tae rules o' logic. Tae a Scot, and particularly a Highland Scot, honor matters mair than life itself. The man hae gi'en his word. Whether wise or foolish, he canna willingly break his oath. We may send him hame, Elbridge, but nae wi' his consent. I say, let him stay. His feet will heal in time, and there is little risk o' imminent action wi' the French or Spanish fleet. He is an inspirational leader, and his reputation fer courage is unquestioned. He is also an exceptional fencer, and I would like naething mair than an opportunity tae learn his techniques. Why, scarcely able tae walk and weak frae imprisonment, he bested me." He raised a questioning eyebrow.

Pomeroy snorted. "Two headstrong Scots! Although I claim that logic and common sense are on my side, you overwhelm me." He turned to his desk, picked up the release, dipped a quill in the inkpot, and scribbled his signature. He said, "'Tis against my judgment, but here is your release, Mr. Drummond."

Jamie accepted it with relief. "I canna express my gratitude fer this favor. Ye hae my thanks, sir."

Dragon's physician nodded but waved a long finger under Maxwell's nose. "He is now your charge, and I admonish you to be a tyrant in fulfilling every particular of the recovery regimen that I suggested. I wish both of you the very best of luck on *Marlborough*."

Jamie's spirits soared as he swung the seabag containing his uniforms, books, and rapier down to a seaman in the jolly boat bobbing alongside. He had given Jock Armstrong the news of his transfer and promised to visit often during their stay in Havana harbor. As the oarsmen pulled across to *Marlborough*, Jonathan Maxwell leaned back in the stern sheets. He said, "Rumors abound o' *Marlborough* joining the convoy that Admiral Pocock is sending back tae England. It will be a tight race tae make her seaworthy, fer there was much damage frae El Morro's guns."

Jamie inquired, "Wi'oot a proper dry dock, is it possible?"

The surgeon shrugged. "In the words o' Captain Burnett, we must make sensible compromises. We canna careen her tae repair the hull damage, but wi' pumping, the leaking is manageable. We need a month and a' hands laboring tae repair masts, spars, bulwarks, hatches, and rudder. Life aboard is an endless round o' working parties, but morale is guid."

The boat steered under the ship's shadow. Jamie was first to grab the swaying ladder as they bumped the side. As he reached the top and saluted the officer of the watch, Jamie could easily see that it would be some time before *Marlborough* would be ready to sail. Carpenters and their mates swarmed over the rigging and woodwork. Stacks of lumber, rope, and buckets of oakum and tar filled the waist. A blacksmith was hammering on a sheave at a small anvil while his assistant worked the bellows, keeping the coals glowing. Fire was always feared aboard a wooden ship, but the smiths had taken the precaution of surrounding the hot forge with wet tarpaulins while seamen stood ready with buckets of seawater to defend against sparks.

Maxwell led Jamie below to the row of cabins where junior officers swung their hammocks, followed by a sweating seaman carrying his seabag and other luggage. Jamie swung open the door, wrinkling his nose at the musty smell of a space seldom used. Jonathan grinned at Jamie's reaction. "Aye, Marlborough is auld, every timber reeks o' age. Be joyfu' that ye hae a space o' yer ain."

Jamie nodded. "After my accommodations in Havana's prisons, I am heartily pleased."

Jonathan tipped his hat. "Remember, dinner at the captain's table is in an hour. He is maist insistent that all officers be punctual." He clapped Jamie on the back and took his leave.

○———————○

"Before dinner is served, introductions are in order, gentlemen." Captain Thomas Burnett stood at the head of the table in his cabin, with ship's officers arrayed on both sides. The captain's orderly placed pots of tea on the table.

A tall officer with traces of a blue-black beard shadowing his chin nodded and said, "Commander Elisha Corey, ship's first lieutenant. I believe that I once met Captain Drummond before the battle at Quiberon Bay, when weather bottled up the fleet in Torbay."

Jamie nodded in recognition.

A stocky lieutenant with a florid, beefy face said, "Benjamin Thorpe, second lieutenant. 'Tis our first meeting, Mr. Drummond. Welcome to *Marlborough*."

A youthful smooth-faced officer with dark curly hair waved a hand languidly. "Gideon Marsh, third lieutenant. I have heard from our good doctor that our newly reported marine commander is an expert fencer. I am itching to test your skills."

The surgeon shook his head. "Nay, Gideon, ye need tae temper yer enthusiasm long enough fer Mr. Drummond tae regain his strength and heal his feet. Many victims o' the Spanish bastinado can scarcely walk, let alain recover enough tae fence. I promise ye that when he recovers, Mr. Drummond will gie ye a' the fight ye wish."

A deep baritone interrupted the conversation. "I am Noah Keigwein, *Marlborough's* master for the last eighteen years. I will be retiring at the end of this deployment and returning home to Penzance."

Jamie said, "Hae ye served wi' a sailor frae Mousehole, Ephraim Northcutt by name?"

The master's face crinkled in a broad smile. "A fine mariner, with a knowledge of every cove and embayment along the southwest coast." He sobered. "A courageous man in a fight or storm. We served together at Portobello more years ago than I care to remember."

Jamie smiled. "I couldna hae asked fer a better teacher. I learned gunnery frae him and, maist important o' a', how tae fairly treat men. He will be missed."

The master frowned. "He died? When? Where?"

Jamie said, "Nae, he was unco lucky. He retired and took employment as a steersman and mate on a revenue cutter."

Keigwein burst out laughing. "The old scoundrel! He spent years escaping their nets and now they entrust him to catch smugglers! 'Tis akin to entrusting the guarding of lettuce to hares!" Laughter rippled around the table.

Jamie shook his head. "I think nae, Master Keigwein. Ephraim may hae been a smuggler in the past, but he is a man o' honor. If he gies his word, ye can trust him entirely."

The master nodded. "That you can. Perhaps the old rascal can put in a word for me."

Captain Burnett interrupted the conversation by clattering a knife blade on a glass. "We are in luck, gentlemen. Kelly informs me that he is ready to serve our victuals. He tells me that we have a respite from bully beef, with fish, pork, rice, and vegetables procured from Havana merchants. Enjoy the tropical bounty, for we shall soon be at sea and doomed to consume brined meat frae the barrels thrice daily."

Jamie's eyes swept the rest of the room. While nearly all were strangers to him, a familiar face stood out. Marine Lieutenant Jeremy Faircloth, late of *Stirling Castle*, smiled and waved a hand when Jamie's eyes locked on his.

The meal grew convivial as the conversation and wine flowed. While Jamie had been a stranger to most of *Marlborough*'s officers when he entered the wardroom, by the time the orderlies served dessert—a delectable pudding with a brandy-laced sauce—free-spirited camaraderie was evident. Jamie mused that the Royal Navy and Marines constituted an exceptional brotherhood. He felt great pride in being a part of it. While he missed old friends with whom he had served on previous ships, *Marlborough's* captain and officers promised to be a friendly and gregarious community. The singular disturbing exception appeared to be the ship's third lieutenant, Gideon Marsh. More than once, Jamie caught the dark-eyed young officer staring unsmiling in his direction.

Aye, weel, he thought. *The lad fears his run as best blade on this ship will end and is piqued that I will supplant him. He dinna understand that my objective is nae tae dominate but simply tae enjoy the sport.*

There was another surprise the next morning when Jamie called Jeremy Faircloth to his cabin. The lieutenant presented the detachment roster. Jamie's eyes widened when he recognized Sergeant Hoyt's name. "Tell me, Jeremy, how many o' the lads frae *Stirling Castle* are aboard? Nae, let me review the names." His eyes flew down the list. "Kennedy, Malone, Powell, Eastman, and Burke, in addition tae Hoyt and yerself."

The lieutenant said, "Stirling Castle's contingent was distributed across the fleet, sir, to fill shortages almost immediately after capsizing. While we got the crew off safely, it was some days before we could complete the salvage under cover of darkness.

The hull provided cover once the carpenters knocked a hole in the bulwarks."

Jamie nodded. "I must gie ye thanks fer recovering my kit, uniforms, books, and a'."

Faircloth said, "There was no news, Captain, but we all trusted to Providence that ye would survive imprisonment, eventually return, and need them."

Jamie said softly, "It was an unco unpleasant experience, Jeremy, wi' much hunger, fear, and pain. 'Tis strange, but at the last, it was precisely those emotions that sustained me and gie me resolve tae survive, as weel as the conviction that I hae a purpose in living."

They discussed the marines, assignments, and level of training at length. Jamie said, "I see nae reason tae revise any watch lists, Jeremy. Ye hae done everything I would hae expected since Littlefield's death. I may be hard pressed tae find a role fer myself."

Faircloth chuckled. "No worries, sir. I have already heard the rumor that the captain intends to assign you the same position on *Marlborough* that you held on *Stirling Castle*—to command all guns."

Captain Burnett sent for Jamie the next morning and confirmed what Jeremy Faircloth had told him, that he would command all gun sections. He said, "I am satisfied with neither our accuracy nor ability to run out quickly. While working parties will consume our resources until we join the convoy for the return to Portsmouth, I insist that we hold daily gun drills once we sail. My gun commander has been somewhat lax in training. That betrayed us during the attack on El Morro." He stared moodily out the stern windows.

Jamie waited, but the captain did not seem inclined to break the silence. Jamie broke protocol by asking, "Does the gun commander ken that he is being replaced?"

Captain Burnett nodded. "I told Mr. Marsh yesterday morning before you came aboard that I was intent on reassigning him. He is third lieutenant and overloaded with responsibilities. He should welcome the reassignment, but is taking this rather badly. His pride is wounded and his confidence shaken. He was a protégé of Captain John Holwell, who had commanded since *Marlborough's* recommissioning. Marsh has not been happy since his mentor's departure."

Jamie said, "I hae served on several ships in a multitude o' assignments. Naething is permanent, and we should make the best o' our circumstances. I would be willing tae serve under Mr. Marsh—"

Captain Burnett shook his head. "That would be worse, for then he would not be able to claim any credit for improvement, for all would see that it was your doing. Nay, I am determined to make the change. Gideon Marsh is a fine officer who must swallow his pride and perfect himself in his role of third officer. Your task is to raise the efficiency of the gun captains and crews."

Jamie nodded but with foreboding. The hostility in Marsh's eyes at dinner the evening before portended trouble. While anger over being replaced appeared to drive it rather than rivalry over fencing ability, the consequences could be damaging to them both. Jamie was resolved not to allow unreasoning emotion to control his actions.

For two weeks, the press of repair activities left little time for leisure. No one had time for fencing, but Jamie steeled himself to enduring an hour daily traversing every deck and ladder on the ship to condition his feet. Jamie slipped easily into his role as commander of the marine detachment. Except for a single meeting to take over as gun commander from Gideon Marsh, he and the third lieutenant had no interactions. Jamie credited the captain or the first lieutenant for arranging the watch schedule to restrict their contacts.

While days were filled with activity, Jamie came to dread the nights. The stifling humidity of midsummer had abated, but the buildup of heat below decks still made sleeping difficult. Stern discipline of the mind gave way during sleep, and recurrent dreams of his imprisonment returned. The vividness of these scenes punished all his senses. He felt the shackles that held him to the table in the torture chamber bite into his ankles and wrists. Mind-numbing pain lanced through his feet, swollen by blows wielded by Gaspar Ortega, Molina's torturer. Lieutenant Molina's grinning face, lit by the flickering torches, was a nightmare jack-o'-lantern. When the pain reached a crescendo and Jamie could bear it no longer, he would wake with a gasp, choking on the bile in his throat. He lay awake for long hours, his temples throbbing and heart thudding from the physical trauma brought on by the dream.

Jamie told no one of his nightly ordeal. Jonathan Maxwell took his elbow one day and steered him to a quiet corner of the bridge. "I expected that ye would recover swiftly frae yer time in the prison, Jamie, but yer woefu' countenance troubles me. I saw ye dozing at the captain's table mair than once. Can ye no sleep at night?"

Jamie shifted uncomfortably. The warrior's code that governed his behavior made it easy to acknowledge physical injury and illness, but not the effects of a troubled mind. He fumbled for words. Evasively, he said, "The heat below decks disturbs my sleep."

The physician searched Jamie's face. "Ye hae been at sea fer years, wi' much o' that service in the tropics. I sense that yer ailment is o' recent genesis. May I hazard a guess that it dates frae yer imprisonment and torture?"

Jamie nodded but could find no words to describe his tumultuous thoughts. Maxwell touched his temple and then felt for the pulse in his wrist. When he released it, he said, "The mere remembrance o' what ye endured has yer heart pounding fair tae burst. Ye are a brave man, Jamie Drummond. I ken that ye hae ne'er lacked fer courage in the face o' battle. There is nae shame in battling foes in yer mind, but ye need rest at night in order tae perform yer duties in the day. If you wish, I could prescribe laudanum to permit ye tae sleep."

Jamie shook his head. "I hae taken the potion when injured tae suppress pain and promote sleep but hae heard tales o' the hold it can place on a man wha uses it excessively. I recall men wha hungered fer it until they nearly lost their minds. I wilna take it. Likewise, rum and gin may promote sleep for the troubled, but excessive use can destroy a man's body and mind."

Maxwell yielded, but asked Jamie to wake him if he had a change of heart. The repetitive dreams of torture persisted until the strange night when they suddenly ended. Abruptly, he woke, convinced that a strange presence had entered his cabin. Jamie struggled, almost upsetting his hammock to open his eyes, which fluttered and stayed shut, although his mind told him that he was fully awake. His panting sounded harsh in the small cabin. At last, the muscles holding his lids shut relaxed, and he opened his eyes. He expected darkness, for he remembered pinching the candlewick before beginning the nightly struggle to sleep, but he could make out a faint light, and his head snapped to the left when he detected movement. He was scrabbling for his sword when in the darkness there was a low raspy laugh.

"Ah, ye are awake, lad."

4

The small stuffy room was not fully dark. Two shadowed figures too small to be men sat hunched on the rope that attached his hammock to the eyebolt in the bulkhead. A faint glow emanated from some place behind them, illuminating their unnaturally large heads, hooked noses, and the deep-set sockets of their eyes. Both had long gray beards tucked into their belts and black boots reaching to the tops of their thighs.

One of the dwarvish figures spoke in a gravelly voice that sounded like grinding stones. "Ye dinna remember us, but we ken ye weel."

Jamie yawned hugely, suddenly amused by the strange visitors, for they were clearly not human. "Aye, I feel awake but must be dreaming. Ye are nae as frightful as other denizens o' the night, but ye are nae real. Since ye are nae mair than apparitions and I need my sleep, begone." So saying, he closed his eyes and lay back.

A second voice spoke, more gravelly than the first. "We are as real as the images that haunt yer dreams. We would hae a word or twa wi' ye."

Jamie opened his eyes, propped himself on an elbow, and regarded the pair with interest. The light that illuminated their forms was steady but seemed to come from no source. Their long hair was concealed by their blue bonnets. Their beards and craggy features bore the marks of extreme age. But their eyes were lively and attentive—ageless.

Jamie smiled, and the ancient figures smiled back. "Ye are real, ye say? Name yerselves."

"Tae Highland folk, we are *gruagach* while Lowland Scots call us *urisk*. I am hight Peallaidh an Spùit." He hooked a gnarled thumb at his companion. "He calls himself Stochdail."

Jamie's mouth fell open. "Peallaidh? King o' the gruagach, the little people? I remember lang syne when the brewer at Strathallan would pour wort into a hole in a stane fer ye and the crofters' wives sprinkled milk and set oot butter fer yer people in every corner o' the byre, but come, that was a child's tale, and unreal, albeit a pleasing tale."

Peallaidh scratched his long nose with an equally long finger. "Aye, it was a child's tale, but ye remember. Ofttimes, bards and storytellers invoke our names and retell the auld stories. When they do, we are as real as the wind, rain, and cold ootside the castle or croft. Are we real? Are dreams real? We live through the memories o' men that bring the past tae life wi' the fears, pleasures, and fierce joy o' past events great and common."

Jamie nodded, lost in the recollection of childhood evenings spent before a crackling fire, listening to tales told by his mother and father, uncles, and cousins.

Stochdail's rumbling voice broke his reverie. "When ye were sma', ye shook wi' fear at tales of ogres, trolls, dragons, and evil men. Now that ye are grown and recall them, do such fearsome tales beset ye?" He did not wait for Jamie's response. "Nae. Memories make them seem real, but ye ken that these denizens and events are in the past and hae nae power tae afflict ye. Yer heart beats faster and ice grips yer heart at the recollection, but they canna harm ye, fer they exist only in yer mind."

When he paused, Peallaidh spoke, "Ye bore muckle afflictions frae yer imprisonment, and ye will always remember them. The pain and frequency o' remembrance can be less if ye concentrate on what ye must do in the present. School yer mind tae choose which memories dominate yer thoughts. Dinna bid them forth.

If ye succeed in that effort, lad, ye will hae the restfu' sleep that ye need. Perhaps ye will dream o' us and other pleasant creatures and nae o' pain and suffering."

Jamie said, "I dinna intend tae be presumptuous, gentlemen, but ye make it sound magical."

The hammock rope shook as Stochdail clambered close enough to shake a bony finger under Jamie's nose. "'Tis nae magic tae use the power o' yer mind. Neither potions nor incantations will avail fer mair than a single nicht. Only ye can cleanse yerself o' the evil influence o' bad dreams."

Jamie extended his hand to touch the little man, but he scrambled out of reach. "Wha sent ye wi' this message? Surely, it was at the behest o' someone?"

Peallaidh's beard wagged as he shook his head. "Since we exist in yer memory, it was ye wha called us forth."

Jamie rubbed his chin. "Truly, the human mind is a wondrously complex machine. I dinna recall doing that."

The little man nodded vigorously. "Aye, ye ken the secret. The affliction and cure are baith in yer mind and subject tae yer will if ye hae strength tae call it forth."

Stochdail spoke, "We must depart, fer dawn approaches. We admonish ye tae nae speak o' our visit tae others."

Jamie chuckled. "Ye can count on it, fer they would consider me mad tae be discoursing wi' the wee folk."

In a blink, the little men vanished, and the light faded. Distantly, *Marlborough*'s bell chimed eight times. A chorus of thuds resounded through the timbers as the crew tumbled out of their hammocks.

The next evening, after coming off watch at midnight, Jamie undressed and swung into his hammock. He did not remember dozing off but snapped awake from a dreamless sleep. The gruagach had returned. They repeated their advice, expressing pleasure that Jamie's sleep was dreamless. They appeared twice more and then inexplicably did not return. Neither did the visions of torture. Jonathan Maxwell took him aside after the evening meal, questioning him closely about his dreams. Mindful of the gruagach's warning to not mention them, Jamie attributed the disappearance of the wrenching dreams to the daily regimen of hard work. Maxwell's face was a study in contrast; it showed skepticism that Jamie had been cured so easily and relief that he had.

Captain Burnett informed the officers at dinner that they would sail to Martinique, where the return convoy to England would assemble by the end of October. Repairs ended a week before the scheduled date for departure from Havana. The ship's officers conducted a thorough inspection and found only minor details to be corrected. Working parties shifted to restocking and rewatering for the coming voyage. Faced with pleas from a majority of the ship's officers to set aside a clear area in the hold to allow them to hold fencing drills, he gave in, but insisted that the ship would not sail short in supplies. The officers would have to ingeniously find storage for the boxes and barrels planned for the space.

As they approached completion of preparations to sail, the captain announced shore leave. The city of Havana was securely in control of the British Army, with garrisons in place at El Morro, La Punta, and citadels throughout the city's populous precincts. While not all debris from battle had been cleared away and repairs completed, the city's merchants welcomed trade with their conquerors. With pay jingling in their pockets, sailors and marines prepared to descend on Havana to sample its legendary delights.

Jamie was below at the magazine, supervising inventory of shot and powder when a midshipman nudged his elbow. "Mr. Sharpe sent me to invite you to meet him on the quarterdeck, sir. A shore boat brought a Cuban servant to the gangway carrying this note for you. He is waiting for your reply."

Jamie took the note and broke the red wax seal. He moved close to the lantern suspended in the passageway. The note was written in English in an ornate hand. The signature at the bottom was that of Tomas Gomez. The physician had heard the rumor that British ships were preparing to sail and was extending an invitation for Jamie and a companion to dine with his family two days hence.

"Sergeant Hoyt, continue the inventory. I will return shortly."

As Jamie reached the quarterdeck, the liveried Cuban servant bowed low. "I was major domo for His Excellency, Don José Antonio Gómez, *alcalde* of Guanabacoa. Now I am honored to serve his son, the physician Tomas Antonio Gomez, in the same capacity. I see from your walk, Captain Drummond, that you are recovered from the injuries you received at La Punta. May I confirm to my master that you will attend him?"

Jamie responded, "I will attend. I greatly desire tae see Tomas before we depart. I wish tae thank him again fer saving me at the risk o' his ain life."

The servant's smooth brow wrinkled momentarily at the Scottish brogue, but he was imperturbable. "The hospitality of habaneros is renowned. You will find a visit to Guanabacoa delightful, for my master has many friends in the town. Although the criollos of the capital disdain those who live outside the walls, our town has festive entertainment and the finest food in the Caribbean. I will return conveying your acceptance."

Given that Tomas Gomez was a physician, it seemed appropriate to extend an invitation to Jonathan Maxwell to accompany him. The doctor was delighted to accept.

The two Scottish officers took the shore boat to the dock below La Punta two hours early. While they had assurances that the streets were safe, they would be returning late at night. Both officers wore rapiers, carried a knife in the boot, and concealed a pistol beneath their jacket. They were confident enough in their skill with weapons to ward off local toughs.

To show their gratitude for their host's hospitality, Jamie was intent on finding an appropriate gift. They wandered shops along the thoroughfares, where merchants and their hired boys bedeviled them with offers of bargains. After considering the variety of excellent goods in a shop displaying blown and cut glass, Jamie settled on a magnificent crystal decanter imported from Austria, which he carefully filled with the contents of a bottle of well-aged Scotch whiskey contributed by Jonathan Maxwell. The decanter went into a box, carefully wrapped in paper and soft white linen.

As the time for their dinner appointment approached, Jamie hailed a hansom cab. He was relieved to find that the driver spoke passable English and gave him the address of Tomas Gomez's residence.

The driver looked doubtful. "Guanabacoa? I live there and love my town, but you will find many more delightful places here in the center of Havana. Our great capital is most hospitable to visitors. It is the greatest city in the New World. Let me suggest—"

Jamie cut him off. "We hae an invitation frae Senor Tomas Gomez, the son of Don Jose Antonio Gomez, lately the alcalde of Guanabacoa."

The driver goggled. "Pepe Antonio? He who led the peasant army armed only with machetes against the British, only to be dismissed by the comandante?" He looked about and then back to Jamie and Jonathan Maxwell. "But you are British. Why would you visit his son?"

Jamie frowned. "Ye forget yer station as a driver, but I will answer only this question. I was captured and made a prisoner in El Morro. The good physician Tomas Gomez gave me the means to escape."

The driver whistled his astonishment. "Then you are the man who slew Molina, the comandante of the prison, and released his prisoners. You are a hero to the people of Guanabacoa, senor. It will be my pleasure to take you there."

The splendor of the buildings, parks, and wide avenues faded as they left the city center, passed through the gates, and entered the suburb of Guanabacoa, home to many of the city's artisans, shopkeepers, and workmen. Pedestrians found the sight of two British officers unusual and shouted questions in Spanish. The driver responded, but his passengers were unaware of what he was saying until groups of people began to trot alongside the vehicle. Soon they had also accumulated a crowd of shrieking children. The cab delivered Jamie and Jonathan before the black iron gates of a modest whitewashed mansion on a residential street paved with blue stones and shaded by rows of trees.

The driver refused to accept the money that Jamie proffered. Dismounting, he approached the gate, where he loudly called for Tomas Gomez. The wide brassbound door opened, and the physician emerged, waving to the cheering crowd that had gathered around the cab. He shouldered his way through the press, shaking hands and calling greetings. At last, he reached the place where Jamie and Jonathan had dismounted. They too had begun to shake hands and accept flowers, not knowing how else to behave. The physician turned to face the crowd.

In a voice that startled the birds in the nearby trees and sent them airborne, he shouted, "Los vecinos y ciudadanos de Guanabacoa, estos oficiales británicos son nuestros invitados de festividades de esta noche. Yo soy su anfitrión y la garantía de su seguridad. Mostrarles la hospitalidad debida a los héroes y buenos amigos. El capitán Drummond es el hombre, preso mismo quien sufrió la bastinado, mató al malvado comandante Molina y liberó a los hombres a los que torturaron. Gracias a él, a sus hermanos y padres han regresado a sus hogares. ¡Celebremos!"

When the huzzahs subsided, he translated his message into English. "Neighbors and citizens of Guanabacoa, these British officers are our guests for tonight's festivities. I am their host and guarantee for their safety. Show them the hospitality due to heroes and good friends. Captain Drummond, a prisoner himself who suffered the bastinado, is the man who killed the wicked comandante Molina and freed those men he tortured. Because of him, your brothers and fathers have returned home. Let us celebrate!"

Gomez led his guests into an inner courtyard, where tables had been placed and an entire pig had been roasting on a spit above a bed of charcoal. The trees were hung with garishly colored lanterns and paper streamers.

The evening was a riot of color, festive music, teary embraces, toasts in English and Spanish, and an endless supply of delicious food and drink. Former prisoners in the crowd pushed through the small courtyard to proudly introduce Jamie to their families. The inevitable result was a flurry of embraces, drinks thrust forward, and kisses from wives, daughters, and sons. Tipsy from rum and the fruity sangria, the laughing young British officers allowed themselves to be pulled into a circle of girls for lessons in Cuban dancing.

Later, the men gathered around a table at one end of the courtyard while women and children drifted to the kitchen or to the street. As the conversation quieted, Jonathan Maxwell asked, "Senor Gomez, why is it that your neighbors are so hospitable to those who so recently conquered their city?"

The physician set down his cup of sangria so favored by habaneros and pursed his lips. "To answer your question is more difficult than you may expect. You must understand that we here in Guanabacoa are not the same as those who administer the government of this island. You may consider us all Spanish and all totally loyal to the king, who sits on his throne in far-off Madrid. I tell you that it is not so. The criollos, aristocrats, and military officers who held power in the city and were charged to defend this island against the British, whom they told us were our enemies, are not the same as the people who live here." His long finger swept the courtyard. Here you will find Cubanos—some criollos, but most others merchants, artisans, workers, and even slaves. My father, Pepe Antonio"—he paused, for the people in the courtyard raised a cheer at mention of the name of their alcalde, so recently buried—"my father loved these people so often ignored and poorly treated by the authorities. He considered them the bone and sinews of the community. He trusted them enough that when the authorities failed to prepare for the coming of the British army and navy, he organized several hundred, armed mostly with machetes and other tools, to defend against the invasion. The militia failed to prepare or fight as they should. The city authorities dithered and could not decide what to do, so Pepe Antonio took action. He surprised the oncoming British, fought them off, and captured many. He paraded the captives before the authorities to show them what the people could do to defend their homes and families."

Jonathan Maxwell started to ask a question, but Jamie touched his forearm. Tomas Gomez had more to say. "The comandante of the city refused to listen. He dismissed my father in a most shameful way. He died of apoplexy, brought on by the public indignities that he suffered, along with the realization that the Spanish authorities would not defend us. The citadels and the city would be lost. The only man with spine enough to resist was Velasco, who bravely died defending El Morro."

The physician spread his arms and turned his tear-streaked face to his visitors. Jamie could hear muttered oaths around the long table. "I ask you, who is the enemy of my people? We came from many places, but this is our homeland. We have no voice in the convocations that will decide who will rule over us. The coming of the British will improve commerce on this island for a time, but they will not stay. This island is merely a token to be bartered. The Spanish will return, and hopefully, they will have learned a lesson and provide more resources to fortify our land and improve our economy. I declare to you that we must force the authorities sent here from Madrid to listen to us who live here. We can and will fight for our homes. They now know that and should beware, for true power and indomitable will rests with the people, be they criollos, merchants, free workers, or even slaves. Our loyalty is to our land and people, not to a faraway crown."

Jamie replied, "Such resolve is admirable, but heroic actions dinna always bring success, as my ain family learned in Scotland. Thousands died because my people trusted in leaders wha failed tae agree and friends wha dinna come tae their aid."

Tomas shook his head. "All who enter heaven do so by washing their feet in the blood of martyrs."

Jonathan tapped his head. "Ye must use this, my friend. A wise man judges events and waits fer the opportune time. It may take years—many years."

Jamie said softly, "If ye canna win freedom by arms, ye must nurture it in yer soul. Tyrants may bind ye and force ye tae labor against yer will, but yer soul is always free."

The men discussed these and other topics late into the night. The two physicians became engrossed in medical details. Jamie dozed. Gradually, the women and children went off to bed. The bottles emptied, and the lanterns guttered and went out one by one. Befuddled and maudlin, the men rose for a final toast and embraces all around.

Tomas Gomez held Jamie close for a long time. At last, he said, "Vaya con Dios" and released him. "When a friend departs, it is customary to pronounce a benediction on his head. Go with God, mi amigo. Our lives are bound by our experiences in the prison. Perhaps we may meet again, but I do not think so. I saved your life, and in turn, you saved mine and that of my friends. We will always be grateful. I will welcome you if your travels ever bring you back to Havana. My home is your home."

Jamie promised to write. There was a final round of embraces, and the British officers reboarded the cab for the ride back through the deserted streets to the harbor.

The last larboard twenty-six pounder slammed against *Marlborough's* oaken bulwark. Sergeant Hoyt shouted, "Six minutes, Captain!" as the sweat-streaked gun crew collapsed to their knees, gasping for breath. Gunner Joshua York looked down in shame as Jamie Drummond's shadow fell over him. The rattan cane beat a tattoo against the railing. The silence stretched as Jamie stared across the turquoise water to where blue-gray mountains rose from the sea.

"Six minutes, Mr. Thorpe. Three days o' twice-daily practice hae nae improved this crew's performance. Ye hae three gun crews failing tae complete a run out in the five minutes desired by Captain Burnett." The tip of the cane hovered over first one man's head and then another's. "Loaders must be braw, and these lads are sma'. I suggest reassignments tae balance the strength and agility of the crews. None o' us desire a lang swim wi' the sharks when a French corsair sails in under our guns while we are unready tae fire."

The chagrined second lieutenant bit his lip but only responded, "Aye, aye, sir!" Captain Drummond was a welcome but cruelly demanding change from the languid leadership of Gideon Marsh, his predecessor as gun commander. That officer watched the twice-daily drills from the far corner of the quarterdeck with ill-concealed displeasure. The gun crews, in spite of grousing about the hard drills in the hot Caribbean sun, were pleased with the change in leadership, for they recognized the need for improved readiness since their departure from the relative safety of Havana harbor to skirt the unguarded coast of western Cuba. Deep bays and coves abounded, where privateers might lurk, intent on surprising a lone ship lagging behind the Martinique-bound convoy, as *Marlborough* was doing. Although the seas were moderate, her bluff bottom was showing signs of fouling and leaking, slowing her progress. The convoy was already hull down after only three days.

Captain Bennett was relieved when they cleared the western tip of Cuba and entered the channel separating the island from Mexico's Yucatan. Yet, there was still risk, for *Marlborough's* easterly coursing lay dangerously close to the Cayman Islands, long a haven for pirates and privateers.

Although it was now late September, notorious as the hurricane season in the Caribbean, the seas remained calm, with skies of puffy white clouds and persistent easterly winds that further slowed their progress. *Marlborough* was alone on the chalky blue sea, forced into long tacks to make progress toward Martinique, where the assembling convoy would form for the return voyage to England.

At last, even Jamie tired of driving the gun crews and reduced training to an hour a day. The carpenters completed what repairs were possible, put away their tools, and sought shade from the sun beneath spare sails rigged as awnings. The officers fenced in the relative cool of midmorning as soon as the decks dried from the daily scrubbing and holystoning. Except for Captain Bennett and Noah Keigwein, all the officers participated. For a time, Gideon Marsh was content to be an observer. One morning, teased beyond endurance by Jonathan Maxwell, he stalked off, only to return the next morning with a belted rapier at his waist.

Jamie watched the slender Marsh swiftly disarm two of the senior midshipmen who volunteered to face him. Benjamin Thorpe was a more able opponent, but he yielded to the third lieutenant's furious attack and lowered his blade. Marsh nodded to acknowledge the scattered applause and pointed to Jamie.

"Do you consider yourself sufficiently recovered, Mr. Drummond, to teach me a lesson?"

Eyes turned to Jamie, who shrugged and said, "It seems, Mr. Marsh, that ye hae sufficient skills tae need nae lessons."

Jonathan Maxwell pulled his rapier from its scabbard. The thin blade sang in the still air. "If ye are thirsting fer a lesson, sir, I would enjoy tutoring ye."

Gideon Marsh's eyes remained fixed on Jamie's. "I have already tested myself against your style, physician. While I may need your help if wounded in battle, I find your skills with the blade unworthy of emulation. I seek lessons from the self-professed master."

Jamie shifted his position from where he lounged against the railing. "I hae ne'er styled myself a master, but was fortunate tae be tutored by such a man." He shook his head. "We are a society o' friends, Mr. Marsh, enjoying the exercise, nae rivals seeking domination. I dinna seek an encounter tae satisfy honor or reputation and advise ye tae avoid it as weel."

No one spoke. Crewmen lounging nearby rose and moved off. Benjamin Thorpe glanced toward the quarterdeck. Commander Corey was on watch, preparing instruments for the noon sighting. Captain Burnett was nowhere to be seen. The second lieutenant spoke in a low voice, "I suggest that we end our fencing exercise, gentlemen. The crew senses the enmity and is clearing off. I suggest, Lieutenant Marsh, that you curb your temper. If you wish to engage Mr. Drummond to satisfy your pique or honor, then do so out of sight of the crew, and especially Captain Burnett, who takes a dim view of conflicts among his officers. I have not heard Mr. Drummond say anything provocative. If he does, then I would give him the same stern advice."

Gideon Marsh's face betrayed his anger. He sheathed his rapier, violently ramming the blade into the scabbard. He turned stiffly and stalked away. The others remained together, talking in low voices, but the fencing session was over.

The officers gathered for dinner in the captain's quarters, but Third Lieutenant Marsh was not among them. Kelly, the captain's steward, reported that Mr. Marsh had requested permission to sup in his cabin, complaining that he suffered from an intestinal complaint. The Irishman said, "'Tis a strange ailment. Fer faith, it dinna curb his appetite."

Watch duties kept Jamie and Gideon Marsh from encountering each other. Mr. Marsh's absence at dinner finally drew a rebuke from the captain, who sent Kelly to fetch him. Five minutes later, the scowling young officer appeared but said not a word. Conversations lagged, and the frivolity that prevailed during the meal faded away. Captain Burnett was clearly irritated with his junior officer but said nothing, dismissing him to sup alone.

A week later, the lumbering *Marlborough* raised the island of Jamaica, the dark green canopy of its forests glowing with invitation as they neared the opening of the harbor to Port Royal and Kingston. The scene brought painful nostalgia to Jamie's mind, for it was there that he and Sarah Cotes, the admiral's daughter, had fallen in love and experienced an idyllic beginning to a romance that had perished, victim to a father's political ambition and ruin of the hopes of the Drummond family for restoration of lost titles and estates.

They laid over in the harbor for two days. Native divers used long-handled rakes and scrapers to remove the barnacles and other impediments that they could reach from *Marlborough's* befouled hull. They filled a lighter full with the slimy greenish debris.

Much of the crew and most of the officers took a day's holiday in Kingston, but a disconsolate Jamie remained aboard, supervising restocking and watering. Commander Corey said nothing, but regarded Jamie gravely, for it was unusual for any officer to skip an opportunity for revelry in the famous port.

The ship weighed anchor and moved ponderously down the narrow channel, past Fort Charles, looming on the cliff above the harbor. Her guns boomed a farewell. Jamie nodded to Benjamin Thorpe, the larboard gun captain, who ordered a smoky broadside in response. Captain Burnett ordered topmen aloft to spread canvas. By the time they cleared Morant Bay and hauled all sails, it was obvious that two days of scraping and cleaning had moderately increased the ship's speed and maneuverability. There was relief on the quarterdeck with the call from below that there was no leaking after four hours of cresting a light swell.

The easterly winds lessened, and four days later, *Marlborough* raised the mountainous profile of Martinique. The sun was low in the west when they followed the pilot boat to anchorage. Benjamin Thorpe joined Jamie where he stood against the starboard railing in the waist, gazing at the anchored formation. "There must be at least fifty ships assembled already."

Jamie nodded. "Aye, it seems that we will hae considerable company on our journey back tae Portsmouth."

Benjamin rubbed his chin. "Has the captain spoken of the route that we will follow?"

Jamie shook his head. "Nae, but a northerly passage would be less risky. If there is a French fleet in the Atlantic, I think that it would patrol between the Leeward Islands and Azores, hoping tae pick off stragglers. If 'twere me plotting the route, it would be north following the great current flowing in that direction, skirting the coast o' Spanish Florida and the Bahamas but weel tae the east, then past the Virginia Capes, tae put in at New York. From there, the northward passage would also avoid the great tropical storms o' this season."

Jamie's prediction proved true, for Captain Burnett's gig returned from a commander's conference with news that the convoy would sail in five days and take the northeastward passage. Anxious to complete the return to England, Vice Admiral Pocock had rejected the proposal of his captains to permit a stop in North America before crossing the Atlantic. With no stop to restock, Captain Burnett ordered loading of additional victuals, wood, and water. With two days before sailing and loading were complete, he granted shore liberty to half the officers and crew on each of their remaining days in port.

Realizing that this might be his only opportunity to revisit the island, Jamie invited Benjamin Thorpe and Jonathan Maxwell on a shore excursion. Procuring horses at a stable near the landing, the young officers trotted through the busy portside streets to the western suburb to view the battlefields. The site of the first and abortive landing across the bay was too distant from Fort Royal, so they rode to the beach at Casa des Navires. They dismounted to explore on foot, for the sand was too dry and soft for the horses. The beach and French redoubts were still littered with debris, although bodies from both sides had been taken away for burial long since. Somberly, they remounted and moved along the road that skirted the hills where ten months before, General Monckton's dogged troops endured incessant French bombardment from cannon emplaced on the heights of Morne Tortenson and Morne Grenier as they forced their way toward the city of Fort Royal.

A gasping Jamie wiped sweat from his brow and leaned on his knees. It had been a struggle climbing Morne Grenier, for he was not yet fully recovered from the rigors of his captivity. He led his companions to the summit so that they could appreciate the fortitude of the marines and soldiers who had driven the French from the summit. Once British cannon were emplaced on the heights, they had sealed the doom of the garrison defending the city below.

They descended and remounted to ride slowly through the suburbs of Fort Royal, where many of the damaged buildings remained unrepaired. They skirted mounds of accumulated brick, tile, block, and timber, where residents of the city silently picked through rubble, scavenging for materials for their own houses.

As they reached the waterfront, Jonathan Maxwell pointed to a likely restaurant packed with customers at small tables under umbrellas. Filled with fresh fish and shrimp grilled over the coals in makeshift fire pits nearby and locally brewed beer, they sat reflecting on what they had seen. Benjamin Thorpe pulled on his white clay pipe and then spoke. "The locals seem friendly enough, although less than a year ago, they were ducking our cannon fire."

Jamie said, "Ye misunderstand the nature o' people caught in warfare. While they were loyal tae the French nation that provides much o' their culture, they were here when the war caught them and did what they must tae survive. We came wi' shillings in our pockets, and they are happy tae serve us in exchange. They dinna blame us o'ermuch fer the destruction we showered on them. If we treat them fairly and help them rebuild their city and farms, they wilna cause trouble, although they will be happier if the island reverted tae French control. It is mair akin tae their culture. I saw the same tendencies wi' enterprising farmers and shopkeepers when we landed on Belle Isle." He paused. "It is nae universally true. The people o' Quebec were different. They are French tae the core and wilna accept foreign domination and suppression o' their culture. Native pride runs deep, as it does in the Highlands. Armed might may restrain their restless spirits frae ootright rebellion fer a space, but resentment and a yearning fer freedom wilna fade in a hundred years."

There was a faraway look in Jonathan Maxwell's eyes as he nodded agreement. Benjamin Thorpe took a final puff and knocked out the ashes from his pipe. "Ye may think it best that the crown give Canada back to the French since the cost and effort to maintain garrisons over fractious populations promise to be bothersome expenditures. I tell you, gentlemen, that after this war ends and a peace treaty is forced upon the reluctant French and Spanish, that Great Britain will be the most powerful colonizing force in the world. The conquests of this war are only the beginning of a great empire."

Jamie smiled. "Perhaps ye are correct, Ben, but fractious races are devilishly resistant tae accepting order and discipline. Speaking as a member o' a conquered race, it will be a perilous undertaking, fer people will accept such an empire fer nae mair than a short while. People o' spirit will ne'er forget their heritage nor love o' independence. If Great Britain establishes an empire of exploitation and nae o' accommodation wi' reasonable freedoms, as I fear, it wilna last. Whether it be a few years or decades, or even centuries, conquered people will seize the opportunity to regain their freedom. Mark my words."

Benjamin Thorpe tapped the table. "I cannot gainsay you, Jamie. I fear that peace for an empire, no matter how great, can be as arduous and expensive as war. The history of Rome, while lengthy, is our best example. However, these are weighty matters for ministers, not junior officers in the king's service. Let us enjoy our few remaining hours in this tropical splendor. Pass the brandy."

Two hours later, the trio paid their reckoning, waved to the military and civilian patrons, and walked blinking into the late afternoon sunlight. Not finding a carriage for rent, they decided to cross a small park to an adjoining avenue, where they saw several carriages through the palms that dotted the greensward. They were halfway across when Jamie heard the distinctive sound of metal rasping on metal. He went cold, recognizing the sound of a blade clearing a scabbard, and gripped the hilt of his rapier. A blue-coated man stepped out of the shadows of a mass of purple bougainvillea draped over an arbor. Gideon Marsh stood with gloved hands clasped over the pommel, with the blade resting on the tip of one boot. "I offer you belated greetings. You were supping and drinking for so long that I despaired of waiting, as I have for over an hour, for your appearance."

He looked past the trees at the blue sky and smiled. "We have sufficient daylight before returning to the ship to engage in some sport. I have been waiting for such an opportunity to engage you, Drummond, where it is difficult for you to refuse me." He raised his sword and motioned to the clearing between the trees. "Here is a better place than that cramped space below decks or even the waist. Do you not agree, Benjamin?"

Thorpe shook his head. "You understand the prohibition against dueling, do you not, Mr. Marsh?"

Marsh smiled, but there was no humor in his eyes. "I have said nothing about dueling. I merely seek a little friendly sport with a very reluctant shipmate. I find his reticence puzzling. Can it be that he is afraid to engage me?" He turned to face Jamie. "I see that you are armed, so you cannot concoct a tale that you have no weapon at hand."

Marsh lifted his sword and almost lazily waved the point at Jamie.

Jamie glared at the lieutenant as he eyed the moving tip of the blade. He gripped the pommel of his rapier tightly.

Marsh's voice was soft yet filled with menace. "Are you too cowardly to face me, Drummond? Simply acknowledge the fact, and I will be satisfied."

Jamie's voice was harsh. "Ye are drunk, man. I have nae wish to sport with a man besotted or filled wi' a spirit o' revenge unless ye wish satisfaction. There is nae need, fer I hae ne'er insulted ye. We are shipmates and honor bound tae support and succor each other." He looked around. Curious strollers were stopping to watch.

Jonathan Maxwell stepped between them, arms upraised. "Sheathe yer weapon, Gideon! This is nae place tae fight a duel, man."

Marsh growled. "Move aside, physician! I am not drunk and seek no duel, merely a bit of sport. Drummond can decline on the grounds that he fears me, acknowledges that I am the better fencer, or draws his weapon to exercise with me. What say you, marine?"

Jamie shook his head slowly. "I am nae coward. I hae proven that in six years o' warfare, Gideon Marsh. Wi' yer state o' mind, ye are nae a fit opponent fer a friendly bout."

Marsh exploded. "My state of mind! You wish to see my state of mind?" He sprang to a fencer's en garde position and advanced. Jamie backed against the spiny branches of a palm as he reached for his rapier. Marsh's blade snaked out and snagged Jamie's jacket pocket. A button popped loose and bounced on the close-clipped grass.

Moving laterally and ignoring the shouts of dismay from his companions, Jamie freed himself from the palm fronds and yanked his rapier from the scabbard. He flung his hat to Jonathan Maxwell. Gideon March was on him instantly.

The clash of weapons rang across the small park, bringing more spectators from nearby streets. The fencers were of equal height, build, and stamina. A few minutes of vigorous testing revealed that they were well-matched in skill. They battled back and forth within a grassy area between the palms that was ideally suited for the sport. There were no obstacles, and the grass was smooth and dry, providing good footing.

Gideon Marsh seemed to be genuinely enjoying the sport, making no deliberate attempt to wound Jamie. In return, Jamie settled into a routine of alternating advance and retreat typical of mock bouts. His initial irritation at Marsh's challenge turned gradually to pleasure, for he did love the sport. Marsh pinked him in the forearm, and Jamie retaliated with a thrust that tore a seam in his opponent's dark blue coat. Neither officer seemed able to get an advantage, and the bout promised to be a long one, decided by physical conditioning and not skill.

The crowd cheered and shouted out wagers. Ludicrously, two vendors trundled small carts to the edge of the grass and began hawking beverages to the growing crowd. Although it was late fall, it was a warm day, and the combatants began to sweat heavily, staining their uniform coats. Jamie wished that he had shed his before beginning the bout.

As the minutes passed, Jamie detected a repetitive pattern in Gideon Marsh's high-line attacks. There was a brief instant when his right side was uncovered that might be exploited by a swift advance. He had nearly decided to act when he heard clattering hoofbeats.

Benjamin Thorpe said with urgency in his voice, "Gentlemen, you have drawn the attention of a military patrol! Disengage!"

His voice distracted Gideon Marsh, who slowed his attack and turned his head slightly. Jamie seized the moment. He took two swift steps, ducked inside his opponent's guard, and punched the lieutenant in the jaw with the hilt of the rapier. Startled and stunned, Marsh fell to his knees and dropped his blade. Jamie stepped back to permit him to recover.

The mounted patrol surrounded the park. A British Army officer gigged his horse to the center of the clearing. He sheathed his saber and cleared his throat. The crowd of colonials edged backward.

"I am Major Henry Wheeler, provost marshal for Fort Royal. What is the meaning of this disturbance?"

Jamie slid his rapier into its scabbard and stepped forward. "Sir, I am Marine Captain James Drummond." He gestured to his companions, including the still-addled Gideon Marsh, who was being helped to his feet. "We are officers aboard HMS *Marlborough*, soon to depart with the convoy for Portsmouth. We enjoyed a fine meal on this, our only day of shore leave. We are all devotees of the sport of fencing and were discussing tactics. Lieutenant Marsh requested that I demonstrate some of the more advanced moves. I invited him to join me so that the instruction could be more personal. We were just now completing the lesson. I am embarrassed that we drew a crowd of locals also interested in the art."

Major Wheeler snorted. "It must have been a most vigorous lesson, for I watched you clout him in the jaw as we rode up." He pointed to Gideon Marsh, who stood leaning unsteadily on Jonathan Maxwell's shoulder. After a long pause, he spoke. "Do you agree with this unlikely tale, Lieutenant? You look worsted in this 'lesson' rather than instructed."

Gideon's smile was forced. "The lesson was vigorous, rather more than I expected. I..." He paused, befuddled. "I was distracted and did not expect such a well-timed move. I apologize for what may appear to be a disturbance, but the park is such an inviting place for sport."

The major turned his basilisk stare on the other officers.

"Lieutenant Jonathan Maxwell, Major, ship's physician aboard *Marlborough*," Benjamin Thorpe also identified himself. Major Wheeler pulled on his mustache to hide a widening grin. "Colonial gentlemen have been known to frequent this park for the purpose of dueling but usually only at dawn. When I heard the report, I was shocked to see British officers engaged in what appeared to be mortal combat, an event highly disturbing to the order I am charged to maintain. We need no incident to provoke the locals into rioting. I am highly inclined to report the lot of you to your ship's captain."

Jamie spoke as the others shook their heads in denial. "Nae, sir. There is nae need fer such extreme measures. We hae spent our coin and are ready tae return tae our ship. We love action and dinna think that the local populace would take it as a pretext tae violence. If you wish, sir, since I speak French, I can reassure them o' our guid intentions and apologize."

The major's face softened. "I would appreciate that, Captain Drummond, for I do not speak a word o' the language. Please tell them that and order them to quietly disperse."

Jamie turned to the silent crowd. "Messieurs, il nous fait grand plaisir de vous divertir. Ce n'était pas une affaire d'honneur, mais simplement le sport. Nous vous invitons à utiliser ce merveilleux parc de ces passe-temps agréable, plutôt que de tuer ou de mutiler un autre. De cette façon, tout le monde peut être heureux, et pas seulement celui qui a le privilège de vivre tandis que son adversaire meurt! Le principal ne parle pas votre langue, et m'ordonne de vous dire qu'il serait préférable pour vous de disperser pacifiquement. Il vous remercie pour l'honneur de servir dans votre belle ville."

The crowd applauded, whistled, and waved their hats. Two beaming middle-aged men stepped forward to embrace Jamie and Gideon Marsh and kiss them on both cheeks.

The major growled, "What did you tell them, Captain? I have never seen them so happy."

Jamie shrugged. "I said, 'Gentlemen, it gave us great pleasure tae entertain ye. This was nae an affair o' honor but merely sport. We urge ye tae use this wonderful park fer such enjoyable pastimes, rather than killing and maiming each other. In that way, all can be happy and nae just the ane wha is privileged tae live while his opponent dies! The major dinna speak yer language and bids me tae tell ye that it would be advisable fer ye tae disperse peaceably. He thanks ye fer the honor o' serving in yer beautiful city.' That is what I said."

The provost marshal appeared mollified, but suspicion lingered in his eyes. He turned to stare at the crowd. The cheerful people smiled and waved. He leaned down to address *Marlborough's* officers. "I do not entirely believe your story, gentlemen. There is too much of the 'cock and bull' about it. I want you out of my jurisdiction before trouble flares again. March yourselves directly back to the dock. I have no wish to explain why I felt it necessary to arrest four officers for misbehavior ashore. It would require far more red tape than I am willing to produce. Do I need to detail a squad to escort you on your journey?"

There was a squeak of leather as Major Wheeler leaned back in the saddle and crossed his arms. The *Marlborough's* officers all shook their heads vigorously. The provost marshal raised a beefy forearm to order his troop to circle the park to continue their patrol. With Jamie supporting his erstwhile opponent, the four officers resumed their journey back to the landing. By the time they reached the shore boat, the dispute that had led to the fencing bout was forgotten. The conversation was amiable as the four avidly laid plans for daily fencing practice on the lengthy voyage home.

5

The eastern Caribbean sky was royal blue over a turquoise sea as the great convoy formed off the coastline of Martinique. *Marlborough* waited for two hours as ship after ship weighed and spread white canvas. The notes of capstan shanties and tread of stamping feet on many decks floated over the water as the bowers came up and the ships floated free.

Noah Keigwein saw the signal flag for *Marlborough* to weigh hoisted to the trucks on the flagship and roared the welcome orders. Topmen balanced on swaying lines far overhead recognized the signal and were in motion as soon as the master raised his speaking trumpet.

Jamie's spirits soared as he watched the familiar ritual at the capstans, where seamen inserted oaken bars into the drums and took their places. Their tramping was swift as the cables rose, then slowed to a grunting push as the flukes of the bowers slowly pulled free of the muck of the bottom. A glad shout resounded and the shantyman changed to a lively tune to cheer the men, who were almost racing as they spun the capstans. There was a loud huzzah as the heavy anchors broke the surface. Jamie pumped his fist in sheer exhilaration. He turned from his position at the quarterdeck rail to find Gideon Marsh, the officer of the watch, grinning at his boyish enthusiasm.

"Well, Mr. Drummond, one might think that you had never before seen the departure of a ship of the line from a harbor."

Jamie replied, "I canna but think o' my first experience, Gideon, standing barefoot at the capstan bar o' *Reliant* in '56. It was at the start o' the war, over six lang years in the past. Although those days are far behind me, I must say that in spite o' all, they were happy times. I am nae ashamed o' having served in such a lowly station."

The third lieutenant seemed lost in reflection. "Aye, it was the same for me. I came aboard my first ship as a midshipman at the age of thirteen. My life ashore in my father's house in Norwich seems an alien world now. I have been at sea for more years than my previous life ashore." He faced the breeze and breathed deeply. "The life of a scrivening clerk in my father's counting house, which now belongs to my elder brother, would have been miserable— nay, intolerable. This is the life for me, and I will accept no other."

Jamie sobered. "I pray that you are weel-situated and someday receive preferment that will lead to command, Gideon. I think that my prospects are mair limited, with the war undoubtedly ending soon. There are rumors of a great reduction in the fleet if peace is proclaimed."

Marsh shook his head. "Oh, perhaps there may be a year or two of half pay for some, but peace will not last. Great Britain desires to be a great nation, and great nations require powerful navies. You and I are valuable commodities. The crown and Admiralty will not throw us over, but enough of gloom. My watch ends within the hour. What say you to some vigorous exercise?"

Jamie pointed to Gideon's jaw, which still showed signs of bruising. Marsh nodded emphatically. "Oh, I feel sufficiently healed to risk my face. You will not catch me so unawares again. Beware a retaliatory love tap."

Jamie could not suppress a chuckle. Gideon Marsh's rapid transition from implacable foe to warm friend still surprised him. The man was an uncompromising competitor who would challenge him at every turn. Their newfound relationship was built on mutual respect, for the two were much alike.

Under clear skies, they sailed northward, skirting Dominica, Guadalupe, and the Dutch-held Antilles. The convoy spread from horizon to horizon, guided by signal flags passed from ship to ship. They passed some coastal merchant traffic but no privateers or hostile vessels. They waited off Turks and Caicos for several ships from Havana to join them, then proceeded northward, where they picked up the warm current that skirted the North American coast.

Noah Keigwein was jubilant as he calculated their daily run. At dinner in *Marlborough's* wardroom, he passed the good news. "We are now north of the tip of Florida. I ken that it sounds incomprehensible, but spending several days coursing northwestward to encounter this current was beneficial. Today's run is fifty-five nautical miles greater than yesterday. We are sailing nearly two and a half knots faster pushed by this mighty stream of water. It was discovered by that wrongheaded Spanish dreamer Ponce de Leon, who wandered around Florida searching for the fountain of youth. He never found it, but this stream of warm water has the power to shorten the trans-Atlantic journey by two weeks. I am grateful that we have a wise admiral commanding this convoy. Many ignore it and waste precious time searching for a beneficial wind, failing to realize that it is directly under their hulls."

Jamie insisted on a strict regimen of training for gun crews, exercising them in the tropical air for at least two hours every day. Officers and mates kept the crew busy with household chores and inspections above and below decks all morning. There was still plenty of time in the afternoon for the men not on watch to laze in the bright sunshine while light winds and a following swell speeded their transit of the islands that appeared only occasionally as dark smudges on the western horizon.

Late afternoon was also the time when the officers not on watch and older midshipmen gathered in *Marlborough*'s commodious hold to engage in fencing exercises and instruction. Captain Burnett and the master did not participate but visited occasionally to watch the bouts in the dim light cast by the horn lanterns.

Before departure from Martinique, Benjamin Thorpe had urged the ship's quartermaster to lay in a goodly stock of fresh vegetables, fruits, and smoked meat for the voyage, which had to be eaten before they spoiled. This practice conserved their limited stock of barrels of salted beef, pork, and live chickens and hogs for later in the voyage. It also made for pleasant meals, since there was also an adequate supply of spirits, and Captain Burnett loved the old tradition of singing and musical entertainment following dinner. Jamie found it impossible to avoid playing his mandolin on such occasions once Captain Burnett discovered his skill. His assignment to *Marlborough* had come by chance, but he appreciated the pleasant fellowship that prevailed.

Jamie tugged off his boots and settled himself into his hammock with great contentment. He was not scheduled to go on watch until the next morning. He stretched, yawned hugely, and blew out the flame in the horn lantern that swung from an overhead beam. He closed his eyes in the sudden darkness. Inexplicably, a light grew in the room, growing redly behind his lids. His eyes snapped open.

"Peallaidh!"

The small wizened figure of the ancient king perched above him in the shadows. He grinned toothily at Jamie, his enormous warty nose casting a long shadow beneath his blue bonnet. In his grinding voice, he said, "Ye feel mightily content, fer the stream o' events hae been favorable o' late."

Jamie nodded. "Aye, I am headed hame. Wha could be better?"

When the little figure remained silent, a chill of premonition crept over Jamie. The stony voice spoke, "Beware when matters are sae favorable. It is unco pleasant tae e'er hope fer the best, but ye must be prepared fer misfortune and hard trials, laddie. The sea road is fraught wi' peril. Take heart when the sky is black and the thunder rolls, fer wi' courage, ye will survive. Ye are honor bound on a prophetic mission but must gang warily. It is on the land road that the greater challenges will come tae test ye. Remember that the unexpected path leads tae the right place. Ye will recognize it when ye arrive. Ye are called tae endure much and accomplish much not fer yer ain pleasure and gain but fer a great purpose."

Jamie called out, "A great purpose? What great purpose?" The amber light dimmed and began to gather in on itself. Jamie struggled to sit up. He lunged to seize the brownie king's leg but grasped only air. He shouted, "Peallaidh!" but the light blinked out. The gruagach was gone.

o———o

Jamie was on watch with Gideon Marsh as the third lieutenant struggled to make the noon sun shot, for a high thin layer of cloud had slowly overtaken them from the south. The pale sun was no more than an indistinct ball that faded quickly. The ship maintained a mercury barometer in a glass case stored in the binnacle on the quarterdeck. Jamie opened the wooden cabinet, eyed the level, and recorded the instrument's reading in the ship's log. The two officers' eyes met. Gideon muttered, "The glass has been falling all morning, and the swell is now coming from sou'east and rising in strength."

Jamie responded, "Aye, and the sea state and wind are rising as weel."

Gideon nodded. "The signs of a massive storm are unmistakable. I had best inform the captain and Mr. Keigwein."

Captain Burnett and the master came on deck just as new signals bloomed on the trucks of the flagship nearly two miles away. "The admiral is ordering us to spread the formation, Noah. We are in for a blow. Mr. Drummond, secure double lashings on all guns. Mr. Marsh, reduce canvas. Order all gear on deck and below secured. Man pumps in readiness. Although we are running with the swell, I fear any pounding at all may induce leaking."

The wind rose as the bloodred sun sank in the west, driving spray off the crests of the waves. The convoy had been steering northeast for a day and a half to gain separation from the coastline of North Carolina, and especially Cape Hatteras, renowned as a graveyard of ships wrecked by hurricane-force storms. The coast of North America was a treacherous lee shore, with barrier islands, spits, and shallow beaches all the way from the Florida Straits to Cape Cod.

Captain Burnett called a council of his officers in his wardroom. Elisha Corey, *Marlborough*'s first lieutenant spread the large chart on the table. Gideon Marsh plotted the estimated position of the ship off the coast, determined from the imperfect noon sighting to fix latitude and dead reckoning from the day's log runs. He looked at the captain's jowly face and the stress lines circling his eyes.

"Sir, I estimate that we cleared Cape Hatteras two hours before dusk and are approaching the entrance to Hampton Roads but are still ten to twelve leagues off the coast."

The captain put on his wire-rimmed spectacles and peered at the chart. He sighed heavily. "The admiral's signal is to alter course to nor'east. He has decided to not risk attempting to get the entire convoy into the Roads, Delaware Bay northward, or New York. He intends to ride out the storm by continuing on course for Ushant and the Channel. Any captain who feels that his ship would be endangered may seek safety in whatever coastal port he can reach."

No one spoke. The ticking of the clock in its wooden case was loud. The wind buffeted the shutters. The deck swayed under their feet. A loud bang resounded from forward. Something had broken loose.

The captain looked at Benjamin Thorpe, the ship's third lieutenant. "Mr. Thorpe, what is the state of the leaking? Can the pumps manage it?"

Thorpe rubbed his eyes. "The pounding has been growing as the height of the waves and the wind increase."

Captain Burnett growled, "Stow it, man! I understand the physics of water and wind. Tell me of the pumping."

Abashed, the young officer said, "The leaking is growing more pronounced, sir. The pumps are working well, but we now have two feet of water below, whereas we had scarcely half that at the changing of the watch at four."

Elisha Corey said softly, "Sir, the storm center is gaining on us, as if it intends to drive us aground. We must expect to see nearly a fathom of water below by midnight and possibly much more by dawn. We are already wallowing and cannot keep up with the convoy. We must run for shelter, wherever we can find it, even if we run aground in inland waters."

The captain spread his large hands on the chart. "Order signal lanterns hung, Mr. Corey. The convoy must go on without us. Wear ship to nor'west. Let us take our chances attempting to enter the Roads. If we must sink, I would prefer to sink in shallow water, with at least the possibility of rescue from shore."

The rain started, gently at first, driven stinging into faces by the whistling wind. By midnight, dead reckoning placed them five leagues off the light at Cape Henry, the entrance to Chesapeake Bay and the relative safety of Hampton Roads. Noah Keigwein ordered repeated larboard course changes, but the wind rose to a gale, blowing them across the crashing waves northward. The light at Cape Henry faded and then winked out behind the headlands of Maryland's Eastern Shore.

The master drew his oilskins around himself and shouted to be heard over the bellowing wind. "'Tis no use, Captain! We cannot make the entrance. We must wear away or risk being swept ashore. The whole of the Maryland coast is shallow marsh and back bays. There is no safe entrance short of Cape May and the entrance to Delaware Bay!"

Reluctantly, Captain Burnett issued the order. The ship shuddered under the weight of water in her hold. Everyone on deck looked fearfully to larboard, watching for the white water that would mark the line of surf that would cause them to wreck and capsize in the shallow water. Thirty minutes passed, an hour. The storm continued to grow in intensity. The bow of the third rate dipped into still deeper troughs. Every plunge brought tons of dark water over her bowsprit, which brought terror that it would break off under the terrible strain. Water roared over the waist, carrying off cargo and livestock in pens that had broken loose.

Jamie's watch ended, but he could not bring himself to leave the quarterdeck while the ship was in mortal peril. Hours crawled by, with every report from the pumps bringing graver news of the rising water level. Mercifully, the pumps had not failed, but the men could not stop the water from rising. Exhausted sailors tottered from below while fresh hands trooped into the noisome confines to offer their strength to what was increasingly a futile effort.

Dawn revealed a wild world of raving wind, tumultuous waves, and blinding spray. In the wan light, the sky was completely covered with black clouds that billowed and writhed, lit luridly from within by jagged flashes of brilliant light. The air was filled with the mutter and clamor of nearly continuous thunder. *Marlborough* was alone on the heaving gray sea. If a coastline was nearby, no amount of peering revealed it.

Gideon Marsh gripped Jamie's arm. It was impossible for him to hide his terror, though duty forced a semblance of calm. "We are lost, Jamie. We cannot find the sun or any celestial body for a fix. The waves are so chaotic that logging is impossible. We can only press onward, praying that we are not driven onto the coast by this wind."

Jamie responded grimly, "The leaking continues unabated. We must stay afloat until the storm blows itself oot. We are the sole ship on the water and canna hope fer rescue. Nothing on earth will stop the rising water and our eventual sinking, except tae lighten ship tae buy time. We must persuade the captain tae order the water and stores o'er the side. We hae sixty guns that would reduce our weight by over a hundred tonnes if we can get them safely off."

Together they approached Captain Burnett, hatless and clinging to a lifeline on the quarterdeck. The captain listened and nodded vehemently. "Throw water and beer, victuals, and movable stores overboard if casks and crates can be safely brought on deck. Put bow chasers and upper gun deck cannon over the side. But unchocking a heavy gun on an unstable deck could cause a runaway that may sink us, accomplishing swiftly what we hope to avoid."

Sailors and marines hooked to lifelines worked at the grim task, booming stuff into the waist through open hatches, swinging mallets to smash in the heads of casks, and unlashing everything that could be removed to lighten ship. The gun crews managed to get the forecastle and quarterdeck six pounders over the side. The iron barrels, weighing less than eight hundred pounds, were a manageable load, even on the rain-slick pitching deck. Gun crews even succeeded in getting most middle–gun deck eighteen pounders over the side.

A determined Jamie attempted to unload one of the lower–gun deck thirty-two pounders through a gap smashed in the bulwarks. He ordered lashings removed and the gun rolled to the opening, where the crew could lever it into the sea. When the ship rolled suddenly, the unchecked gun careened across the deck with its trucks shrieking. It slammed into the inner bulkhead, staving in planks, then rumbled down the slick deck as the ship plunged into a trough. Quaking with fear, the gun crew managed to throw enough hammocks under the chocks to bring it to a stop so they could relash it. They had succeeded in getting the lighter guns over the side, but it was impossible to deal with the thirty two pounders of the lower gun decks. The crew of *Marlborough* would either survive with the heavy guns or sink with them.

Elisha Corey examined the ship's boats. All were seaworthy and stocked with water and rations. Their combined capacity was less than two hundred men, without overloading. The mathematics of rescue and death were inexorable. More than half the crew could not be saved. Attempting to put extra men into the boats in waves running fifteen to twenty feet would certainly capsize them, leading to the death of all. Fear was palpable on every face, but they went about their work stoically. The crew was a hardened lot and knew the danger and probable outcome of a sinking or wreck.

Jamie went down to where the men were pumping. The men looked at him hopefully, but he shook his head. "Ye must keep pumping. Ye are our only hope tae stay afloat. Wi' a will, lads. I need a measurement o' water depth."

The answer was depressing—two inches short of a fathom and a half. He could say nothing to reassure the men manning the elmwood pumps. In the wardroom, he and Elisha Corey hurriedly calculated the probable center of *Marlborough*'s mass and the rate of increase in depth while Captain Burnett hovered over them. The answer would tell them how long they had until the mass of the ship and water in her hold would exceed her ability to stay above the waves.

Elisha Corey pushed back from the table, his eyes wide. "Captain, I have checked and rechecked the numbers. Unless the men at the pumps can stop the increase in depth, we cannot remain afloat more than another twelve hours, perhaps less."

The captain's voice was hoarse with emotion. "Drummond, if we knocked more holes in the bulwarks, could we get the thirty two pounders overboard?"

Jamie shook his head. "We tried, Captain. Even if we could synchronize the effort, the risk o' capsizing by offloading such a weight on one side before the other could roll the ship onto her beam ends. She is already pitching heavily wi' the buffeting o' the waves. The men dinna have the strength tae resist a heavy gun rolling backward as the deck tilts up or chock it until she rolls back. In less violent seas, it might be possible, but nae here."

Captain Burnett turned toward his first lieutenant. "Mr. Corey, how far off the coast do we lay?"

Elisha Corey shrugged. "We have only dead reckoning to guide us since the last sun shot two days past. Perhaps twenty leagues, perhaps less, certainly not more with the swell and wind pushing us westward."

The captain sat head down with his eyes closed. He rose slowly, planting his fists on the table. "Gentlemen, I cannot sacrifice so many men to the sea, myself included, without performing every act possible to give them a chance to live, no matter how slim. Suspend all efforts to lighten ship. Put as many men over the side as the boats will safely carry." He paused as a rumble of thunder drowned out his voice. "Hoist as much canvas as she will carry without blowing out. Those of us who remain will steer for the Maryland coast, where I intend to ground this ship on the sand. She may topple or capsize, but even in the storm surge and waves, men will have a chance to reach shore and survive."

Suddenly, there was a wild yell from outside that carried over the howling of the wind. The master yanked the door open. The swirling wind snatched papers from the table and flung them around the wardroom. Noah Keigwein thrust his bulk against the door and managed to get it latched. He turned around, dripping water onto the wardroom deck.

The master was weeping. "God be praised! Sail ho, Captain, coming up to starboard and flying the Union Jack. A fourth rate, sir."

The six officers in the wardroom, heedless of the wind and storm, pried the door open and rushed on deck bareheaded. The sight that greeted them was overwhelming. Riding the violent waves scarcely a half mile distant lay HMS *Antelope*, a fifty-gun frigate, her topmen shivering sails. Sailors were already lowering a boat.

The wind whipped away the master's shouted orders to sailors crowding *Marlborough*'s rails to return to stations. Many were capering foolishly while others stood weeping helplessly in the sudden expectation that they might yet live through the terror of the storm. Boatswain's mates were forced to seize men by an arm or prod them with a belaying pin.

As soon as *Antelope*'s second lieutenant Pliny Graves mounted *Marlborough*'s quarterdeck, he understood the danger. He addressed the captain and the ship's officers in the wardroom. "We were on station at Placentia Bay in Newfoundland prepared to resist an expected French fleet sailing from Brest. Fifteen hundred troops sailed into Saint John's and captured the town in late June. We blockaded the French and brought troops over from Louisburg ten weeks ago. The French relief convoy evaded the blockade and, abandoning the troops, sailed back to France. The frogs surrendered, so we were no longer needed. We sailed for England, but encountered the convoy sailing from Martinique. At the admiral's urging, we came south to find *Marlborough* and offer help if needed. We did not expect to find you sinking."

Captain Burnett said, "My officers tell me that we have perhaps as little as ten hours before the decks are awash, Lieutenant Graves. Except for the heavy cannon, we have little left to throw overboard. How many men can *Antelope* accommodate? I do not wish to leave men in open boats at the mercy of the waves."

Pliny Graves smiled. "You are fortunate, Captain. We are shorthanded and not carrying external cargo. Captain Webb instructed me to tell you to bring all your crew aboard, along with a limited amount of their personal possessions and all victuals that you have not yet consigned to the waves. We can accommodate about half below decks, with the remainder in the waist under tarpaulins once the wind subsides. The exposure to wind and water will be brutal, but better than sailing in open boats. It is impossible for us to take all of your men to Portsmouth."

Captain Burnett agreed that the two-day sail to New York would be easier to accomplish than reversing course to reach Hampton Roads in Virginia. Fortunately, the wind and waves began to subside as sailors from both ships manned boats to rescue *Marlborough's* crew. There were some heart-stopping episodes, with several crewmen plucked from chilly water and one boat lost in the five hours required to empty the ship.

Sitting in the stern sheets in one of the last boats off-loading officers and mates from the doomed ship's waist, Jamie reflected on the similarities between the capsizing of *Invincible* on Dean Sands four years before and this rescue. A combination of fortitude and stern professionalism had saved the entirety of both crews. While forty seamen had abandoned *Invincible* and risked punishment as mutineers, *Marlborough's* crew remained loyally at their stations until sent to the rescue boats. Jamie was also relieved not to leap from the deck, nor crawl through broken wreckage to rescue those left behind.

Safely aboard *Antelope*, Jamie gathered at the rail with the rest of *Marlborough's* officers. As minutes passed and the doomed ship settled lower, he brooded on his future. Once more, he was bereft of an assignment and a ship, but fortunate to live. Thirty minutes after boarding the rescue ship, with no shouts or cheers accompanying departure, *Marlborough's* stern settled and her prow rose clear of the water.

The sun sank into a cloud bank westward. A white moon rode low in the darkening sky. The sinking ship's rising bowsprit touched the rim of the moon, then slid backward into the swirling dark water. HMS *Marlborough* was gone. Except for the tightly folded ensign tucked under Lieutenant Elisha Corey's arm, nothing remained of the magnificent old warship.

6

Bundled against the bitter wind that sliced across the deck of HMS *Lion*, the three officers resisted the impulse to retire to the wardroom. They had been absent from Great Britain for more than a year and relished the view as the ancient sixty-gun fourth rate followed the pilot boat to anchorage off Gosport. Jamie nudged Jonathan Maxwell, who broke off his conversation with Gideon Marsh. "Hae ye e'er heard sae many bells ringing? I ne'er heard that the thirteenth o' February was a notable holiday." His companions shrugged their ignorance. Jamie extracted a small glass from his pocket and extended it toward the late afternoon skyline. He braced his hip against the railing and studied the view. "Bunting on the front o' every building on the waterfront. Bunting and bells. Whate'er can be happening?"

They were passengers aboard the warship on its journey from New York City to Gosport and privy to neither fleet intelligence nor coded signals. Following *Marlborough's* loss, they were no longer a crew. Three days after *Antelope* reached port, she had sailed for Plymouth, carrying ninety survivors as passengers. A hundred were commandeered by the Admiralty office in New York and distributed to warships in the harbor. The remainder waited two weeks for assignments as passengers aboard naval and merchant craft returning to England with berthing space available. Captain Burnett, Noah Keigwein, and Benjamin Thorpe departed aboard ninety-gun HMS *Blenheim*, another ancient ship of the line, eighty years old, on the same day that *Lion* sailed. When they received their orders, Jonathan Maxwell had whispered grimly, "It is indeed ill luck, tae step frae ane sinking ship onto the deck o' another as unlikely tae reach England."

Lion survived a rough and slow trans-Atlantic passage, with nearly continuous pumping. It was fortunate that the ship carried extra sails, for the topsails had blown out twice before they struck soundings. The sky cleared as they entered the Channel, although the wind still blew at nearly gale force. They made good time up the channel with following seas, but the fearsome pounding had sickened all but the most seaworthy. In spite of storms, the ship dubbed "that wallowing old sea hog" swung to her anchor cables two hours before sunset, with everyone curious about the incessant bell ringing and colorful bunting whipping in the cold wind, not only across the harbor front but from the rigging of every anchored ship.

Ten minutes after the anchors struck bottom, the harbor master and a commander from the Admiralty office at the dockyard mounted the gangway. They huddled briefly with the *Lion*'s captain and then announced the glad news that a peace treaty had been signed by the British and French governments in Paris three days earlier. The war that had lasted for nearly seven years was over. The cheers of the crew and passengers were thunderous. Sailors tossed their tarpaulin hats in the air and danced in mad circles. When the noise subsided, the captain shouted for a double ration of rum for all hands.

Jamie remembered nothing of the captain's speech but seized on the announcement that the embarked passengers were free to go ashore. Senior officers departed in the captain's gig, while junior officers waited their turn in *Lion*'s shore boats. Late in the afternoon, with the winter sun casting long shadows, Jamie swung his seabag down to a sailor and dropped from the ladder. He had been so long at sea that his legs automatically took up the rise and slight corkscrew motion of the boat. However, once they reached the Gosport landing, his legs betrayed him, for he swayed precariously during his first few steps on the dock's planking. Gideon Marsh and Jonathan Maxwell also had difficulty maintaining their balance, which prompted unseemly hilarity from all three, as well as some of the passersby.

A carriage took them to a nearby hotel, for the transient officer's quarters at the dockyard across the channel were full. After depositing their belongings, they walked the length of the harborside to the Fox Tavern, which Jamie had frequented during his stay in Haslar Hospital following his wounding at Quiberon Bay.

In spite of the cold weather, crowds jammed the esplanade in an indiscriminate mix of workmen, wives, soldiers, sailors, doxies, and children. The taverns were so full that drinking and dancing spilled outdoors. The cacophony of voices, drums, horns, and whistles was deafening. In spite of the crush, the crowd was wary of the three officers and pushed aside to make a path for them.

They passed a crowd of sailors and soldiers alternately cheering and hooting a group of doxies loudly chanting a ribald lyric.

> Sailors get all the silver,
> Soldiers get naught but brass,
> I do love a jolly sailor,
> Soldiers can kiss my arse.

A little further along, crowds jamming the esplanade were less noisy.

Jonathan said, "Do ye ken the Lovely Nans' doggerel?"

Jamie chuckled. "Aye, prize money paid tae sailors may look sma' compared tae the huge amounts paid captains and admirals, but still 'tis a modest pile o' gold and siller compared tae naething. Soldiers wha dinna receive prize money earn sae little that they receive nae mair than brass coins. Girls grant favors tae those wha can afford tae gie them gifts, food, and entertainment. It is a cruel economy fer puir soldiers. I also pity the girls, fer soon there will be far fewer sailors than during wartime and nae soldiers at a'."

Gideon Marsh added, "The innkeepers will also make a tidy profit this night. The town is awash in gin, rum, and beer. Tomorrow, they will add to their profits from those suffering from their excesses by peddling useless nostrums to cure their ailments. It is the nature of seamen and marines to spend what they have until it is gone or stolen. They dream of shore leave during all those lonely months afloat while they endure incredible danger. They are incapable of rationing their pay to prolong the pleasurable experiences once they reach port. A three- or four-day spree can easily dissipate six months' pay. Fortunately, few married men are here. They are hame wi' their bairns while their gimlet-eyed wives already hae their pay."

Maxwell said, "As a ship's surgeon, I am familiar wi' the results. Drunkenness and brawling kept me endlessly busy as lang as we were in port. Indeed, this night will be lively, fer they and we hae much tae celebrate. Others must deal wi' the excesses, fer we are at loose ends, wi' nae assignments, at least until tomorrow, when we report tae the Admiralty office."

In the darkness, where Trinity Green joined the esplanade, the lights of the inn welcomed them. Jamie put his arms around his two companions as they walked inside. "My friends, let us enjoy these few hours wi'oot responsibility. While it hae been mair than three years since I hae visited the Fox Inn, I expect that we will be weel-fed after sae many days o' bully beef, biscuit, and stale beer."

They entered the common room and were dismayed that every table was occupied. While they surveyed the room, a group of boisterous merchants shouted an invitation to join them. Their table, in a far corner, was cramped, but adequate to seat three more. As soon as they placed their order for ale, a bulky gray-haired naval officer stood and, in an excellent tenor, began a song. He was quickly joined by the entire room, for it was a favorite with the nautical community. Within seconds, fists were thumping tables at a rate that rattled the dishes and cutlery.

> Come all ye brave Britons, let no one complain,
> 'Britannia! Britannia!' once more rules the main,
> With bumpers o'erflowing, we'll jovially sing,
> And tell the high deeds o' the year fifty nine!

They continued through a medley of the popular music hall ditties composed by the immensely popular David Garrick, who praised the British Navy and army's victories in Canada, India, the Caribbean, and the high seas.

At length, the singing flagged, and conversation became possible. Introductions went around the table. The merchants flung questions about their service and raised a cheer when they discovered that veterans of some of the most illustrious victories of the war were among them. The eldest among the civilians, quite red of cheek and expansive of girth, rose with great solemnity to propose a toast to those who had fallen. His voice was slurred from the great quantity of spirits he had consumed.

"We are grateful to have peace, but this peace is scarcely honorable. It deprecates the lifeblood shed to conquer Cuba, Martinique, Guadalupe, and other lands handed back to the French and Spanish." He slammed his tankard on the table. "I tell you that I am ashamed of ministers and a monarch without the manhood to hold what brave men conquered!"

Looking around with apprehension, his companions pulled at his coattails in a futile attempt to quiet him. An annoyed diner at another table shouted, "Treason!" but no one raised a voice in support.

The first man rounded on the sole defender of the government. "Fie! 'Tis no treason to speak plainly! Am I not a loyal Englishman and pay my taxes? Are not we all?" After the hubbub subsided, Jamie rose to face the crowd, which quieted to hear him.

"Gentlemen, I pray my Scottish voice dinna confuse ye. We arrived only this day frae the Caribbean wi' nae information aboot the agreement wi' the French and Spanish, which we defeated at Havana, Martinique, Louisburg, Quebec, and Quiberon Bay, or the logic employed by government ministers tae achieve the peace. I dinna ken whether the agreement is guid or harmfu' tae the kingdom. Clearly, we should celebrate something on which we can agree." He raised his glass. "Let us toast the memory o' those wha fought and died, whose blood stained the soil o' foreign lands, and whose courage inspired their comrades. They sacrificed, and we endured tae gain the victory. Gentlemen, I gie ye the unnamed heroes o' this war wha fought fer honor!" He sat down to tumultuous applause.

Many bumpers of ale and bowls of punch later, the outspoken merchant slid into the seat next to Jamie, who was amazed that the man could think and speak with any clarity. He pointed to the military officers scattered around the large room. "I tell you, the fate of this nation lies in the hands of those who braved the enemy and elements to serve. The gentry of this nation, which now stands astride the globe, have too few willing to endure discomfort, let alone risk their lives and limbs. They prefer to sit in sedan chairs drawn by those of what they consider the lower classes, who are far more manly than they. They prefer warm salons and carriages to walking or riding strenuously. Young men whose speech is of macaroni fashions, wigs, cards, dicing, whist, and dissolute unspeakable vices are lacking in public spirit and love of country, although they profit handsomely from other men's sacrifices and labor. If we do not correct the imbalance and find a way to encourage the brave to continue in service for the good of this nation, we will soon slip from today's lofty standing. We have many enemies who would rejoice to see our downfall. Thank God for men of action like yourselves, for they give me hope."

Jamie felt a stab of déjà vu, for he had heard the same admonition from Major General James Wolfe long ago in his childhood as they rode together over the cold hills north of Inverness.

After many toasts and compliments, the three managed to find their way back to the hotel, though the celebrating crowds were little diminished. At one point, a group of local toughs began to trail them. Jamie and Gideon turned, ostentatiously thrusting back their coats to expose their weapons. Both had left their ornate rapiers behind, choosing to be armed with heavy broadswords. The locals, perhaps expecting to confront men armed with dress weapons, chose to withdraw into the shadows rather than face such deadly blades.

In the morning, they made their way to the new Admiralty office, for the dockyard fire had destroyed its predecessor. Jamie found that there was no marine officer on the much-diminished staff. While his companions met with officers authorized to process their orders and discuss postings, Jamie received only a cursory review of his paperwork. An overloaded Commander Benjamin Fairfield gave him ten minutes. "All assignments for marine officers come from London, Captain Drummond. With peace, postings and ship assignments are in an uproar. I see that you came in on *Lion*, which is headed to survey, with her crew available for reassignment. All the barely sufficient ships, along with their officers and crews, are awaiting orders. There is no shortage of available officers and few openings for sea service. 'Tis not a gamble to say that with long years in foreign service, ye will most likely receive a lengthy home leave. Good luck." He pressed a stamp into an inked pad, whacked it noisily on Jamie's orders, and added his signature. He extended a warm handshake, and their business was over.

That night, the shipmates compared results. Gideon Marsh was assigned to duty as a third lieutenant on an elderly fourth rate patrolling the Channel coast, a significant comedown for a junior officer aspiring to command. Jonathan Maxwell was assigned to

Haslar Hospital. He was overjoyed at the opportunity to serve and learn under James Lind.

"At least these are meaningful assignments," growled Jamie. "I am still in limbo until I reach London."

They enjoyed a final meal at the Fox Inn. In the morning, as a few flakes of snow sifted down, Jamie had his bag hoisted into the boot of a carriage making the run from Gosport to the Dockyards and then on to London.

Jamie stared at Lieutenant Colonel Raibert MacKenzie with ill-concealed frustration. In an hour, the senior officer who had built his reputation as a man of action had dashed Jamie's hopes of a lengthy home leave. "Nae, Captain Drummond. I hae the greatest regard fer yer bravery and devotion tae duty. It is true that the Peace o' Paris concludes hostilities, but our forces are in critical disarray. We must hae them in an entirely different posture now that the need for expeditionary concentration is o'er. The Admiralty already hae orders tae reduce the number o' warships and auxiliary craft. It is imperative that we evaluate and reposition officers, men, weapons, and supplies. I dinna need tae tell ye that war costs money, and we are spending far mair than government ministers are prepared tae supply. I hae been told that the national debt is approaching one hundred million pounds. Such a burden will bring a level o' taxation on the nation that will be difficult tae manage in the downturn that inevitably follows war. In spite o' our need tae maintain our naval power, we must spend less and reduce our forces. I need competent and dedicated officers tae help me perform the necessary planning o'er the next twa months. We canna wait until spring. When that work is complete, I will be pleased tae honor yer request fer hame leave."

Jamie focused on his boots, uncertain how to reply. He spoke in a low voice, "Sir, I hae dedicated nearly seven years o' my life tae this war, wi' less than a handful o' opportunities o' seein' my family awa' in the north. Perhaps placing my name at the top o' the list o' expendable officers would be fitting, fer I am heartily sick o' war."

MacKenzie fingered the scar that ran down his cheek—a memento of the battle for Fort Royal. He shook his head vehemently. "I would find that damnably unacceptable, Drummond. I am weel acquainted wi' yer sacrifices. Ye'd be a great loss tae the corps o' Royal Marines. However, I ken ye need rest and diversion frae weighty duties. Many men's desires would be quenched wi' a few days and nights o' carousing, drinking, and wenching. Ye are nae that sort." His face softened. He said, "Take a week tae hunt up auld friends and enjoy London's attractions. I am sorry that I canna grant ye mair time, for I need ye tae report back by eight in the morning Monday week. I must bid ye guid day, fer I am needed elsewhere." He stood up, cutting off the possibility of further conversation.

Jamie sagged, for he recognized the futility of argument with the obdurate senior officer. Captain Ambrose Newton of MacKenzie's staff showed Jamie the office where he would be working, which had a magnificent view over Whitehall Street. He also recommended a comfortable rooming house three blocks away that catered to transient naval and marine officers.

Admiralty House, facing Whitehall in Westminster, was ideally situated for the enjoyment of the great city's attractions. The Whitehall Theater was adjacent to the three-story building of yellow brick. An evening walk in a light drizzle down to the Thames and back to his lodgings by way of the Strand and Haymarket Street convinced Jamie that while he considered his assignment onerous, the neighborhood bustled with opportunities for diversion and enjoyment, with theaters, bookstores, coffee shops, taverns, and gentlemen's clubs.

He joined Ambrose Newton for dinner, but not before sending letters to Peter Gordon and Joseph Cotes. He was somewhat reluctant about contacting Sarah Cotes's uncle, for he considered that chapter of his life closed. It was only to fulfill a promise to the old gentleman, who had worked hard to promote Jamie's suit for Sarah's hand that had failed at last in the face of her father's political ambitions.

The rain stopped, so Jamie spent a day or two prowling the nearby districts. His lodging on Cockspur Court was only yards from elegant Warwick House and the grand houses of Pall Mall, frequented by London's lesser gentry. Carriages came and went with great frequency, conveying laughing parties of well-dressed men and women, colorful as tropical birds, who had obviously spent the greater part of the morning with their wardrobe, coiffure, and makeup.

He found the London streets endlessly fascinating. His nose was assaulted by the mingled scents of roasting meat, baking bread, fresh horse droppings and coal smoke, which also induced a gray haze that hung gauze-like over the streets. Along Haymarket, the clamor was a mercantile symphony of clanging bells, shouts, squealing axles, clattering hooves, and insistent spiels by pitchmen haranguing crowds before every storefront.

When he tired of wandering, he rejected the elegant clubs along Pall Mall and around Saint James' Square. He headed for the theater district stretching along Haymarket Street. He found an open supper club across the street from the King's Theater that did not require a membership and ducked in out of the cold.

Jamie handed his great coat to a solicitous attendant, who escorted him to a table with a view of a lush glass-enclosed garden across the entire back of the room. The midday crowd had departed. Most tables were vacant, with only one young couple seated at a nearby table, engaged in an intense whispered conversation. Jamie's ear quickly picked up the dark-haired man's Scottish accent. He glanced with interest at the girl, pretty and blonde. She was shaking her head vigorously. She rose suddenly, clutching her tiny bag and fled for the entrance. The young man did not rise but called after her, "Please, Fanny, ye misunderstand me!" But she was gone.

Jamie studied the bill of fare. A serving girl approached the table to take his order. The young man at the nearby table had turned to stare at him. Jamie inquired politely, "I see that I hae attracted yer interest. May I help ye, sir?"

The young man wore no wig. His dark hair was medium length and curly, swept back. His face was round and ruddy, his eyes dark and penetrating. He wore a burgundy vest and knickers under a dark green jacket fringed with fur. Jamie judged his age at twenty. "Ye are Scottish!" the stranger blurted.

Jamie smiled. "Aye. Do ye find a Scot unusual in London?"

The young man smiled in return. "Nae, but I always feel a surge o' comradeship when encountering a fellow countryman." He rose, approached Jamie's table, and extended a hand. Jamie noted that he wore no rings or other ostentatious jewelry. Jamie pushed back his chair and got to his feet. He towered over the stranger, who was of slight build, with slender hands. However, his grip was firm and his countenance open. "I am James Boswell, eldest son o' Alexander Boswell, advocate and judge in Edinburgh. I hae been in London fer aboot four months."

Jamie introduced himself and invited Boswell to join him. The young man proved to be an engaging conversationalist. Jamie asked him about his career plans. Boswell's face grew moody. "My father and I hae frequently clashed o'er that subject. I despise the thought o' pursuing law, which is my father's great dream, since I am firstborn. I prefer the company o' theater people and authors, fer I admire their minds and merry natures much mair than the dry logic o' the law."

Jamie chuckled. "I hear that maist theater people, fer all their gaudy attire and gay spirits, hae leetle money. Unless ye can attract the interest o' a wealthy patron, ye will gnaw stones and sleep in a garret."

Boswell nodded. "I ken that may be true. A man wi' such interests needs a steady income. Therefore, I hae resolved tae seek a military commission tae provide it."

Jamie sat back, stunned by the young man's naiveté. He said, "I must caution ye, James, that military pay, unless yer father can afford a commission at senior rank, is puir. Naval and marine officers share prize money, but such commissions are rarely bought. War is a dangerous profession, and army service is often in bleak foreign parts. We are also at the end o' war fer a space, wi' many mair officers and men than needed."

Boswell was silent as he took in this news. "I am nae surprised tae hear that. My hope is that my father's connections will make an appointment possible." He brightened. "My agreement with him is tae spend a year in London, and I still hae some months before I must return. I hae met many interesting people and hae some fascinating experiences, which I am recounting in a journal that I hope tae see printed."

Jamie rubbed his chin. "Interesting people? Apparently, ane o' the maist interesting just rejected ye and departed."

Boswell burst out laughing. "Aye, weel. London is noted fer guid female sport."

Jamie smiled. "She dinna look like the Lovely Nans that haunt port towns. Perhaps ye are mistaken."

Boswell shook his head. "Ye misunderstand me. Fanny is nae a prostitute, but an aspiring actress whose favors may be gained by gifts and sweet words but nae money."

Jamie said drily, "I fail tae discern the difference, except fer the effort ye must expend and the cost tae attain yer objective. I misdoubt that the risk tae yer health is any the less."

Boswell said, "I must ruefully admit that my lust has already caused me tae suffer. I hae an amorous nature and fear that my desires are stronger than my ability tae withstand."

Jamie sighed. "I dinna desire tae lecture ye on morality, James, but I hae taken a liking tae ye. I hae advised the young marines in my command tae avoid the perils o' the street, wi' varying results. There is sae much mair misery than happiness, on the whole, produced by engaging in such illicit entertainment. The momentary pleasure that ye experience is nae worth the danger tae body and spirit. The cost tae yer dignity and the purity that ye should bring tae the marital state wi' an innocent bride wha loves and trusts ye is far greater than ye should pay."

Boswell seemed to shrink inside himself and nodded dumbly. "Every time, I am remorseful and resolve ne'er again tae violate my oath tae maintain virtue, though lust rages inside me. I begin each morning wi' purpose tae guard against this great evil, but I am weak and my resolve crumbles wi' each setting sun."

The food arrived, and they fell to it hungrily. Jamie, in a generous mood, paid the reckoning, for he detected that James Boswell had a spare living from his father and had not yet learned to live within his frugal means. Their conversation was so amiable that Jamie promised to sup with his fellow Scot from time to time as long as they both remained in London.

7

On the Thursday before he was due to report back to the Admiralty, Jamie returned from an afternoon's excursion to the venerable Tower of London and a stroll along the Thames. The porter at his lodgings passed him two envelopes. Cracking the red wax seal on the larger, Jamie withdrew an engraved invitation. The letterhead depicted a line drawing of Chesterfield House, one of the great houses recently completed in Mayfair. He quickly scanned the announcement. His was the final name on a list of those invited to join Philip Stanhope, Lord Chesterfield, for dinner at 7:00 p.m. on Friday night. Unfamiliar with court politics, Jamie recognized only three names in the list—Charles Townsend, a former Lord of the Admiralty, Joseph Cotes, and his cousin Peter Gordon. The small envelope contained a note from Peter informing him that his carriage would arrive at six thirty.

Jamie was puzzled by the invitation since nothing had been said on Sunday afternoon, during his visit to the home of Peter and Rachel Gordon. That had been a pleasant time with play and storytelling with the four Gordon children. After the children had been packed off to bed, Peter had spoken of affairs at Abergeldie in the north but had said nothing about the family's petition to the crown for restoration of lands and titles. Jamie was reluctant to ask since silence implied no good news. He reread the invitation and felt hope rising. Why was he invited to a meeting with such men?

Seated in a fine carriage with Italianate appointments that reflected well on his rising prominence in professional legal circles, Peter was enigmatic while Jamie plied him with questions. At last, he spoke, "Dear cousin, whatever I can say aboot this meeting will all be explained in due course. I admit that I conspired wi' Joseph Cotes tae arrange it fer yer benefit. He hae a great admiration fer ye, in spite o' the sudden turn in his brother's political intentions that brought an abrupt end tae yer hopes o' courting his daughter." He shook his head. "Maist unfortunate. The admiral's death was quite unexpected."

Jamie started. He finally found his voice. "Admiral Cotes died? When?"

Peter said, "O' course ye hae nae heard. It was shortly after he returned frae the Caribbean and took up the seat in Parliament tae which he hae been elected wi' the influence o' Sarah's new husband. Apoplexy gies little warning. His wife declined and died within months, leaving Sarah as the heiress of the family estates."

The news troubled Jamie, who stared through the curtains as the horses drew the carriage toward Mayfair. "I dinna wish tae discuss these matters further, Peter, fer they bring back painful memories o' what might hae been, except tae ask if Sarah and Jessica are weel-placed and happy in marriage."

Peter tapped the knob of his walking stick on his palm. At last, he spoke. "Sarah seems happy enough, according tae Uncle Joseph. She now hae a bairn, and that always brings happiness tae a mother. The child is a boy wha also pleases the father, wha yearned fer an heir. Jessica hae been a grass widow o' sorts, yet unmarried, while she waited fer John Anthony tae return frae India."

Jamie murmured, "She must be in a dither, waiting fer the fleet tae return frae around the Cape and preparing fer marriage."

Peter shook his head. "A letter came that John Anthony hae resigned his commission now that India hae been won by Robert Clive. That young worthy is a national hero fer defeating the French and securing control o' the Eastern markets fer the East India Company. Joseph tells me that Anthony received a highly lucrative offer frae Clive tae stay in the East and engage wi' him and his minions in building a great mercantile empire and militarily subduing the remainder o' Bengal and the Carnatic. Many young worthies are heading there tae seek their fortunes. John sent a message telling Jessica o' the offer and asking her tae make the lang voyage tae India, promising marriage once she arrived. She was sae incensed that she burned his letter. Apparently, there will be nae marriage." Peter stared speculatively at Jamie. "I understand that in Jamaica, the lass was once quite taken wi' ye before she transferred her affections tae young Anthony."

Jamie glared at his cousin. "I understand that is quite fashionable at court fer young men o' humble means but aristocratic birth tae pursue women o' wealth. I carry a burden o' memories o' love lost. I hae nae interest in such demeaning activities, cousin, nor an association that would bring me into regular contact wi' her sister." His voice quavered. "God help me, Peter! I still love Sarah." He held up a palm. "I pity Jessica's misfortune tae wait years fer John Anthony, only tae see him lured awa' by a promise o' wealth, but canna bring myself tae imagine a romantic liaison. Let us nae speak further o' these misfortunes. Although ye refuse tae discuss the purpose, tell me of tonight's guests."

Peter said, "Chesterfield House is the home o' Philip Stanhope, fourth Earl o' Chesterfield, and he will host our meeting. William Dowdeswell is an Oxford-educated man of rising importance in the Whig party and has held a seat in Parliament for nearly twenty years. Charles Townsend is another rising member o' Parliament frae Norfolk, second son of the Third Viscount Townsend. He is married tae Caroline Campbell, daughter o' the Duke o' Argyll."

Jamie gaped. "Then he is in the sway o' the Campbells."

Peter shook his head. "Nae. He is independently minded in spite o' the connection. Another guest is Dr. Samuel Johnson, wha is a poet, essayist, moralist, literary critic, biographer, and editor."

Jamie smiled. "Wi' such credentials, he is clearly a mortal enemy o' politicians."

Peter said, "They consider him dangerous tae their interests but a powerful man tae placate and cultivate. I consider him an insufferable egotist and yet possibly the most interesting man in Britain. He canna sit still fer five minutes wi'out expressing his opinion on any subject."

Jamie chuckled. "He should enliven the conversation and create a fascinating battle o' wits wi' those headstrong enough tae challenge his opinions."

Peter said, "The most interesting guest tonight is an Irishman—Edmund Burke. He is my age, a man of manifold talents and author of treatises on politics and philosophy since he was nineteen. He is a rising figure in Whig circles wi' the uncanny ability tae appeal tae the passions o' conservatives and liberals alike. He aspires to Parliament but has not yet stood for a seat."

Peter fell silent, and Jamie was left to ponder the purpose of the meeting and his invitation to join such an august group. The driver slowed the spirited horses as the carriage made a turn onto Curzon Street and another through the open gate in the high wrought-iron fence. He expertly steered the carriage between rows of glowing post lanterns to the pillared entrance of the massive four-story mansion.

Inside, Jamie was confronted with the rich grandeur of the magnificent furniture and decorations. He was lost in remembrance of the beauty of Strathallan Castle, his childhood home, from which his family had fled before the collapse of the hopes of a Jacobite victory and the flight of the Bonnie Prince from Culloden Moor in the spring of 1746.

Glittering chandeliers hung on heavy chains from the high ceiling. A black iron double staircase rose to the second level from the spacious marble foyer. Grecian urns and statuary, portraits, and tapestries abounded. Chesterfield House was a treasure into which Philip Stanhope had poured his vibrant personality and wealth.

A group was gathered outside the drawing room. One man stood somewhat apart from the others. He had a lean face, with prominent nose and deep-set eyes. His coat bore the arms that denoted his rank. Jamie and Peter approached and began to make the traditional leg expected when addressing an earl.

Stanhope smiled and waved his hand dismissively. "Please, gentlemen. We are not at court, and such acts are not expected. I desire a convivial gathering in which guests are welcome to participate freely and enjoy themselves." He extended his hand to grip Jamie's. "Welcome, Captain Drummond." He turned to Peter. "And since we are dispensing with titles for tonight, I will welcome my barrister friend without addressing him as Esquire. I find it perplexing, Mr. Gordon, that armigers and lawyers are appropriating the term once used to describe a man who held a horse for a knight. I wonder what else they will appropriate."

Everyone laughed at the earl's jest.

The drawing room was also sumptuously appointed, with a long table and ornate chairs that appeared too delicate to support a man as big as Samuel Johnson. Jamie held his breath when the man settled his bulk into his chair opposite, with Peter on his right, Joseph Cotes on Jamie's right, and Edmund Burke on his left. The earl had invited everyone to sample the view into two composite mirrors imported from France. They were placed facing each other, so that the viewer saw multiple reflections of himself in the mirrors, stretching out and endlessly repeating.

Jamie exclaimed, "I hae an eerie feeling that I am looking into eternity, both forwards and backwards."

This comment started a vigorous conversation between Samuel Johnson and Edmund Burke on the nature of infinity and eternity, which continued until the earl's steward drew their attention by coughing loudly but discreetly, for the servers were filing in with platters and tureens wafting delicious scents.

The food was tasty, and the wines were excellent choices from France, Germany, and Italy. Charles Townsend acclaimed their quality and remarked that he was happy to once again enjoy the French vintages now that peace was restored. William Dowdeswell harrumphed and observed that he had great admiration for the diligence of smugglers, who could always be depended on to deliver in spite of the blockade of the British Navy.

Jamie remarked that he had spent many nights staring into the blackness to discover the elusive smugglers but that few could be caught in the treacherous waters and thick fogs of the French coast. "I do recall one ship we surprised loaded with wines, brandies, and fine French lace. We may hae disappointed many ladies and gentlemen on this side o' the Channel, but the prize was a rich reward fer the lang days and nights we patrolled on that treacherous coast."

The side conversations rose and fell for over an hour. At last, the earl rose and began the traditional round of toasts to the king, followed by others who offered them to generals and admirals who had distinguished themselves in the war. Jamie took his turn, standing to toast General James Wolfe, the hero of Louisburg and Quebec. Joseph Cotes rose, faced the earl, and raised his glass.

"I think it proper, my lord and gentlemen, that we toast a man who has served this nation with great distinction, but without the accolades extended to those of higher rank. We are fortunate to have many hundreds—nay, thousands—like him. He and they exemplify the fiber and sinew of this nation. He entered service in a lowly station and rose to higher rank because of his uncommon qualities, which are deserving of greater reward than he has received. He fought with great distinction in the

Mediterranean, on the coast of France, at Île-d'Aix, Louisburg, Quebec, Quiberon Bay, Belle Isle, Martinique, and Cuba. As a prisoner of war of the Spanish, he suffered the indignity of the bastinado and barely escaped with his life. He survived capsizing and sinking. I give you Captain James William Drummond of the Royal Marines."

Jamie sat red-faced while the men toasted him.

Lord Chesterfield tapped his glass, and the drawing room quieted. He looked intently at Jamie and then began speaking. "I am appreciative to you all for accepting my invitation. I am now an old man, nearing seventy, and greatly enjoy the privilege that my rank gives me to invite the association of men with brilliant minds and whose advice I respect. I am pleased to warm myself in the reflected glow of your abilities and promise. We have gathered from time to time to discuss and take up various causes important to our society and nation. I am very grateful to my old friend Joseph Cotes, who has stated today's issue so distinctly."

Charles Townsend began the conversation by saying, "Jacobitism has been a persistent threat to the stability of the realm for three generations. The means taken to suppress it have required excessive measures against the population of the far north while little was done to reduce the threat at its source—France. We have now prevailed against the French. Rather than join them, the military prowess of the men of the Highlands served on our side. I say that we should provide their families relief and encouragement to continue to be loyal to King George."

Samuel Johnson raised a hand and growled, "While the majority of this group may be Whiggish in their sympathies, I am not. I am a dyed-in-the-wool Tory and stand with the current government, which is correct in not considering relief from the Act of Attainder. There is little to admire in the culture of the Highland people or the land itself. The country consists of two things—stone and water. There is, indeed, earth above the stone in some places, but very little, and the stone is always appearing.

It is like a man in rags. The naked skin is still peeping out." The remark provoked laughter, but Jamie turned to face the big man in indignation.

He asked, "Sir, hae ye e'er traveled there and met the people?"

Johnson said calmly, "I have met enough Scotchmen in my time to develop a reliable gauge of their temper and state of development. Knowledge is divided among the Scots, like bread in a besieged town—to every man a mouthful, to no man a bellyful."

Jamie reddened but kept his voice level. "I suggest that a great man of letters should withhold judgment on a subject until he has gained a sufficiency of knowledge. Ken ye nae that the Enlightenment hae lit a flame o' enlightenment in the great universities o' the north? Scholars throughout Great Britain, and even on the continent, hae embraced their advances in ethics, rhetoric, science, economics, and political thought. While many o' my countrymen are ignorant o' literacy and fine manners, they are uncommonly brave, fiercely loyal, and trustworthy. Ye would benefit frae spending time among them."

Dr. Johnson smiled. "Well said, Captain Drummond. You are an admirable defender of your homeland and its people. I am a civilized man and loathe discomfort, but I have had thoughts of traveling to the far north. I accept your challenge."

Jamie nodded and, abashed at Johnson's mild response, sat down.

After a brief silence, William Dowdeswell said, "My lord, we are a small number, and none of us serve in the current government. Although we may arrive at a unanimity of opinion that Captain Drummond and others who served in the recent conflict are deserving of restoration of their hereditary properties and rights, how could we influence Parliament and the crown?"

The earl said, "The current government is quite unstable. Lord Bute and his friends appear formidable, but their support rests on sand. For the benefit of Captain Drummond, let me explain their objections to restoration. Lord Bute is closely allied with the Duke of Argyll. John Campbell has been staunchly opposed to restoration for any of the Highland families who came out for James in the Rising of 1745. He is now quite elderly, but his son and heir shares his father's prejudices and will continue to wield uncommon influence with Tory ministers for decades. There are rumors that Lord Bute is losing favor with the king, but several of his young protégés will be influential for decades. A prime example is Frederick North, with close connections to the young king. Anyone who doubts the reason for North's strong connections has only to stare at portraits of the two. The familial likeness is startling. Conditions may improve under a successor government, particularly if it is Whig. I predict that George Grenville, First Lord of the Admiralty will be asked to serve as Prime Minister. If so, we may have an opportunity to press the issue with one or more of his ministers. He is uncertain himself, but our estimable friend Charles Townsend may be asked to serve."

Jamie's heart lurched as he thought of the strange circumstances that were about to place the fate and fortune of his family in the hands of Charles Townsend, married to a Campbell. The Dukes of Argyll had long been the principal power in the western Highlands, just as the Drummonds had been in the central Highlands. Would the Campbells quietly acquiesce to a restoration that could weaken their own preeminent position in British politics?

The conversation continued, heated at times. Servers passed silently through the diners, distributing plates of pastries, bowls of cream, coffee and tea services, and snifters of brandy. The evening grew late. At length, the earl rose to his feet. "Gentlemen, I grow weary. It seems that except for encouraging any of us who may be called into a new government to initiate steps to promote restoration, there is little any of us can do under the present circumstances. We can importune current ministers to consider the wholesome benefits of a restoration of titles and estates to loyal and deserving heirs, although I hold out little hope for action at the present. Dr. Johnson is considering making a progress through the Highlands and writing about his experiences. That will bring the subject of conditions in the north to the sympathetic attention of many. Mr. Burke will collaborate with our barrister colleague Mr. Gordon in writing a thoughtful series of letters for me to use to good effect. I intend to solicit support from members of that select group of young gentlemen of yore, well-known now only to the older generation as Cobham's Cubs. While they have evolved to hold diverse political persuasions both Whig and Tory, we were ever supportive of the oppressed and disadvantaged."

He glanced at Jamie. "These are thin reeds indeed and may do little to promote your cause, Captain Drummond. Tell me, do you intend to remain in active military service, or will you return home?"

Jamie rose to address the earl. "My lord, I am maist appreciative o' yer patronage and the consideration of sae many worthy gentlemen. While none here hae felt the loss o' hereditary titles and lands because o' a father's loyalty tae a cause, it appears that ye understand that it can be devastating. In my case, it may hae been beneficial. I was raised in comfortable but constrained circumstances. Pressed military service tested my ability tae survive privation and forced me tae rely on my ain merits tae survive. War, wi' all its trials, is a crucible that tests the mettle o' those wha fight. Nae matter the outcome o' my petition, I feel worthy tae contribute o' my abilities to serve this nation. Whether that will be in military service, I dinna ken. That decision appears tae lie wi' others. My preference is tae return hame fer a time. Fer me, there will be nae grand tour o' European capitals, nae riding tae the hounds, nae leisurely dining nor card playing in swank clubs. Wi'out income, I will be forced tae seek employment, which I understand is nae the habit o' young aristocrats. I possess some admirable skills that may attract future employers. I can direct artillery and volleys o' musketry tae devastating effect, and I am a fair hand wi' rapier and cutlass."

The room erupted in laughter, followed by hearty handshakes and requests for visits before Jamie left London. Peter and Jamie donned their coats, but Lord Chesterfield detained them at the door. As he shook Jamie's hand, he said, "I intend to call my friends together in three months' time to discuss whether we are achieving progress in your behalf. If you receive orders to depart London before that time, you must notify me immediately. May I hae your word on that?"

Jamie nodded, but Peter assured the earl that he would stand as Jamie's proxy in the event of unexpected military deployment.

○―――――○

Lieutenant Colonel Mackenzie tapped the list that Jamie had presented to him earlier that morning. "I dinna find this list complete, Captain Drummond. It must be reworked. The salvage boards hae condemned four ships only this week, which means that their officers and crews lack assignments. Conducting reviews o' their performance will take time, time that we canna spare. We hae orders tae cut, and cut we must."

Jamie objected, "But, sir, some o' these officers and men are mair experienced than many wi' secure positions. It is nae tae the benefit o' the service tae lose the better simply because they were unlucky enough tae ride auld vessels made unseaworthy in valorous combat!"

Mackenzie rubbed his chin and then turned to stare out the window at the glistening rain-soaked street. "Time is our enemy, Drummond. I must fulfill the Admiralty's orders and soon. Henceforth, you will put the name o' any officer or enlisted man wi'oot assignment tae a ship or station on the list tae be either discharged or placed on half pay based on the rules I already prescribed."

Jamie gaped and then said slowly, "Sir, I am nae assigned at present. I will place my name on the list."

Mackenzie frowned, and his voice rose dangerously. "Ye are assigned, Drummond! Ye are assigned tae the Admiralty! Ye are an officer o' such promise that it would cost me my head if I submitted yer name on the half-pay list, which will be reviewed by several admirals and the First Lord himself. Nae, my lad. Yer position is secure. Now leave me and return in the morning wi' a revised list."

Jamie received letters from his mother and sisters in Abergeldie filled with elation that the war was over and that he had returned safely to England after the sinking of HMS *Marlborough*. Euphemia Drummond wrote that conditions in the north were restless, with rising prices and rents outpacing profits to be made in farming and running cattle as in the old days. Some Gordon tenants had gathered their families and pitiful possessions and taken them to Inverness, Aberdeen, and cities in the Lowlands where they could find work. Those with the means to emigrate to the American colonies and Canada were doing so, but few could afford the ticket prices without signing papers indenturing themselves for years. Luckily, there were so many farmers begging for land that replacing those who departed was not difficult. Some younger sons of aristocratic families were gathering farmers, tacksmen, skilled artisans, and clerks and taking a ship to Jamaica and other Caribbean islands for the purpose of clearing land for sugar plantations. Indeed, as she commiserated, it seemed that all worthwhile opportunities lay elsewhere. His mother urged him to come north but to take care. Brigands and even destitute farmers and herders were haunting the moors and turnpikes, preying on unwary travelers.

Reading the salvage reports, Jamie saw that Major Jock Armstrong, his first commander and great friend, was in a secure assignment, but disconsolate when a name that he was forced to add to the list was that of Major Gerald MacIntyre. Gerry of the wild Irish fiddle music, who had suffered a gunshot wound in Canada that nearly ended his career, was slated to lose it after all due to the misfortune of being caught out without an assignment.

Additions to the lists seemed endless, for decisions by the salvage board were announced more than once a week. The Admiralty was under stringent orders to force reductions by early May. Jamie spent much of March and early April shuttling between London and the ports from Bristol, Plymouth, and Portsmouth in the southwest to Deptford on the outskirts of London. He met with port authorities and warship captains to discover openings that would provide opportunities for placing unassigned officers and rated men in marine contingents.

Through these efforts, he was successful in removing nearly seventy names from the lists of those slated to be discharged or placed on half pay until the Royal Marines recalled them, which could be months or years in the future. More opportunities emerged when warships and transports of the Indian fleet docked at Deptford. Most were shorthanded, for Clive's victories had secured a bonanza of trade opportunities across the subcontinent. Deaths and debilitating illness from disease and battle had drawn down their crews. Many officers and men were allowed to resign to immediately go to India to take up lucrative positions with the East India Company as administrators, craftsmen, shopkeepers, and even military positions for the company had its own army and a small but growing fleet.

Jamie worked long into the night revising the lists to satisfy Lieutenant Colonel Mackenzie's schedule. He rubbed his burning eyes and yawned. Exhausted, he rested his head on his arms, frustrated by the impossibility of saving any more careers. His eyelids grew heavy, his breathing slowed, and he slept. After a time, the candle in the lantern hung over the desk guttered and went out. Cold moonlight flooded the darkened room.

Jamie sat up with a jerk. The room was filled with a lambent yellow glow that seemed to come from no obvious source. Two gnarled faces peered at him from the shadowed rafters.

Jamie put his head in his hands and groaned. "Gruagach! Why must ye bedevil me wi' yer gloomy pronouncements?"

Although both sprites were elderly, the one who appeared older rubbed the wart on his hook-shaped nose. He spoke, "Ye might remember me, Jamie Drummond. I hight Stochdail, companion o' King Peallaidh. He sent me tae ye again, along wi' Brùnaidh an Easain, the brownie o' the little waterfall."

Jamie sighed. "Why hae ye come? Yer appearances are a curse. Ye disturb my sleep to croak mysterious sayings that are naething mair than confusing riddles."

Brùnaidh's voice rumbled. "We are here tae convince ye, now that ye hae safely returned frae the sea, that ye must be aboot the great business o' fulfilling the prophecy pronounced by the bard wi' the Sight."

Jamie stood to get a better view of the two sprites, who scuttled further into the shadows over his head. He shouted, "I am sick tae death o' being directed aboot by creatures frae legends and dreams! If ye canna tell me the purpose o' the prophecy, I wilna listen further tae yer infernal hounding! I am beginning tae think that ye are nae here at a', that ye are naething mair than creatures o' my fevered mind!"

Stochdail uttered a croaking laugh. "O' a certainty, child o' the Highlands. We exist only in yer memories and yer sense o' duty tae yer heritage. As our king told ye once, ye will us tae yer presence. We hae nae power o'er yer mind except as ye choose. A powerful part o' yer soul wishes tae pursue the prophecy and achieve great deeds. We are only reminders o' that desire." The light began to gather around the pair.

Jamie stretched out his hands and pleaded, "Please, Stochdail! Dinna leave wi'out telling me the purpose! Wha is the purpose o' the prophecy?"

A voice echoed from the remaining orb of light. "Ye will come tae understand the purpose as ye seek tae fulfill it." The light slowly vanished. Jamie fumbled in the faint moonlight to find a candle and flint. When he had relit the lantern, he gathered the lists and placed them in the leather courier case. That done, he locked up and walked back to his lodgings, musing on the strange dream, if dream it was.

He rose before dawn, for sleep had been filled with disturbing dreams, in one of which he climbed stairs and wandered down endless corridors trying doors and finding them locked. He faintly recalled another vision of riding through a deep forest during a storm, looking in vain for shelter and not finding it. He dined alone on the sunny patio at the inn, unwilling to share his gloomy thoughts with other lodgers.

8

Late April was glorious in London, and he decided to stroll the two miles that lay between his lodgings and the Admiralty. Tenants had hung flower boxes from upper balconies of the grand houses and hotels lining the avenues. Manicured lawns, trees, and flower beds flourished with a kaleidoscope of colors. There were many strollers enjoying the fine weather, and nearly every person he passed greeted him cheerily. His spirits lifted, for the young cannot remain grim in the face of such beauty and pleasantness.

He reflected on the decision he had made in the depths of the night just past, for it was momentous. It was not just the recurrent dreams about his nocturnal visitors from Highland legend, for he admitted to himself that he had been drifting to such an action for some time. *Since I hae decided, it hae best been done quickly*, he thought to himself.

He saluted the marine guards standing watch before the great doors at the entrance to Admiralty House, climbed the stairs to the second level, and walked to his small office halfway down the echoing corridor. He hung his hat on a peg and placed the attaché case on the corner of his desk. He sat down, selected a new quill, and carefully cut a point, using the small knife reserved for that purpose. He had rehearsed the text in his mind a dozen times. He selected a sheet of paper and inked the point. In bold strokes, he wrote the words of his resignation, reinked the pen, and applied his signature. He laid the single sheet on the desk and stared at it. The letter said little about his reasons, only declaring that Captain James William Drummond was resigning his commission because he had a great need to return to his family. It was a cryptic epitaph to the end of a career that had consumed nearly a third of his life. It said nothing of the dangers faced, deeds done, killings inflicted and wounds suffered, lessons learned, or the camaraderie that sustained him and his companions through the long days and nights for seven years. The scars, lessons, and memories would sustain him for a lifetime. His military career would end because of his own resolve, not because he was no longer needed or wanted. An impulse stabbed him, and he almost reached out to crumple the sheet in his fist, but he fought it down. He was not destitute. He had reviewed his prize account, which, by only prudent withdrawals for his mother's maintenance and wise investments, had grown to over thirty thousand pounds. Although he was more hopeful than ever that his petition for restoration would eventually be honored, he could not be a spendthrift or base his whole future on that hope. If he lived modestly, this fund would sustain him for years, at least until he could acquire and prove himself in some profession. Steeling himself to endure the criticism that would surely come from Lieutenant Colonel Mackenzie, Jamie rose. He picked up the letter and attaché case with the lists of officers and men recommended for discharge or half-pay assignment.

To say that Raibert Mackenzie was skilled in profanity would be understating an ability developed over a long career at sea. The wrathful tongue-lashing Jamie received that morning overwhelmed any that he had ever received. The letter that he had laid on Mackenzie's desk lay in shreds on the polished floor. Jamie stood ramrod straight, waiting for his superior's passion to cool. To the older officer, voluntary resignation was an unacceptable affront to the service, which had accepted a callow youth, turned him into a man of whom the nation was justifiably proud, and enriched him with a small fortune in prize money. To Raibert Mackenzie, who had served for twenty-eight years, Jamie owed a debt of gratitude to the Royal Marines that could only be repaid through a career of service; anything less was a breach of faith. At last, the senior officer's tirade ended, and he sat back, his blue eyes glaring frostily at Jamie.

"I advise ye tae return tae yer duties, Drummond. I will approve sixty days o' leave in the Highlands. That is sufficient time fer ye tae gain an appreciation that the Corps o' Marines is yer rightfu' hame."

Jamie's resolve was intact. He shook his head. "Sir, when I was pressed tae service, I accepted fer the sake o' an oath o' loyalty fer four years or the duration o' the war. I hae served faithfully fer seven, and the war is now o'er. It is difficult fer me tae find the words tae tell ye that as the years passed, I hae changed. I still love the Corps o' Marines and hae learned much through blood, sweat, and toil, but my destiny lies elsewhere. I hae made my decision and canna look back."

The breath seemed to go out of Lieutenant Colonel Mackenzie. He sat staring out the window for a long time. His chair squeaked as he rose. He walked around the wide desk. His hands gripped Jamie's shoulders. "Lad, I remember Martinique, when I assigned ye tae take the redoubt. I can ne'er doubt yer integrity, spirit, or courage. We dinna ken the future, and circumstances may change. Fer the guid o' the service, I canna bring myself tae accept yer resignation. I propose a compromise that preserves yer future ability tae choose. I will add yer name tae the half-pay list, although the Admiralty commissioners may refuse tae accept it. Admiral Lord Viscount Richard Howe is the maist likely member tae be assigned tae review and approve the lists. He is a fair man but zealous concerning the readiness o' the fleet tae fight."

Jamie said, "He was captain o' *Magnanime* when I was commissioned. He will remember me weel. He is a fair man.

Howe'r, I am nae sae sanguine that he will release me frae active service. I dinna realize that resigning would be sae difficult since the Admiralty is anxious tae shed extra officers. How lang must I wait fer a decision?"

Lieutenant Colonel Mackenzie shrugged. "Take the leave, lad. Surely the Admiralty will act on the lists by the time ye return. Ye must remember that although we are now at peace wi' the French and Spanish, it is a parlous peace that may end at any time. If it does, the needs o' the nation must take precedence o'er the needs o' men. If ye will prepare a new letter, I will see that it accompanies the lists."

Armed with his leave orders, Jamie arranged a final dinner with James Boswell. Jamie confided that he was departing soon for the Highlands. Boswell moodily stirred his finger in his wineglass and then shared the news that he had failed to obtain an army commission. "I have nae choice but tae accept my father's will and return tae the university tae study law." He brightened. "My father, the judge, hae a softer heart than I expected. He will permit me a summer's miniature grand tour o' the continent before beginning study at the University o' Utrecht."

Jamie chuckled. "Aye, it is time tae pursue a career, James. Since I am leaving the military, I am faced wi' the challenge o' finding a new path as weel. Hae ye turned awa' altogether frae writing?"

Boswell shook his head. "Writing is a dream that haunts my nights—when I am nae pursuing the opposite sex."

Jamie scowled his disapproval. "Ye live a dangerous life, wi' a greater likelihood o' severe wounding and painful death than frae battle. Ye should resist such temptations if ye value yer health."

Boswell was rueful. "I struggle at times and burn wi' guilt when I succumb, but I canna help myself. I love the lasses and take much pleasure frae the sport. Is there such a pleasant disease as this?"

Jamie said, "Calling a weakness a disease may assuage a man's feelings o' guilt, but it is a sham. Ye will ne'er rise above it until ye acknowledge that fact."

Boswell lowered his head, shoulders shaking. Jamie thought that he was weeping, but at length his friend looked up, grinning. Jamie growled, "Ye are incorrigible, James Boswell. I am done wi' attempting tae reform ye. Ye may live a merry life, but shorter than if ye hae a stronger moral sense."

Boswell told Jamie of the journal he was writing and his hopes to eventually have it published. Jamie was impressed by his passion and sincerity. "At a dinner, I met the maist interestin' man o' letters wha is thinking o' a grand tour o' the Highlands. Since ye are a Scot and a journalist, ye may profit frae meeting him. His name is Dr. Samuel Johnson. I was impressed wi' his intellect, but that pretentious man has a serious fault."

Boswell looked up. "What fault is that? Does he also pursue the ladies?"

Jamie laughed. "Although he is not a dashing fellow, he is a great man, with many admirers. Many o' those are undoubtedly female. Nay, I find his fault tae be that he is insufferably prejudiced against the Scottish people. If ye could tolerate such a man, ye may find employment wi' him someday."

Boswell said, "I thank ye fer the recommendation. I will seek tae meet Dr. Johnson, for he may be helpful in getting my journal printed, but I hae nae interest in returning tae Scotland at present, fer fear that my father will detain me. My heart is set on pursuing my fortune on the Continent."

Over coffee, Boswell turned morose. Jamie prodded him for the reason since he had been so exuberant earlier. He sipped from his cup and then put it down. In a strained voice, he said, "I am suffering because o' my curiosity. There are some things that are nae guid fer a man tae experience. I wish wi' great fervency that I could erase a memory. A week ago, Tuesday, I conceded tae an impulse tae visit Newgate."

Jamie stared. "Newgate? Why, James?"

Boswell said, "I read newspaper accounts o' prisoners and their trip tae Tyburn. I decided tae make a visit. I stopped in a sort o' court before the cells. They are surely maist dismal places."

Jamie nodded. "Aye, they are indeed. I spent weeks in that forecourt but nae in a cell. They are far worse."

Boswell continued. "There are three stacks o' cells, four in a row. They hae double iron windows, and within these are strong iron rails and in these dark cages are the unhappy criminals confined. I dinna gae in but stood in the court, where were a number of blackguards with sad countenances milling aboot, maist o' them friends o' those under sentence o' death. In the cells, I hae been told, were Paul Lewis for robbery and Hannah Diego for theft. I saw them pass by in leg irons tae a chapel service. The woman was a huge blowsy creature, ugly and ungainly in the extreme. The man hae been in the sea service and called captain, fer his affected manners. He was a genteel, spirited young fellow. He was dressed in a white coat and blue silk vest, with his hair neatly queued and a silver laced hat smartly cocked. Poor fellow! I really took a great concern fer him. He appeared much too fine tae suffer such a fate. He walked a firm tread and with a guid air, with his chains rattling, as if they were jewelry and nae an impediment."

"I discovered after his demise that Paul Lewis was the son o' a clergyman wha hae run awa' tae sea after having run up debts wi' his tailor. After some time in the navy, where he became known fer cheating money frae mess mates, he returned tae England, where he was caught committing robbery on the highway." He sighed deeply and busied himself in draining his cup.

"My curiosity tae see the melancholy spectacle o' the executions was sae strong that I couldna resist it. I was sensible that I would suffer much frae it. In my younger years I hae read in the lives o' convicts sae much aboot Tyburn that I had a horrid eagerness tae be there."

Jamie observed drily, "It seems that ye find it impossible tae resist any impulse."

Boswell smiled faintly. He said, "I also wished tae see the last behavior of Paul Lewis, the handsome and haughty fellow wha I had seen the day before. Accordingly I took Captain Temple with me, and he and I got up on a scaffold very near the fatal crosstree sae that we could clearly see the dismal scene. There was a maist prodigious crowd of spectators, ranging frae gentry—men and women mixed—in the boxes and the rabble a' aboot, sitting in trees and balancing on cart wheels. Paul Lewis was a consummate actor, fer he lost none o' his spirit, smiling and waving tae the audience. I was maist terribly affected by his bravery and thrown intae a very deep melancholy."

Jamie laid a hand on his arm. "There is nae need fer ye tae harrow yer soul o'er these events."

Boswell shook off the hand and continued, "Hannah Diego was a brawny harridan, an auld offender wha had spent much time in prison fer a multitude o' offenses. She stabbed a man in Newgate fer testifying against her. At Tyburn, when the gaolers were lifting her oot o' the cart, she got her hands loose, struggled with the executioner tae avoid his black hood, and gave him such a blow as to almost beat him tae the ground. When he staggered aboot, she laughed and cursed him in the maist obscene manner. She threw off her hat and clothes to spite him, and as soon as the rope was yanked aboot her neck, she tied a handkerchief o'er her eyes wi' her ain hands. She stunned the crowd by unexpectedly throwing herself frae the cart wi' such violence that she broke her neck and died instantly."

Jamie was transfixed by Boswell's quavering voice. "Paul Lewis waved gaily tae the crowd a final time but refused tae make a speech. He accepted the executioner's hood readily before having his hands bound. He died wi' dignity while the crowd cheered and children clapped. It was a ghastly sight, nae at all wha I expected, and I heartily wish I could erase the vision frae my memory.

Gloomy terrors came upon me sae much as night approached that I durst nae stay by myself."

He shivered violently but pressed on with his story. "I was sae fearful that I begged a bed or rather half a bed frae my friend Erskine, which he kindly gie me, and he stayed wi' me a' nicht. He is a guid man wha really had compassion on me." Boswell wiped tears from his face. Huskily, he said, "I am grateful tae ye, Jamie Drummond, fer listening tae my foolish tale, fer I ken that ye understand my wild emotions, although ye dinna approve. I am easily affected, man. It is a weakness o' my mind. I own it."

Jamie put an arm around his friend's shoulder. "Aye, if we could erase such terrible memories. I commanded the guard during an execution o' traitors in the Caribbean as a young officer. I hae ne'er been tae Tyburn, but a condemned man befriended me in Newgate. He was a highwayman wha was hanged, but I found his character noble in such a hellish place. As a lad, I was easy pickings fer the brutal guards and desperate prisoners. He protected me and taught me tae cope wi' my misfortune in being consigned tae such a place. When ye introduced yerself that first night, ye gie me a start because o' the similarity in names. Ye see, my condemned friend's name was also Boswell—John Boswell."

James Boswell gaped, unable to speak. After a moment, he began to guffaw. Jamie joined him, for the grim humor of the coincidence was amusing. They laughed so hard that the publican rushed over, red-faced and demanded that they desist or leave. The laughter also served as a curative for Boswell's depressed spirits for the rest of the evening.

The heavily laden coach clattered through the village of High Wycombe, striking sparks as a wheel hub hit a milepost. The sound wakened Jamie, who had drifted off shortly after they had left the northern environs of London. He had traveled so much by coach that sleep was his preference to the inane conversations that usually preoccupied coach travelers. The two vicars sitting opposite had nattered endlessly about benefices, livings, and the torturous labor of preparing sermons every Saturday night. He was squeezed into a corner by the bulk of Nicholas Blodgett, Esq. Jamie's dislike began when, at mention of Peter Gordon's name, the enormous barrister's jowls quivered, and he proceeded to deliver a lecture on the sins of excessive "Whiggishness" and liberality among the younger members of the bar. Jamie took the rebuke to include his cousin and decided to sleep.

He had greatly enjoyed his last week in London, which included two dinner parties staged by Peter and Rachel Gordon and an outing to Hyde Park to allow the children to ride the marvelous horse-powered carousel. Jamie was stunned by the massive expanse of trees, gardens, and lawns contiguous with Kensington Gardens, which stretched over six hundred acres, separated into two parts by the Long Water and Serpentine. The carousel had been constructed in Italy, with cunningly crafted horses, cows, pigs, sheep, and a mechanical harpsichord. The gaily painted animals rose and fell in rhythm with the tinkling music. Scores of shrieking children battled for places in line and refused to leave when their parents tired of the attraction. Jamie's engineering interest was piqued by the gears, levers, and pulleys that drove the machine.

While Rachel tended the children, Peter and Jamie walked around the Serpentine, discussing political developments that might affect chances for restoration. Peter said, "Now that Grenville hae replaced Lord Bute as lead minister, I am encouraged. Charles Townsend expects tae be offered a position in the new government, as weel as others favorable tae yer case. I advise ye tae enjoy yer respite while events unfold."

Jamie growled, "I would as lief watch paint drying or hay growing." Impulsively, he told Peter of his strange dreams of the little men visiting him.

Peter's eyebrows rose.

"As I said lang ago, when Maggie prophesied at the Crieff cattle fair, I hae respect fer the Sight but dinna expect anyone tae plan their life or make crucial decisions based on the vague pronouncements o' a seer." He tapped Jamie on the arm. "Yer mind is o'erwrought by uncertainty and the rigors o' battle, imprisonment, and work. Ye are clearly in need o' rest after years frae hame. A sojourn in the Highlands, a guid horse under yer thighs, and the Cairngorms tae beguile ye will hae a tonic effect on yer mind and ability tae sleep dreamlessly, undisturbed by wee strangers o' legend."

The conversation turned to career prospects if the Admiralty accepted Jamie's resignation. Peter advised caution. "The Highlands are dominated by the clan chiefs, wi' their ain followers. The magnates o' industry are Lowlanders and English. They hae nae interest in investing money tae develop the region. Will ye seek a position as a tacksman collecting rents fer Frasers, McKays, Sinclairs, or Sutherlands? 'Tis far below yer birth and upbringing, Jamie. As much as ye may yearn tae stay in the north, ye must eventually leave. What will ye do?"

Jamie walked in silence for a time before speaking. "Except fer the military arts, I hae few skills. Dinna take offense, cousin, but I hae little interest in law or commerce. I could return tae university, but I am already twenty-five. I would be twenty-eight or nine before I graduated. That is far beyond when men begin careers. If I am heartily sick o' military service, why would I seek a position as a mercenary fer a foreign government?"

Peter stopped and faced Jamie. "Ye could stand fer Parliament. Ye hae a heroic record, a probing mind, and ye speak well. Yer political deficiency is yer unwillingness tae subvert yer sense o' honor. It would be difficult tae obtain a patron wha will nae attempt tae subvert ye. Honest politicians are a rare breed."

Jamie laughed. "Ye are correct, cousin. My temper and sense o' outrage would make my political career short-lived, particularly among ministers o' a king sae stubborn and opinionated aboot my family. Perhaps I will move tae Ireland and raise horses wi' my guid friend, Gerry MacIntyre." They finished their excursion in silence and rejoined Rachel, who had finally pried the children away from the carousel.

The heavily laden post coach lurched as a wheel hub struck sparks from a tilted milepost. The jolt woke Jamie, who gently pushed away the intruding bulk of the snoring Mr. Blodgett, his seatmate on the journey from Smithfield Market in Clerkenwell, in the heart of London's commercial district. With the warm May weather, the window shades were up. Jamie peered at the roadway sign that announced that they were on the outskirts of the town of Alconbury.

In the opposite backward-facing seat, the Right Reverend Josiah Wright slept with his head lolling backward and mouth open, leaning on the arm of his cadaverous black-robed beadle, who had stared at Jamie with tight-lipped disapproval since they had boarded. Jamie had joked during the customary introductions about the appropriateness of the Right Reverend's name of Wright. The bishop had smiled indulgently, and other passengers chuckled, but Mordecai Grimsby muttered that the comment was insulting and sacrilegious.

Samuel Newberry, a burly gray-haired squire from Derbyshire snorted. "A pox on your indignation, sir! I am certain that Captain Drummond's comment was not intended as an insult. Even men of the cloth must appreciate a sense of humor, which gladdens the heart. Excessive rectitude cramps the bowels and renders the countenance odious."

The other passengers laughed, gleeful at the beadle's discomfiture, and even the bishop chuckled at the squire's crude jest before remarking that he had heard comparisons aplenty concerning his surname.

"I must strive constantly to be worthy to be judged right."

Jamie spoke up. "Yer pardon. I dinna intend tae cause offense. Twas merely a guid-hearted jest, sir."

There was a murmur of approval at Jamie's mild remark. However, Mr. Grimsby's thin lips clamped in a bloodless grimace. He remained silent and scowling, arms tightly crossed over his thin chest while other passengers engaged in friendly conversation with his employer. The coach lumbered through the northern precincts of the vast city, with many delays for slow drays and skittish draft animals before entering the tollgate to the turnpike north.

Hours later, Jamie stretched his arms and yawned hugely as he disembarked at the post house in Alconbury. He was fascinated by the garrulous squire and regretted his choice of seat in the after compartment, squeezed into a corner by the corpulent Mr. Blodgett on the short distance to Derby, where Newberry would depart the coach. In the tavern, they struck up a conversation. The squire rapped his walking stick on the floor and said, "You may not be aware of the history of this inn beyond it's role as a post house. Tis said that the notorious highwayman Dick Turpin supped here during his flight north to York from London. Of course, other inns make the same claim to fame. If Dick had stopped at all of them, he would have been caught and never reached York."

The squire remarked on Jamie's accent. "I see that you are a Highlander, sir. Are you returning home?"

Jamie nodded. "Aye, sir. I hae been lang awa' in the war. It is a brief leave o' sixty days, but I hope tae make it permanent. I hae resigned my commission, but the Admiralty hae nae approved as yet."

The man raised his glass. "I understand. You are a king's officer and serve at his pleasure. I was too old and gouty to be called up in

'56. Instead, I remained at home. My service was and still is to pay taxes, a duty that stretches out endlessly, for the cost of defeating the king's enemies is enormous. If you become a civilian, I pray that your lands and profits are sufficient, for the government taxes crush an enterprising man at every turn. Ministers while away nights inventing new taxes, fees, and imposts."

Jamie put down his glass and wiped the foam from his lip. "Nae chance o' that. My family was attainted during the '45 Rising, wi' titles and lands stripped. Except fer my prize account and the money in my purse, I hae naething."

Samuel Newberry's eyes widened. "Then you were forced to rise by your own merit. I commend you, sir. I am one who admires that ability, rare in our aristocratic society. It has been nearly twenty years, but I remember a Drummond in the force that came through Derby before turning back for Scotland. He commanded a rebel regiment. His troops camped on my land. He paid me generously for the inconvenience." His eyes closed for a moment. "Yes, his name was also James Drummond. I recall him during the few days while the Jacobite army was at Derby as an uncommonly inspirational leader. Are you related, perchance?"

Jamie said, "Aye, he is my father, whom I hae nae seen fer years. He helped rally the scattered forces after the disastrous loss at Culloden, when the Bonnie Prince refused tae fight on and abandoned the loyal men tae their fate. They hae nae choices but surrender or flee. My father chose exile." Bitterness filled his voice. "Fer him there is nae hope o' restoration, fer he sought tae carry on the struggle. He will end his days banished frae his native land, ne'er tae enjoy that fraternity that comes naturally wi' a family and relations. His hae been a lonely life."

The squire smiled. "Perhaps, but perhaps not. Although my parliamentary colleagues treat me as a country bumpkin with horse dung clinging to my boots, I sense that a vast number are sanguine about prospects for peace and amity in Ireland and the north of Scotland now that the war is over. It is in the best interests of the nation to promote it. I bid you be of good cheer and exercise a little patience, although that is a detested word among the young."

Jamie grinned. "I hae heard that advice all my life, although it is unco difficult tae bear."

The squire insisted on paying the reckoning as they rose to heed the driver's insistent call to reboard the post coach for the next leg of their journey along the Great North Road. They waited for the footmen to stuff the last mail sack into the boot and lash down the leathern cover before resuming their seats in the crowded passenger compartment.

The odious beadle and the Right Reverend Wright departed at Stilton and the friendly squire at Stamford. The coach remained full, for others boarded and engaged in the customary round of introductions before settling in for the long ride. Jamie elected to remain aboard during the nights rather than endure the discomfort of sharing a bed in an overcrowded post inn. Three days wheeled away as the coach progressed northward, with accents in the inns varying with the locale until they crossed the old stone bridge into Newcastle, the last post station before the road passed out of England at Berwick-upon-Tweed and entered the East Lothian hills on the Scottish side of the border.

Since he was required to change post coaches in Edinburgh, Jamie decided to get a night's sleep at an inn he found on Leith Street near Calton Hill and depart northward to Aberdeen the following afternoon. Following a leisurely breakfast in the garden of the inn with its smoky panorama of the old city and the newer residential districts westward, he walked a mile up the steep cobbled street from Holyrood Palace to the castle on its rocky eminence. Although impressed with the sights and history of the city—the venerable "auld reekie", as it was known—Jamie was disappointed at the rundown condition of the buildings surrounding Saint Giles cathedral and the acrid smoke pouring from countless chimneys that created a persistent haze that hung as a vast dark shroud over the city, the chief cause of black stains on every roof and wall, as well as on stones of many streets. The bleak and dreary aspect of the city stiffened his resolve not to choose Edinburgh as a future place of residence.

The next morning, a cab took him from the inn and deposited him and his luggage at the Queensferry wharf, where he joined other passengers waiting for the boat that would cross the fast-running spring flood of the Forth to the post coach station on the northern shore. The wind was fresh from the northwest, creating a moderate chop in the gray-blue waters that stretched a mile wide. The rough water was of no concern to Jamie, but several passengers expressed their uneasiness.

A slender dark-haired man in his early twenties spoke soothing words to an agitated gray-haired couple, who soon retreated to stand guard over their luggage. The young man's speech marked him as having a nautical background. Jamie moved closer and introduced himself. The other man knuckled his forehead, habitual for juniors in the presence of those of higher rank, and replied in kind.

Jamie smiled. "I ken that ye hae recent service, John Robison. Ye have nae lost the habits o' a navy man."

Robison colored slightly and replied, "Indeed, Captain Drummond, I was in the navy fer five years and only recently discharged as a midshipman. I am frae Baldernock, close by Stirling. Four years I served afloat, in Canada and then Portugal. I spent the final year at Greenwich working fer the Board o' Longitude on various studies and experiments. I passed my lieutenant's examination but was forced tae depart the service before promotion."

They stopped as dockworkers pushed past them to catch hawsers tossed from the bobbing boat approaching the wharf. The pilot warped the blunt bow of the flat-bottomed ferry shoreward. In spite of tossing waves, the experienced hands brought her in smoothly. The craft scarcely bumped as it kissed the hempenwrapped timbers. Jamie looked back at the squat ramshackle South Queensferry Priory Church as the bells tolled seven times.

Boarding the passengers and their luggage took only minutes. The ferry crew pushed off, anxious to cross the choppy Forth as quickly as possible. While most passengers were soon miserable from the rolling motion, Jamie and John Robison were both seasoned mariners and took seats forward to enjoy the view. They had nearly an hour before the ferry reached the north shore. Jamie described his experiences on the team mapping the Saint Lawrence and the approach to Quebec, after which he peppered the former midshipman with questions about his voyage to test an experimental marine chronometer to determine longitude.

"John Harrison hae been working on what he calls his sea clocks fer nearly thirty years. I met him several times, although he dinna accompany us tae Jamaica on HMS *Deptford*. He is near seventy and suffering frae inflammation in the joints. He sent his son William tae tend the device, which took six years tae construct. William set it tae local time at Greenwich before we sailed. As part o' the trial, we measured the azimuth and elevation o' the moon, which moves across the sky nearly thirteen degrees per day. The mathematics tae calculate longitude by this lunar distance method were onerous and my principal responsibility. We found it useful, but cloud cover prevented us frae making daily sightings o' the sun and moon. When we reached Port Royal, we found the error in the lunar method tae be thirty miles while Harrison's chronometer was only five seconds slow, corresponding tae an error o' a leetle o'er a minute o' longitude." He grinned hugely when Jamie whistled in amazement.

"Scarcely a mile in error! Then Mr. Harrison deservedly won the great prize offered by the Admiralty fer a practical solution tae the longitude problem!" John Robison shook his head.

"Nae. He applied fer the award, but the board is requiring yet mair experiments, which require another trans-Atlantic voyage and rigorous testing o' both methods. The Harrisons are furious, fer they hae lang labored wi'oot much reward. In their anger, they hae said hard things tae the board. They were granted a pittance tae build twa new timepieces, but the prize o' twenty thousand pounds is still unawarded. Auld John Harrison may nae live tae collect it. William told me that his father feels ill-used and is considering appealing tae the king fer redress."

Jamie grimaced. "I hae heard mair than I care tae hear o' the fecklessness o' Admiralty functionaries. I dinna trust their weasely lack o' principles. Wi' other officers o' *Invincible*, I endured a court-martial in '58, when they blamed the officers fer the foundering o' the ship on an unexpectedly high sandbar. Fortunately fer our careers and the cause o' justice, officers o' the court defied the Admiralty and absolved us."

The landsmen were relieved when the crew warped the ferry to the dock in Inverkeithing harbor. They fled, ashen-faced, to the end of the pier to where two post coaches waited. Jamie and John Robison sauntered after them, still deeply engrossed in their conversation about longitude, time pieces, and inventions.

The coachmen held up lettered placards to direct passengers to appropriate coaches. One was headed northeastward along the Fife coast to Kirkcaldy, Pittenweem, and the venerable university town of Saint Andrews. The other was headed north to Perth and then along the Firth of Tay and North Sea coast to Dundee and Aberdeen. The late spring day was long, and no one was disturbed by news that they would reach their evening destination of Dundee near twilight.

In deference to other passengers, the young veterans suspended their conversation on inventions to listen to a lively conversation about the recent shift in government ministers, the threat of higher taxes to pay for the war, and hopes for economic stability in the north. One bold and articulate businessman was adamant that higher taxes would greatly depress commerce and lead to massive unemployment and civil unrest. After dinner, the others seemed played out and inclined to nap. In low tones, John Robison spoke of his excitement in accepting a position working for James Watt on a steam-powered coach. Jamie envied his companion's good fortune in working on such a visionary invention.

"Obstacles posed by such an invention are towering. Yet I am sanguine aboot our prospects. The skill o' Scottish engineers is highly respected across the island, drawing bright minds and opening purses o' canny investors. Mr. Watt is young, scarcely twenty-six. Yet he hae a considerable reputation and following in Glasgow. He began as an instrument maker at the university but became interested in the science o' steam. While he dinna invent the steam engine, he quickly detected that Newcomen's original design fer a contrivance tae pump water hae great inefficiencies. Watt designed a separate condenser tae radically improve the power and efficiency o' steam engines." Robison stopped speaking to look around. The other passengers were all dozing. He dropped the level of his speech to a near whisper. "Watt's maist innovative improvement remains tae be demonstrated, but the theory is excellent. It is tae drive motion in a rotary direction through an assemblage o' gears and wheels o' different diameters tae perform work."

Jamie's mind was whirling. Robison had difficulty containing his rising excitement and gripped Jamie's arm.

"The idea tae create a steam-powered coach is nae dream. I can see the design in my mind already. Unfortunately, the size and weight o' the contraption will pose great problems, wi' the large condenser, engine, and drive mechanism. Also, the coach must carry a supply o' wood or coke and water tae replenish steam lost during operation. The size and weight o' such a contrivance would be considerable."

John Robison put a finger to his lips. "Aye, there are problems aplenty, but this is nae a guid place tae discuss them. Ye seem tae hae the kind o' inquiring mind and energy that James Watt would desire tae attract. While ye may hae other plans fer yer future, ye might consider coming tae Glasgow tae participate in the venture wi' us. While there is nae guarantee o' success, think o' the joy o' invention and the opportunity tae solve such challenges."

Jamie had great difficulty sleeping that night at the post tavern in Dundee. He and Robison agreed not to discuss the project during the next day's run to Aberdeen but exchanged many penciled notes. By the time he bade farewell the next evening, Jamie had resolved to accept the invitation to visit Glasgow and pursue the opportunity—if the Admiralty released him from active service.

Jamie could not resist taking an evening walk in the blue twilight around the shadowed buildings of King's College, which he had left so abruptly on a winter's evening seven years past. Standing before the dormitory where he and Andy Hay had lived during their short sojourn as university students, time fled away, and nostalgia recreated the tryst with his father and Andy's agreement to courier the fateful Jacobite letters to Dumfries. He recalled Andy's illness, which had led to his death from consumption, his own acceptance of the assignment, the pursuit and capture, his incarceration in Carlisle castle, the journey to London, and the weeks of languishing behind the gray walls of Newgate Prison before his cousins Hugh Drummond and Peter Gordon secured the agreement whereby Jamie was pressed to service in the Royal Marines to avoid prison.

The next day was unseasonably warm until a brisk breeze blew in from the sea, bringing cooler air. Jamie was disappointed that his old tutor and professor Archibald Thompson was on sabbatical and absent from Aberdeen until the autumn term. He wandered the buildings and pathways of the lushly green campus steeped in nostalgia. He scarcely noticed that the students looked painfully adolescent. They seemed reluctant to encounter the tall sun-darkened marine officer, scurrying to the opposite side of pathways and lawns as if they were sheep avoiding a sheepdog.

Jamie listened to a few conversations among the loitering students and convinced himself that socially and intellectually, he had moved far beyond academia. He concluded that while he would greatly enjoy the challenge of research, military life and frequent near-death experiences had moved him in such practical orbits that a return to university would be a retreat to a cloistered existence that no longer appealed to him. By midmorning, he was ready to board the post coach headed westward into the fastnesses of the Cairngorm Mountains and up the heather-stained straths of Deeside to the Gordon castle at Abergeldie.

9

The coach swayed as the team turned off the military road and crossed the foaming Dee, clattering over its rocky bed. Emerging into bright sunlight after a half-mile ride through the trees, the driver applied his whip a final time as he expertly steered the six-horse team around the gravel drive to the foot of the staircase that led to the four-story blocky castle. Chuckling, he called a warning as Jamie opened the door to a shrieking crowd of girls and women. Lanky twelve-year-old Margaret vaulted into his arms, propelling him backward onto the coach seat. Eight-year-old Elizabeth, her face flushed apple-ruddy, straddled Jamie. His mother, Euphemia, smiling through tears, crowded into the coach, followed by Aunt Allison and wee Jock, who, at five years old, was a sturdy near replica of his older brother. Jamie pulled himself out of the pile of petticoats and waved to his uncle Charles, who stood smiling benignly on the stone steps with his arm around Jamie's cousin David.

The footman pulled the luggage from the boot. Jamie extended a hand from the tangle to pay him a gratuity. Allison and Euphemia extricated the children, Jamie stepped down, and the driver cracked his whip. The wheels crunched the gravel, and the post coach moved off to return to the main road northward. The family trooped up the stone steps and through the venerable castle to the solar facing the sprawling garden, where servants had laid a cold lunch.

Jamie poked his cousin David, who no longer wore an army uniform, and raised an eyebrow. "I see that ye hae dispensed wi' army brown. Ye look quite dashing in burgundy and dove gray."

David explained, "I came hame a month past released on half pay. I appreciate the stipend, but doubt that I will ever wear the uniform again. My skills as an infantry officer are nae exceptional. I am finding it difficult tae adjust tae the rhythm o' civilian life, but Papa says that I am a godsend in helping manage the estates."

Uncle Charles nodded. "Wi' Peter ensconced in London as a noted barrister, I need David." He brushed at his gray hair. "As ye can see, nephew, age is laying its claim on me."

Jamie sneaked a glance at Aunt Allison, who said crisply, "Ye are an impertinent lad tae think such thoughts, Jamie Drummond. The cares and concerns o' a household and raising children age women. Yer dear mother appears tae be an exception. Her hair, and face, as weel, are nearly the same as when she was eighteen and marrying yer father. It would be impossible fer a stranger to guess her age as forty-four."

Euphemia smiled. "Dear Allison, I may not seem tae be aging, but it is true. Ye canna see its outward effects, but I feel it on chill mornings as an ache in my fingers, toes, and knees." She giggled suddenly. "Perhaps it will all happen in a single night. I will lie doon tae sleep a winsome lass and awake a toothless auld crone wi' white hair!"

Jamie chuckled and wrapped his arms around his mother. "Ach, I dinna believe it. Ye are like the princess in the tales o' the Arabian Nights, Mama. Ye hae an uncanny power tae make time stand still."

Euphemia smiled pensively and laid her head against her son's dark blond hair.

"Nae. Allison's words are true. The cares and concerns o' life, drop by drop, sap our strength and bring us doon at last. Our hopes lie in the resurrection o' the just and dreams fer our children." Her voice rose in pitch as she exclaimed, "Fer seven years, I hae prayed nightly fer ye, my son, in the midst o' war and imprisonment. I am a blessed mother tae hae all my children gathered safely in this refuge frae a violent and dangerous world." She burst into sudden tears while everyone waited awkwardly. Margaret and Elizabeth Marie rushed to their mother, who hugged them fiercely.

Jamie was relieved when the tears ended and the conversation returned to pleasant topics. David and Jamie vowed that they would spend part of each day in the saddle, revisiting their childhood haunts.

David grinned. "I must make frequent rounds o' estates and settle accounts wi' tacksmen, but surely it will be a simple matter o' extending the day's wark tae revisit such sights."

David urged Euphemia, who enjoyed riding, to accompany them. She brightened at the suggestion. "Lachin-y-gair in such weather will put a sonsie face on everyone. It hae been lang years since we hae been up the Muick or climbed Craig-na-Ban. We should bring Meg. She is quite skilled in the saddle. I would also see ye attend lessons wi' the girls. Ye will be astonished by their agile and inquiring minds. Wee Jock hae a million questions, fer he dreams constantly o' battles and weapons. He is astonishingly similar tae ye at the same age, Jamie. He will follow ye as a barnacle attaches itself tae a ship's hull."

Jamie chuckled and nodded.

Euphemia closed her eyes in recollection. "The resemblance is uncanny. He told me that he intends to question ye aboot every voyage and battle. He hae a great dream tae be like his brother and someday be a general."

Jamie stared out the glass at the trees that bent to a suddenly stiff breeze. "Aye, I hae such dreams lang syne. The thought o' military glory and noble deeds stirred my heart, as they do nearly a' lads. I dinna wish tae quench his desire, but after seven years, the reality o' war is far different from those childish dreams. I hae seen and experienced glory, sacrifice, and suffering in equal measures. I may find it difficult tae describe war in the rosy terms that he expects."

Euphemia laid a cool hand on her son's arm. "Then it is needfu' that ye take time tae wander the straths and glens. They hae an unco restorative ability tae heal the spirit, but dinna discourage the lad. His mind dwells on heroic deeds, as did ye at the same age. There will be time later fer him tae grasp the reality."

It was a joyful reunion. They ate and talked far into the night before retiring. No one disturbed Jamie in the morning. Sunk into warm comforters, he did not wake until the sun was well up a sky of cerulean blue, with wisps of cloud. David hammered on the door, ignoring Jamie's protests. After a gargantuan breakfast of porridge, eggs, ham, and mugs of black tea, they were in the stable getting acquainted with the horses. Jamie selected a bay gelding and saddled him, crooning and talking to the beast all the while.

David said, "We will ride wi'out yer mama and the girls this morning, fer they are in classes. We will take the trail southeastward across the grazing lands below Balmoral Forest. I must obtain an inventory o' sheep on those lands frae the tacksmen. We will cross the Dee at Invercauld Bridge to the military road, which will bring us tae Crathie. Ye might recall a fine inn there above the Dee. We will dine with Archie Munroe, wha hae been tacksman tae my father fer certain properties fer twenty years. He is a trustworthy man but hae suffered severe losses o' cattle recently. I suspect that a band o' thieves hae infested the Cairngorms, fer other landlords hae lost cattle as weel. They hae been there fer years, fugitives frae the sheriff, waylaying the unwary but taking few kine. He looked at Jamie speculatively. "Lately, they hae become bolder and begun preying on herders and shepherds. If we encounter them, there may be violence."

Jamie patted the front of his jacket. "I carry twa loaded pistols, cousin, and hae uncommon skill wi' the rapier."

David shook his head. "I dinna think that we will encounter them in daylight, but there is always the risk o' a surprise. I expect that we must soon seek a writ frae the sheriff and pursue them through the hills tae their den. We need intelligence concerning its location and the paths by which they drive stolen cattle tae market. By midsummer, it will not be difficult tae persuade our neighbors tae join a hot-trod tae put these thieves awa'."

Jamie grinned broadly. "A bit o' hot action against reivers could be excellent sport. I volunteer!"

David frowned. "It could be an ugly sport, cousin. Cornered men are dangerous when they realize that a scaffold awaits them if they are captured. The Cairngorms were once relatively safe but ne'er completely so. Wi' war and reductions in garrisons in the north, lawlessness grew year by year. 'Tis nae the danger o' armed conflict wi' these rascals that causes the greatest damage. It is the loss o' revenue tae herders, shepherds, tacksmen, and lairds that impoverishes the district."

They reined up and dismounted where a freshet of water tumbled down a rock face and fell foaming into a rivulet that cascaded below the trail. Jamie stepped around a thicket of gorse and scarlet bell heather. He drank, refilled his cup, and passed it to David. The horses waited impatiently, nickering and pushing until the men held up leather buckets full of the icy water.

Jamie looked about as the bay gelding whuffled greedily at the bucket. "Can ye imagine a lovelier site on God's earth than this? I recall Martinique and Cuba, surrounded by lovely vegetation but blasted by infernal heat. Canada was a wilderness o' green, but either frozen or baking in heat, filled wi' flying pests and few flowers as lovely as our native heather and broom. Aboard ship, we saw little green and ne'er a flower tae break the monotony o' the heaving seas."

His cousin smiled crookedly and said, "Think o' the adventures ye will miss!"

Jamie said, "I would yield them a' tae those wha love wandering tae enjoy such lovely sites as these Highlands, even in the grayness and short days o' winter. 'Tis a pity that Maggie McRae hae pronounced a prophecy that I am doomed tae wander far awa'. I dinna wish it."

David gave him a questioning look, and Jamie rapidly told him the tale of Maggie's prophecies. David said, "Dreams and portents are unco powerful, but these words are vague wi' respect tae time and place. I dinna see any actions that ye can take or avoid, except tae accept what may happen. A man canna lay plans fer his life under such an ominous cloud, which I sense is troubling ye, Jamie. What will ye do when yer leave is done?"

Jamie shrugged. "I hope that they accept my resignation sae I may seek employment in Scotland, but Lieutenant Colonel Mackenzie was adamant that they wouldna. I am in limbo until they gie me an assignment or release me. Since the crown is nae disposed tae restore the Drummond fortunes, I must find wark. I hae nae interest in a university life. Law and government bore me, and life as a mercenary abroad hae nae appeal. I am intrigued by an opportunity tae wark wi' a professor at Glasgow University inventing a carriage that would run on steam. Such employment would satisfy my thirst fer adventure and yet allow me tae live in Scotland. However, until the Admiralty makes its decision, I fret, dither, and wait."

David consulted his pocket watch and then slapped Jamie on the back. "Awa' wi' gloomy thoughts, cousin. The future will come, as it always does, wi' action aplenty. The tacksmen maintain a cottage in Balmoral Forest and are expecting us in an hour."

They gave the horses another bucketful of water apiece, remounted, and rode into a final patch of bright sunlight before entering the dark fastness of the forest. The narrow trail ran past thickets of rhododendrons, azaleas, campions, and bogs dotted with craneberry and bilberry bushes.

David commented, "Balmoral hae always been Gordon land, but it passed to Charles Farquharson o' Inverey a hundred years past. James Farquharson o' Balmoral was Jacobite and involved in the '15 and '45 rebellions. He was wounded at Falkirk. His estates were declared forfeit and passed to the Farquharsons of Auchendryne. They leased the lands tae my father tae manage. If they remain profitable, we will retain them, but fer fifteen years revenue hae been in slow decline."

Jamie looked up. "Due tae thefts?"

David shrugged. "Perhaps. Perhaps fraud. That is the reason fer conducting the inventory."

Jamie suddenly did not envy David his position managing Gordon estates. Trust with the tacksmen and loyalty with tenants must exist for the system to prosper, in addition to favorable weather, prices, and a host of other factors.

The trail grew narrower as it wound through Scotch pine, birch, rowan, aspen, juniper, and oak. Jamie heard a fluttering and thrumming of wings as a covey of grouse burst from the undergrowth. The bay gelding, startled by the sudden movement, whinnied and reared. Jamie fought him down and spoke to him soothingly.

David said, "There is much game throughout the Caledonian Forest. Another day, we will hunt those grouse. They are fine eating. There is a herd of red deer that ranges higher up the slopes, and elk hae been spotted, but seldom. I hae seen ospreys and erns soaring, but their eyries are high in the craigs. This is the remaining remnant o' the forest that, before the Romans came, spread o'er the eastern and western Highlands and even doon into Wales and Cornwall."

Jamie listened to his cousin's lecture, admiring the scenery until they topped a rise and glimpsed the tackmen's cottage in a clearing close by a burn. They tethered their horses where others stood cropping the long grass.

Jamie pointed away from the cottage. "I canna contribute aught tae the inventory or conversation. If ye hae nae objection, I will walk aboot while ye conduct the meeting."

David nodded but said, "First, I wish ye tae meet them. Ye may hae seen them frae time tae time when we were lads, fer they hae been in my father's employment since before the Rising o' '45. In spite o' that, I dinna wish any tae hear o' a search fer the reiver's hideout. That will be a secret hidden tae all but the sheriff, wha I expect will appoint Thomas Elphinstone, the undersheriff fer this district, tae conduct the search and pursuit. Dinna breathe a word."

The door of the lodge opened, and three dour gray-haired men in heavy coats emerged. Jamie smiled, for they were recognizable across the gap of fifteen years since he had seen them.

David supplied the names, for Jamie had forgotten. "My cousin Captain James Drummond, my tacksmen, Mr. John Alford."

Jamie shook hands with the tall herder, who grinned around several missing teeth.

"Charles Dalrymple." David turned to a shorter man with flowing locks, gray at the edges.

"Rabbie Duncan." Another handshake.

David continued, "As a military officer hame on leave, my cousin hae little interest in our proceedings. Let us inspect the inventory, fer we hae much tae discuss and little time."

They went inside, the door shut, and Jamie was free to view the old stone bridge and enjoy the water tumbling down from the heights.

Jamie was surprised to see a young man leaning casually against the stones of the bridge. Jamie introduced himself, whereupon the young man explained in Lowland accents that he was Harry Pringle, son-in-law to Robert Duncan. He had drifted north from the border country three years ago. With experience as a herder, he accepted employment and, within a year, had wooed and married the tacksman's eldest daughter. His manner was pleasant, but he would not look directly at Jamie. Jamie had to admit to himself that he was uncommonly bold and direct in his manner, which may have enhanced young Pringle's deference in the presence of a member of the family of the Laird of Abergeldie.

An hour later, the door of the lodge banged open, and David Gordon emerged, visibly angry, trailed by the tacksmen, who were attempting to mollify him. Turning, David demanded loudly, "I am requiring that ye repeat the inventory. I canna believe that winter losses were sae severe and count o' lambs and yearlings sae puir. Another year wi' such numbers, and we are undone. Expect me at this time Monday week." He ignored the tacksmen's pleas and walked away, motioning to Jamie.

They mounted and rode across the bridge toward the road. Jamie waited for David's temper to subside, which required nearly a half hour before he broke silence. "If the remaining inventories are nae better, we hae little choice. Carried off by wolves indeed! Last winter was severe, wi' much drifted snaw and ice. I expect that we lost a few sheep and kine tae predators but not three hundred head! I find it unusual that the tacksmen reported few carcasses found."

Jamie gasped. "Three hundred?"

David nodded grimly. "Aye, wi' inventories already completed, I will be forced tae report the loss o' a thousand head in less than a year, perhaps mair wi' Archie Munroe's accounts!" He roweled his horse savagely, which sprang ahead nervously. Jamie spurred his horse to catch up.

David growled, "Tae replace the stock will require all revenue we hae gained frae these pasturages fer three years. Since we must provide the lease payments tae Farquharson wi'out fail, the losses will amount tae mair than five thousand pounds. I tell ye, Jamie, there is nae other answer than tae suspect a band o' weel-organized reivers and secret buyers. I canna bring myself tae deprive herders and shepherds unless they prove complicit in the crime. After informing my father o' this ill news, I expect that we must mount a search throughout the Cairngorms fer their hiding places. If we canna find them, setting a trap will be impossible. Only if we can locate them will the sheriff issue the hue and cry and authorize Mr. Elphinstone tae gather a posse comitatus tae apprehend these villains."

David Gordon's thunderous mood did not improve during the interview with Archie Munroe, though the food was excellent and the tacksman's accounts showed only modest losses.

Jamie interjected a comment. "I ken frae yer discussions that there are losses throughout the properties, but they are mair severe in Balmoral. Might it be that the reivers hae their hideout nearby and hae the assistance o' an informant?"

David pushed back his plate. Reaching into his jacket, he extracted and unfolded a small hand-drawn map. No one spoke while he studied it.

Archie Munroe jabbed a horny fingernail at Aviemore on the map. "The Grant drovers were complaining just last week aboot heavy losses, although the snaw is nae deep in the northern glens." He looked at David from under white-thatched brows. "Beggin' yer lairdship's pardon, but if 'twere me huntin' these rascals, I would look tae Braenach. The glens are lonely, wi' few herders willin' tae abide thereaboots because o' the hauntin' sperits aroon Loch Coire an Lochain."

David sat with eyes closed for a long moment and then sat bolt upright, staring at the tacksman. "Do ye hae the Sight, man?"

Munroe shook his head vigorously.

David grinned suddenly. "Of course! There is a bridge o'er the Dee at Braemar and an easy trail intae the mountains towards Braenach. From there, drovers could take any o' a dozen trails tae bypass Ben Macdui doon tae Pitlochry or Aberfeldy or further westward tae Rannoch Muir tae sell the cattle and sheep. Few herders or travelers would see them. That explains Grant losses and why our losses are centered in Balmoral." He jabbed Archie Munroe, startling the old tacksman.

"Ye must keep the secret, Archie, fer there must be an informant, wha must nae suspect that we are huntin' fer their camp."

Munroe protested the thought that he was other than a loyal employee. "I hae served the Laird o' Abergeldie fer forty years and owe him my comfortable life and loyalty."

Jamie said, "Loyalty means naething tae men tempted tae gain money wi' little effort. 'Tis nae stretch tae such men tae blame men o' property if they are nae wealthy themselves and justify stealing as fair. They dinna appreciate the risk tae their life and limb. The gibbets on the crossroads make nae impression on their minds."

In spite of the warm day, Archie shivered. "Aye, 'tis an evil course such men hae chosen. The cost o' their theft deprives many o' food, shelter, and raiment. 'Tis a foolish notion that only lairds are deprived by losses."

Charles Gordon was not slow to make a decision. The next morning, he penned a request for a writ from the undersheriff and took a carriage to Aberdeen to deliver it. He was gone three days and returned with news that he shared only with David, Jamie, and a small number of his family members and employees, who were all sworn to deepest secrecy. In one week, two groups of about twenty riders each would converge on the suspected location of the reivers' hideout in Braenach, one starting from Braemar to the south and another from Aviemore in Strathspey to the north. The undersheriff would accompany the northern posse, consisting mostly of Grants, and David Gordon would lead the southern group, recruited with care from Gordons, Stewarts, Alfords, Forbes, and Farquharsons with lands along Deeside.

Jamie's blood was stirred by the prospect, for while he enjoyed riding daily with his sisters, playing, and telling stories in the evenings, he welcomed the opportunity for action. Too little activity was making him restless. The evening before the rendezvous of the posse at the inn in Crathie, he went over weapons he would carry. As an afterthought, he took down a length of rope from a peg in the stable, fashioned a noose in one end, and coiled it. He recalled seeing a rider use such a rope to restrain a steer in Martinique and thought it a useful weapon to capture a man if need be.

David supervised the logistics for the posse, which might require a week or more. Additional horses, food, water, tents, ammunition, medicines—the list of required items was lengthy. Luckily, the estate was well equipped with trained grooms, a farrier to reshoe the horses, and an extensive stable. A successful posse was far more than an eager body of men on the hunt.

David and Jamie led eight other Gordon riders by torchlight through the darkness across the stone bridge and down the military road along Deeside toward Crathie. The light was faint, for the moon was down, but the men knew the road as well as the floor of their own homes. The group rode slowly but still arrived at the inn before sunrise. The innkeeper had laid a hearty breakfast for the hungry men of the posse, for it was impossible to say when they would eat a substantial meal again. They all carried rations appropriate for long rides, which were more substantial than tasty. Riders trailed in by twos and threes from north and south, tethered their horses, and trooped into the inn to eat. An hour later, the rising sun flooded the ground, and the last riders appeared.

David conducted an inventory of weapons and supplies of the grim-faced men. He nodded his satisfaction. "Thirty-three men and twenty-four extra horses. Nine packhorses wi' supplies. We hae nine mair riders than requested by the undersheriff, but I am nae inclined to reject them, fer the supplies appear adequate." He organized them into five groups of six each, with three appointed as messengers. He conferred with the leaders of the five groups, which included Jamie. He was not well-known to the men, but his reputation was legendary.

"We ride tae Braemar along the road, then leave it tae follow the Dee where the road turns south. There is a trail on the strath, but'tis narrow and steep in places. Around midday, we come tae a fork in the river. I will send ane group tae explore the westward glen and seal it off. A second group will ascend a steep glen tae the right, where a burn feeding the Dee arises. The remaining three groups will pass Ben Macdui on the right tae another fork. The rightmost glen ends in a series of three glacks below a long ridge. Loch Eanaich lies on the other side. Someone must ascend the ridge tae maintain watch on movements on the far side. The reivers could easily hae cattle in pens in any o' these glacks. Tae escape, they must ascend the ridge in full view. There is another lang glen that leads tae three glacks on the northern face o' Ben Macdui. We will rendezvous wi' the other posse, which will explore them, along with those whose burns feed into Loch Eanaich. The groups will converge if they discover the reivers. I canna tell ye how the pursuit will proceed, but I will use messengers tae convey further instructions."

Jamie shrugged. It was a sketchy plan, but the broken country they faced made any more elaborate scheme impossible to implement. All the men were skilled riders, familiar with the terrain, and no one lacked for either courage or ability to shoot. At least half the men in the posse had ridden to war for Bonnie Prince Charlie eighteen years before, in spite of the neutrality declared by the Gordons, and would not quail under fire.

Their ascent of the upper reaches of the Dee was slow, for the trail was flooded in many places shortly after leaving Braemar. The river, although narrowing as they went, was in spate from the late snow melt, which made treacherous footing for the skittish horses. In places, riders were forced to dismount and wade through knee-deep water. The sun was sliding toward the horizon when David called a halt. He glanced at Jamie. "Ye are an excellent navigator, cousin. How far up the Dee frae Braemar do ye ken we hae come, and where should we camp?"

Jamie responded, "It hae been six hours since the bridge. Aboot ten or eleven miles, I would say. I see the fork ahead betwixt those trees. There is a grove up a gentle slope on the far side. The ground under the trees wilna be as boggy as further doon. I would camp there." The other leaders stood in their stirrups to look over the site and grunted their agreement.

It was a good choice, and tents were soon erected under the spreading branches. David forbade fires, for their light would be visible for many miles in the open country. The men fed the horses, ate, and rolled themselves in their blankets, for it had been a difficult climb. Everyone was weary. The team leaders gathered to discuss the next day's strategy.

George Geddes, a herdsman and minor factor, scanned the sky apprehensively. "The moon is up, but sheeting mist is eating it up frae the west. I fear a downpour on the morrow. How far is it tae the first glen?"

Jamie said, "I am nae familiar wi' the ground, but the map shows the distance as six miles."

Geddes rocked back and forth in the darkness. "If we must travel in heavy rain on a flooded strath, the path will be unco treacherous. We will be lucky tae reach it in half a day. Tae set up a' the other positions will take the rest o' the day."

Someone growled, "If we are hindered by rain, the reivers will nae be expecting us."

David spoke, "I agree and am inclined tae proceed. We are in the Highlands, and every day brings the risk o' rain. Pistols may be o' little use in the damp. If there must be fighting, it will be wi' cold steel, in the auld way." There was a ripple of laughter at this jest. Conversation fell away, and the leaders prepared for sleep, for late May would bring dawn a little after four thirty in the morning.

Dawn brought leaden skies and a cold drenching rain. Drifting sheets of mist obstructed visibility. Only a few scrambled out from under the dripping tents to relieve themselves until an insistent David Gordon called for action. Voluble complaints were voiced, although in muted tones, for David was insistent. The men gave the horses oats from their saddlebags and ate cold rations hunkered under the tents. By five thirty, tents had been struck and folded, although dripping wet, and horses saddled. As the double column of riders moved upslope, there was plentiful grousing.

Jamie observed cheerfully, "Tis Scotland, lads, where the weather is as fickle and changeable as a woman's heart. We might be under blue skies and sweating by midday!"

Another voice replied, "Or we could have muckle mud in our boots and rain beating in our faces!"

David Gordon said, "Slow and steady, lads. The mire will tire the horses. We dinna wish tae founder them. Change mounts at each rest stop." His advice was unnecessary. Within fifteen minutes, every rider was leading his horse, splashing head down through torrents of sluicing water on the uphill track.

An hour passed, and the rain slowed to a drizzle. Progress slowed further because a heavy ground fog overtook them. Jamie tapped David's arm. "Yonder lies the first glen, barely visible through this damnable mist. We are traveling blind and in ignorance o' the progress o' the other posse coming frae Strathspay. Do ye wish me tae take the first group?"

David shook his head. "Nae, send Geddes. This glen is a box wi' nae exit except here. Once he hae explored it, have him advance and report. I will then reassign his group further upslope." David assigned a second group to explore the glen eastward, hidden in the mist, before he led the remaining three groups north.

An hour later, the mist lifted, and the rain stopped. Tiny patches of blue dotted the gray cloud cover, driven eastward by a brisk wind. David, riding ahead, called a halt and motioned the three remaining leaders to join him. After they gathered, he said,

"Jamie, ye will take the next glen, which leads tae Braenach itself. It is where I expect tae find the reivers if they are here at all—in those three glacks below the ridge. Take a messenger wi' ye. Geddes will be yer reinforcement. If ye encounter trouble, send fer him, fer he will be closest. Ye must remember that we are unco spread oot. Although the ground is somewhat firmer after the rain, it may take an hour or mair fer reinforcements tae join ye."

Jamie nodded. "I expected as much. We hae nae better intelligence. Since the day is passing quickly, let us be aboot it." He turned the gelding's head and motioned the five riders to join him.

The slightly sloping strath on either side of the burn was about two hundred yards wide and clothed thickly in heather, gorse, and broom. Jamie motioned the riders to form a skirmish line across the wide opening of the glen. When they were in place, he nudged the gelding forward, breasting wet vegetation up to the horse's withers. Luckily, the runoff had been so intense that the footing was better than on the boggy ground around the burn.

Two riders moved to investigate a structure that appeared to be a corral. They returned at a gallop. One rider called, "Mair than a hundred black cattle in pens but nae reivers in sight."

Jamie sent two more riders ahead a quarter mile and upslope into the second glack. Fifteen minutes later, it was obvious that they were close to the reiver hideout, for the riders had discovered another two hundred head in makeshift corrals.

Jamie stood in his stirrups with a small glass to his eye, studying the terrain ahead. "Plenty o' trees and exactly what we expected tae find—a croft standing in a clearing. There are horses, four, five—nae, six cropping grass in a wee meadow. He snapped the glass shut and took out his pocket watch. "Nearly seven. The reivers dinna suspect a raid, fer I see nae sentry. They are either awa' or sleeping. Let us discover which." He motioned the riders forward in a V formation.

As they neared the croft, Jamie motioned two riders through the trees to the back of the thatched structure while the rest rode slowly to where they could see the front entrance. There was a sheepfold to the left but no other structure. Jamie cantered forward until he was less than thirty feet from the door and stopped. The leather curtain covering the door rustled and drew back. Jamie pushed the bay in a left-hand turn to shield himself from anyone coming outside.

There was a crackle of gunfire, and Jamie's hat flew off. Frightened by the report and a whirring ball, the bay reared, exposing Jamie. He slid to the ground, yanking his pistols from his jacket. The ratcheting of the cocking was loud in the silence. A flung shovel sailed inches over his head, followed by a hatchet. Jamie dove under the horse's belly as a thick-bodied man charged from the door with a pistol in his left hand and broadsword in his right. The man fired, the shot striking a puddle, showering mud and water. Jamie swiveled the pistol in his left hand to the center of the approaching dark silhouette. The ball took the reiver in the chest, slamming him back against the stone wall of the croft. A scarlet splotch blossomed on the man's tunic. He howled in pain, his heels drumming the hard-packed earth and then went still. A second reiver burst from the entrance, rolling across the mud and then up on the balls of his feet. He tore around the corner of the croft and away. Jamie snapped off a shot, but it went wild. With no time to reload, Jamie dropped the pistols and drew his saber. He could not concern himself with the escapee. He had positioned two riders behind the croft who would deal with him.

Bracing his feet, Jamie slashed at the leather door covering. The saber splintered the wood. He tried the latch. Someone inside the croft had slammed and bolted the door. His first kick demolished a hinge. The second kick ripped the door from its casing, shattering the wooden pegs holding it together. He heard stertorious breathing at his shoulder. Two of the posse had dismounted and taken positions on either side of the darkened entrance, sabers raised.

Jamie shouted, "Drop yer weapons! Raise yer hands and come oot walkin' on yer knees!" He repeated the command in Gaelic. There was silence from the darkened croft. Behind him, the messenger had retrieved his pistols and was busily recharging them. Jamie repeated his warning, adding that the reivers had only to the count of ten to surrender. While he counted, he sheathed his saber and took the reloaded pistols held out to him. At the count of nine, there was a strangled wail from the croft house, followed by scuffling sounds. A tousled downcast head and thin upraised arms emerged. A terrified face looked up at the drawn blades. A boot hit the lad in the back, smashing him face-first into the mud. In seconds, he was a prisoner, dragged out of the line of fire and trussed hand and foot.

A horse trotted around the corner, dragging the reiver who had attempted to escape by his heels. Jamie snapped his fingers, motioning two of his posse to search the croft house. The messenger remounted and cantered around the wall. Looking up, he shouted, "Captain Drummond, one hae gotten tae the corral. He's mounting a horse!"

Jamie shoved his pistols into his jacket and leaped for the gelding, calling the messenger to join him. As the corral came into view, Jamie could see a black horse two hundred yards away, heading down the glen. He grinned at the prospect of the chase. Trusting the bay to maintain good footing, Jamie urged him into a gallop. What Jamie did not know was if the man was the only escapee or what armament he carried.

The distance narrowed as the horses galloped downslope. After a mile, Jamie had closed the gap by half. Jamie roared a command for the reiver to surrender. The man turned suddenly, as if making a stand. He drew a pistol and fired. Jamie flung himself violently to the left, almost falling from the saddle. The ball whined harmlessly. The reiver galloped past, fleeing back upstream.

Jamie swung himself erect. "I hae ye trapped now, bucko." Reaching back, he grabbed the rope hanging from a saddle loop. Guiding the galloping horse with his knees, he loosened the running noose. The faithful bay had reserves of stamina and ate up the gap separating him from the fleeing reiver's black horse.

When he had closed to less than fifty feet, Jamie began swinging the rope's noose in a slow circle. Overtaking the flagging quarry, Jamie tossed the loop, which settled over the rider's head until it engulfed his torso. Jamie pulled back abruptly on the reins. The bay's rear legs dug in, hooves skidding in the mud and tearing gouts in the brushy gorse. Jamie whipped his gloved hands around two twists of the rope. The loop about the reiver's body snapped taut. The horse ran from under him as the man rose in the air. Seconds later, he crashed down heavily in the brush. Jamie dismounted, looping coils of rope in his hands as he moved toward the fallen body. Although the reiver was undoubtedly stunned, he could still be dangerous if he carried a hidden weapon.

Standing twenty feet away from the fallen man, who lay facedown, Jamie kept the rope taut and waited for the messenger to canter to his side and dismount. Archie Forbes walked to the stunned reiver. Seizing his shoulders, he rolled him over roughly and then recoiled in surprise. "Ach, this news will break Mollie Duncan's heart as weel as her father's." A stab of apprehension shook Jamie.

"Ye need nae tell me that my rope hae caught Harry Pringle. My cousin's prediction proves correct. His presence here makes me wonder if he was acting alain or if others betrayed their employers. Weel, let us bind him and return tae the croft. We hae much work sorting and returning the stock."

"Beggin' ye pardon, Captain Drummond, but I dinna think that the men will be satisfied wi'oot discovering the identity o' a' the reivers, whether there are others we hae nae yet caught or if there are other informers. Tis an unco rough business, but we will hae the truth frae the prisoners before we take them tae the tollbooth."

Jamie's stomach clenched, for he disliked such methods. However, he knew that Forbes understood the mood of the posse better than he. The final decision on torture lay with David Gordon.

Harry Pringle regained consciousness on the ride back but refused to talk, even when the messenger gloatingly described the treatment awaiting him. No torture or other coercion was necessary. When they returned, the posse had found Harry Pringle's fourteen-year-old brother hiding behind sacks of oats in the croft house. The lad nearly fainted from fear as the riders yanked him outside. Without a smile, although they were shamming torture they had no intention of carrying out, members of the posse put a noose around the boy's neck. They balanced him on a barrel, flung the rope over a tree branch, and blindfolded him. The lad voided his bladder, choking as the rope tightened around his throat. Richard Pringle, quaking on his barrelhead, talked at length, implicating three reivers tending stock in glens on the far side of Ben Macdui and two grooms in the employment of the Grants of Strathspey.

By midmorning, David Gordon arrived with Undersheriff Elphinstone, who maintained a grave demeanor, although he was obviously elated at the capture and recovery of so many animals and prisoners. Riders were sent out to capture the remaining reivers and their informants and search their hideouts. Systematic probing of the croft's hard-packed dirt floor revealed a stash of coins amounting to over two thousand pounds. If there were other stashes, none of the captured reivers admitted any knowledge, and none were ever found. Jamie's accurate shot had killed their leader, who would have had such knowledge.

In the morning, the undersheriff took possession of the money, inventoried the kine and sheep, and appointed a group of riders to drive them back to Strathspay and Balmoral, where the lairds would settle on the distribution. His greatest praise was for the riders who had fought and captured the reivers. "It seems that we owe a great debt tae a man wi' no stake in this hot-trod. Captain Drummond hae mair than any man's share o' danger in the late war, and here he is in the midst o' mair adventure."

Elphinstone smiled. "Perhaps Aberdeenshire would be best served wi' ye as undersheriff sae that I may retire tae a warm hearth."

Jamie reddened, and everyone chuckled. In retrospect, he was exhilarated at the adventure but shocked at how close he had come to sudden death in the brief Battle of Braenach, as the tussle came to be known.

10

Within days, word of the successful raid and Jamie's heroic role had been heard across the eastern Highlands. Local lairds came by to extend congratulations and offers to dinner—more than Jamie could possibly accept. One unannounced visitor he received joyously was Cousin Hugh Drummond down from Inverness on his way back to offices he shared with Peter Gordon in London. Jamie enjoyed Hugh's company, but his visit resurrected the issue of the family's moribund petition for restoration. His mother looked archly at Hugh as he advised Jamie to forget about the issue for several years.

"The government is going through a change in ministers, and everyone is waiting to discover if relations wi' the French will be stable or return tae the normal pattern o' suspicion and intrigue o'er the Jacobite cause. Ye must wait fer the tumult at the close o' war tae die doon." He crinkled his shaggy gray brows at Jamie's mother. "Do ye agree, Euphemia?"

She rose. Her tense body and tight lips betrayed her turbulent emotions, but her voice was dead calm. "We hae nae choice, Cousin Hugh. My husband will be in an exile's grave and I will be a white-haired crone before King Geordie will deign tae extend a favor tae the Drummonds. Ye ken which clans and great magnates control Scotland. Perhaps millions o' pounds fer his Exchequer would receive his attention, but naething less." She flung her napkin on the low table spread with refreshments and marched stiffly from the room.

Hugh watched her go with troubled eyes and sighed. "She was always difficult, even as a young wife, mair than maist Highland women, wha are excessive in their emotional speeches. I always felt that she would relish flaying my hide fer my moderate stances. She thinks like a soldier, nae a tender maiden."

Jamie chuckled. "She is my mama, and ever protective, although I canna gainsay yer words."

Hugh said soberly, "Ye ken that Peter and I canna possibly deliver what she expects, Jamie." He placed a chubby hand on his cousin's knee. "Service in foreign parts if ye remain in the military is best. If ye are permitted tae resign, it would be best that ye nae remain in the Highlands. Seek employment in the Lowlands or England if ye can find ought appropriate tae yer station in life and liking. There is nae commerce worth yer investment in the north. I wish ye loved the law and jurisprudence. Ye hae a fine mind, lad, and would qualify fer the bar in less than three years. Ye could join our firm in London or open an office in Edinburgh or Glasgow."

Jamie shook his head and related the story of James Watt's work with steam engines and John Robison's offer to introduce him to the inventor. They talked long of prospects and pitfalls for such industry. Hugh warned him, "Commit ainly yer mind and hands tae the enterprise, nae yer savings. Exercise financial prudence, lad. That should be yer course until the invented devices prove their worth, which may require years."

Spring advanced, and there was still no word from the Admiralty. Jamie accompanied David Gordon on visits in the surrounding area until he felt suffocated by the admiring attention of lairds and herdsmen alike. After a tavern lunch, the two fended off pleas to stay for "just another round."

Jamie muttered as they rode away from the inn, "I dinna relish the duties o' a hero, which would leave me a sodden drunk. Ye canna avoid the adulation, fer ye must meet oft wi' these men. Fer my part, I will take my leave and ride wi' my sisters in the hills."

He was good to his word. As soon as they could escape morning classes, Meg and Elizabeth were in the saddle, with Jamie trotting behind. The weather proved congenial to their preoccupation with exploring every hill and glen surrounding Abergeldie. A tearful Wee Jock was left behind with a promise that when he turned six, he would begin riding lessons.

Their routine seldom varied. They rode vigorously for an hour through fields and trees dappled by sun glinting through a mosaic of fluffy clouds—sheepbacks, as Elizabeth playfully named them. Jamie would signal a stop, and the girls would spread a cloth and unpack a generously provisioned hamper.

After lunch, Jamie braced himself against a tree, tuned his mandolin, and played minstrel while the girls sang old ballads and airs. One day, Meg's face turned solemn. She said, "It hae been a glorious six weeks, Jamie. Since I was a bairn, I hae seen yer picture and wondered if ye would e'er return. Mama says that ye must be leaving soon. I wish—" Her voice broke, and her sister took her hand, concern evident in her puckered eyebrows. Meg continued in a rush. "I wish that ye could stay and that Papa could come hame. Uncle Charles and Aunt Allison are sae kind, but it would be wonderful tae be a complete family in our ain hame, nae matter how simple."

Jamie put his arms around his sisters, hugging them tightly. He was silent a long time, struggling for words. His voice husky with emotion, he said, "Ye ken that the war is scarcely o'er, and our family hae lived through great difficulty. We must be strong and patient." Meg shifted restlessly, as if she would speak, but Jamie plowed ahead. "I promise ye that I will work ceaselessly tae protect ye and Mama. Perhaps I can restore the family fortunes, but it may take a very lang time before we are all together again." Impulsively, he added, "If circumstances permit, I will make a trip tae France tae visit papa." He instantly regretted his rashness, for if that trip were discovered by agents of the British government, it could doom the Drummond family's prospects for restoration. The girls sat absorbing his words. At last, they nodded.

That night, he recounted the conversation to his mother, whose face grew thunderous. "Ye canna do that, Jamie! Ye are a king's officer. It matters nae a whit that there is nae war betwixt the nations. 'Twould bring doon the wrath o' the government upon us."

Jamie gripped his mother's hand. "Mama, 'tis a notion fer the possible time when and if I am nae langer a king's officer."

Euphemia Drummond subsided but wryly observed, "Yer sister Meg is much like me, lad. She is mair strong-willed than ye realize. She will hold ye tae yer promise. If the impediments tae travel are removed, ye will hae nae peace wi' that lass."

It had been years since Jamie had sat in Charles Gordon's study. He dimly remembered the carved oaken desk, comfortable leather chairs, and magnificent view of the slopes of Craig-na-ban through the tall glass windows framed in burgundy silk.

His uncle sat with slender fingers templed, observing him over the rims of his reading glasses. Jamie was struck by how little the man had changed over two decades. His hair, always thin and receding, was now gray, and his face had gathered wrinkles softened by candlelight. In every other respect, his mother's oldest brother was still the reticent figure of old. Charles had always professed loyalty to the banished house of Stewart but had stood apart from the rebels during the Rising of '45. However, his loyalty to family, in spite of his often-proclaimed fears of government reprisals, had provided the refuge that Jamie and his mother needed when the Drummonds of Strathallan were dispossessed and forced to flee their home. Although Jamie had never been close to his uncle, he harbored a deep appreciation for the risks that the Laird of Abergeldie had taken to shelter his sister's family.

Charles Gordon interrupted Jamie's reverie. "I returned frae Aberdeen on Friday, where I met wi' the high sheriff. He is highly satisfied wi' our success in apprehending the thieves and their informants. The assizes met scarcely a week past. The trials were short, and the judge and jury pronounced doom on the miscreants. Their stay in the tollbooth was mercifully short." He sat back and sighed. "I broke the news tae Rabbie Duncan, wha must tell his daughter Molly that she is now a widow. Harry Pringle and the twa informants danced the Flibber Tae Gibbet on Heiden Hill Wednesday last. 'Tis a sad but necessary end o' their thieving ways." He fell silent.

Jamie prompted, "And the remaining reivers?"

Charles said, "Although they are reprobates, the assizes judge deemed them capable o' reformation. He sentenced them tae banishment fer fourteen years and transportation. Their skills wi' horses and cattle may redeem them in their new hame o' South Carolina."

Jamie asked, "Wha became o' the lad—Harry Pringle's young brother Richard? Was he transported as weel?"

Uncle Charles smiled. "It seems that Rabbie Duncan hae a soft heart fer the lad and wishes tae provide him that which our system o' justice rarely grants. My tacksman hae a blacksmith brother in Kirriemuir in Angus, that wee red toun, wha agreed tae purchase the lad's indenture fer four years. 'Tis a far better fate fer the lad than where the judge intended tae send him— tae Barbados."

Jamie sat lost in reflection, for he himself had once believed transportation to be his fate as he sat in Newgate Prison. Charles interrupted his reverie.

"Tell me o' the letters and yer decision."

Jamie removed papers from his jacket pocket and spread them on the desk. "Ye ken, Uncle, that I was preparing to return tae London, fer my leave was scheduled tae expire soon." Charles nodded. Jamie tapped one of the pages. "That journey is nae langer necessary. This letter from Lieutenant Colonel MacKenzie, my commanding officer, informs me that the Admiralty hae accepted his recommendation tae reject my resignation. I hae been placed on ha' pay in my current rank o' captain. That action consigns me tae a limbo that, as the colonel states, may last months or perhaps years. It is his opinion that unless war is declared, I will nae be recalled. I canna live on ha' pay but hae sufficient funds in my prize account fer a guid lang time."

His uncle shifted in his chair and gestured at the papers. "I see that there is some uncertainty in such a status. I surmise that there are nae restrictions on yer place o' residence or civilian employment. I suspect that ye hae plans, fer ye hae nae explained the rest o' the letters."

Jamie nodded. "I canna live a life o' leisure and must seek some manner o' employment. I hae a letter from a faculty member at the University o' Glasgow. Professor James Watt is a foremost expert in building and improving devices using steam fer motive power. At the urging o' a chap I met on the journey north, he hae made me an offer tae help build a steam-powered carriage."

The look on his uncle's face was a mixture of wonder and skepticism.

Jamie rushed on. "I verra much appreciate the refuge that Abergeldie hae been fer my mama, sisters, and brother. I ask yer indulgence in continuing tae provide shelter while I seek a position and place o' residence."

Charles waved his hand emphatically. "'Tis nae the practice o' Gordons tae turn oot family when there is need. Dinna concern yerself, lad. Provide yer mother whate'er ye can spare. I ken that ye prefer this opportunity in Glasgow, but I wish ye tae consider an unusual proposal closer tae hame."

Jamie's eyebrows rose.

Charles turned his chair so he could look outside. In the dim twilight, two does were feeding peacefully at the edge of the lawn that extended from the castle to the forest canopy. The silence stretched. Charles turned to face Jamie. "I wish ye tae listen tae the entire proposal before responding."

Jamie nodded but said nothing.

"Eastward, in Aberdeenshire, near Fyvie, lives a family which is a sept o' the Gordons o' Huntly. At this time, I wilna disclose their identity. The laird o' that house and his wife hae three daughters but nae sons. He married late in life, and his health is in decline. The eldest daughter is in her late twenties, and her sisters are younger. A naturally frugal man w' considerable skills in management, the laird hae accumulated a considerable fortune and is favored wi' excellent and extensive lands and herds. The auld laird and his wife are casting aboot fer a husband wha can also manage the estates." Jamie stirred restlessly, but Uncle Charles raised a warning hand. "Hear me oot, lad. Arranged marriages between weel-connected families hae been the salvation o' many astute young men o' guid family but wi'out wealth. Ye must admit that ye are o' that class and circumstances through nae fault o' yer own."

He stared at Jamie, who remained seated wi' an enigmatic smile on his face. Charles blew out a breath, which gave Jamie an opening to say, "I am aware that I was born tae an aristocratic family, and I ken the practicality and value o' marriages arranged between powerful families. But ye fair take my breath awa', Uncle. The proposal reeks o' desperation tae offer a pig in a poke. She is years beyond the age at which daughters typically marry. The lass must lack the qualities that attract suitors. Is she sae deficient that her father would stoop tae peddle her?"

Charles Gordon kept his face passive, but Jamie could see that he was nettled by the comment. "I expected a fair amount o' reluctance, but yer comment is insolent, sir. Ye remember that I asked ye tae withhold comment until I had explained the entire proposal. I hear that while suitors hae been rare and she is nae a beauty, she is nae unattractive and withal hae an amiable disposition."

Jamie retorted, "Come, Uncle. Surely, there must be some defect fer her father tae offer sae much tae obtain a husband o' guid family but modest means."

Charles sighed. He was losing control of the conversation. "Allow me tae summarize the offer. If ye will contract tae serve as the laird's manager fer a year, wi' residence on the estate, he will grant his permission fer ye tae court his daughter. If ye marry the lass in that year's time, the properties will pass tae ye upon the laird's death, as confirmed in his will."

Jamie shook his head vehemently. He kept his voice low and controlled, although his emotions were seething. "Uncle Charles, I am gratefu' beyond measure at yer attempts tae settle wealth and status on me. I ken that ye are only thinking o' my guid." He took a breath and let it out slowly. "It matters nae a whit if the heiress is plain or as lovely as the Queen of Sheba, or whether she would bring fifty thousand pounds or a million to a marriage. If I canna inherit lands and titles that are rightfully mine, I dinna wish tae inherit wealth by marrying it. I ken that aristocrats dinna share my thinking in rejecting such an advantage, but I wish tae earn wealth only through my ain efforts."

His uncle lifted a warning finger. "Ye sound as if ye hae imbibed a strange brew o' republicanism, such as that which I understand is becoming a popular notion on the Continent and in the colonies. I would beware o' stating such beliefs in influential circles. While we here in the country tolerate such beliefs tae a degree, they are anathema at court."

Jamie responded, "I hae been in parlous circumstances where merit and effort are what saved me, nae another man's titles or prerogatives. I believe in the virtue of common sense, Uncle, which is rapidly convincing me that the aristocracy hae nae monopoly o'er common people in its application fer the guid o' mankind."

Jamie was implacable. Uncle Charles was soon convinced that his attempt to assure the economic success and security of the Drummonds through marriage into a staunchly Hanoverian family was doomed. The conversation was at loggerheads and soon took other avenues.

Bidding farewell to his mother and siblings went better than Jamie expected. They viewed his trip to Glasgow as a transitory stage before he returned to the Highlands to settle down. In a last attempt to make his mother understand his motivation in leaving, he recounted the strange nocturnal visits of the gruagach, with their unending refrain of his need to heed the prophecy. Euphemia Drummond listened without interrupting, an enigmatic smile playing around her lips.

"Ach, Jamie, ye canna believe such tales. They are the maunderings o' dreams. Do ye nae remember when I told ye aboot French Kate, wha haunts this castle? Ye believed and were frightened because ye were an impressionable child."

Jamie laid a hand on hers. "Mama, ye hae said that ye sometimes believe in the Sight. I dinna wish tae believe Maggie's prophecy, but it came true. It hae a purpose and was fulfilled during my voyage tae Canada. She pronounced another prophecy, which Flora MacDonald took pains tae confirm. I believe in reason, Mama, and choose tae guide my life by it, but some hidden portion o' my mind is bedeviled by such dreams, and I canna suppress them. Am I such a creature sae ruled by reason and logic that I can deny all the passions, beliefs, and prejudices o' my heritage? My mind persuades me that I canna do it."

Euphemia did not speak for a long time but hugged her son tightly. Finally, she found her voice and whispered, "I hae nae guid answer, fer I am o' like mind and canna shake off beliefs frae the past. There are many mysteries hidden in the core o' these Highland hills. I can only offer this motherly advice. Pure reason is mair worthy o' trust. Ye must beware o' auld passions and all else that inflame the spirit. They may bring great joy and fulfillment, but they also bring great sadness when unleashed tae satisfy base desires and hatreds. It was a lesson that yer papa dinna learn when he impulsively pledged his loyalty tae a young prince and his doomed cause. When confronted wi' a dilemma, ye must carefully examine it, then ask yerself if it feels right before ye decide." She released him to dab away tears that sparkled in her dark lashes.

Jamie could not pack away his uniforms in a stout oaken chest that had once held his long-dead grandfather William Gordon's cloaks, coats, and other clothing without recalling voyages and battles, along with a tinge of regret at the choice he had made. In accordance with his mother's advice, he dropped in several small linen bags packed with camphor crystals to protect the woolens from insect damage and resolutely shut the lid. He did not pack away his pistols or blades, although he decided to leave his beloved Andrea Ferrara rapier behind. Later, servants hoisted the chest up to the castle's spacious attic.

A considerable group of Drummonds, Gordons, and liveried servants gathered before the castle's entrance to await the post coach that would convey Jamie on his journey to Glasgow. With his little brother perched on his shoulders and wearing his beaver hat, he listened politely to advice poured into his ears by his mother, Aunt Allison, and sisters. He was somewhat befuddled, for they were merely repeating all that had been discussed the previous evening, accompanied by copious tears. A groom trotted up from the road, shouting, "The coach is crossing the bridge."

Jamie set Wee Jock down from his perch and retrieved his hat. The driver loudly announced that he was behind schedule. Jamie, in an aside to David Gordon, noted that in all his experience, drivers were invariably late and anxious to transfer the guilt to their passengers. Nevertheless, the farewells were soon over, and Jamie waved cheerily to his family as the driver negotiated the return to the military road and turned southward.

After exchanging small talk with other passengers, Jamie reread the letter from John Robison, filled with glowing descriptions of great advances in steam power being made by James Watt's team of students and employees. Professor Watt's offer letter itself promised only a modest stipend from university funds, with instructions to lodge at a nearby rooming house frequented by the university's visitors.

○────────○

In the small square before the great doors of Saint Giles Cathedral on the Royal Mile in Edinburgh, passengers waited for the post coaches. They had gathered in the hour after dawn from nearby hotels. Porters trundled luggage and stacked trunks, boxes, and bags on the cobbles in spots marked in chalk for their destinations. Six men huddled under a lamppost from which hung a tattered banner that bore the single word—Glasgow. A group of four men in dark suits chatted about mercantile matters. Jamie marked them as businessmen traveling together. He moved close to a ruddy-faced fellow in his thirties and introduced himself. The man smiled and gripped Jamie's hand. "John Anderson o' Glasgow. I teach natural philosophy at the university. I am returning hame after lecturing on physics." He paused. "I see frae yer countenance that ye hae an interest in the subject."

Jamie nodded. "Aye, when I was a student at King's College, I studied natural sciences and mathematics. Tis my first experience in Glasgow. I hae an offer o' employment frae James Watt, o' the university faculty tae help him wi' his explorations and inventions using steam power."

John Anderson's round face crinkled with pleasure. "Excellent! We will hae a stimulating conversation, much mair enjoyable than that between the mongers and merchants accompanying us." He was good to his word, for the two spent the five hours of the journey deeply immersed in their topic. Jamie discovered that his companion was acquainted with Benjamin Franklin and had hosted the great American inventor on the trip to Scotland on which he had received his honorary doctorate. He had also sponsored James Watt's early work in steam and had been influential in that young scientist's obtaining a position at the university. However, he deflated some of Jamie's enthusiasm with his next statement. Anderson bent toward him and lowered his voice. "I must warn ye that all is nae favorable fer James at present. While his early work hae been weel received, there is concern among his benefactors and investors that progress in his inventions hae been slow. They wish tae turn a profit quickly. Such men hae little idea o' difficulties bedeviling the creative process and are hasty in judging success and failure. For James Watt's ideas tae succeed, he needs progress in a wide range o' technologies. That hae been lacking, and his backers are dissatisfied. If they withhold funding, I fear fer his future." Anderson recognized the symptoms of concern on Jamie's face. He patted his knee and tried to lighten the impact of his words. "Nae, I hae spoken o' matters best discussed by the inventor himself. He hae overcome such difficulties in the past and always come through unscathed. I beg yer pardon."

The passengers caught their first view of the city as the coach rattled along the turnpike that ran east-west between Edinburgh and Glasgow. The spires of the city's historic cathedral and clock tower of the university gracing the skyline appeared, causing one of the merchant passengers to exclaim over the city's beauty as the "cleanest and most beautiful in the north." Jamie smiled but did not contradict him, for he had seen London. Approaching from the northeast, the coach passed attractive recently built estates surrounded by lush orchards and parklands. As they reached the ancient city wall, the businessman opened a small volume and began to read to his companions. "The great physician and geographer Robert Sibbald wrote concerning Glasgow thusly: 'Glasgow is the maist famous emporium o' a' the west o' Scotland. Notwithstanding it is inferior tae many in antiquity, yet if we respect the largeness o' the city, number and stateliness o' its public and private buildings, its commerce wi' foreign nations, and opulence o' its inhabitants, it is the chief o' all cities in the kingdom, next tae Edinburgh. The city stands maist pleasantly on the east bank o' Clyde, navigable up tae the tower, by ships o' small burden; but New Glasgow is a haven fer vessels o' the greatest size. The city is joined tae the suburbs, which stand on the west brink, by a beautiful bridge o' eight arches, built of square hewn stane. The maist part of the city stands on a plain, and is in a manner four-square. In the middle is the tollbooth, built of hewn stane, with a very high tower, and bells which sound melodiously at every hour's end. At the tollbooth, principal streets cross each other tae divide the city into four equal parts, every one o' which is adorned wi' public buildings. In the higher part o' the city, stands the cathedral church, commonly called Saint Mungo's. It amazes beholders fer its bigness and artifice o' its structure. The pillars and high towers show a wonderful architecture. Near to the church is the Archbishop's castle, fenced with an exceeding high wall o' hewn stone and looks down tae the city. The college is remarkable, consisting of diverse courts. The forepart is an excellent structure o' hewn stane. The precincts o' the college are enlarged by some acres, purchased by money granted by the king, separated frae the toun by an exceeding high wall.'"

Yet Jamie scarcely heard the professor's words. The appearance of the grounds of Glasgow's venerable university absorbed his attention. Above the massive stone façade rose the impressive tower, with shorter corner spires reaching skyward around it. The size and extent of the buildings dwarfed Jamie's recollection of King's College in Aberdeen. He asked John Anderson, "In which building does James Watt perform his experiments?"

Anderson replied, "There is a great fear among the faculty o' explosions and noxious odors frae the furnaces and workshops. Master Watt's efforts are confined tae sheds constructed behind the buildings where professors conduct classes. 'Tis a decidedly unacademic place that he and his companions inhabit, surrounded by mechanics and blacksmiths. Maist professors avoid the place, but the mair curious students o' natural science hae a great love fer it, sensing that great discoveries lie just below the surface."

Jamie nodded. "Aye, 'tis what draws me here. I relish the opportunity tae advance science."

John Anderson frowned. "I pray that yer soaring hopes may be satisfied, fer material progress hae been slow of late and costs mair excessive than planned."

Jamie did not know what to make of the professor's pessimism and said nothing. The coach driver brought his conveyance to a halt. The footmen swung down and quickly pulled valises and trunks from the commodious boot. Jamie agreed to Professor Anderson's invitation to dinner at his residence on Granby Lane the following Friday night. A roughly dressed lad with pox-marked cheeks, taller than his companions, elbowed them aside to offer his services carrying Jamie's luggage. Not wishing to challenge the protocol of the group, Jamie nodded.

Together, they strode uphill toward to a street lined with small shops and residences, most of which displayed signs offering rooms for rent. Consulting his letter from James Watt, Jamie read the address: Curlers Rest 256 Byres Road. The location housed a whitewashed inn on the ground floor, with four inviting windows above displays of flowers in baskets hanging from a wrought-iron railing above a row of iron-cased lanterns.

A cheerful publican met them at the entrance. Sweating under his load of luggage, the young porter struggled up a narrow staircase but was all smiles when Jamie rewarded his toil with a half-crown coin. With long experience of crowded inns, Jamie had haggled for a room to himself, which cost him rather more than he expected. Reviewing the menu as he sat at a big oak table in the crowded public room that evening, Jamie concluded that to live in Glasgow for a lengthy period would easily consume the stipend offered by James Watt and force him to spend much of his half-pay allowance to support himself. The publican noted his scowl and hastened to remark, "Prithee dinna take offense, sire. 'Tis the fault o' the government, wi' wartime prices still high and taxes and a'."

Jamie laid aside the menu and rubbed his eyes tiredly. "Nae offense taken, man. As ye can surmise frae my accent, I am o' the north, where life and prices are simpler. I must be frugal but must live. Instead o' wine and roast fowl, bring me a pint o' porter and a meat pie. I hae been at sea and abroad fer many years and mair familiar wi' rough fare than dainties."

The publican laughed jovially. "I life on such simple fare myself, and ye can see that it nourishes my body adequately."

Jamie smiled, for the innkeeper was round as a tub. "Aye, weel. Beef and porter make guid belly mortar."

The jest drew amused chuckles from other diners and led to friendly conversations. Jamie retired to his room on the second story, well-filled with good food and wishes for success in his new endeavor. He was pleased to find clean sheets and, at least by the light of the single lamp in the room, no vermin crawling in the bedding.

In spite of two pints of porter that had left him light-headed the evening before, he rose at dawn and flung back the curtains. The cobbled pavement glittered from a brief overnight shower.

The sky was dappled with clouds fleeing eastward and clearing rapidly to the west, promising a sunny day.

Jamie poured water into a basin from a china pitcher and began swirling a wet brush in a cup holding a cake of shaving soap, stirring up creamy lather. After stropping his razor on a length of leather, he began to shave. When he was finished, he examined his face in a small mirror for nicks. Finding none, he winked insouciantly at his reflection, combed his hair, and tied it off with a strip of leather. Most young men preferred silk in colorful hues, but his long military service had left its conservative stamp on his habits.

He changed his small clothes, donned a white linen shirt, and wriggled into brown breeches. A simple cravat, dark green coat, and horsehair wig completed his attire. He was better dressed than any mechanic or other laborer but far from wearing the finery affected by young dandies of the upper classes. He was satisfied, for he would blend in with the young professionals of the city—solicitors, bankers, and merchants—who preferred subdued colors.

There was a sharp rap on the door. Jamie swung it open. John Robison stood grinning like a schoolboy. "I am here tae guid ye tae Master Watt's workshops, since I stood as sponsor fer yer employment. On yer first day, it wouldna do tae hae ye lost in the maze o' buildings o' our great university."

Jamie responded, "Then I invite ye tae breakfast wi' me, fer I canna labor wi'oot nourishment! The publican assured me that the Curlers Rest lays a table tae satisfy the maist ravenous appetites." John Robison eagerly accepted. Jamie grabbed his old greatcoat, for Glasgow weather at any season was fickle. In five minutes, the pair was huddled over trenchers of shirred eggs, smoky fat-popping sausages, black pudding, and piles of crisp toast, accompanied by a carafe of milk and a pot of strong Indian tea.

John Robison led the way across the hill to the back of the university grounds. He headed for a row of three long low-roofed whitewashed buildings. Across a wide lawn rose the imposing gray stone tracery of the soaring tower that marked the center of the venerable campus. They skirted the lawn and followed a cobbled lane to an entrance. Inside, Jamie was astonished to see only a simple foundry where two blacksmiths in leather aprons were beating a sheet of tin into a curved shape with small hammers. Nearby, a cabinet housed pipes of various diameters and lengths nested in pigeonholes. A partially assembled metallic cylinder as tall as a man sat on a stand supported with clamps and braces. The blacksmiths stopped their work and looked at John Robison expectantly. John waved them back to work. "They are building a condensing chamber, which will be attached tae the Newcomen steam engine. Mr. Watt believes that it will prevent losses o' steam and improve its efficiency. They are hammering oot the curved sections according tae Mr. Watt's design, and they are tae be joined at the seams. Tae hold the steam under pressure is unco difficult, requiring crimping and then welding o' the edges by synchronized hammering inside and ootside. The work takes days fer each piece and many sessions o' heating and pounding."

At the far end of the workshop, a makeshift tower stood, resembling a hayloft. Under it stood a tall mysterious device with its top hidden in the gloom. Robison explained, "'Tis a Newcomen engine that belongs tae the university. Mr. Watt's task is tae study it and make improvements upon it." He pointed to various components as he talked. "This potbellied beastie is the boiler, filled wi' water that generates steam as it heats. A series o' valves control the steam as a piston is forced alternately up and doon by the walking beam at the top o' the tower. The arrangement permits the piston tae fall and rise twelve times a minute, lifting and discharging aboot ten gallons o' water a stroke. That is why the earliest use o' the engine was tae pump flooded mines. Mr. Watt intends tae nae only improve the efficiency o' the engine but attach the piston tae a drive wheel tae translate the back-and-forth action tae circular motion."

The second building housed rows of wide workbenches. The entire building was well lit, with sunshine streaming through large glass panes mounted in the low-pitched ceiling. Two rows of lamps hung on centerline beams down the length of the building. A dozen workmen sat or stood hunched over instruments. Jamie expressed his astonishment at the delicacy of their work.

John nodded. "Ye must remember that this was James Watt's instrument laboratory when he was employed by the university tae service their precision devices. All the university timepieces, measuring equipment, and surveying tools are either created or repaired in this workshop. Here is also where we are attempting tae develop a gauge tae measure the pressure o' steam fer Mr. Watt's experimental engines."

The third building was as quiet as a library since it housed James Watt's office, an auditorium for meetings, and tables where clerks were sketching diagrams. James Watt detached himself from a huddle of professors in his office and hurried to greet Jamie, who was taken aback by the inventor's youth and unruly shock of brown hair falling over his eyes.

Any notion that Watt was a callow or indolent young man were quickly dispelled. While his manner was friendly and amiable, his instructions were direct and his questions shrewd. It was also clear that his time was precious and he was beset by many problems and issues. He assured himself that Jamie was settled in housing and assigned John Robison to secure Jamie a worktable and a craftsman and apprentice to assist him. His first work assignment was to develop a wooden model of a gearing mechanism to convert the Newcomen piston thrust to centrifugal motion to drive a spinning shaft. John Robison would advise him and help attach a model Newcomen engine. Watt announced that he expected the two to conduct a demonstration two months hence. Assuring himself that they understood his instructions, Watt left to rejoin his meeting with the professors. He apologized for his hastiness and said in a low voice, "Ye must understand that these men are fools, but I canna afford tae treat them as they deserve. They control my funding, and they are dyspeptic at the best of times and uncommonly vile at the worst. Right now, they are demanding mair progress than reason and science can produce. I must abase myself and make hollow promises to placate them." So saying, he rushed off.

Most of the craftsmen were of mature skills and already assigned to other projects. Jamie inherited a newly made and talkative journeyman who introduced himself as Sim Johnston, with skills on the lathe and in woodworking. He showed Jamie examples of geared wheels and cams that he had carved. The apprentice was Alan Sandilands, a quiet lad of fourteen whose father was a mechanic in Edinburgh. The son had done only menial work in his father's shop and had been an apprentice scarcely a year. John Robison confided that the boy's woodworking skills were rudimentary. His most obvious abilities seemed to be artistic. He was excellent at sketching and copying drawings. Jamie philosophized, "Aye, weel. I ken that this task will require a variety o' skills. We a' must learn quickly. Desire and great effort must substitute fer experience."

Robison showed Jamie other wooden models that Watt's team had produced. While two months would be a considerable challenge, Jamie was determined to make a good showing for his new employer and not above pressuring his friend for further help. "John, ye hae much knowledge o' mechanics and the Newcomen engine that I lack. Fer this project tae succeed, I am insistent that ye sacrifice a bit o' sleep tae tutor me or lead me tae others wha can stuff my brain. I am like the proverbial ox stuck in the mire and unable tae get oot nae matter how I labor."

Robison was agreeable, and the two spent much of the first two weeks engaged in discussions on principles of motion, power, force, pressure, and the devices that could translate back-and-forth motion into driving a shaft clockwise at variable speeds through a series of cogged wheels. Jamie pawed through Sim

Johnston's boxes of carvings for examples to help them in their design discussions. He invited the apprentice Alan Sandilands into these sessions, where the lad began to sketch, translating concepts into drawings of interacting components.

11

The two months passed quickly. Work days lasted from shortly after dawn to well past midnight, with only Sundays off. Jamie was pleased with the contributions of his craftsman and apprentice, for both enthusiastically embraced the difficult task. Slowly, Alan Sandilands's drawings took shape in wood as Sim Johnston's skillful hands whittled and sanded. The lathe yielded driveshafts from seasoned elm, chosen for its supple toughness. The team's spirits soared as the two months came to an end. They labored all night to assemble the wheels, gears, shafts, pulleys, and leather bands that made up the model. Jamie mounted a metal-bound cart wheel on the shaft.

The sun had not yet risen when Sim Johnston spit on his hands and grasped the drive rod connected to the Newcomen engine. Grunting with the effort, he shoved it back and forth. Jamie held his breath as he watched the shaft push a heavy flywheel downward, then upward on the backward thrust as it rotated. Toothed wooden gears, well-greased beforehand, rotated forward, and the laterally mounted shaft began to spin. Five minutes later, a thoroughly exhausted Sim Johnston dropped the pry bar he had been using to push the driveshaft and raised his hands in triumph.

John Robison smiled as he watched the three cavort like demented schoolboys, flushed with their success after a difficult night. At least ten times they had attempted the experiment and failed. Misalignment of the wheels and shafts was the principal culprit, and heat was also a great enemy. Fighting disappointment, time after time they had disassembled, adjusted, and reassembled the parts. They used up most of a tub of grease used by drivers to lubricate carriage axles and wheel bearings. The contrivance almost dripped liquid. Jamie observed that heat and misalignment would rapidly wear out the toothed wheels. John Robison replied that cast metal wheels would resist warping and that encasing the device in an oil bath would help dissipate the heat. Jamie said, "These are a' vital considerations fer the future. I am hoping that Mr. Watt will be satisfied that we hae demonstrated the practicality o' providing motive power tae vehicles."

John Robinson replied, "Perhaps he is ready tae consider these matters and watch yer demonstration, fer he hae called us tae a meeting in his office at ten o'clock. I suggest that ye a' get wha sleep ye can."

Jamie nodded agreement and dismissed his workers. He was so energized by their success that sleep would not come. Instead, he spent the morning bathing, shaving, dressing, and consuming a large breakfast and copious quantities of strong tea in the public room of the Curlers Rest.

James Watt listened without expression to Jamie's report, buttressed by favorable comments from John Robison. Jamie was puzzled, for the inventor had expressed great enthusiasm during previous reports of the project's progress.

Jamie asked, "When would ye care tae attend a demonstration, Mr. Watt? I can arrange it fer this very afternoon."

Watt sat forward, templed his long fingers, rested his forehead against them, and closed his eyes. Jamie glanced at John Robison with apprehension. At last, the inventor spoke, his voice strained with tension. "I expected that ye would succeed in demonstrating rotary motion frae a walking beam, Jamie, although the resources and time I granted ye were sparse in the extreme. I can see that ye hae extraordinary ability and a keen imagination. Gi'en the opportunity, ye could make yer mark. I regret that I must convey bitter news that hae curdled my spirits since I was informed o' it yesterday. I was called tae the provost's office and told that my financial backers hae withdrawn half o' their support. They hae determined that I need less money tae produce the results that they demand. In particular, they insist that all collateral projects be stopped. I am permitted only that funding needed tae make approved changes tae the Newcomen engine. I told them o' my concept o' a separate condensation chamber and how it would improve efficiency. They were unmoved. I confided that if we could bore a precise cylinder, it would create a chamber that could hold much greater pressure wi'oot leakage than wi' hammered seams. They were unimpressed. " He slammed his hands down on the desk. "Utter fools! They canna possibly comprehend their ain stupidity! We hae the potential tae make such changes tae industry and manufacturing that canna be comprehended." His voice sank to nearly a whisper. "I regret that I must dismiss half o' my staff. John Robison will remain tae aid me, but he must support himself by teaching in the college." Miserably, Watt concluded, "I hae nae position fer ye, Jamie Drummond. Furthermore, I doubt that I kin offer hope fer improvement tae prospects fer several years. I can pay ye fer the past weeks but naething further beyond today."

Jamie rose, pressing his hands firmly on the table. Taking a deep breath, he said, "I canna express my disappointment in this setback. However, I hae faith that ye will succeed, albeit wi'out my help. Ye dare tae dream o' great success in spite o' towering obstacles. Just as yer spirits hae been brought low by disappointment, they will rise again, fer I sense a great resolve in ye, James Watt, and ye, John Robison. I hae only myself tae blame fer dreaming excessively o' success and being unmindfu' o' the likelihood o' setbacks. Although others warned me o' the risks, I dinna listen. Unfortunately, I canna gamble my future on such dreams. I wish that I could remain here at nae pay fer a year or twa. I dinna hae that luxury and must seek gainfu' employment soon. In spite o' feelings o' blame that my anger encourages me tae express, I wish ye baith weel as ye invest years in this endeavor. Come, let us demonstrate our success wi' rotary motion and the ingenious linkage that enables it. I will leave ye my notes and drawings. Perhaps some day they will aid ye in building such an engine."

That evening, John Robison shared a last meal with Jamie, commiserating over the ill fortune that had befallen the project. The demonstration of the rotary motion model had greatly impressed James Watt. The inventor berated himself for not being sufficiently eloquent in attempting to persuade his investors to continue its funding. Jamie had only succeeded in offending the inventor by blaming his meekness for not selling his projects more forcefully. Watt had reddened at the accusation but could not be pushed to make another attempt.

Robison shook his head sadly. "I fear that ye are correct, Jamie. Fer a' his brilliance and the respect in which he is held by the university dons, he dinna ken how tae advocate fer his ain benefit."

Jamie said, "Then ye must assume that task, John, if ye wish tae see success for Mr. Watt's ventures. English, German, Swedish, and Dutch industrialists wilna wait."

The young ex-naval officer nodded slowly. "I fear that ye are correct, although that time is still somewhat distant. I still see nae opportunity fer ye, man. Do ye hae any other prospects, except a return tae military or mercenary service?"

Jamie shrugged. "I hae nae intention o' risking my life further in military service unless the cause is the safety o' my ain family. I think that my natural stock o' luck hae been greatly depleted. I hae sufficient means tae avoid starvation, but I am at loose ends." He stopped, for a thought to which he had never yet given voice intruded. "Tae tell ye truly, John, I yearn tae resolve a mystery aboot my family which bedevils my mind. I hae the liberty which unemployment provides tae pursue it. I wilna explain further until I hae the facts in hand, although I sense that ye are burning wi' curiosity." Taking a purse from his pocket, Jamie pressed John Robison to share it between his workman and apprentice, who faced imminent loss of employment.

In the morning, Jamie packed and bought a coach ticket, not for return to Abergeldie but southward to Carlisle and then southeastward along Hadrian's Wall to Yorkshire. After a lengthy day that took the coach across the border into England and over the high moorland to Hexham, with its tall church spire and Corbridge, the road wound down to the city of Newcastle-on-Tyne. In the morning, he hired a cab to take him to South Shields, where the Tyne met the sea. Turning south on the turnpike, a few more miles brought him to the square in the middle of Sunderland.

After supper in the public room, Jamie sat before a glowing fire nursing a tankard of the local ale that had been heartily recommended by the tavern keeper. He reflected on a long-ago conversation with cousin Hugh Drummond, which had brought a devastating revelation about his father. Hugh had revealed that he had hired a spy to trail James Drummond. The man reported that Jamie's father had not returned to the Low Countries but hidden in a small town in Yorkshire. There he had lodged with a miller's family and committed the folly of wooing and then marrying the daughter, sired her three children, and then fled the country. Hugh had presented the evidence as overwhelming, but Jamie's mind gave him no satisfaction. He had always desired to see the proof firsthand. With this quest in mind, Jamie had persisted in worming information out of Cousin Hugh. It had taken two hours late one night and many drinks before the name of the town had slipped out—South Biddick. Another evening was required before Jamie extracted the name of the miller's daughter—Elizabeth.

After a night in a lumpy bed with dirty linen, he checked his body thoroughly for lice. Relieved at finding none, he bathed from the jug standing on a rickety and scarred table, dressed, eyed himself sourly in the cracked mirror, and sought the breakfast room. He asked the innkeeper to recommend a reliable stable.

He found it two blocks away on Burdon Road, at the corner of Mowbray Park, favored for riding by city dwellers. On the way, he passed a greengrocer's stall, where he purchased a sack of apples. Rejecting the first horses offered, his eye lit on a dark gray mare whose eyes followed him as he moved around the stalls. He saddled her and tried her about the yard. Satisfied with the mare's responsiveness, he dismounted and offered her an apple from the sack. A whinny of appreciation confirmed that a bond had formed between them. A few minutes of haggling over the rental price were enough to rent the horse for a week. Returning to the inn to load his luggage, Jamie asked directions to the tiny village of South Biddick on the banks of the River Wear. The innkeeper stared at him curiously, but Jamie simply muttered, "I seek an auld friend frae the war wha may hae passed that way some months past." He had no intention of arousing undue interest in his quest. He was apprehensive about approaching the village that had supposedly been the hiding place of his father and now the residence of the miller's daughter and her children.

The day was warm, and Jamie took his time cantering out of town on the Penshaw Road. The houses of Sunderland, set back from the busy road behind white pickets, quickly gave way to rolling emerald hills and straight-edged fields of waving yellow grain. Traffic on the road dwindled, with only an occasional pony cart or farm wagon. Two hours of pleasant riding brought him to the crossroads with the turnpike connecting Newcastle and Leeds. Jamie rode into an innyard by the turnpike to draw water for himself and the horse.

After Penshaw, Jamie followed the innkeeper's advice and took the next road north toward the bridge across the River Wear and then along the river. It was past noon when he spied the mill on the north bank, where Biddick Burn ran into the Wear. The wheel was turning slowly, and small children were playing in the field below the mill. Rather than approach the mill directly, Jamie wheeled the mare and returned to the road south and across the river that led to the village of South Biddick.

Except for the two-story red brick magnificence of Biddick Hall, South Biddick consisted of small buildings and thatched cottages, housing perhaps a hundred families. Jamie cantered the mare up a steep rise in the road to the only inn—the Coach and Crown. Receiving affirmation that there was room at the inn, he followed the groom to the stable, helped him unsaddle the horse, and tramped to the entrance to rent a room for the few days he expected would be needed for his investigation.

The balding and portly innkeeper sidled from behind the bar in the public room and introduced himself as Phineas Fowler. Smiling toothily, he asked, "And who might ye be, and what is yer purpose in coming to our fine village?"

In response to the innkeeper's query, Jamie named himself Mr. James and gave as his purpose that he was seeking an older former comrade in arms—a Highlander who might be living under an assumed name. The innkeeper led him to a table in the far corner of the nearly empty public room and signaled a wench for ale. Jamie placed two silver coins on his palm. The wench serving the drinks plucked one, but the second disappeared into the innkeeper's pocket. Jamie drank deeply, wiped the foam from his lip, and sat back expectantly.

"South Biddick is a small place, and strangers seldom pass this way. Ye undoubtedly saw Biddick Hall. 'Tis impossible to miss. Squire Nicholas Lambton lives there on an estate of nearly five hundred acres. He controls the commerce hereabouts but not every enterprise, for many are not quite legal. I warn ye to be circumspect about the town, for Biddick is also a place of tough coal miners and smugglers. It is well known for unlicensed manufacture and transport of spirits. The sheriff of Durham and his constables avoid it after dark, as do the excisemen. More than one has ended up disappearing from sight, never to be found again."

Jamie nodded at this strange news, for the village gave every appearance of being a peaceful place. The innkeeper continued in low tones. "The villagers are widely known in the county as the Bloody Biddickers. If the friend ye are seeking is afoul of the law, 'tis the perfect place for a man wishing to go to ground. There are many houses lying in hollows hereabouts that ye cannot enter without a troop accompanying ye. Now ye appear to be a well-set-up young man and mayhap proficient with a blade, but ye cannot hope to best a gang of rough pitmen and smuggler's bullyboys."

Jamie produced a gold coin, which disappeared swiftly. Jamie said, "My friend hae been missing a great lang while. He may hae flown but perchance left family behind. Do ye ken if a stranger frae Scotland married a local girl, say five or mair years past, and then went missing?"

The innkeeper stared at Jamie a long time. Another gold coin appeared and was pocketed. The innkeeper leaned so close that his forehead brushed Jamie's. "Ye are speaking of the stranger who married the daughter of the pitman, who then came into unexpected wealth, bought a tract o' timber, and erected a sawmill. He was away for a time but has returned. He found his wife friendly with another man, who fled for the stranger is not unskilled with weapons. All is now happiness for the Scot and the miller's daughter."

A thrill ran through Jamie's innards, but he did not move. He did not expect his investigation to proceed so smoothly. He said softly, "Aye, perhaps he is the same."

The innkeeper left briefly to resolve an issue at the bar and then returned. "Ye are intruding into dangerous country, Mr. James. The squire himself, Nicholas Lambton, has an interest in John Armstrong's sawmill and is known to be protecting the Scottish stranger. He believes him to be of aristocratic origins but attainted by the crown. I hesitate to mention the name, but Jacobite feeling still runs strongly in these Yorkshire lands."

Jamie's pulse began to race. So Hugh Drummond's story was proving true! He said quietly, "Dinna mistake my intentions. My family was also involved in the failed Rising o' '45. Be assured that I am nae neither an agent o' the King o'er the Water or the king that the Bonnie Prince sought tae replace. I am only seeking an auld friend."

The innkeeper gripped Jamie's arm tightly. "I believe ye, but ye must beware o' loose talk. Ye may end up in a bolt-hole with no way to save yerself. Do not meander around South Biddick asking questions. If ye wish tae see and speak with the Scottish stranger, who is not so much a stranger hereabouts, I can arrange it fer a sizable reward."

The haggling was brief. For twenty pounds, Phineas Fowler agreed to arrange the tryst, with payment of half before and half after the meeting. Jamie paid over the coins, convinced that he was being fleeced but anxious to resolve the mystery. The thought that he might be only one night away from a reunion with his fugitive father kept him awake until nearly dawn. He had scarcely shut his eyes when a light began to grow in his room. Sitting at the foot of the bed was one of the wizened little gruagach who had pestered his dreams aboard ship.

The gnome's message was curt. "A' is nae as it seems, lad. Hae a care fer yer ain safety." He repeated the words three times and vanished. Jamie lay wide awake on his side with his fist under his chin, musing on how to interpret the strange dream until dawn lightened the sky.

He did not see Phineas Fowler at breakfast. Concerned about his warning of the rough elements about, Jamie restricted his exploration of the town to the few shops along the high street. When he returned, the innkeeper signaled him from his station behind the bar. Drawing two tankards of ale, he joined Jamie at the same corner table, well away from other diners.

"The Scottish stranger bids ye attend him tonight at his house at the boat landing hard by the mill. 'Tis easy to find. There will be a lantern hung on the stoop to guide ye. The meeting is set for nine o'clock, after the children have been sent to bed. But ye must come unarmed, fer he is wary o' being taken."

Jamie demurred. "Why canna he meet me here at the inn?"

"He makes it a practice to not venture out after dark and seldom comes to the village. There are always agents o' the sheriff sniffing about."

"How can I trust yer information wi' ye yerself warning me tae be cautious? Will ye accompany me?"

Phineas Fowler shook his head. "I dare not. I maintain a delicate balance betwixt the elements hereabouts, but the Scot gave me a word to speak to ye to promote trust."

Jamie frowned. "And what is this word that would dispel my concerns?"

The innkeeper smiled. "Strathallan."

Jamie heart leaped at mention of his childhood home, which had been seized by Cumberland's forces when he and his mother had been forced to flee to the northern Highlands during the failed rising. He nodded. "I will make the journey tae his hoose and will pay o'er the remainder o' the money after I return."

The afternoon crawled by. Having slept little during the night, Jamie dozed, only to have the little gruagach return to spoil his rest by repeating the warning of the previous night.

His eyes flew open. The sun had westered, and long shadows filled the room. After supper in the public room and not entirely trusting the talkative innkeeper, he returned to the upstairs chamber determined to "hae a care." He packed his luggage, and locking the door, carried it down the back way to the unattended stable, where he saddled the mare and strapped the bags on her rump. Although he hoped that he was headed to a glad reunion with his father and had paid well for the favor, he decided to heed the dream's repeated warning. He carried a *sgian dubh*, a razor-sharp blade in a scabbard inside his boot that would escape detection if he were searched. The meeting instructions might require him to be unarmed, but he wanted weapons close by. He loaded his pistols and placed each in a bag that he hung on either side of the saddle. He strapped his heavy cavalry saber within easy reach.

The night was moonless. He had to wait a few anxious minutes to regain his night vision. A gate behind the stable that he had discovered on his earlier walk through the town meant that he could avoid leading the horse through the yard to the busy front entrance to the inn. He took his time threading a way through the narrow close to a quiet tree-lined residential street. A block from the inn, he mounted and walked the mare slowly along a lane to where it converged with the high street, only yards from the bridge across the River Wear.

Once across, he turned the horse's head onto the path westward along the river. Less than half a mile after he crossed the bridge, with the lights of the miller's house in view, he dismounted and led the mare into the trees. He filled a nose bag with oats to settle the horse and fed her an apple from his dwindling bag. "Ach, ye glutton! Ye hae a great hankering fer apples. Ye hae already eaten ha' the bag!" He patted her cheeks affectionately, laced the reins around a tree trunk, and counted thirty paces back to the lane. With his knife, he cut a wedge of bark from a nearby tree until the wound shone whitely in the sliver of moon riding over the trees.

Judging that the time was near nine, he hastened his steps to the boat landing. The sawmill was silent, the wheel still. Behind the mill on the landward side stood a large one-and-a–half-story house that must belong to John Armstrong, the miller. Lights glimmered in several windows. There were two buildings at the landing itself. One was dark, but the moonlight was sufficient for him to make out a white board with black lettering mounted on the roof proclaiming it a grocery and dry goods store. Set back from the landing was a one-story house of good size with a stoop in the Dutch style. A lantern glowed in a stand, illuminating the entry door. A light also shone from a wide window facing the stoop of what Jamie took to be a dining room from the dark outline of a large table and chairs.

Jamie stepped onto the stoop just as the door opened. A slender dark-haired woman his own age faced him. She wore a smock over her dress and was obviously well along in pregnancy. She did not curtsy but extended her hand to take his in a firm grip as a man would.

Jamie inclined his head and said, "My lady. My name is Mr. James, and I am here frae Scotland seeking information aboot an auld friend."

She looked at him intently and released his hand. "I am Elizabeth Drummond. From yer fair words, Mr. James, yer mission seems innocent. You must appreciate why we are cautious when strangers seek my husband, for others arrive with intent to bring harm. Ye must excuse my forwardness, but I must search ye fer weapons."

Jamie raised his arms. She patted his torso and the sleeves of his jacket, then bent to feel around his waist. She stepped back, satisfied that he carried neither pistols, sword, nor dirk.

She gestured to a grouping of chairs on the stoop. "Please make yourself comfortable. My husband will join you shortly. Ye must excuse me, for I must put my children to bed." She bowed and turned away, her long skirts flaring as she left.

Jamie sank into the chair closest to the lampstand. He did not have to wait long. A silent shadowy figure came around the side of the house and took a seat in a rocker at the edge of the lamplight. He was wearing a broad-brimmed hat that left his face in shadow. The creak of the rocker and an occasional croak from the direction of the boat landing were the only sounds.

At last, a voice spoke from the shadows. "Wha comes seeking me frae the far north? Be ye friend or foe?"

Jamie's breath caught. The speech was obviously Scottish, but the Highland burr was somehow subdued. Perhaps long residence in Yorkshire and the Continent had altered his father's voice. "I am nae foe, sir, fer I came wi'oot weapons. We may be friends o' long association or, perchance, relationship."

The shadowy figure sat forward. "Relationship? Are ye then frae Strathallan?"

Jamie peered intently but could see nothing under the hat except for the man's smooth-shaven chin. An uneasy conviction was growing that this man was not James Drummond, his father. "Aye, I hae dwelt in Strathallan, but that was lang syne. Yer speech marks ye as Scottish and probably Highland, but yer tones dinna reflect an origin in Strathallan or other places in Perthshire."

The response was wary, evasive. "Many years hae past since I was there. Since the bill o' attainder, I canna claim my rightfu' title."

Jamie said musingly, "The man I seek returned tae the Highlands mair than once. When I met him last, there was nae change in his voice. Ye are tall, as is he. He was bearded tae conceal his appearance and tending tae gray, yet ye are smooth-shaven. I misdoubt that ye are the same man. Ye claim that ye are James Drummond, but I am convinced that ye are nae the James Drummond I seek." He stood up.

There was a quick movement in the shadows. He caught the glint of metal and the unmistakably ratcheting sound of a pistol being cocked. Jamie said, "Ye hae the advantage o' me since I came unarmed. Ye masquerade as a banished Jacobite aristocrat. I dinna ken why. Would ye risk hanging by shooting an unarmed man to maintain yer thin disguise?"

The man's voice grew hard. "Sit doon! I canna allow ye tae depart tae tell others, but there is nae harm in revealing mair. Ye are correct. I am nae James Drummond, the rightfu' Earl o' Strathallan. I hae maintained that fiction hereabouts fer fourteen years, but it is nae the name wi' which I was christened. Years hae piled on years since I was an honest man."

Jamie sat. "Wha are ye then?"

The man in the shadows sighed. "I will ne'er reveal my true name. I met the Bonnie Prince that day at Glenfinnan when he stepped ashore. Full o' youthful zeal, I raised my dirk wi' my clansmen as we swore tae follow him. Prestonpans, Edinburgh, Derby then northward, Falkirk, and Culloden—I marched as a common soldier in General James Drummond's command. Wi' luck, I survived tae flee tae the Continent wi' other exiles. Fer three years, I was a mercenary fer the French. In 1749, James Drummond hired me tae courier letters and a vast amount o' money tae the loyal families in the Highlands. Following his instructions and disguised as a Flemish clerk, I took ship frae Antwerp fer Newcastle. When we landed, I succeeded in passing customs but feared that I hae been followed by government agents. Rather than attempt tae proceed north tae Scotland, I came west until I reached Biddick. I met Phineas Fowler at the Coach and Crown, wha introduced me tae John Armstrong. Tae hide frae pursuit, I lodged wi' his family, wha proved sympathetic tae the Jacobite cause, especially his intelligent and beautiful high-spirited daughter Elizabeth."

Jamie interrupted with a sneer, "Sae the innkeeper colluded wi' ye frae the beginning! Yer fear fer yer ain safety, and lust triumphed o'er a commitment tae honor a pledge?"

A low laugh came from the shadowed rocker. "My corruption was gradual, nae immediate. I hid the letters and gold beneath the floorboards, taking only what I needed tae maintain myself. Elizabeth was only thirteen. I was beguiled by her intelligence. We sat up late, discussing high-minded principles."

"Such as integrity?" Jamie goaded.

"Aye, in those days, I had some. I was a fugitive and forced tae deceive others tae protect myself. It took nearly three years for me tae conclude that the cause was lost and that I must see tae myself. The gold that I carried amounted tae nearly a thousand pounds, sufficient for me to buy the favor of Squire Lambton, John Armstrong, and others in return fer protection. Adopting the Drummond name was essential tae the scheme since the local people are loyal Jacobites, albeit a rough and violent lot. They may lack scruples in maist affairs, but they will protect me."

The imposter paused. "And now that I hae revealed myself, ye must do the same."

Jamie laughed. "Must I? Ye realize that I am nae alain in hearing the tale o' James Drummond hiding in Yorkshire. There are others."

"Perhaps, but why would ye risk yerself tae come here?" There was a sharp intake of breath from the shadows. "Ye are a Drummond! The earl spoke o' a son. Ye are the correct age, although I canna see yer features clearly in the lamplight! Sae perchance ye are the heir, thinking tae unmask me tae preserve yer claim tae the title and property!"

Three dark figures emerged from the shadows. The man stood up from the rocker, his pistol unwaveringly pointed at Jamie's midsection. "Ho! My bullyboys are here tae escort ye tae an abandoned pit, which will serve as an excellent bolt-hole. There they will imprison ye until I say otherwise, perhaps ne'er. Ye will surely vanish frae the sight o' men."

A swipe from Jamie's hand sent the lantern flying from the stand. It shattered, plunging the stoop into darkness. Jamie flung himself onto the wooden planks, drew the blade from his boot, and rolled toward the rocker where the false James Drummond stood. The pistol fired with a bright flash and a crack that rattled the windows. The ball plowed splinters from the planks, narrowly missing Jamie's eyes.

Rising, he smashed his left fist into his assailant's face. The man toppled backward with an oath, as Jamie struck with the knife. The blade missed the imposter's vitals but sank deep into his upper arm. A vicious twist, and blood spattered. Spasmodically, the wounded man doubled up and screamed. The pistol flew from his hand and skittered across the boards.

Jamie leaped off the stoop. A shot thudded into a post as he swerved around the corner and raced for the shrubbery behind the house. Running a lurching zigzag pattern, he expected the hot sting from being shot in the back by one of the surprised henchmen before he could reach the concealment of the forest only tantalizing yards away.

"A stupid gullible fool ye are, Jamie Drummond!" he panted, plunging into a hazel thicket. Yells and the baying of dogs excited by the shots resounded behind him. A woman's shrill scream pierced the night. Obviously, the wounded imposter's wife had found him.

Jamie wormed his way through the thicket, ripping his jacket and scratching his face on the thorn-edged foliage. Sweating profusely, although the misty evening was cool, he finally reached the edge of the trees. He pushed aside slick, dew-coated leaves enough to view the path that shone whitely in the moonlight. There was shouting in the distance and torches bobbing toward the mill and boat landing.

He was about to push his way through the last branches to the road when he heard thudding hoofbeats. Two men on horseback charged past. There was now no clear path back to the road. He had assailants ahead on the path as well as behind. He had to follow the path, for he doubted that he could get the horse through the undergrowth to reach the open moorland that lay northward. Perhaps he could in daylight, but not at night.

On all fours, Jamie padded through the inches-deep mulch of the forest floor, moving parallel to the path. A single rider galloped past back toward the mill. Perhaps there was only one sentinel blocking the road, although reinforcements might come soon.

Jamie rose and started down the road, keeping to the verge in case he had to make a sudden dive into the brush. The white slash mark, high up on the tree came into view. He veered onto the path and slowed down to count the paces. When he reached thirty, he stopped and mimicked a birdcall. There was a low whicker from a dark mass of foliage to his left. Moving cautiously, he pulled the branches aside. The mare nuzzled his hand.

Damp with relief, he felt for the bag of apples to reward the horse's patience. He pulled the pistols from their bags, primed them, thrust one into his belt and the other into his jacket. He untied the reins and swung into the saddle. Back on the path, he drew the heavy cavalry saber from its scabbard. Shooting in the wan moonlight on a forest path was so chancy that Jamie decided to trust his life to a blade rather than an uncertain pistol shot.

He walked the mare slowly back to the lane. To the right lay the mill and boat landing and the blocked path to the left. He paused, listening intently for hoofbeats. There were none. His only choice was to force his way past the lone sentinel blocking his return to the road leading to North Biddick and the Yorkshire moorlands.

Suddenly, there were riders coming up the lane from the direction of the mill and boat landing. The net that he hoped to escape was closing! There was no time for any other decision. He swung the horse's head to the left and gigged the mare. Fighting in a score of battles had taught him that bold and swift action was almost always more successful than vacillation and timidity. He urged the horse to a gallop as he headed into a shadowed stretch between trees where the moonlight did not penetrate.

There was a chance that the sentinel ahead of him would be indecisive, uncertain of his identity in the darkness and unlikely to risk a shot. If he was wrong or there was more than a single rider ahead, he would die. A hundred yards away, a blurry shadow moved. The sentinel sat his horse in the center of the narrow lane and shouted a challenge, but his voice was drowned by the mare's drumming hoofbeats.

The fingers of Jamie's left hand gripped the underside of the pommel tightly as he flung his body to the right until he was riding perpendicular to the saddle. There was a flash and the *boom!* of a pistol shot. The ball whirred harmlessly, and the mare reared, pawing the air. Jamie had just enough time to jerk his body upright before the two horses collided. He swung the saber in a scything motion that swept the opposing rider from his seat as neatly as if he had ridden under a low-hanging bough. The body thumped to the ground, and the riderless horse sprang free. There was an awkward lurch as the mare leaped forward, almost unhorsing him.

The hoofbeats were louder, and the pursuing riders began yelling as Jamie pushed the mare to a reckless speed. Another quarter mile and the mare galloped clear of the trees, up a short incline, and onto the cobbles of the bridge, sparks flying from her iron-shod hooves. A sharp tug of the reins and she veered left. The hour was late, and there was no traffic. As he rode down into North Biddick, Jamie chanced a look back. Six or more riders were pursuing him. Mercifully, the village was small and the high street straight. He was soon back on hard-packed dirt, riding directly northward along Biddick Lane.

Jamie had studied a map of the unfamiliar area during the day. He knew that a few more miles would bring him to the bridge over the Tyne and the outskirts of the city of Newcastle. He had no concern about his pursuers enlisting the resources of a local undersheriff, for he would be long gone before they could muster reinforcements. All that mattered was whether the mare could outrun the pursuit. While he hoped that those following him, being local men, would give up the chase before they reached the river, he did not know the stamina of the mare.

Another glance behind revealed two riders keeping pace. The others had fallen well back. The mare galloped through a sleeping hamlet where a venturous dog rushed barking into the street, only to retreat ki-yiing from her flashing hooves.

As he neared the bridge over the Tyne, Jamie saw that the approach was well-lit and the toll barrier down. Jamie steered the mare onto a road that ran westward along the bank of the river. The signposts were invisible in the darkness, but he knew that this had to be the road that wound along the river and onto the high moors until it came to Hexham, where a ruined Roman fort brooded over the town.

The map had shown a bridge where he could cross the shrinking Ware. If it was blocked, he would swim the horse across and take the ancient road that ran westward to Carlisle. A better course of action, he concluded, would be to leave the road and head directly north across open country, where there were no towns until after he crossed the border into Scotland. This was all reiver country, where even now constables and the law had little hold, where he could hide in a deep glen until the pursuit abandoned the chase. After a decent rest for himself and the gallant mare, he could wend his way down to Jedburgh or Hawick. He chuckled at the irony, for it was at Hawick seven years before that thieftakers had caught him, chained him to the Mercat Cross, and turned him over to the tender mercies of Captain Ian Hamilton.

The mare clattered through Hexham, where Jamie found the stone bridge across the Tyne without a tollgate. The lead pursuit riders were not in sight, so he stopped briefly to water the horse and allow her to eat some oats. Remounting, he held her speed down to a canter to conserve her strength. The countryside opened up to stunning vistas of wide moors, with no trees anywhere, except in low burns and swales. He was utterly alone in the late night, with no other light but the setting moon.

At dawn, he rode through the hamlet of Byrness, encountering shepherds gigging their flock across the road. Jamie, anxious about pursuit, refused to wait for their passing, for hundreds of animals crowded the road. He veered across country to where the shepherds told him he would regain the winding road.

A signpost marked the border of Scotland. Just beyond, he came to a fork where one road led down to Jedburgh and the other westward to Hawick. Hoping to confuse the pursuing riders, he took to the moor for a mile before reentering the road to Hawick.

The mare was flagging badly when Jamie reached Jed Water. Her nostrils were encrusted with dried foam and blood. She was panting raggedly, close to foundering. He gave her fifteen minutes of rest, all he dared allow as he looked back for the pursuers. The landscape was uniformly bleak, with no sign of any place where he and the horse could safely go to ground. His only hope of escape was to remount and trot onward.

Two hours passed. The mare was so exhausted that she was stumbling. Jamie dismounted to give her some relief, running alongside and murmuring encouragement. The road tipped downward to cross a chuckling burn. The steeple of Hawick Kirk had just come into view when Jamie heard the sounds of pursuit—hooves thudding on the dirt track. A despairing glance backward confirmed it; two riders crested a rise behind him. Hastily, Jamie remounted. Perhaps he would be safe in the town coming to life ahead of him.

The mare had incredible heart, but she was near the end of her strength. Jamie guided her downhill to where the road met the Teviot and then turned toward town, the church steeple serving as his compass. Every backward glance confirmed that the pursuer's mounts were stronger, for they ate up the gap at a tremendous rate. Jamie rode into the town square, marked by a ten-foot-tall wooden Mercat Cross. On one side of the square sat a stone watering trough. Jamie allowed the mare to drop her head, whuffling her nostrils as she plunged into the cold water. The admission was painful. He was trapped. The horse could go no further. Jamie had decided to dismount to find shelter in one of the shops lining the square when two horses bearing begrimed riders trotted into view.

They stopped and sat silently, yards from Jamie, while their sweat-streaked horses panted. Townspeople sensed the danger and moved silently out of the way. Jamie's spirits sank, for there was no escape. He had to fight against unfair odds. During his ride, Jamie had sheathed his saber. Now he drew it. His pursuers did the same. The older of the two men smirked as he raised his weapon in a mocking salute before wheeling his mount to attack Jamie's right side. The other rider moved to his left to attack from the opposite direction.

Exhausted as she was, the mare was still responsive to her rider's knees and pressure on the bridle. Jamie pulled her in a tight circle, during which he pulled the pistol from his belt with his left hand and cocked it. As the horse came out of the circle, the barrel of the weapon swung laterally toward the rightmost rider, now only yards away with sword upraised.

In spite of his exhaustion, Jamie's hand was steady. The sixteen-inch barrel of the elegant Queen Anne pistol hovered on the rider's torso. He squeezed the trigger. The crash of the shot echoed in the small square. The heavy shot, larger than the barrel, moved up the tapered breech, which compressed the ball as it moved forward at the moment of firing to tightly fit the bore. High gas pressure drove the round out of the sixteen inch barrel, which pointed directly at the center of the rider's torso.

The rider jerked convulsively backward. He staggered in the saddle and looked down at his right shoulder incredulously. Bright blood was bubbling through the rip in his jerkin where the ball had entered to smash through flesh and shatter the bones. He turned his gaze on Jamie, and his mouth worked spasmodically. Blood poured from the wound. The rider lost his grip on the reins and slid from the saddle as he lost consciousness, his knees collapsing as his body hit the ground. The sword fell from his fingers, clattering on the pavement stones.

Jamie thrust the smoking pistol into his jacket and drew the second, cocking and aiming in one motion. The younger pursuer gaped at the gun as the barrel swung toward him. He hastily dropped his blade, signaling defeat. He dismounted and ran to aid his companion.

A gray-haired jowly man wearing a leather apron approached Jamie. "I dinna ken yer disagreement wi' these men, but if ye value freedom, young sir, ye should get ye gone and swiftly. We hae nae constable here in Hawick, but Squire Guthrie will hae heard the shot and will be here shortly wi' his men. He hae the force o' law hereabouts."

Jamie touched the brim of his hat and nodded. "My horse in spent, but I will gang hence. These twa scoundrels chased me frae south o' Newcastle all nicht lang fer nae fault o' mine, fer I refused tae become their prisoner. Do wi' these ruffians as ye will. I wish ye a guid morning."

He turned away, stopping at the edge of the square to purchase a sack of bannocks and a jug of cider before riding out of town, never once looking back. He steered the stumbling horse at a gentle walk into the trees on the far side of Ashkirk Loch, where he found a deep glen.

He unsaddled the horse and tethered her, although in her exhaustion he had no fear that she would wander. He fed her the rest of the oats, watered her, and settled back against the saddle to munch the currant-and sultana-stuffed bannocks and swig cider. He forced himself to stay awake long enough to clean his pistol, recharge, and prime it. There was no guarantee that he was quit of his pursuers.

He slept undisturbed and woke as the sun sank low in the sky. The mare had pulled her tether loose but had not wandered. She was nuzzling his unshaven cheek. Stretching and yawning hugely, Jamie finished the now-stiff pastries and drank his fill of water, for the strong cider had left his head muzzy. As the sky darkened, he lay reflecting on his visit to South Biddick and how closely he had come to becoming a prisoner of the false James Drummond and his gang of ruffians. He shivered, not entirely from the cold wind that swept the moors and stirred the long grass. He had been warned in a dream and had heedlessly persisted, compelled to solve the mystery of the tale of his father's infidelity. He had narrowly escaped being imprisoned in a dank coal pit, perhaps to waste away long years, with his family ignorant of his fate.

Aye, he thought ruefully, *I owe my freedom tae that dream o' the little people and the courage o' this horse. Unco strange are the twists o' fortune. I am nae such a rational person after all.* He sat wrapped in reminiscence until after the sun sank in red-tinged splendor behind clouds and the stars came out.

After two nights of sleep but little food, Jamie slowly rode the limping mare the remaining miles to Selkirk. His first task was at a farrier's, where he paid well to have the mare reshod and her hooves pared. The second was to eat his fill at a tavern. The third was to find a scrivener so he could pen and post a letter to the stable owner in Sunderland, apologizing for not returning the mare and asking the price at which he could buy her. The two had been through a great trial together that formed a bond that he had no desire to break.

12

The cold seemed to intensify in the pines soughing in the stiffening wind. The sky was leaden in the fading blue light of evening as the riders slowly picked their way down the steep snow-covered trail. Except for the breathing of their tired mounts, all was silent. Jamie and David Gordon had left that morning under a blue sky to revisit the glens around Ben Macdui, the site of their summer raid on the reivers to verify that no other thieves were preying on their cattle and herds of sheep. The cattle pens were sagging, their flimsy wattle and wood decaying; the croft empty and shuttered. There were no signs of human activity in the camps or on the tortuous trails that wound between the glens and glacks of the high country.

During the afternoon, fleecy clouds had been succeeded by a uniform gray sheet that crept eastward. Mist billowed through the glens. Trees and boulders faded from sight. Snowflakes swirled and settled. Realizing the danger of being trapped by a snowstorm, the riders turned their horses' heads down the trail toward the old military road that ran between Abergeldie and Braemar.

The snowfall grew and began to stick as the short afternoon wore away. The riders did not panic; both were experienced and well-equipped. The horses were recently shod and sure-footed. David broke the silence. "The English mare hae ta'en tae the Highlands as if she was bred hereaboots."

Jamie tweaked the horse's ears affectionately. "Aye. I was pleased that her owner was agreeable tae selling her fer a fair price. Ye will care fer her, Davey, while I am awa'?"

His cousin turned in the saddle to regard him. "Ye are determined tae make the journey in spite o' yer mama's and my father's objections?"

Jamie heaved a great sigh. "When will they realize that we are grown men, used tae danger, wha hae survived a great war wi' their prayers fer our safety, but capable o' making responsible decisions and taking care fer our ain affairs?"

David grinned. "Perhaps ne'er. My ain mama tries tae avoid being domineering, but as lang as I live at Abergeldie, it will be difficult."

Jamie shifted uneasily, the saddle creaking in the pervasive silence. "Aye, my mama persists in reminding me that my venture into Yorkshire was dangerous. At least three times a day, she says, 'Jamie, ye could hae been killed!' She forgets that in seven years o' war, I was in mortal danger mair times than I can count. I acknowledge that seeking the answer tae the mystery o' my father's whereaboots was hazardous, but it was a mystery that needed solving. I am angry wi' my father fer his decision tae honor a vow tae a feckless prince, wha is now probably lying drunk in Rome wi' his Polish mistress while loyal and brave men languish in exile. I couldna bear my father betraying my mama by living a dissolute lie, siring children wi' another woman. My father fulfilled his oath, an honorable, although ultimately costly decision. It cost him and us mightily, but he was ne'er disloyal tae my mama. Fer that, I honor him."

David broke in. "The reports are that he is broken in health and may nae survive his sickness. Will ye hazard yer inheritance tae visit him?"

Jamie's face hardened. "Aye, a hundred times aye, in spite o' advice frae every direction. My mama, Uncle Charles, Peter, Cousin Hugh all counsel nae, fer the government could discover that I hae been visiting the refuge o' Jacobite rebellion in Sens. David! The rebellion is o'er. Sens is where auld rebels hae gathered tae reminisce o' their brave deeds that came tae naught, take solace frae each other, and grieving, die far frae hame and loved ones. I am a loyal son and love my father in spite o' his deeds. I will be circumspect, but in spite o' the risks, I will gae tae see him, perhaps fer the final time. Do ye also advise against it?"

David's face softened. "Nae, Jamie. We lived through those joyous and then dreadfu' times together. The blood is still strang. I ken that the advice ye hae received is weel-intended, but dinna place a high enough value on loyalty tae kith and kin and auld loyalties. I feel it in ye and admire ye fer it. Ye must gae, but gang warily. Nae everyone ye meet values that quality."

Euphemia Drummond relented and embraced her son with a full heart but with her eyes brimming. Meg, Elizabeth Marie, and wee Jock were of a different mood and joyfully endorsed their brother's journey, pressing letters and small portraits on him to present to their father. Charles Gordon recognized the inevitability of the trip and took it with grace. However, he also took Jamie aside to advise caution through the use of disguises and assumed names and travel by circuitous routes to avoid being followed. Jamie quietly agreed, recognizing his uncle's concern for his safety and inheritance. In parting, Charles once again urged Jamie to consider an arranged marriage with the Gordon heiress, who was being courted by two other swains but still available. Jamie struggled to keep a grimace off his face, reaffirming his determination to seek his fortune by other means.

The sea crossing from Aberdeen to Rotterdam was rough, for it was the onset of winter. Crew and passengers on the small merchant ship endured several gale-force blows during the ten-day passage, which was lengthened by being forced to backtrack. The storms had blown the ship well eastward along the flat and sandy Dutch coast to find the narrow channel that led upstream to the seaport.

A population of forty thousand called Rotterdam home. The port city had been inhabited since Roman times and grew along the Meuse river into the most important trading and shipping center in northern Europe. Renowned as the home base of the Dutch East India Company, the city enjoyed an enormous advantage through the trade with that far-flung colony, with Dutch ships dominating the Moluccan spice trade with Europe. Vast warehouses lined the waterfront, where dozens of deep-draft vessels docked alongside dozens more coastal luggers supporting trade along the North Sea and Baltic coasts.

Jamie was apprehensive about border security in a foreign land, but his fears were quickly dismissed. The Dutch government welcomed visitors of clearly aristocratic origins with full purses. The officials asked few questions, stamped his paperwork, and passed him and his luggage through customs control with an affable wave. He found money exchange an easy but expensive process. A friendly Dutch fellow passenger guided him around the clots of noisy locals pestering travelers with offers of transport, lodging, entertainment, and food to a stolid establishment in Vlaardingen that catered to British travelers. Jamie rewarded the man with an invitation to join him for dinner before he departed for his home in Charlois.

On the ship south, Jamie had determined that he could most easily escape detection by crossing the border into France far to the south. It took two days to arrange travel by coach and then riverboat for distant Basel on the Rhine at the border between France, the duchy of Baden-Württemberg and the Swiss Confederation. There were few sights to be seen, for the flat, rainy landscape was uniformly uninteresting and officious guards at the numerous border crossings rude. He did take the time to view the mighty cathedral in Cologne, the medieval city of Strasbourg, and the remnants of castles along the Rhine. Conversations with fellow travelers were amiable and conducted in French, for his Highland accent made discourse difficult with those whose native language was not English.

The journey up the Rhine required a week, with teams of draft horses hauling the flat-bottomed river craft against the current. Although the late autumn days were short, the plodding teams made good time. The rain stopped as the riverboat passed Karlsruhe and skirted the thickly wooded hills of the Black Forest. Passengers flocked on deck in spite of the cold to exclaim over the brooding ruins of castles destroyed by invaders during the Thirty Years' War a century and a half before.

Shortly before they docked in Basel, Jamie listened while a passenger regaled him with the history of the origins of Basel. He listened with half an ear to stories of Celts, Romans, Germanic tribes, and Magyars building, destroying, and rebuilding the old city, followed by religious conflict. What whetted his interest was a story about Joachim Meyer, who had written the influential sixteenth-century text *Kunst des Fechten* or *Art of Fencing*.

Debarking in Basel, Jamie spent the day arranging a coach trip to the French border and onward to Dijon, where he could obtain a coach to Sens, for it lay on the major route north to Paris. Jamie had thought about his uncle's advice about disguises and assumed names, but the penalty for being caught as an imposter by foreign authorities and his reasonable fears of imprisonment dissuaded him.

At the border, the guards ushered the passengers into a comfortable parlor to present their papers. There was no rush, no queue, but genteel service of tea and pastries, for the passengers were all well-dressed and aristocratic.

Jamie passed his papers to the commandant, who addressed him in clipped, only slightly-accented English. That official smiled when Jamie replied in French, but returned to English.

"What is your destination and purpose in visiting France?"

Jamie had decided to use his real name and hope that he would not draw unusual attention on this unorthodox route into the center of France. He said, "I am traveling tae Sens, where my father took up residence wi' other Scottish expatriates."

The official scribbled some notes and looked up. "My government no longer supports the ambitions of the exiled dynasty, but our countries have had a long alliance. It is a pity that it came to naught. Your command of French is excellent, monsieur. Perfectly understandable Parisian. Have you spent much time in France?"

Jamie bowed slightly. "You are kind. I learned the language as a schoolboy and have spent only a few days in your country."

The official asked, "Only a few days? I must ask you where, for your papers show no such visit."

Jamie fidgeted, reluctant to extend the conversation. He said, "There was nae passport control on Belle Isle. The accommodations were terrible. Although the populace was friendly, the French soldiers were inhospitable."

The official grinned. "I understand. I was also in the war and spent time engaging with your countrymen at Louisburg, who afforded me free transportation to a prison. Luckily, I was repatriated early and ended my service safely."

Jamie nodded and closed his eyes. "I was there as weel, wi' the attacking force besieging the citadel."

The official stamped Jamie's papers and held them out. There was no rancor in his eyes. "We were soldiers, monsieur, enemies and allies at different times. We did what was required for honor's sake. I welcome you to France, but not all of my countrymen are so generous or understanding. You must be discreet about your past and reasons for being here."

Jamie said, "Should I use French and avoid English?"

The official shook his head and laughed. "Probably for my people's sake, for your English is so abominable that everyone will immediately recognize you as Scottish. Now I understand that you are traveling to Sens and, when you are finished, to visit

Paris. It is my home and the greatest city in the world. You will have a wonderful visit."

Jamie was surprised to find Dijon, traditional home of the Dukes of Burgundy, jammed with visitors. Finding a room at an inn took several hours, for the city was hosting a popular fair devoted to food and wine. Finding restaurants and taverns jammed, he satisfied his appetite while wandering the fair, sampling grilled meats, cheeses, bread, and wine from the stalls.

Beaune and Avallon slipped away as the coach rattled and jounced northwestward on the muddy roads. Jamie had heard that European roads were superior to those of such a poor country as Scotland but found the truth far different. He was convinced that coaches lacked adequate cushioning and that all roads were designed to rattle the teeth and loosen bones in their sockets.

The coach lost an axle, shattered by a jarring drop into a deep water-filled rut. The driver and passengers cursed volubly, but the delay could not be helped. The prediction of a two-day wait for a replacement was too much for Jamie, who shouldered his bag and stolidly plodded six miles in the muck to Auxerre. He rented a horse from the first stable he passed. Armed with directions to Sens, he set out. The weather did not cooperate, with wind and rain driven by a persistent westerly wind. It took Jamie two more days to cover the fifty miles to Sens, where he stopped by the city's southern gate to scrape the thick mud from the exhausted horse's hooves.

Sens was a city of modest size, lying on the eastern bank of the lead-colored Yonne. The city bore a somber appearance under the darkening sky of late afternoon. Jamie guided the horse along the Quay, heading for the spire of the Cathédrale Saint-Étienne. He knew from his father's last letter to Abergeldie that he was rooming with Madame Hilbert, along with several other expatriate Scots. She lived in the mansion on Rue de l'Épée and let rooms in a massive apartment building that backed onto thick woods that fringed the city wall.

He saw no sign for Rue de l'Épée and stopped where a boat-shaped islet split the river to ask directions to Madame Hilbert's residence from a man fishing from the embankment.

"Bonjour, messieur. Pouvez-vous me diriger vers la résidence de Madame de Hilbert. Elle vit sur la rue de l'Épée et permet de chambres."

The man pointed and said, "Certainement et bienvenue à Sens, monsieur. Le chemin le plus facile à la maison de la bonne madame est d'aller à mi-hauteur du quai, là-bas et tourner à droite. A la rue, tournez à droite et la maison est sur la droite. Directions simples, droit , à droite, et de droite."

Smiling, Jamie tossed him a coin. The man grinned toothily and caught it in midair. As he turned away, he said, "Merci, jeune homme. Cependant, Mme Hilbert loue seulement aux vieillards, et non les jeunes dames de la ville que vous devriez être à la recherche."

Jamie chuckled, for the fisherman had wondered why he was looking for Madam Hilbert, who only rented to old men, and not ladies. The directions were simple and clear enough, halfway up the quay, followed by three right turns would bring him to the house he was seeking.

Repeated knocking finally brought a man servant in green livery. Through the half-open door, the man stolidly listened as Jamie asked for James Drummond and then shut the door. Minutes passed before it reopened to reveal a tiny white-haired woman dressed entirely in black. The man servant spoke in heavily accented English. "Madam Hilbert vishes you to join her for tea and to explain your business. Please come to her parlor."

Jamie took a seat facing his hostess, warmed by a crackling fire. A maid placed tea, cream, sugar, and a plate of cakes on the table between them. Silence hung heavy in the small room decorated with ornate furniture and paintings of rural scenes. The scent of lavender was pervasive in the room. Madame Hilbert stared over the gilt-trimmed rim of her porcelain cup, her black eyes, under white wrinkled brows expressionless.

Suddenly, she spoke in perfectly clear Scots. "My man servant tells me that ye are here tae find a James Drummond. I dinna hae any guest in my lodgings wi' that name. I hae been letting rooms tae Scottish gentlemen fer o'er thirty years and doubt that a man wi' that name hae e'er lived in Sens."

Jamie was taken aback until he remembered that his father often went by the alias of James Williamson, a patronymic name form, for he was James the son of William Drummond.

Cautiously, he said, "Madam Hilbert, hae ye e'er met a James Williamson wha came tae Sens frae Antwerp some years past?" He watched the woman's withered face closely for a reaction.

She kept her face impassive and responded with another question. "Why would ye believe that such a man lives at my lodgings?" Jamie wordlessly passed her the envelope from his father's last letter, which clearly bore Madame Hilbert's address.

She took out a pair of small wire-rimmed spectacles and examined the paper. She sighed and passed it back to Jamie. "Ye must understand that the Scottish men wha live in these lodgings are here and nae at hame because o' their past deeds and the implacable hatred o' the British government, which continues tae spy on them. These unfortunates hae few loyal friends and many enemies. They deserve what sma' measure o' security that I can provide. If James Williamson, as he chooses tae be called, is yer father, then I bid ye welcome. The light in this room is nae the best, but I can see some resemblance in the face in spite o' the years betwixt ye." She leaned forward and took one of Jamie's hands. Hers were gnarled and spotted but smooth and warm. Her voice was tense and high-pitched.

"It is guid that ye are here. Ye may hae little time, fer he is weak and in low spirits. The physicians despair o' improvement."

Ice gripped Jamie's heart. He inquired, "Is he then bedridden?"

Madam Hilbert shook her head. "He is nae an invalid but is sae weak that he canna leave his rooms. He is pale and thin beyond measure and finds it difficult tae eat."

The same man servant who had taken him to Madame Hilbert's parlor escorted him along a winding path to the two-story apartment block that lay on the fringe of the forest. The leafless trees and piles of drifted yellow and brown leaves multiplied Jamie's sense of foreboding.

In response to the servant's knock, a faint voice invited them to enter. The sitting room was cluttered with books and papers, and the door to the bedroom stood open. The bed was empty. James Drummond sat barefooted and unshaven in a rocker, bundled in a dark brown robe, his graying hair tousled. He turned his head slowly as Jamie strode through the door.

Surprise and wonder were in his whispery voice. "Ach, Jamie! I dinna expect tae e'er see ye again, son!"

Jamie knelt to embrace his father as the servant discreetly withdrew. Many minutes passed before tumultuous emotions were spent and father and son could speak.

James Drummond wiped his eyes and ran fingers through his disheveled hair and beard. "Ye find me in parlous circumstances, son. Ye are a fit and noble figure, the essence o' manhood itself. I wish I could hae seen ye in uniform. Can ye e'er forgive a foolhardy father, fer it was my zeal fer the Jacobites that brought ye into great danger? I couldna hae been prouder o' yer service fer ye o'ercame a'. I am unco pleased that I could see ye before I die."

Jamie nodded and embraced his father once again. "Papa, there is naething tae forgive, fer I took the letters o' my ain choice as a final favor tae Andy Hay. I will hear nae speech aboot dyin'. We will hae much time tae recount our histories, fer I intend tae remain until ye are healed o' this affliction."

James's face hardened. "I would say the same encouraging words in yer place, son, but the best physicians hae assured me that they hae done all that they can. I still weaken, grow thinner, and fall victim tae sweats and fevers repeatedly. Nae, I hae suffered much grief since the failed rising and my exile frae friends and family. I ken that it is the fate o' those attainted tae suffer in body and spirit and then die at an untimely age."

Jamie rose and sat facing his father. "Tae pine and grieve shortens life, Papa. As lang as life persists, there is hope. Ye hae a faithful wife and four children wha hae nae lost faith in ye. The cause fer which ye fought and sacrificed hae been lost, and naething will bring it back, but ye are our papa, and we will ne'er abandon ye."

Evening came on, and Jamie lit the candles. The liveried man servant, who at last introduced himself as Jacques, announced dinner. Against his father's objections, Jamie accepted, helped him dress, and led him at a slow shuffle to the refectory. They joined a dozen other roomers, mostly expatriate Scots, who greeted James Drummond warmly, for it had been many days since he had eaten with them.

After the evening meal, his father was exhausted by his exertions. Jamie put him to bed and walked to the stables to look in on his rented horse. He reflected ruefully as the gelding nuzzled him. "Aye, I am a great fool and love the companionship o' horses. Fer sairtain, I will spend o'ermuch fer yer services while I am here." The horse nickered agreement and ducked his head into the bag of oats that Jamie had filled for him.

Madame Hilbert provided a two-room suite with a fireplace. Jamie settled down to write a letter to his mother recounting his journey and the low state in which he had found his father but fell asleep before he finished. Military service had inured him to short sleep. He woke before dawn, walked to the stables, and surprised the young groom, who hastily saddled the gelding.

The weather was still gloomy, with dark clouds obscuring the sky, but the weather was dry enough for a ride along the river to the north end of the city and through the impromptu farmer's market assembling on the square. He stopped to purchase a wheel of local cheese, two dozen eggs, and a lean piece of smoky bacon, which he contributed to the cook with the stipulation that a fine omelet would make an excellent breakfast for Jamie's father.

Over the course of the next week, Jamie made a series of discoveries about his father. The first was that he was gripped in a baffling depression that sapped his appetite, distanced him from old friends, and left him withdrawn and bitter. The second was that he had placed himself under the care of a physician who other Scots roomers described as a "bit o' a seer" who consulted an astrologer and spiritualist. Etienne Fouche was a tall graybeard who prescribed bloodletting for every ailment. While Jamie snorted at this practice, it was uncommonly popular in Great Britain as well as in every country on the Continent. Fouche also prescribed soaking sweats, fasting, and sitting in a darkened overheated room for hours on end.

Jamie returned from his ride to find his father listless in a chair while blood dripped from a wound in his lower arm into a white basin. Dr. Fouche was sitting in a chair, writing notes in a bound journal. Hearing the jingling of spurs, he looked up at Jamie.

Forgetting to speak in French, Jamie shouted, "Here, sir! What are ye aboot wi' my father? Wha authorized ye tae let blood? I left instructions that he would hae nae mair o' that pernicious practice!"

Fouche put down his quill and rose. "This man is my patient, sir. May I inquire of your interest in him?"

Jamie said, "Aye, he is my father and near death frae weakness. How much blood hae ye taken frae his body?"

The doctor sneered. "For phlebotomy to be effective, it must be copious. I am the authority in this matter."

Jamie seized the journal and opened it, fending off the doctor's clutching hands. "I must protest this intrusion. You have no right to read my notes. Give them to me."

Jamie put out a hand and shoved the doctor, who abruptly sat down. He opened his mouth to speak, but one look at Jamie's thunderous face deterred him. His mouth closed with a snap.

Jamie read out loud from the journal, translating the French into English. "On October fifteenth, I immediately bled him o' twenty ounces tae prevent inflammation. October sixteenth, in the morning, he was bled another twenty-four ounces. Early the next morning, the seventeenth, I bled the patient another ten ounces. During the next fourteen hours, I bled him five mair times. I was forced tae intentionally remove mair than half the patient's normal blood supply tae alleviate the symptoms of lassitude and weakness. Bleedings continued o'er the next several days. On the first day of November, I applied thirty-twa leeches tae the abdomen and lower legs, yet the weakness and lassitude returned."

He turned more pages. "O'er the next month, conducted mair bleedings, applying six leeches, then eight, and at last twenty leeches. Then ye hae the temerity tae make this entry: by the large quantity of blood lost, amounting tae one hundred and seventy ounces, besides that drawn by application o' leeches amounting tae at least thirty-twa ounces, the health o' the patient was improved."

Jamie flung the journal across the room, where it slid under the sofa. He towered over the physician. "Ye withdrew nearly fifteen pints o' blood and imposed a regimen o' fasting and sweats? How many men hae ye killed in this manner? Is there any doubt that my father is sae weak and listless solely because o' such practices? A pox on yer pernicious methods, sir! Ye are surely condemning him tae an early death! Did muttering spirits and astrologers convince ye tae take such measures tae destroy him?"

Fouche struggled out of the chair, his face a mask of fear, and began gathering his tools with shaking hands. Jamie hovered over him, grating, "Get ye gone, ye fraud. I hae a mind tae impose my ain form o' bloodletting on ye wi' a rapier in yer innards!"

In his towering rage, Jamie had forgotten that others were surely hearing his shouts. Fouche pushed through a growing crowd at the door who called questions in Scots and French as he stumbled down the stairs. Jamie ignored the questioning crowd. He gently withdrew the lancet from his father's arm and pressed a cloth against the flesh to stop the bleeding.

Madame Hilbert arrived to argue vehemently that Fouche was well-respected in the town and not a barber who let blood indiscriminately. Jamie listened respectfully but insisted on implementing the regimen he had seen practiced by James Lind at Haslar Hospital. He oversaw a thorough cleaning of his father's rooms and ordered daily changes of bed linen, frequent bathing, fresh air, and nourishing food.

He found a craftsman in town who constructed a wheeled chair. As James Drummond slowly recovered, Jamie bundled him in warm blankets for a daily push around the parkland behind Madame Hilbert's property. Within a month, his father was walking on his own with the use of a pair of canes and gradually extending the length of his exercise. At last, the day came on which he confidently laid the canes aside, accepting no more than his son's arm.

Most importantly, James Drummond's recovery to health was the product of lively sociability. Jamie drew his father into dinner discussions with Madame Hilbert's other roomers, most of whom were Jacobite veterans of long acquaintance. While nostalgia for the events of the lost cause brought depression to the fore, Jamie guided the older men away from their sense of loss to joyful remembrances of marches, battles, songs, and the camaraderie that they had shared with their comrades.

One evening, James Drummond was in a particularly pleasant mood after dinner. They lingered at table as he recounted amusing tales of the march the Jacobite army had made through northern England to Derby. Afterward, the men drifted away to their rooms, but James was still wide-awake. Jamie rose to add a log to the fire. As it blazed up, father and son sat reminiscing of bygone days in Strathallan, cracking walnuts, nibbling crumbly Langres cheese, and sipping the burgundy thoughtfully provided by Madame Hilbert's servant.

James stroked his beard, his eyes crinkling in a smile. "Aye, lad. Life was guid until that day we rode tae Crieff, where we made the commitment tae follow the Bonnie Prince." His smile vanished, replaced by such a look of remorse that Jamie thought that his father would weep. "If I could spend but a single year wi' yer dear mother and the children, I would forfeit all the rest of the years that God hae planned fer me."

Jamie put down his glass. "Papa, ye will soon be fit tae travel. Perhaps, the new year will bring an opportunity fer a tryst at the auld place near Aberdeen."

His father stretched out his long legs. "Aye, perhaps. I still hae friends in the Highlands wha will help me maintain my disguise as James Williamson. I am feeling the effects of my age, son, but thanks tae yer ministrations, I am faring better than I hae any right tae expect." He looked at his son earnestly. "Ye are a man now, Jamie lad, and able tae understand the loneliness o' the solitary life. I must tell ye that I hae e'er been faithful tae yer mama, although it was unco difficult at times."

Jamie gripped his father's arm. "Then ye must listen tae the tale brought tae me and Peter by cousin Hugh. It infected my thinking and obsessed my spirits fer several years, fer Hugh hired a detective tae follow a man wha claimed he was ye. Hugh heard that ye hae taken up wi' a Yorkshire lass, married her, and sired her bairns." Swiftly, Jamie told his father the story of Elizabeth Armstrong, the pitman's daughter, and the man who had masqueraded as James Drummond.

James sat back and did not speak for several minutes. "That explains wha happened tae the courier wha disappeared lang syne wi' the money and letters."

Jamie teased his father. "Papa, ye must be mair careful entrusting clandestine missions tae untrustworthy characters."

James grimaced. "I hae been, excepting twa occasions. In ye ain case, ye were betrayed by a chance conversation overheard by a government agent, which led ye tae Carlisle and Newgate, pressed service fer transporting letters and a lang imprisonment fer the bookseller. I am truly sorry fer that mistake, but ye rose by yer wits and uncommon courage, laddie. Ye canna imagine how my heart swelled tae hear o' yer exploits. Ye are a warrior fit tae stand wi' those o' auld times. The other occasion was tae entrust a large sum o' money tae a man wha hae proven himself faithful yet became a scoundrel when the opportunity tae take advantage arose. Many families were harmed by his actions."

Jamie smiled thinly. "It would be a simple matter tae exact revenge."

His father nodded. "Aye, a single stroke would send him tae a deserved perdition." He sighed. "Nae, wi' help frae certain parties, I hae lang since made good the shortage. My zeal fer the cause hae been burnt tae ashes, and I hae nae desire fer revenge. He deserves retribution but canna be brought tae justice. There is nae court on earth wi' authority tae lawfully convict him. I would rather that man spend a lifetime dreading every nightfall, the sound of hooves in the darkness, and creak of the floorboards. I wish him tae cringe at the appearance o' every stranger, fearing the sudden slash o' a blade across his miserable gullet. Aye, he deserves nae less."

Jamie persisted. "Will ye no tell me his name? I could easily find him again. His plan was tae confine me in a mining pit, perhaps fer eternity. It took much tae escape the claws o' his henchmen. I could introduce him tae the bite o' cold steel wi' nae blot on my conscience."

His father smiled and cuffed him gently. "Let it pass, Jamie lad. I dinna wish tae hear o' a man dying tae erase a single blot on my already besmirched reputation or ye risking yerself on such a mission."

An early spring succeeded a mild winter, with green shoots poking forth, crocuses blooming, and scant traces of dirty snow disappearing from shaded hollows. James Drummond, with a bounce in his stride, accompanied Jamie on long walks in the countryside around Sens. It was not long before they were in the saddle, cantering across the rolling hills that lay between Sens and the great Palace of Fontainbleau. Jamie's confidence in his father's recovery soared, although he still received sour glances from barbers and physicians on every journey into town.

As James recovered, Madame Hilbert began to invite the former Jacobite general and his son to late afternoon tea in her suite. Surrounded by exquisite paintings and tasteful appointments, Jamie found the previously taciturn widow in somber black and gray charming and talkative. He had been mystified since his arrival by the old woman's fluency in Scots until his father revealed the key to the puzzle.

While most of Madame Hilbert's paintings were of flowered gardens and landscape, a large portrait hung facing the sofa. A military officer stared out in stolid rectitude, dressed in a dark blue coat with white facings and frothy lace cuffs. When they were alone, he asked his father the identity of the soldier. James smiled.

"I remember him weel. Although he was far older than I, he was uncommonly brave. Let me begin by describing Genevieve Hilbert. Fifty years ago, as a dazzling young beauty from Sens, she had gone to Paris to serve the queen. While there, she attracted the attention of a dashing young officer of the renowned Garde Écossaise, composed of Scottish soldiers in the service of the French king since the thirteenth century. Angus McLeod had been banished from his homeland after the failed Jacobite rising of 1715. He had risen rapidly and became a captain of one of the four companies of mostly Scottish soldiers. They married, and the couple lived in Paris for many years, happy in the Scottish enclave. The only blot on their happiness was a lack of children."

James stared into the fire, lost in reverie. Jamie waited until his father resumed his tale. "In 1745, the aged soldier left his wife to return tae Scotland with his troops under the leadership o' yer Uncle John tae fight fer the Bonnie Prince and to restore the rightfu' king. Angus fell during the charge that routed the government forces during a wild storm at Falkirk. His soldiers laid him in a hasty grave before retreating northward tae the Highlands, where we met crushing defeat at Culloden and the end o' a' our hopes. Genevieve McLeod received the sad news wi' the reaction expected o' a widow. She put off her gay clothing, donned black, and scarcely spoke fer months. She ignored the traditional end of mourning after one year and refused to put off the black. When her parents died, tae inherit the house, she restored her maiden name. She returned to Sens and took up managing this large rooming house for exiled Scottish officers behind her family's ancestral home. She had spent most of her adult life associating with Scots and preferred their company. She provided housing and meals, consoled them in their sickness and sorrow, and attended tae their affairs when they died. The depth of her devotion extends beyond the grave. Every week, this faithful woman treks tae the small cemetery to tend the graves o' the Scottish soldiers she considers her lads. She is as much a Highland Scot as any wha hae been born in that land. It is at her persuading that I abandoned Antwerp tae associate wi' my auld comrades in this place."

In late April, James reminded his son that he was restored to health and that his mission was accomplished. After a farewell dinner with the other exiled Scots, they made plans for a family tryst in late summer at the old hunting lodge on Pitfour Loch in Buchan.

James sternly reminded Jamie, "We must assume that the government is as vigilant as in the auld days. I will return tae

Antwerp before making the crossing tae Aberdeen, although commerce wi' France hae been restored somewhat. The customs cutters are vigilant. It would be guid fer ye tae make the arrangements fer lodging since I canna risk an earlier crossing tae accomplish that task."

Jamie nodded and turned to Madame Hilbert. Startling the frail widow, he impulsively threw his arms around her.

"Madame, ye are as guid a friend as these men could hae in their sojourn in this land. I gie ye thanks fer yer hospitality. Here these lonely men hae found mair than a hame, they hae found a wee bit o' Scotland. Take care o' my papa."

Her red-rimmed eyes brimmed over, and tears trickled down her withered cheeks. She gently touched his face and nodded. Jamie embraced his father, impressed by his robust vigor, and then pushed back, for the groom had brought the saddled horse from the stables. Jamie had extravagantly rented the gelding for the duration of the winter. To return the horse meant retracing his steps to Basel rather than enjoying the shorter journey northward. He would not see Paris but was anxious to return homeward to relate all to his mother and sisters. His arrival in Abergeldie would be joyous but would also restore the anxiety of unemployment. Neither daytime musings nor night dreams had brought any enlightenment about his future. The gruagach had been silent.

13

The journey home was swift and uneventful. The weather was mild and the roads dry. The spring flood sped the barge down the Rhine to Rotterdam. Jamie was forced to wait only three days for a ship to Aberdeen, providing scarcely time to view the venerable old city. With fair winds and following seas, the journey was brief. Twenty-eight days after leaving Sens, the coach deposited Jamie before the steps of Abergeldie Castle.

His mother waited until the tumult subsided, tales were told, and the children departed to hand him a letter. "It arrived three weeks ago. I dinna ken its contents, but I sent a note tae Lord Lockhart-Ross informing him that ye were returning frae the Continent. His reply indicates that wishes ye tae visit soon."

Jamie broke the brittle wax seal and unfolded the brief letter. His mother watched him as he read. When he was finished, her face was expectant. "'Tis an offer o' employment, Mama. Lord Lockhart-Ross is Captain John Lockhart. He retired abruptly when he inherited a vast estate. He was born o' aristocratic parents and embarked on a naval career nae thinking that he would inherit. His mother was the third daughter o' William, the twelfth Lord Ross. I remember him first as captain o' HMS *Tartar*. He was highly successful against French privateers in the English Channel. He next commanded *Chatham*, serving under Admiral Edward Hawke and was at Quiberon Bay. While I was recovering frae being shot, he succeeded John Campbell as commander o' Hawke's flagship, *Royal George*, when Captain Campbell returned hame wi' the glad news o' the victory. When the flagship reached Spithead, Lockhart shifted tae command *Bedford*. He was weel on the way tae a flag when his brother died and he succeeded tae the Ross estate of Balnagown. That made him a Ross. Shortly after, he was placed on half pay since he also hae been elected tae Parliament."

He snorted. "Aye, imagine if ye can, such a dilemma, Mama. Forced tae abandon a naval career tae become a lord and a belted knight. He spends his time shifting between estates in Lanark and Balnagown."

Euphemia murmured, "How does his success affect ye, Jamie? What is it he wishes tae discuss?"

Jamie shrugged. "It seems that he is embarking on a vast program o' land reform. He wishes tae survey his estates, so that he can be better informed o' their extent and usage. He heard o' my experience in surveying in North America frae Captain Campbell. Indeed, I am amazed that he remembered me. I met him while the fleet sought refuge in Torbay before the Battle o' Quiberon Bay. He hae been much involved in experiments wi' navigation instruments, and he was curious about the survey that enabled the invasion fleet's ascent o' the Saint Lawrence. That was only a chance encounter, but John Campbell remembered me. Lord Lockhart-Ross wishes me tae come tae Balnagown tae discuss a contract. He expects that the work will require a year."

Euphemia Drummond asked, "Can ye tell me the location o' Balnagown? The Highlands are vast, and I dinna recognize the name."

Jamie ruminated for a moment before replying. "In Easter Ross, north o' the Black Isle, on the road frae Dingwall tae Dornoch."

His mother replied, "That is north o' Inverness. I hae nae been there, but it must be bleak and barren. How does he think he can improve such lands?"

Jamie smiled. "'Tis nae my concern, Mama. He wishes tae employ me, and that is sufficient enticement. I wilna wait fer a coach. The weather is guid, and the mare is anxious tae stretch her legs. In truth, I welcome the opportunity."

The journey from Abergeldie along the Dee to Crathie was familiar territory. He stopped in the village long enough to inspect the mare's hooves. While they were tender from stabling through the long northern winter, the grooms assured him that she would hold up if not pushed excessively. Jamie was in no hurry since Lord Lockhart-Ross was not expecting him on any particular day. The ride north would require three days to cover the one hundred and thirty miles. A coach would require two days on poor roads, where winter frost heaving would have left potholes that jarred teeth and damaged axles.

North of Crathie, the road threaded a narrow course between the looming hills of An Creagan and Geallaig Hill. Rotting snow still clung to the heights, but the road was passable. The mare deftly sidestepped water-filled holes and scattered rocks. The roar of the river was a constant accompaniment, for spring runoff was strong.

The miles rolled away, and Jamie began to whistle. The gray overcast had broken, and the sun peeked through. Overhead, clouds of birds migrating north filled the sky he could see through the budding canopy of trees. He waved to the occasional coach or wagon that rolled past, but few travelers were on this road deep in the mountains.

He stopped under the brow of a high hill, where a massive stone bordered the road. Tethering the horse, he took down a leather bucket and scrambled down a steep slope to fetch water, pushing aside thick ferns to reach the burn. The horse turned up her nose at the oats, preferring to crop the sweet spring grass. Jamie perched on the rock and spread the meat, cheese, and bread that his mother had insisted on packing for him. He fondled the bottle of burgundy and put it back in his pack, content to drink his fill of the cold mountain water. He reflected that he had gone months when at sea with only tepid water from barrels, stinking of whatever dregs had settled to the bottom and thinking of such a treat."

The first night's stop was halfway to Inverness. It was close to Grantoun-on-Spey, deep in the territory of Clan Grant, where Jamie accepted the hospitality of one of the leaders who had participated in the raid that had netted the cattle reivers the previous year. Although tired after dinner, Jamie complied with the protocol that dictated recitation of the particulars of the hunt, battle, and capture, which had marked the greatest excitement in the region since the battle on nearby Drummossie Muir that had ended the last rising. Highland Scots reveled in a well-told tale. As a visitor and participant in the events, he was expected to play the role of bard. When the cider was gone and toasts with the traditional whiskey drunk, Jamie's obligations were at an end, and he was allowed to sleep.

The next day dawned with a strong westerly breeze scudding away the last of the clouds. The Grants plied him with a sumptuous breakfast, after which he crossed the bridge over the Spey. He followed the road down toward Nairn rather than the straight road to Inverness, for he had a great desire to see the town where he had spent much of his boyhood. The town had grown little. It was not difficult to find the house on the High Street where he and his mother had found refuge and where his little sisters had been born.

He rode to the house where Andy Hay had lived and died from consumption, but a short inquiry revealed that his parents had sold out and gone to Glasgow. Consumed in nostalgia, Jamie guided the mare to the strand and galloped north to the brooding walls of Fort George. He pulled up before the moat and sat watching the guards walking on the parapet. A sentinel glanced his way, but no one challenged him. The threat of Jacobite spying on the fortifications lay in the past, and there was no longer any requirement for passes or curfews.

Jamie had one more nostalgic errand to perform. He rode the sixteen miles from Fort George to Inverness and pulled up in the square. The Mercat Cross still stood, as well as the two whipping posts with their shackle mountings. He dropped the reins and rubbed his eyes, for the memory of that winter day when soldiers had chained his mother and Mr. MacAlister to them for punishment was indelibly imprinted in his mind.

It had been a monstrous cruelty planned by a vengeful Ian Hamilton that was abruptly interrupted by Lieutenant Colonel James Wolfe. Now both were gone. He could never forget that terrible day, the fear and loathing that had nearly strangled a young boy striving to protect his mother. Yet it had strangely led to beneficial events. If not for that day, would James Wolfe have taken him under his protection and introduced him to Master Everard Gascoyne who taught him fencing? The lessons these men had taught were more than physical skills, they were lessons of the spirit, of honor, fortitude, and devotion to duty. He wiped his wet cheeks and turned away to find an inn, for the sun was sinking behind the western hills.

North of Inverness, he trotted the mare onto the deck of a small ferry. Although uneasy with the rolling motion, she stood obediently, with Jamie plied her with small apples. On the north side, the road crossed the land known locally as the Black Isle or Cromarty Peninsula. Fields stretched away, with crofters and their wives busily engaged in turning and raking the dark earth in preparation for spring planting. It was midmorning when he crossed the stone bridge across the Conon River and entered the town of Dingwall, which Jamie knew to be the birthplace of King MacBeth and the site of the largest castle north of Stirling. He fought down an urge to explore the historic place, anxious to press on to Balnagown.

North of Dingwall, the road skirted the north shore of the Cromarty Firth. It was low tide, and small fishing boats painted in colorful hues lay with their keels embedded in mud, awaiting the tidal surge that would float them free. The garish sign for a roadside inn twelve miles up the Firth attracted him. He dismounted slowly on aching legs, for the miles were exacting a toll. The mare regarded him and shook her head. Jamie grinned. "Aye, a month o' riding in carriage, barge, and boat hae taken a toll on my fitness tae ride. Ye are faring much better than I, lass."

A youthful groom with a shock of carroty hair deftly caught the coin he tossed and led the horse to the stable. An hour later, Jamie patted the red sign with a white stork and crown and belched with contentment. He had stopped in Alness by chance and had found good food and friendly service. The garrulous innkeeper had insisted on telling the tale of the village's notoriety as the site of a battle fifty years ago during the 1715 rebellion. Jacobite clansmen had driven a government force of Munroes, Rosses, and MacKays from the field. Jamie observed, "Twas lang syne, and yet the people remember?"

The innkeeper nodded. "Aye, now they are peaceful except when roaring drunk. We hae lang memories here in the north, lad, and much rivalry." Uncertain where the innkeeper's sympathies lay in this politically fractured land, Jamie kept his own counsel.

He took his time covering the final eight miles to the village of Kildary. Balnagown Castle loomed over the landscape, a confection of colorful towers and turrets. Its older walls were a pleasing mix of pink and gray stone. Newer portions were finished in stucco. Remembering the splendor of the gardens of Strathallan, Jamie noted that those at Balnagown were ill-kept, with shaggy trees crowding in on all sides. *Weel*, he mused. *The laird's letter stated that he was engaged in a massive restoration project. That must include the castle and gardens, as weel as the fields and forests.*

A man servant had scarcely seated Jamie in the solar when Sir John Lockhart-Ross flung open the outer doors leading from the gardens and slipped off his muddy boots. He wore no wig, and his bushy red hair was tousled by the wind. Jamie rose to greet him.

Sir John was short and slender and exuded vitality. He shook hands with a strong grip, flung himself into a seat, and extended his stockinged feet on a dainty table. The manservant wrinkled his nose but turned away to hide his disapproval. Lockhart-Ross's boyish grin was completely disarming. "I must say, Master Drummond, that I hae begun tae despair o' obtaining yer services. I am pleased that ye accepted my invitation." His accent was Lowland, yet they were in the northern part of the Highlands, with little between them and the northern seas except barren Sutherland.

Jamie said, "My lord, I was detained on the Continent much later than I intended but came as soon as I received yer letter."

Sir John waved a hand in dismissal. "Nae matter. Ye are here safely, although solitary travel in these times can be hazardous."

Jamie smiled. "I was nae concerned o'ermuch. I hae experience wi' weapons, am an excellent shot, and ride weel-armed."

The baronet nodded. "Ye hae obviously read my proposal. Ye also hae sufficient interest tae spend three days in the saddle. Frae the tale told by those wha were in Canada and hae reason tae be familiar wi' the team that surveyed the Saint Lawrence, I hae nae fears fer yer competency." He stopped as the man servant returned to lay out refreshments. He waited until Jamie had wolfed down two cakes and stirred sugar and cream into his tea.

"I hae been a naval officer fer nearly all my adult life. My reasons for seeking yer services are that I hae recently inherited this vast estate, which hae forced me tae seek half-pay status tae manage them, fer they hae been sair neglected fer many years. I am ill-prepared fer the task and hae been seeking help frae many quarters." He leaned forward and stared at Jamie earnestly. "Tae undertake improvements requires that I understand the nature and extent o' the estates. I need a map and inventory o' the fields, forests, waters, and other features o' this inheritance."

Jamie nodded. "While I will require helpers fer the survey, I am competent tae conduct it, My lord. Howe'er the case, I hae nae equipment."

Sir John smiled. "That deficiency can be quickly remedied. I am sairtain that adequate devices can be purchased, if nae in Inverness, then further south in Glasgow or Edinburgh. If we conclude an agreement, I am prepared tae issue a draft on Barclays tae permit ye tae purchase whate'er is needfu' and then return tae begin the survey. Please dispense wi' the honorific, Master Drummond. I prefer *Captain* in friendly conversation. In return, I will address ye as Captain Drummond. That tends tae put us on an equal footing." Jamie chuckled and agreed. He felt himself warming to the sixth Baronet but was still aware of the great social gap that separated a peer of the realm from a commoner and prospective employee like himself.

Lockhart-Ross was not talking of anything so simple as a physical survey and map of his holdings. He spent the next half hour discussing the additional data he required from the survey. He wanted information gathered from tacksmen and factors on livestock, croft houses, byres, shielings, farm animals, crop types and yields, and tree species and counts. Jamie's estimate of a task that might require three to four months greatly expanded. Ross-shire extended from the Irish Sea to the North Sea. Excluding Cromarty scarcely reduced the daunting task. He would have to survey all the land between Inverness in the east to Loch Carron in the west and northward to the border that separated Ross from Sutherland.

When he told Sir John that perhaps an entire year might be required, the laird was not shocked. He scratched his red locks and pursed his lips. "Aye, that schedule fits perfectly wi' the seasons. If ye require assistants, I will see that ye can select them from bright, weel-educated lads in my employ. Ye may commission the factors wi' the task o' gathering crop yield and stock inventories during the summer and autumn. Ye could even return hame tae Abergeldie during the winter and return next spring wi' the completed maps." Jamie nodded, for he knew that his family would find it hard to accept a yearlong absence after his extended journey to the Continent. By the time a servant arrived to announce dinner, Jamie had decided to accept the commission. It was a task well-suited to his skills and temperament. Sir John increased his resolve with mention of a stipend of two thousand pounds, far more than Jamie imagined the task was worth.

The next day, Lockhart-Ross introduced Jamie to his principal factor, Hugh MacTaggart, a barrel-chested man with a wild coppery mane and beard who spoke both Gaelic and Scots in a low growl. Visiting the entirety of Ross-shire would take many days, for it was a vast domain of mountains, deep glens, and two coastlines. However, they agreed that a brief visit of the lands and villages surrounding Balnagown would prove helpful. Sir John remained behind to draw up the terms of the employment contract.

The castle faded from view as they took the road toward Tain. The burly factor pointed to a nearby croft. "I ken that ye see a difference betwixt Easter Ross and yer hame in Abergeldie?"

Jamie replied, "Aye. The landscape hereaboots is maistly level, akin tae the Lowlands, wi' much land fer field crops and pasturage. In the Cairngorms, the soil is thinner and the growing season short. Howe'er, there is considerable pasturage fer cattle and sheep in the hills. Agriculture is precarious, except on the haws beside streams, but the crofters hae worked the soil fer generations. Wi' manuring and allowing the land tae lie fallow every few seasons, they reap decent crops."

MacTaggart swung his beefy arm eastward. "Around Baile an Todhair, frae Cromarty Firth tae Dornoch, beside the sea is flatland. Some is marshy, but there is land fer crofting. I ken that ye came up the road along Cromarty Firth. There is a strip o' guid land aboot three miles wide below the hills and some distance up the glens." He turned in the saddle and pointed west.

"Wester Ross is wild country, Master Drummond. I grant ye that it hae spectacular mountain scenery, but it yields only a precarious existence fer crofting and even herding. There are guid fishing grounds."

Jamie interrupted, "The weather is brutal?"

MacTaggart chuckled. "Aye, deep snaw and ice. The wind is fierce and chills a man tae the bone. There are times when the mist is sae thick that a man can be hopelessly lost fer days. There are few settlements, except fishing villages in inlets along the western sea and gatherings of crofters in the sheltered glens."

Jamie said, "What o' the people?"

MacTaggart rubbed his grizzled beard. "Here in Easter Ross lang syne, the king settled many Lowlanders and Flemings under Norman aristocrats. Wester Ross adheres tae the auld way o' life. The clan chiefs still rule and inflict their ain brand o' justice. Ye will find chiefly Rosses, Munroes, MacLeods, MacDonalds, and MacKenzies. There is now relative peace between the clans, but auld rivalries and jealousies cause occasional flare-ups. Sadly, those rivalries are naething compared tae the risks posed by reivers and bandits throughout all o' Wester Ross." He pointed a thick finger westward. "Where the hills rise abruptly marks the end o' the sheriff's regular patrols. When the reivers' thieving becomes intolerable, armed posses must enter the hills on hot-trods. Those caught are frequently hanged on the spot because o' the difficulty o' getting them oot fer trial wi'out rescue. It is a lawless region, is Wester Ross. I advise ye, Master Drummond, tae begin yer surveys in Easter Ross, at Baile an Todhair and further north, around the shore o' the Dornoch Firth up tae Bonar Bridge. When ye enter Wester Ross, ye should bring as many armed men as my employer will gie ye. Ye wilna find much that is useful."

Jamie frowned. "Sir John also mentioned his plan tae greatly expand forests. He boasted that he desires tae hae one million trees. It seems tae me that wi' sae much mountainous country, that will be difficult."

Hugh shrugged. "Weel, ye hae nae seen the forests o' Clais Mor, Strath Oykel, and aboot some o' the mountainous lochs. While it would be foolish tae plant trees where howling winds sweep the mountains, there are many protected low-lying areas. O' course, that is yer challenge, Master Drummond, tae find districts where mair trees can be successfully grown."

Jamie smiled. "Then I hae little choice but tae survey sufficient land in Wester Ross tae meet that goal, Mr. MacTaggart. 'Tis nae a task fer a lone man. I dinna expect tae find any lads wi' surveying skills. I can train the three I need if they are literate, adept in ciphering, and capable o' following instruction. If their minds are agile, I can hae them serving as rodmen, and even working wi' transit and plane table. I will also require them tae calculate, draw maps, and take notes."

MacTaggart grinned and said, "Nae all are country louts here, Master Drummond. Ye will be pleased tae hear that I can swiftly assemble a likely group, including some wi' a wee bit o' university training."

Jamie said, "We will form a regular cavalcade since we will hae a considerable pile o' equipment, tentage, and stores tae transport. We canna be downing tools and returning hameward every evening. At least while the weather is guid, we will camp where we wark and change locations nearly daily. Time is precious. I expect that we will wark a' daylight hours six days, resting only on the Sabbath. It will be an unco laborious task. I need lads wha hae stamina and the will tae persevere."

MacTaggart shifted his bulk in the saddle. "Ye will require a groom tae tend the horses, a drover fer the cart, and a cook wha will also serve as quartermaster. Ye will be safe in Easter Ross, but when ye ascend into the high country o' Wester Ross, I would add twa weel-armed men tae guard ye." He raised a hand, for Jamie had opened his mouth to object. "I ken ye are adept wi' weapons, but ye will be occupied wi' the business o' surveying. I hae lived in this land maist o' my life. I hae ne'er seen it as dangerous as at present or wi' sae many broken men roaming the hills."

○────────○

Jamie spent a day interviewing one by one the fifteen young men assembled by MacTaggart. After describing the task, he questioned each at length on their knowledge of mathematics, mechanics, and their willingness to spend most of the summer and fall working in the open. There were no ideal candidates, in spite of MacTaggart's promise. When he finished late that evening, he selected three with the fewest deficiencies.

In the morning, he met with John Lockhart-Ross. They resolved the last details of the contract, inked in the changes, signed both copies, and shook hands. The baronet sanded the signatures, carefully creased the pages, and handed one copy to Jamie. He then wrote out a draft on Barclays Bank. "I trust that this provides sufficient funds tae purchase the surveying equipment adequate tae yer specifications. Ye will leave fer Glasgow in the morning? When can ye return?"

Jamie nodded. "I will stable my horse here and travel by coach. It will make it easier tae transport the equipment on the return journey. I will tarry briefly in Abergeldie tae inform my family and pick up clothing. If I am successful in Glasgow, then I should be back in Balnagown in less than ten days. Howe'er, I am nae as confident as ye that I will find what we require in Glasgow. A diversion tae Edinburgh may be needed. I must caution ye that if the equipment is nae available in Scotland, then I will hae nae choice but tae journey tae London. That would perhaps require nearly a month."

Lockhart-Ross scowled. "The delay canna be helped, I suppose. The task must be done by an experienced man wi' the correct equipment. Take the time ye need, but remember that the northern winter wilna wait. Now let us speak o' obtaining helpers."

Jamie presented his choices of David Duthie, Archie Mitchell, and Ian MacTaggart. Jamie had wished to avoid nepotism by not selecting the factor's second son, but the sixteen-year-old's mathematical prowess was so dominant that he changed his mind. Sir John ran his fingers through his red hair for a moment before speaking.

"Ye hae made excellent choices. While the MacTaggart lad is young, he is quite bright. I am familiar wi' Mitchell's family. His father is vicar o' Kildary kirk. He desires tae follow his father as a man o' the cloth. He hae an inquiring mind and will serve ye weel. The Duthie boy hae a year o' university at Saint Andrews and must return in the fall. I suggest that ye train another lad tae fill the shortage."

Jamie raised an eyebrow. "And wha would I take?"

"My nephew Matthew Davidson. He lives at Lockhart Hall in Lanarkshire wi' his parents. He is fifteen and an uncommonly adept scholar. He will matriculate at Glasgow University a year hence."

Jamie hesitated, but Sir John did not amplify his words. At last he said, "I hae reservations wi' assuming responsibility fer the lad wi'out having met him."

Sir John rose. "I dinna wish tae force him on ye, but he will be here when ye return frae obtaining equipment. Ye can train him wi' the others and then decide. It would please me greatly tae see the lad working on this assignment."

Jamie bit his lip. He was familiar with the tendency of families to prefer relatives. He did not wish to offend his new employer with a strenuous objection before the project started.

Jamie visited Abergeldie before journeying onward to Glasgow. His mother was excited by the assignment, although disappointed that her son would not be able to return often. She predicted that if successfully done that it might lead to offers from other large landowners in the largely unmapped north. Meg and Elizabeth Marie were disconsolate, for a summer of daily rides and picnics with their long-absent brother would not happen. He gave them two days and departed.

On arrival in Glasgow, he went straight to the university to seek advice and help from his old friend John Robison. Although James Watt still maintained the instrument shop for the school, he told Jamie that there were no transits and plane tables in stock. The university owned one set, but it was committed to use. Inquiries among engineers operating in the city were fruitless. None were interested in selling their equipment.

Watt gave him references to engineers and optical equipment suppliers in Glasgow, Manchester, Liverpool, and London. The only high point of his visit was that the model that Jamie's team had built that spring demonstrating rotary motion from the Newcomen engine had earned a small stipend from investors. However, it was not enough to tempt Jamie to return. He had made his choice and signed a contract. Thanking Watt and Robison for their help, he took the coach to Edinburgh.

Stiff and sore, Jamie dismounted from the cab in Exeter Exchange, off the Strand. He had been riding in a variety of vehicles for nearly two weeks, vainly seeking surveying equipment. Failing to find any available in every city visited, he had come to London, his last hope in Great Britain. He stared upward at the sign above the shop entrance—a pair of golden spectacles and a sea quadrant. He stared at the display of instruments nestled on green velvet in the window facing the busy thoroughfare. Inside, a well-dressed customer in a white wig was intently examining a brass and leather bound telescope and did not look up. Before Jamie could speak, the man motioned to a man in his thirties busily engaged in wiping the broad glass case that took up much of the shop. "Peter, you have a customer."

Dark-haired and smiling, the young man, who was wearing a leather apron, set down his cloth and extended a hand. "I am Peter Dollond, and this is my shop. I assume that you are interested in telescopes. I assure you that this firm is well-recognized among the Worshipful Company of Spectacle Makers for offering the finest and widest selection of instruments available in Great Britain, all with finely ground lenses by George Bass, of the highest quality. Do you live in London or are ye visiting from elsewhere?"

Dollond's English was only slightly accented. Jamie was surprised by the strength in the man's slender fingers. He said, "I am staying wi' a cousin but hae traveled frae Ross-shire in the far north o' Scotland. Surveying is gaining a great popularity. I hae an imperative need fer equipment, which seem tae be in rather short supply in the cities betwixt here and there."

The proprietor nodded and beckoned Jamie to follow him. A comfortable sitting room occupied the rear of the shop. Peter Dollond whisked a tea service and a plate of cakes onto a small table and invited Jamie to take a seat. Ten minutes and many shrewd questions later, Dollond summarized Jamie's needs. While he was an instrument maker by trade, he had a thorough understanding of the practice of surveying. He scribbled a list of items and prices and showed it to Jamie, who said, "That is sufficient fer a single set o' equipment, but I hae hopes o' training an apprentice sufficiently tae double our productivity in short order."

The proprietor nodded. "Assembling a second set of instruments will take only a little more time."

Jamie leaned forward. "Master Dollond, is it possible tae obtain a third set? While Sir John is bearing the expense o' the other instruments, I wish tae purchase a set fer my ain use once the assignment is complete. I ken that the expense fer rushing the order may cost a higher price. I am willing tae agree tae any reasonable price."

The instrument maker regarded him for a moment. "Master Drummond, I inherited this shop from my father, who died recently. He established a reputation among instrument makers that reaches many nations and principalities of providing quality goods at fair prices. I expect to be operating this shop for many years and desire my customers to return often and recommend me to their friends. My charges will be only what I require to build what you need with a reasonable profit."

Jamie grinned. "I hae nae choice and am grateful tae find an honest merchant. My employer is anxious tae proceed wi' the project and make guid progress this season. How lang must I wait?"

Peter Dollond stared at the ceiling. "I have somewhat of a backlog of work because of an emergency order for Governor Thomas Graves of Newfoundland, who commissioned James Cook last year to survey the entire coast of that land. He sailed not eight weeks past with new instruments with which he expects to complete the work by this autumn."

Jamie chuckled. "This is an amazing tale. I spent a year and half in Canada working wi' James Cook tae prepare the great chart that enabled James Wolfe tae conquer Quebec."

Dollond laughed. "I did not disclose it when you arrived, Master Drummond, but James Cook told me of that great effort under Captain John Simcoe. Your name recalled his tale of your contributions. I am privileged to support you. Without inflicting excessive delays on my other customers, I will send you north with three sets of equipment before the sun rises seven days hence. I only wish that you could have arrived while Master Cook was here. It would have made a jolly reunion."

Jamie nodded his agreement. "Aye. I left Canada abruptly tae fight at Quiberon Bay, frae which place my path led tae hospital, back tae sea, then tae the Caribbean and a Spanish prison. I am done wi' military service, but I sense that we will yet hear much frae Master Cook."

Peter Dollond replied, "I expect that you are correct. He has come to the attention of the Royal Society, which sponsors voyages of discovery and botanical expeditions. I heard from Joseph Banks, a young Oxford student, who came with his friend Daniel Solander, a Swedish naturalist, to procure optical instruments. They are deeply engrossed in natural science and are endeavoring to join the expedition that the Royal Society intends to send next year to Newfoundland, where Master Cook is now developing charts of the coastal lands and waters."

After two hours of watching Peter Dollond's craftsmen polishing lenses, fitting casings, and meticulously engraving markings, Jamie took his leave to spend an evening with Peter Gordon's family at their elegant house in Saint James's Square. After dinner and play with the children, Rachel led the promenade up the stairs, leaving the men sipping Madeira and discussing politics.

"Dear cousin, naething o' any substance will happen. My hopes were elevated when the news came that Charles Townsend is tae be appointed Chancellor of the Exchequer. Many weeks hae passed, and the doleful message hae nae changed. The government's financial situation following the end of the war continues tae worsen as mair debt and damage tae ships, harbors, and armaments are discovered. The cost o' credit continues tae rise. Townsend's situation is precarious. On this side o' the Atlantic, his arguments are reasonable, but I dinna expect that the colonists will be easily persuaded tae accept his view that they ought tae pay any share o' the cost o' defending their settlements. The minister wilna meet wi' me. Others in Lord Chesterfield's circle are quite certain that we will only arouse animosity if we press Townsend at this point. He is obsessed wi' squeezing revenue frae the American colonies, nae wi' restoring attainted properties, which will bring a pittance in new revenue."

Jamie sat sunk in gloom. The hope he had felt during that meeting with Lord Chesterfield's circle had convinced him that the time was ripe. Now it was as far away as ever. Peter leaned forward and slapped his knee.

"Come, ye must look on the sunny side o' the hill. Ye hae returned frae the war with scars but nae permanent impairment. Yer reputation is spotless in many influential circles. Few came hame wi' as large a prize account as ye. Ye hae employment in a profession ye enjoy, in addition tae a ha'-pay stipend. Life is guid if ye can bring yerself tae admit it."

Jamie reflected a moment and then grinned. "Aye, ye are correct, cousin. The task laid before me by Lockhart-Ross is daunting but pleasant. Perhaps it is mair than a single assignment and I am on the threshold o' a worthy profession. I prefer the saddle tae a desk and a transit tae a dusty law book. I am content." He paused, staring into the fireplace. The flames that had warmed their evening had gone out, leaving glowing coals, which winked as they cooled.

Peter interrupted his reverie. "Ye are thinking o' yer father. I advise ye tae let the matter rest. He is restored tae health and may yet find a way tae visit undetected frae time tae time. Ye were lucky that yer journey tae France was nae discovered. It wilna bear repeating."

Jamie stirred. "Nae, I am tranquil wi' regard tae my father's state and fortunes, and my mama hae come tae accept the inevitable—that he may visit but his exile is permanent. She hae chosen tae raise the children in the Highlands and nae join him in exile. It is fer the best." He hesitated and then plunged on. "Maggie's prophecy still hangs o'er me like a dark cloud." He sighed and stretched his legs. "I dinna understand it or any o' the strange dreams aboot the gruagach. I feel possessed."

Peter smiled. "Perhaps we can find a priest tae exorcise them."

Jamie shivered. "Ye jest, cousin and I dinna believe in such supernatural affairs. However, I am also unco cautious and choose tae nae tamper wi' such matters. I refuse tae fret or act foolishly. I am content that someday, all will be clear."

The Royal Military Academy at Woolwich in southeast London was a military academy for the training of commissioned officers of the Royal Artillery and Royal Engineers. Locals referred to it as the Shop since it was housed in a former workshop. It lay on the south side of the Thames, a short walk from the South Pier. After the crowded ferry ride, Jamie felt like strolling. Only a few questions were required to direct him to the entrance off Beresford Street, where a single sentry stood guard. Yes, the guard was familiar with the name Everard Gascoyne, Woolwich's fencing master. No, the master was not about but was expected momentarily. Jamie's friendliness dissolved the guard's reticence, and he confided that the fencing master lived in a comfortable mansion in Plumstead with a charming lady of means whose driver deposited Gascoyne at the entrance precisely at nine each morning.

The bell tower on Church Hill tolled just as a liveried driver slowed the pair of spirited bays pulling a handsome berlin to the entrance. Everard Gascoyne opened the door, leaped down, and then turned back to embrace a woman in billowing satin. Jamie grinned. The charming lady of means was also uncommonly lovely, with a heart-shaped face and jet-black hair under a saucy hat. Gascoyne ignored the bystanders to linger over her hand and whisper in her ear. She reddened prettily and slapped him before pushing him away and closing the door.

The fencing master walked to the entrance as the carriage rolled away. Jamie marveled, for Gascoyne had changed little since abruptly leaving Inverness thirteen years before. His dark hair was flecked with gray, and there were more lines in his face, but his carriage was straight and his step firm. Jamie stepped toward him and drew the Andrea Ferrara. The whisking sound of the blade brought Gascoyne to a halt. He raised a hand. "Monsieur, as you can see, I am not armed. If you are here to demand satisfaction, I can easily arrange to provide it, but not here at my place of employment."

Jamie smiled, for he could see that his old master did not recognize him and was assuming that he was one of many husbands desiring revenge against the amorous Frenchman. "I doubt that ye are as harmless as ye profess, but I am nae here seeking a duel. I see that ye dinna recognize me. Many years hae passed, and I hae changed, but ye hae nae changed a whit. Nae matter, fer ye must recognize the weapon. Examine it closely." He reversed the blade and extended it to Gascoyne. The Frenchman's eyes widened as he recognized the Andrea Ferrara rapier he had given Jamie before he abruptly fled from Scotland. His emotions were unrestrained as he handed back the weapon and gave Jamie time to sheathe it. He embraced his former pupil fervently, shedding tears and babbling his joy in English and French. Gradually, they disengaged, and Gascoyne made the introductions to students and military officers who had gathered to watch the scene.

It was a joyous day followed by a long evening. There was nothing for it, but Jamie had to show his prized rapier to everyone, then join Gascoyne's students for fencing drills. They cheered noisily when the master announced that he and Jamie would engage in a ceremonial bout. While youth and reach were on Jamie's side, he was wary of Gascoyne's skill, honed in thousands of matches over decades. While the master was now in his early fifties, Jamie doubted that he could overcome his great skill. He tried the tactic of wearing down the canny master by adopting a defensive posture. They battled back and forth for many minutes before Gascoyne did something astonishing and unexpected. He pirouetted, kicked the wall vigorously, and flexing his body, sailed over Jamie's blade, to land behind him. Jamie spun, but it was too late. Gascoyne tapped him lightly between the shoulder blades, stepped back, and grinned insouciantly while the class cheered their master. Jamie chuckled and lowered his blade. "Ye auld scoundrel! I canna believe that I was sae easily tricked!"

Gascoyne embraced him sweatily. "It was only one of several possible lines of attack. You are so accomplished a fencer, so fast and strong, that I can no longer defeat you except by surprise. I have always been a dancer, and a dancer's moves are so quick and unexpected that they are very effective methods of attack. My objective was to get behind your fine defenses either by springing over you or sliding under your blade to attack from below. I now teach my students to spin on the floor and then spring up from behind. Very surprising, no?"

Jamie laughed. "Very surprising, aye. But, Master Gascoyne, if the opponent is expecting it, he can spit ye like a chicken."

Gascoyne nodded. "If he expects it. Most fencers do not since they expect their opponent to stand on his feet and fight as a gentleman."

Jamie tapped his forehead. "I hae ne'er forgotten the lessons put here by ye and that auld soldier Jock McRae. 'There are rules and expectations o' chivalrous behavior in sport but no sech rules in warfare.' That hae saved my life many times o'er."

His plans to visit Joseph Cotes before leaving London were dashed when Peter confided that the old gentleman had been laid low by a mysterious fever. He had recovered somewhat but had departed the capital to convalesce in the resort town of Bath, famous for the healing qualities of its thermal spas since Roman times. Jamie spent the remaining days waiting for his surveying equipment to be completed strolling the parks and Thameside and the evenings sampling the plays in the Mayfair district.

Summer was well advanced when Jamie returned to the castle in Ross-shire with his equipment and completed what he considered a bare minimum of training for his apprentice surveyors. As the sun's disk emerged from the sea on the second Monday of August, the little cavalcade set out escorted by the massive factor Hugh MacTaggart on an equally massive horse.

A guard led the way, followed by the four apprentices, Jamie, the cart drover, the cook, and the groom. A second guard trailed the formation. They rode north slowly, with frequent stops to adjust saddle girths and rebalance loads. As the sun rose and the air warmed, they stopped to wrap spare shirts around their faces to deter the swarms of black midges that followed them.

By late morning, they reached the promontory of Tarbat Ness, where the sparkling firth ran into the North Sea. Hugh MacTaggart waved the caravan to a halt and then trotted to where Jamie had dismounted and stood viewing the fields of windswept gorse and yellow broom.

He waved his brawny arm in a semicircle. "Mr. Drummond, since ye hae selected the northeastern border o' the shire along the Dornoch Firth as yer first surveying task, I suggest that ye make camp hereaboot. There is a sma' burn yonder, which will gie ye fresh water. The land is open fer miles, wi' nae relief frae the wind."

Jamie nodded. "Aye, I dinna expect tae find a sheltered place on this headland. Once we move westward up the waterway toward Bonar Bridge, we might find relief. Ah weel, we expected tae be in the open, and the weather will be fine unless a storm blaws in frae the sea. This will be an excellent place fer the lads tae refine their skills before taking on the challenge of mapping Strath Oykel and the high country tae the western sea."

MacTaggart looked at the mountainous mass looming in that direction. "Ye hae perhaps twa months before the first snaw. Once the weather turns evil, ye must retreat to the lowlands of Easter Ross. I suggest that ye map the region north o' the firth of Cromarty westward tae Dingwall and save the remainder o' Wester Ross until spring."

Jamie grinned. "Yer advice is guid. I dinna relish bein' trapped in that wilderness. Come, we are wasting daylight. Lead us on tae the camping place."

Within an hour, the cart had been unloaded, tents erected and staked, water gathered, horses set to pasture, surveying tools unpacked, and lunch eaten standing up. MacTaggart mounted his horse and departed, promising to find the team's encampment in a week. Jamie drew a quick sketch of the terrain, assigned his teams, and the monumental task of surveying the whole of Ross-shire began.

The apprentices took to the work eagerly, and within five days, they had mapped the open fields and pasturage from the high promontory of Tarbat Ness past the tiny fishing villages of Portmahomack and Inver until they faced the marshes and sand beaches where the shore of the firth curved outward before bending in at the ferry landing near Glenmorangie. The enthusiasm of his apprentices faded as they were forced to slog through the muck of the marshes to obtain their sightings. David Duthie, Archie Mitchell, and Ian MacTaggart took on the task in silence, although they sank to their calves in the soft mud and the midges were voracious. However, Lord Lockhart-Ross's nephew Matthew Davidson muttered and cursed throughout the afternoon. Jamie was nearly resolved to speak to the boy, but Ian MacTaggart made any chastisement unnecessary. A smaller version of his father's massive bulk, the lad seized Davidson by his shirtfront and threatened to drag him facedown through the marsh if he did not stop his carping. Jamie smiled inwardly but realized that he might have to answer to his employer if his nephew complained about his treatment.

They changed their encampment to a lovely glade in Glen Morangie, beyond the town of Tain. On Saturday, Jamie treated his team to a dinner at the tavern near the ruined castle, with the guards taking turns at the camp. In addition to tasty food and drink, the building housed the historic Hilton of Cadboll Stone depicting Pictish carvings of mythical creatures, birds, and hunting scenes painstakingly carved into sandstone at a date lost in time. Jamie mused on the mysterious painted people who had made the artifact, as well as carvings and mysterious stones that marked the landscape of his youth in Strathallan.

David Duthie asked, "I ken that we call them Picts because the Romans described them as the painted people. I wonder what they called themselves?"

Jamie said, "I dinna think we will discover that fact, fer while these people left many symbols in their art and decoration, we hae ne'er discovered a key that would help us translate them. My papa called them our ancestors, and perhaps they are. This is an ancient land, lads, perhaps as auld as Egypt or Babylon, although the monuments are cruder. In the far north and the islands, there are tall circles o' standing stones brooding o'er the landscape but hiding their secrets unco weel. Perhaps our mapping will be o' use tae mair purposes than we suspect, even the unlocking o' the mysteries o' sech stones."

In deference to old tradition, Jamie set aside Sunday for rest. He had driven the apprentices hard from before sunup to well after sundown for six days. While the day was set aside for rest, the team members strolled about the town of Tain. No shops were open, for this was the Sabbath, but they found street vendors willing to trade beer and food for coins. They organized a game of football in the afternoon.

Jamie propped himself at the table knocked together by the groom and cook, reviewing and correcting his journal of observations for the week. The air was warm, and bees buzzed pleasingly in the broom that lined their campsite. Jamie dozed but jerked awake at a hail from Hugh MacTaggart as he rode into view. With food and beer in his belly, MacTaggart looked over the rudimentary maps resulting from the week's work. He belched and said, "I hae nae appreciation fer the work, but this seems a fair representation o' the district. I am familiar wi' this land, having spent maist o' my life hereaboots. The laird will be pleased tae hear o' the progress. Hae ye any observations concerning what ye hae recorded?"

Jamie closed his eyes for a moment, considering. At last, he said, "Much o' what we hae seen is wasteland o' broom, marsh grass, and sand. There are some thick patches o' woodland and fields surrounding croft houses south and east o' Tain. We dinna venture south o' Balintore and hae nae yet attempted tae survey westward o' where we sit. Maist land is pasturage. I hae noted cropland, but it seems o' puir yield."

MacTaggart pulled at his mug and nodded emphatically. He rumbled, "The land is fairer westward o' Tain, but ye are seeing already wha I hae seen fer these thirty and mair years that I hae been factor o'er this land. The growing season this far north is short and the soil thin, although it hae been cropped fer centuries. The crofters are hard-pressed, wi' puir yields o' grain, potatoes, turnips, and cabbages. They struggle constantly tae keep the kine oot o' the fields. Whilst they manure as they can before planting, I hae noted a steady decline in yields. Many crofters are hard-pressed tae feed their bairns toward the end o' lang winters. I hae recommended tae the laird that he bring in mair manure, but that is costly." He sighed noisily. "I fear that we hae many mair mouths tae feed than land tae produce food. It is a bitter tale, Mr. Drummond, a bitter tale. Growling bellies stir resentment. Resentment unchecked breeds crime and violence. We already hae many men wha hae fled tae the hills and prey upon the innocent."

Jamie muttered, "Aye, 'tis the same in Abergeldie. We rounded up and either hanged or transported reivers wha were once farmers."

MacTaggart frowned. "The regiments hae ta'en many, but they are braw lads. A few return wi' gold, but most ne'er come hame, dying or settling in foreign lands."

Jamie said, "What aboot emigration? Surely the colonies offer crofters an opportunity fer land."

MacTaggart scuffed his boot in the soft earth. "Aye, they do, but always at a price much dearer than the puir can afford. Someone must pay fer the transportation or sell himself fer a period o' years. Maist canna afford tae depart, fer transporting a family is beyond the means o' nearly everyone. Some drift tae the touns, but if they lack a tradesman's skills and tools, there are few jobs. The guilds take apprentices but charge fer the privilege. They are jealous o' their prerogatives and take violent measures against intruders. Even fer a factor—and my family hae been factors tae the house o' Ross fer o'er a hundred years—times are difficult. I spend a goodly portion o' my ain wages helping my tenants. We are kith, and many are kin. We and the land hae been bound together fer generations, but these are new times, and I fear the future. We hae always bent during hard times, but we are close tae breaking. The laird is a guid man wha cares fer the people and desires tae improve conditions. He is nae like the Sutherlands tae the north and many others in the west wha wilna listen tae the cries o' the hungry. They use the surplus o' good years in riotous living, fine hooses in London and Edinburgh, and fine clothing."

Jamie listened solemnly and shivered slightly in the late afternoon breeze. MacTaggart's words were a dire warning that resonated with what he had come to realize himself. The Highlands were changing forever, but no one knew either how to stop the changes or ease their impact on the people clinging to their fading heritage and livelihoods.

Mapping the crazy-quilt pattern of rigs, ditches, and winding paths of the farmland stretching between Tain and the bridge of Bonar required all of ten arduous days. Jamie had to explain their work and equipment to the curious crofters and herders, detracting from other work. Once the locals understood that the surveyors would be careful around their crops and livestock, they were satisfied.

Arrival at the bridge also meant that David Duthie, the university student who had proven most adept at surveying, had to depart for Saint Andrews. Jamie had come to rely heavily on the quiet lad. With four apprentice surveyors, he was able to run two crews. Reduced to three, in order to maintain two crews, he would have to survey himself, deferring other tasks and slowing the work. Of the three, Lockhart-Ross's nephew Matthew Davidson was not only the youngest but also the most inclined to shirk when given the opportunity. The lad was sufficiently bright, but Jamie gloomily reflected that keeping up his flagging interest in the repetitive and exacting work would be a difficult challenge.

The evening had turned cool, and the light was draining from the sky when Jamie signaled that they had completed the survey of Ardgay, not only as far as the bridge but two miles inland along the south bank of the Carron. Young Duthie would depart the next morning, which was a Friday, and the three remaining apprentices would take Saturday to record their observations and help Jamie ink the verified results on the map. They would rest over the Sabbath before heading west along the Kyle of Sutherland, an inland-reaching extension of the Dornoch Firth that separated Ross from Sutherland. They would find little farmland along the wandering watercourse as the land rose, for the slopes were thickly coated not only with stunted trees but with thickets of hazel and other shrubbery that would make the going difficult. They had been fortunate to work in dry weather, but growing cloud cover presaged the time, only a few days distant, when miserably cold rain and occasional sleet would add to their obstacles.

They mapped the extent of each woodland, following faintly defined paths where they could be found and tramping down the gorse, broom, and small shrubs where they did not. They mapped Balinoe Wood, Carbisdale, Badarach, Rhelonie, and entered the edge of the vast Inveroykel Wood. Midday of the autumnal equinox found them at the fork that separated the dwindling river. Jamie rode along the straths that bounded the two streams for a mile or more, examining the footing. Ian MacTaggart trailed him. Jamie had taken to separating the factor's son from Matthew Davidson, for the animosity between the two boys had caused several flare-ups. Jamie's choices were whether to follow the westward-trending Oykel that skirted the mass of Ben More Assynt on the southward-facing slopes or the Cressley, whose course led northward and appeared to swing around the north shoulder of the massive peak.

Young MacTaggart blew his nose noisily, which startled his mount, which reared, nearly unseating its rider. "I hae heard, Mr. Drummond, that the Cressley ends in a chain o' lochs, the last o' which is Gleann Dubh, which reaches the sea far inside Sutherland."

Jamie urged, "And tell me, Ian, where would following the Oykel bring us? I am anxious tae reach the sea and turn back before snaw finds us."

MacTaggart rubbed his chin while he thought. Slowly, he said, "My father hae been that way. He said that the Oykel ends in a flat bare tableland dotted wi' wee lochs. There is a steep descent tae Loch Broom. There is a weel-used road frae the head o' the loch tae Loch Glascarnoch and frae thence, by a tortuous way, tae Dingwall. Loch Broom is a favorite docking place fer boats plying a route tae Antrim and the Hebrides."

Jamie grinned. "Excellent! I will be pleased tae find some civilization in Wester Ross before our return. Come, we will look for a sheltered camp for tonight. I sense that the wind will rise, and there is already an autumnal bite tae the air."

Jamie ordered a halt a mile up the Oykel, where the crew set up camp on a wide place on the southern strath, where a copse of trees provided some relief from the surging wind. Erecting and staking the tents was a challenge, but they managed a cook fire behind a hastily erected wall of rough stone. It was fully dark before they had a chance to eat. They were finishing their meal when Jamie heard the distinct ratcheting sound of a firearm being cocked. He dropped his wooden trencher and scuttled out of the firelight, waving to his crew to disperse. He squinted to see into the darkness under the trees.

Four shadowy forms materialized and strode into the camp. There had been no alarm from the guards. Jamie was chagrined, for a broadsword hovered over his breastbone before he could draw his weapon. There was shocked silence from the entire crew. A ripple of low laughter came from the intruders, followed by a gruff voice.

"Wha daur enter the territory o' the MacKenzies wi'oot our laird's approval? Wha is in charge o' this company?" More forms emerged from the shadows and took shape in the firelight.

Jamie rose slowly, his eyes never leaving the unwavering blade scarcely six inches from his chest. His small group was completely surrounded by armed men. He raised his hands and stared at the grim face confronting him. The man was tall, of the same height as himself. Jamie spoke with more confidence than he felt.

"I am James Drummond, surveyor. I lead this company by command o' the laird John Lockhart-Ross, wha sent me tae map and inventory all lands in Ross-shire. I hae a commission signed by the laird requesting the assistance o' all factors, tacksmen, and tenants inhabiting these lands in carrying oot my task."

The stranger's voice took on a friendlier tone. "Ye are a Drummond, ye say? A Drummond o' Strathallan?"

Jamie responded slowly, for he could not gauge the man's intent. "Aye. My father was James and my grandfather William o' Strathallan and Machany. But I dinna fight in the Rising o' '45. I was young, my family was attainted, and my father exiled. I myself served seven years in the recent war wi' the French."

The sword was withdrawn and sheathed. The man extended a huge hand. "I am Colin MacKenzie, son o' Kenneth, Laird Fortrose and chief o' Clan MacKenzie. I was captain o' a loyal independent company at Badenoch during the rising. My father supported the Hanoverian king, though his heart was fer the cause, as were many o' the MacKenzies. I bid ye welcome but wish that ye hae notified us o' yer approach. We dinna receive any instructions frae the laird regarding yer visit. These are perilous times and perilous lands, wi' many bands o' rough men roaming the braes and glens. The chief o' our clan may hold a charter fer lands frae the laird and owe him service, but the MacKenzies keeps the peace in these mountains. We canna allow strangers tae wander wi'oot accounting fer themselves. I fear that I must disappoint my men, wha were looking forward tae a fight and perhaps a hanging."

"Wha hae ye done tae the lads I set tae guard our camp? Why did they nae gie any alarm at yer approach?"

Colin MacKenzie grinned, huge teeth shining in the wavering light. "They may be dear lads but useless fer warning o' the approach o' stealthy Highlanders." He jerked a thumb. "Ye will find them trussed and gagged, meek as lambs lying athwart twa horses. Dinna fash yerself. They are unhurt, except in pride. Twas a guid lesson tae teach them vigilance. I suggest that ye test them frequently tae keep them alert." He held up a hand. "Nay, I will accept nae compensation fer the instruction."

Jamie shrugged but could not resist a jest in return. He was coming to like Colin MacKenzie. "Maist o' my crew are mere lads wi' leetle experience. It would be a pity fer them tae depart wi'out learning such a valuable lesson. I insist on payment. Pray, join us wi' what is left o' the coffee and victuals. We live rudely and can offer scant entertainment."

MacKenzie chuckled and motioned to his men to join them. "I accept yer kind overture. Here in the northern lands, we seldom enjoy the luxury o' coffee. Tae satisfy my father, I must insist on reading the laird's commission. If all is in order, I will see that ye receive a' the support ye need in fulfilling it." He motioned to his clansmen. "Come, my guid duniewassals. Put up yer weapons, release the guards, and join us at the fire."

14

The evening was late when Colin MacKenzie led his men from the camp. It was a cruel injustice to rouse his crew before dawn, but Jamie was obdurate. There was hard frost on the heather, and the sky promised snow. Drowsy from lack of sleep, they grumbled but stolidly performed the camp housekeeping chores, and they were fed and in the saddle up the Oykel within an hour.

Except for sparse trees in the glens, the ground rose to a high moorland of barren rock clothed in yellowing grass dimpled with peat bogs. Fearing a horse might break its leg plunging into the unknown depth, Jamie warned his men to steer carefully around them. The sky darkened appreciably as they passed Loch Daimh and started down the slope to the grassy strath bordering the River Rhidorroch, as the stream was called. Shaggy, long-haired cattle grazed or lay peacefully, occasionally looking up through the matted red hair that obscured their faces. While they sported long horns with wickedly sharp tips, they were well used to riders and made no move to attack. The crew worked swiftly to deploy the equipment, construct a baseline, and survey the strath to the shores of Loch Achall. By midday, the cook had prepared a hot meal and served the crew in a level spot sheltered from the steady wind blowing off the sea.

After lunch, the crew was content to spend an hour relaxing, except for young Matthew Davidson, who pointed to the high ridge that marked the edge of the strath. Without waiting for permission, he began to climb. Irritated at the lad's willfulness, Jamie rose to follow him upward. He walked swiftly through a copse of evergreens and, dodging rough rocks studding the thin soil, across soft grass to ascend the concave slope. His breathing was soon labored, but ahead of him, the fifteen-year-old climbed with little apparent effort. Jamie smiled inwardly, for the lad's impulsiveness was much like his own at the same age.

Matthew reached the top of the ridge and turned to stare at Loch Achall, where the river drained into it and from which it tumbled down a steep slope into Loch Broom glittering from a shaft of sunlight penetrating the cloud cover. He extended both arms and laughed. Jamie considered thrashing the impudent youth, but reaching his level and turning, he was struck by the unusual sight of a rainbow floating over the loch and touching from shore to shore against the backdrop of gray stone, black bog, and green strath. For long minutes, man and boy stood enraptured, with the cold wind whipping their hair and numbing their faces. A horn sounded below them, breaking their reverie. The crew was packed and ready to move on.

From Loch Achall, a faint trail led along the bank of the river, ending less than two miles away on the shore of Loch Broom. Several fisher cots and four windowless warehouses dotted the shore. Two short-planked docks extended over the deep blue water of the inlet. With the persistent wind, the water of the loch was ruffled, but there was no evidence of a strong tidal bore from the sea less than five miles distant. Two coastal luggers with reefed canvas bobbed at their moorings. A handful of boats plied the waters close to the far shore, where fishermen pulled in nets.

Racing to complete their tasks before dusk caught them, the crew hurried to the shoreline and broke out their surveying equipment and began to set up camp. The sun sank redly into the regathering cloud bank, and the wind grew bitter. An enterprising fishwife had sold the cook cod, herring, and shrimp from her day's catch. The surveyors followed the tantalizing smell and sizzle of frying seafood back to camp.

In the morning, huddled in his tent to avoid the persistent cold and wind, Jamie reviewed the incomplete map. The serrated coastline southward, with its deep-set sea lochs, steep ridges, and moorland, would have to wait until spring. He knew the names of the inlets from his conversation with Colin MacKenzie: Little Loch Broom, Loch Ewe, Loch Maree, and Loch Torridon down toward the crossing to the Isle of Skye. Northward lay a rocky peninsula and the wide entrance to Loch Garvie. While little of this forbidding country was cultivated, cattle abounded on the grassy uplands and in dark glens bordering the rushing rocky burns. They had been lucky to avoid a deep early snowfall. They would start the survey of the coastline southward, but there was little hope of completing it.

They enjoyed uncharacteristically mild weather that heartened the tired surveying crew. The sun peeked through the overcast, and the air was crisp and still. By the fifth day, they had mapped the crenulated cliffs of the coastline and the headlands between the numerous sea lochs southward for twelve miles. By four in the afternoon, the late autumn sun was well down into a towering wall of mist that had advanced during the day from the Isle of Lewis. The wind had fallen, and Jamie rushed the team to set up camp on the wide strath of Loch Maree, with an exquisite view of the high peaks of Eilean Subhainn and its companion islands rising above the glassy waters of the loch. The thrusting peaks were bare reddish rock rising above an expanse of purple heather, dark green shrubs, and stunted trees at their base.

By morning, thick mist entirely enveloped the camp. There would be no surveying until it lifted. Jamie assigned his apprentices to work under canvas to calculate positions and update the master map. Every half an hour, he poked his head through the tent flaps to assess the fog. By midmorning, it had lifted enough for them to see the road that ran along the lochside. He refastened the flap and announced that he expected the mist to lift enough by noon to enable the survey work to recommence.

A hail from three shadowy riders approaching on the trail from the east brought the camp guards running from their perches on the hillside. All three strangers were bearded and wrapped in heavy tartan hoods. Jamie stepped from the tent to greet them, for they were Colin MacKenzie and two of his tacksmen, David MacKenzie and Peter MacConnach. Plied with hot tea laced liberally with whiskey, the visitors sat before a peat fire in the makeshift fireplace that the crew had erected against a rock face.

Colin MacKenzie took a deep draught and wiped perspiration from his forehead. "'Tis fortunate that we found ye. We come frae Kintail wi' an admonition frae our chief tae quit yer surveying. Ye are frae the east and unaccustomed tae the fierce storms that plague this coast. While the Hebrides absorb some storm energy, the western Highlands are notorious fer high winds, deep snaw, and conditions where air and land are a uniform white, wi' nae landmarks ye can trust. The MacKenzie says tae tell ye that he is thinking o' what he would say tae Lord Lockhart-Ross if ye were tae die o' cold and lack o' nourishment in MacKenzie lands. I dinna relish finding yer frozen arses hereabouts when spring melts the snaw." He fixed Jamie with intensity in his eyes as he leaned toward him. "I dinna expect ye tae leave today. Tomorrow morning will do."

Jamie frowned at his words. "I wish tae finish surveying baith straths o' Loch Maree tae its end at Kinlochewe before departing fer the winter."

David MacKenzie spoke in a hoarse rumble, "'Tis five miles and mair frae where we sit, but the trail is weel-marked. Can ye accomplish the task in ain day?"

Jamie shook his head. "Probably twa."

Colin drained his cup and held it out for a refill, adding whiskey from his own flask, which he passed around the circle. "The risk grows wi' every day that passes." He sighed. "Weel, I dinna wish tae force ye, and we canna stay tae escort ye back tae Dingwall, fer we are expected at Lochcarron soon. But heed my warning. If a storm catches ye, stay on the trail and seek shelter. Ye canna begin tae understand the danger o' bein' lost when the world is swirling white and wind gusts sweep ye frae the saddle."

The cooks served a stew made of grouse shot that day and vegetables bought from a crofter's wife who had trekked out from a tiny settlement where the Talladale burn flowed into the loch. The MacKenzies contributed a small keg of beer, and the gathering grew convivial.

Late in the evening, most of the crew retired to their blankets, but Jamie stayed up with the MacKenzies. The air grew noticeably colder and the mist thicker, but the Highlanders huddled around the fire did not notice.

The conversation drifted to the purpose of the survey. Jamie described how John Lockhart-Ross was looking for ways to better manage the land and raise its productivity.

"It is the same here as in Easter Ross. Maist crofters raise grain and other crops in sma' rigs stretching across the straths and run cattle and sheep on a common pasturage where the land is puir fer cropping. The yields in the east are pitiful, indicating that the soil is exhausted. Here in the west, I see better crops and wonder why."

Colin MacKenzie spoke, "The soil is thin hereabouts and the weather much colder than in the east. Ye would think that crops would fare puirly, but the crofters work in ash frae kelp that they gather and burn by the shore. 'Tis an easy task tae gather and lay it tae dry. Peat is plentiful, and the kelp reduced tae ashes is easy tae shovel and transport."

Jamie mused, "Then why dinna crofters in Easter Ross apply kelp tae their crops?"

David MacKenzie said, "Little washes up on the eastern shore, and crofters follow traditional ways o' enriching their fields by manuring and allowing the land tae lie fallow. They live on their side o' the hills, and we live on our side. The laird may think that factors and tacksmen can order crofters tae adopt the practices o' others, but tradition is an unco difficult habit tae change."

Jamie nodded thoughtfully, then said, "Aye, but if they saw the size o' cabbages, kail, and potatoes raised in the west, it might be easier tae persuade them. I will include such a suggestion in my survey."

In the morning, the mist lifted two hours after dawn. The MacKenzies mounted, waved farewell, and turned southeastward along the loch. By the time the surveyors staked out their baseline, the riders were out of sight.

Far to the northwest, south of the barren mass of Iceland, lay a vast area of low pressure that spawned the Atlantic winter storms that swept across the British Isles and western Europe every winter. Once a cyclonic storm began to move from this region, it picked up energy from the sea. At an average rate of eight to ten miles an hour, a storm could traverse the six hundred miles of open water in as little as sixty hours. Two days earlier, three hundred miles from Scotland, two of these storms coalesced, intensifying their power. As the leading edge of this massive storm approached the Outer Hebrides and the exposed coast of Wester Ross, freezing rain and snow began to fall, but the winds were calm. However, at the storm's core of intense low pressure, the winds rose to hurricane force, lashing the ocean water into mountainous waves.

The surveying crew went to their blankets early, for it had been a tiring day. Jamie sat up for an hour reviewing his notes by lantern light. The air was still, the wall of mist that had enveloped their camp each night was gone. The stars and the sickle moon disappeared as a high cloud bank moved in from the west. Jamie's breath smoked out, and he became aware that the temperature was dropping steadily. He rummaged in his pack for an extra blanket. Although he was restless, he wrapped himself in it, extinguished the lantern, and retired to his tent.

As the temperature of the air dropped, a lacy pattern of frost spread over the ground and water froze in the wooden buckets. It began to snow, flakes falling gently to dot the grass and heather surrounding the campsite. Alastair Ross, the assigned guard for the evening, rose and stretched. He yearned for a cup of hot tea. He added a log to the fire, but it was retreating into ashes under the accumulating flakes. He poked the coals, which flared to life momentarily, but faded under the snowfall. Defeated, he huddled deeper into his coat and wound a woolen shawl around his head. He jerked awake, realizing that he had been dozing. The ashes emitted only a dull glow. A coating of white lay over the camp, and the snow was falling so thickly that he could scarcely make out the tents. Rising, he shook the snow off himself and trudged to wake his relief.

Alastair's anxious voice woke Jamie. "Mr. Drummond, we thought it best tae notify ye that there is heavy snaw falling."

Jamie rubbed his eyes and sat up. He unhooded the lantern that he always kept burning for emergencies. The interior of the tent lit up. He rose and pulled back the tent flap. After staring for a minute, he said, "I dinna hear any wind. Perhaps it will soon pass. I fear that we are done wi' surveying and must pack and depart in the morning. We will be on the trail lang before we find shelter—if we find it at all this side o' Achnasheen and Bran Water. I advise ye tae get some sleep. There is nae need this night fer a guard."

The camp slept peacefully as the silent snowfall accumulated. Four hours later, much more than a foot of snow was on the ground. The wind began as tiny cats paws ruffling the still water of Loch Maree. Soon, it was sighing in the few trees dotting the strath and the islands in the loch, bending them eastward under its inexorable force. Tent ropes vibrated, and poles flexed. Pushed by the wind, the loose snow crystals began to drift, leaving some patches bare and mounding in heaps against obstructions. Canvas flapped noisily, snatching the surveying crew from sleep.

Jamie was instantly awake and on his feet. Long years at sea had trained him to quickly recognize and assess danger. The wall of the tent belled inward, straining the guy ropes and suddenly flew outward with a crack like a gunshot. Two minutes later, Jamie stepped outside with the lantern. He gasped as the wind assaulted his face. It swirled the snow until there was scarcely visibility in any direction.

Jamie staggered sideways under the wind's buffeting force. He regained his footing and ran from tent to tent. None were damaged, but the stakes were pulling out. "Ho, Ian! Archie!" he shouted. "Bring sledges and mair stakes! Hurry!"

The voice of the wind rose in intensity from a full-throated roar to a banshee scream. The young men worked frantically, joined by the groom and cook, to reinforce the tents. In spite of their efforts, one blew away, scattering blankets and clothing across the snow.

Jamie cursed himself for not heeding Colin MacKenzie's warning, and especially for complacently dismissing the guard not four hours earlier. Frail tents could not withstand the storm's blast. They had to seek shelter, but where would they find it? The lochside crofts and warehouses had already been closed for the winter. The folk who had tended them had left days before. The danger was real, but not so great that he felt justified breaking into them. He made a swift decision that they would load food and the precious surveying equipment on the pack animals and head eastward. Achnasheen was a large enough village to shelter them. The cart would be useless in the deep snow. They would leave it behind with a cache of everything they did not need.

He sent Ian MacTaggart with a team to bring the horses and pack animals from their makeshift corral. He and the other crew members fought the raving wind to salvage what they could from the tents. Before they were finished, two more shredded to flying tatters. When the animals were loaded with all that they could carry, Jamie formed them into two columns. Archie Mitchell and Ian MacTaggart roped them together. Jamie gathered his crew into a close circle in the darkness. He had to shout to make himself heard over the shrieking wind.

"I canna show ye the map, but recall that our camp is five hundred feet frae the shore o' the loch by the stream that flows frae Loch Garbhaig. We must cross it by way o' the footbridge. The trail traverses the lochside eastward but lies under the snaw. I dinna wish us tae blunder aboot in the darkness. Dawn will bring but little improvement in visibility, but we will wait. Although I fear the wind-driven flooding along the shore, it is the surest way. We will follow the loch eastward tae its end. Ian will lead, and I will bring up the rear tae prevent straggling. This will be a wearying day, lads, but I dare nae risk ye being separated and lost in the snaw. Keep hold o' yer mount's bridle and call fer help if ye fall."

The sky lightened as they huddled in the snow, facing east to keep the blowing snow out of their faces. With the coming of dawn, the wind subsided briefly, and the air cleared enough that they could see the strath and the water churned to gray foam. As if possessed by a malevolent intelligence, the storm renewed its fury as the cavalcade of men and animals began their slogging trek along its shore.

The wind-driven snow lay in crescent-shaped dunes formed by the wind. It was two to three feet deep in places. Its softness was beguiling. Boots and hooves went in easily but had to be pulled out with every step, sapping energy. Jamie was cheered by a single thought as they trudged. At least they were facing away from the blast. If their backs were taking the force of the wind, their faces were protected. While the wind aided their movement, the slippery surface under the layer of snow made for treacherous footing and many stumbles. As the party neared the flooded lochside, the footing became even more perilous. Ian MacTaggart waved frantically, fell, got up, and changed course to find higher ground.

The trail to the head of the loch covered seven miles. The light was fading from the scud-filled sky when the exhausted survey crew reached it. They did not stop to eat but munched on stale bannocks and dried fish from their saddlebags. The animals were showing signs of distress, and Jamie ordered a halt to feed and give them water dipped from the loch. Kinlochewe was deserted. It was no more than a shieling or summer place used by herders.

There were three roofless bawns with stone walls that offered shelter on three sides from the howling wind. Scraping away the snow in the interior revealed a thick and noisome layer of cattle dung, so the crew hastily pushed the snow back in place. These were filthy places, but they needed shelter from the storm for themselves and the horses.

They lay wrapped in woolens, cocooned in the snow that kept falling, while the wind howled and shrieked demonically around the bawns. At dawn, Jamie gathered his crew, concerned over their glassy eyes and slow movements. They were exhausted, but their survival required them to move on over the mountain trail below the craggy peaks that they could not see. The trail wound upward out of a valley with frowning heights on either side, onto the high moors and past the cold waters of Loch Chroisg, then down to the village of Achnasheen, where they would find shelter.

Ian MacTaggart had broken the trail all the day before, so Jamie made a reluctant decision to take the lead himself. Archie Mitchell seemed in better shape, so he assigned him to serve as rear guard. They fed the horses and ate standing inside the bawns. Stepping outside exposed them all to the inexorable wind, which chilled them to the bone within seconds. The sky was iron-gray, with black scud racing eastward underneath. East of Loch Maree lay a wilderness of snow to where the scene vanished a half mile off into an impenetrable wall of white. With the horses roped together once again, Jamie walked the length of the caravan, encouraging his crew and promising them rest after one more good push. "Eleven miles, lad. That's all tae shelter, warmth, and hot victuals. Most nodded vigorously, but several heard the message in silence with downcast eyes. Matthew Davidson, nephew of Lord Lockhart-Ross, looked piteously at Jamie, who hesitated, then ordered the boy to mount his horse.

The worst of the trail was the four miles of steep uphill to the western side of Loch Chroisg. They had scarcely started when the wind redoubled its fury. Snowflakes filled the air. Visibility shrank until an hour later, Jamie was pushing through drifts in whiteness, with no view of the hills, shrubs, or even his own boots. He stopped and held up a mittened fist. He could scarcely see it. He stopped his mare, patted her flank, and released his grip on the reins. She stood still, snorting her disapproval.

Jamie trudged back along the line of roped-together horses, bent over into the wind, until he reached Archie Mitchell at the rear. All was well, though some of the crew were clearly panicked. He retraced his steps and resumed the trek. The day wore on, and Jamie granted frequent rests, for the uphill climb was exhausting, even with the aid of the inexorable wind.

The brief twilight found them only halfway along the north shore of the narrow mountain loch. Guiding along the water in the blinding whiteness made picking out a path through the deep snow easier. They moved a little faster. Jamie's anxiety for the crew's safety grew until his boots felt the slope change to downhill. He stopped and peered ahead. Colin MacKenzie, utterly familiar with this trail, had told him that he should be able to see the village lying at the bottom of the steep drop off the massive ice-capped Munro of Fionn Bheinn. The settlement was less than a mile below them alongside the river Bran. He peered, straining his eyes to see through the snow-speckled blackness. Nothing. He trusted that the village was there, but it was impossible to see any lights to guide them.

Their nearness to safety made the weary crew careless on the winding descent. Several times, they had to halt while those who had fallen climbed wearily back to their feet before resuming their downward march. Jamie guided them, with frequent shouted warnings, along the river. He caught himself growing careless, and he nearly stepped off the hidden trail, where the drop-off plunged down to the sinuous river. The mare, restrained by the rope tying her to the following horse, moved more and more slowly. Despairing of being forced to stop for the night once more, Jamie shouted exultantly when a yellow glow ahead resolved into a lantern hung from a signboard on the front of a shadowed building.

The snow had been shoveled clear of the raised wooden entrance of what was obviously an inn. In spite of the wind, Jamie could hear shouts from inside the door. "God hae mercy," he croaked. "We are saved!" He turned to wave frantically at his companions, who kept trudging stolidly toward him. Townspeople swiftly surrounded them, untying the horses and pulling the crew toward the golden light and warmth that spilled from the wide-open doorway. In less than a minute, the joy of finding refuge had turned to horror. Matthew Davidson was missing. The horse he had been riding on their tortured journey from Kinlochewe bore an empty saddle.

A frantic Jamie peppered Archie Mitchell, who had been the rear guard of the formation, with questions. Matthew was in the saddle when they had left the bawns that morning. He was still there when they stopped at the westward end of the mountain loch. Ian MacTaggart had spoken to him just before dusk. He had been sagging from exhaustion but refused to be tied to the saddle. He had slipped off somewhere before they had started downhill. In the gathering darkness and blowing snow, no one had seen him fall, and no one had stepped over him.

Mitchell and MacTaggart offered to return to search for Matthew, in addition to several townsmen. Leaving all the crew except Archie, he and the townsmen gathered lanterns for the return hike. MacTaggart was a copy of his massive father and not lacking in courage or stamina. He loudly pleaded to join them.

Jamie refused MacTaggart's pleas. "Nae, lad, stay. Ye are sae far gone in weariness. We canna carry yer bulky carcass when ye collapse, as ye surely will." In spite of the seriousness of the scene, the youth spread his hands in resignation. "Another time then, Mr. Drummond." Jamie nodded and clasped the boy's hand.

The nighttime trail back to Kinlochewe was far harder to travel than Jamie thought possible. The trail was uphill and into the unrelenting wind. Jamie had been battling the deep snow for hours. He felt that knives were being thrust through his calves and shins.

The rescue team was in a hurry, for time was precious for a boy lying in the snow. It was also impossible to guess where along the trail Matthew had fallen and whether he might have rolled or crawled away. They had to examine every hummock on either side of the crew's scarcely identifiable tracks for many yards. They had brought long poles, which they used to thrust into the snow, hallooing all the while in hopes that the boy could hear them and respond.

Jamie's tortured conscience conjured horrific scenarios of Matthew found frozen or so badly injured that survival was improbable. It was true that the lad had been headstrong and careless of sound advice repeatedly during the expedition, but Jamie was the leader and felt a heavy burden of guilt. How could he ever explain his failure to protect the boy to his parents or uncle. He felt bitter shame for the disgrace he would carry for a lifetime for his own carelessness. In that trek up the mountain trail, he mouthed silent prayers for the lad's safety.

It was Archie and the innkeeper, who had promptly removed his leather apron and donned a heavy coat and snug woolen hat to volunteer, who found Matthew's body and called for the others. He lay under a rocky overhang at the edge of the trail, where he must have rolled after falling from the horse. In the lantern light, his face was pale and his eyes closed. Archie removed a mitten and gently brushed away the accumulated snowflakes from his calm face. Jamie picked up his still form, and the innkeeper wrapped two blankets around him. They lay him down, and Archie, shaking with sobs, began rubbing Matthew's hands and cheeks. "Ach, lad! Come back tae us! 'Tis a great wrang tae lose sech a cantie sperit! Come back!"

Jamie reached to pull Archie's hands away when Matthew groaned and opened one eye. His mouth slowly formed words and all the men leaned close around him to hear. "Why are ye disturbing my sleep? I am sae warm and comfortable."

Archie wept, and the men cheered. They managed to get Matthew to a sitting position. The innkeeper growled. "Ye are lucky that ye are still alive, laddie. We feared that ye were freezing tae death, which makes a body feel warm and comfortable. Aye, it may be a pleasant way tae die, but ye hae much mair life tae live. Now rest easy while we bundle ye up and get ye doon the mountain." A gloved hand proffered a flask, and the innkeeper tilted it gently to Matthew's lips. A few drops trickled into his mouth, and he swallowed. Another swallow and he choked on the fiery liquid, erupting into coughing. He grinned weakly and said, "I would like tae try it again. I may need mair practice."

The men laughed heartily. The innkeeper swung the blanket-wrapped figure into his arms and rose easily. He said, "Whiskey can be warming, but there is naething better than Mrs. Murchison's cock-a-leekie soup tae fill yer belly." With firm strides, he led the way back along the loch.

In the morning, the storm clouds fled eastward, the wind subsided, and the sun shone in a blue sky. The weather continued cold, preventing the accumulated snow from melting and making travel hazardous. The conditions provided Jamie an excellent excuse for giving his weakened crew a few days of rest. The rooms in Mr. Murchison's inn at Achnasheen were crowded but warm. Mrs. Murchison's soup and other victuals on the limited bill of fare were all that her publican husband had promised. While the rest of the surveying crew recovered rapidly, Matthew Davidson remained abed for three days with aching joints and the aftereffects of frostbite in his fingers and toes. Jamie found it difficult to convince the fifteen-year-old that the blotchy red of his face and the skin peeling from his nose would not permanently disfigure him. He struggled from his bed on the fourth day and made his way downstairs to the public room, where the crew applauded his grit. This day also marked the end of the cold snap. Rain fell all day, turning the white snow to a gray slush and offering the hope that in a day or two they could start their journey back to Balnagown.

A week after the surveying crew had staggered out of the snow-choked mountains, Jamie paid Mr. Murchison generously for his hospitality and gave the order to leave. Matthew Davidson was still too weak to ride alone, so he sat strapped in front of Archie Mitchell. The two were good friends and chatted amiably as the riders trotted alongside the rocky Brand. The sky was cloudy, but the air sufficiently warm so that the horses were splashing in meltwater as they trotted the sixteen miles to the road junction beyond Loch Luichart.

At the joining of the trails, the road widened. Ian MacTaggart moved up alongside Jamie. "I suggest stopping tae eat somewhere on the strath below where the Brand runs into Loch Garve."

Jamie shook his head. "I would rather allow the crew tae dismount and sup in a village where we can sit at table wi' hot food."

MacTaggart shifted uneasily in the saddle. "The only settlement before the road comes oot o' the mountains is Cunndainn on Blackwaterside. 'Tis a fell place, wi' an evil reputation because o' what happened at the kirk."

Jamie raised an eyebrow. The factor's son had proven himself throughout the summer as a steady hand, unshakeable in dangerous circumstances, yet he was plainly frightened. MacTaggart shook his head. "The ghosts o' the innocent hover o'er the burned church. Many hae seen these souls in torment."

Jamie asked, "Wha happened at the kirk, and when?"

MacTaggart stared at the pine trees that lined the road for a while without answering. In a low voice, he began the tale. "Lang syne, there was a feud between the MacDonalds and their allies wi' the MacKenzies o' Kinellan. Their forces met at Cunndainn and discovered that the women, elderly, and the children o' the place hae taken refuge in the kirk, trusting in the sacred tradition o' sanctuary tae protect them. Alexander Macdonald commanded his men tae bar the doors and surround the building sae none could escape. He gave orders to set the kirk on fire, and everyone inside, perhaps hundreds, were burnt tae death. Vengeance from Mackenzies and MacRaes was swift. After the battle at Pairc, perhaps twa hundred o' a force o' twa thousand Macdonalds and their followers, wha hae come tae rendezvous in the toun, were left tae escape as they might, but many were hacked tae death or shot as they ran awa'. It was lang years before people resettled the toun."

Jamie listened in silence while the horses splashed along the muddy track. He was struck by the vehemence with which young MacTaggart told his tale and the tears that streaked his face. At length, he said, "Every place in Scotland hae a reputation fer dark and bluidy events, yet the folk wha inhabit sech places gae on wi' their lives."

MacTaggart wiped his cheeks. His voice husky with feeling, he said, "Aye, they do, but those o' the affected families dinna easily forget and feed the auld clan feuds. Ye canna expect the McIans tae forget Glencoe, nor the MacDonalds the piper wi' his hands severed by the Campbells. While the MacTaggarts are a sept o' Clan Ross, I am a MacKenzie o' Kinellan on my mother's side."

Jamie said quietly, "'Tis the bane o' the Scottish race tae be e'er divided by auld injuries and jealousies. We are a prickly and pridefu' folk. Twill be seventy and seven generations before we achieve tranquility. I hae noted that Scots lose that sense o' rivalry when ta'en awa'. Wi' military men, pride and loyalty tae the service or a ship becomes paramount and nae nationality or ancestry. Of course, that is true o' maist men and officers but nae the aristocrats."

Ian MacTaggart rode closer and touched Jamie's arm. He leaned in and spoke with intensity, "If my father hae his way, twill nae langer be a concern fer my family or those laboring fer him."

Jamie stared. "What are ye saying, lad? Why will it nae be a concern? Yer family is bound tae the clan chief by generations o' tradition. Lockhart-Ross also told me that all the factors and tacksmen hold charters tae their lands. The laird canna dispossess him wi'out his consent, surely."

MacTaggart colored and muttered, "I hae nae right tae speak fer my father. My words were intemperate."

Jamie put a finger to his lips and drew the factor's son off the trail onto the flooded strath. Looking back, he motioned the rest of the crew onward. He dropped the reins and pulled off his gloves. "Lad, yer father's secret is safe wi' me, but I advise ye sternly tae keep silence on this matter. Weeks o' riding and walking aboot in Ross-shire hae made it plain that the crofter folk, herders, and others dependent on agriculture and grazing are struggling tae harvest sufficient crops tae feed their families. Perhaps some will choose tae relocate tae touns, or even emigrate, but it is too soon. The laird ordered this survey tae support his plan o' improvements tae make the land mair productive. I would think that such a message would be encouraging."

Young MacTaggart wagged his head in denial. "Ye are nae o' this shire and canna learn easily wha those living here already ken. Many will hae faith in the laird, fer they feel that he is a guid man and concerned fer the folk. But he is a laird wi' a laird's manner and thirst fer living weel. Factors hae traditionally lived comfortably. We are nae puir, and my father hae been maist generous wi' those wha depend upon him in forgiving debts and ensuring that those in unfortunate circumstances receive help. I am young but hae seen my father's resources dwindle quickly o'er the years. Wi' high prices and rents and low yields, he can nae langer afford tae be as generous as before. He believes the folk in his care are his children, sae tae speak, as their fathers and mothers were tae his father, and it grieves him mightily tae see them suffer."

Jamie slapped the pommel with his gloves and looked down the road. "We must move on soon, MacTaggart, but what will yer father do?"

The factor's son pulled off his cap and ran his fingers through his curly red hair. "Ye must promise nae tae tell."

Jamie replied, "Ye hae my word. 'Tis a matter only fer yer father and the laird."

MacTaggart took a deep breath and continued, "If he can collect enough money frae rents, subsidies, and other sources, he intends tae charter a ship and leave Ross wi' maist o' his crofters, herders, and their families."

Skepticism was evident in Jamie's reply. "And where will they sail? The weather in Canada is brutal, and the Caribbean is a disease-ridden death trap fer white settlers. There is surely nae place in England or Ireland fer them. The Ulster Scots are fleeing those lands at a great pace, where rents are impossible tae pay."

Ian smiled. "In North Carolina, land is cheap and easily cleared. Reliable folk report that it is a guidly land free o' the fevers o' the tidewater. People hae been settling on the land fer mair than a generation."

Jamie said, "I hae heard the reports, which are excessively favorable, but there they provide that which the folk need."

MacTaggart frowned. "And what is that, Mr. Drummond?"

Jamie grinned. "Hope, my lad. Since the disaster at Darien in Panama where sae many died o' strange tropical diseases, Carolina stirs hope in the hearts o' the Scottish people. I hae a high regard fer yer father and would urge him tae deal honorably wi' the laird. I will keep his secret." He pulled on his gloves. Lifting the reins, he guided the mare back to the road, trotting to catch up to the crew.

Jamie quietly issued the order that they would bypass haunted Cunndainn. They would stop briefly in Tarvie Wood, where the road provided a fine view of the cascading waters of Rogie Falls.

The crew fed their horses and ate in the saddle since the strath was muddy. Jamie permitted only a brief rest, for he was anxious to reach the outskirts of Dingwall before dusk. The road alongside the Blackwater led to Conon Bridge. From there, the level route was easy to navigate to the familiar road that skirted the Cromarty Firth. Thirty-five miles in the saddle made for a long day, but all the crew were experienced riders. They and their mounts had enjoyed a week's rest. It was a happy group that raised a cheer as Jamie led his tired procession past the lights of Balnagown castle to the stables. He checked his watch by the flaring light of the sentry's torch. It was past midnight.

Jamie roused the grooms but insisted that the riders perform the necessary chores of feeding, watering, and rubbing down the horses before dismissing them to the kitchen, where sleepy cooks fed them a cold meal. Only when the animals and men had been settled did Jamie leave word for Lord Lockhart-Ross, who had retired at a sensible hour, that he would provide him a report in the morning.

Early winter daylight came late. He rolled over, luxuriating in the warm comfort of the bed until the rising sun painted the insides of his eyelids a rosy hue. He flung the corner of the blanket across his face to block the light and tried to force his racing mind to still, but it was too late. It had been the first night in months that he could sleep undisturbed by care for others under his charge. He regretted that he would be unable to sleep any longer, for although the crew had returned safely, the survey remained incomplete. Lord Lockhart-Ross was an exacting employer and would require a thorough accounting of the team's progress, difficulties encountered, monies spent, and plans for spring less than four months away. He had been captain of a British warship, and Jamie was well-acquainted with the restless minds of commanders and the questions requiring answers. He rose and padded across the cold stone floor in his bare feet to pick up the white envelope lying where a discreet servant had pushed it under the door. He tore it open and stared at the letter. Lord Lockhart-Ross requested that he report to him at ten thirty in the solar, with his notes, observations, accounts, and maps.

Jamie remained standing while Lord Ross studied the partially completed map, knuckles planted firmly on the table. He uttered an occasional *humph*, his eyes flicking back and forth between the chart and the notes spread before him. At length, he straightened, rubbing his back. He chuckled ruefully. "I hae grown soft since leaving sea duty and coming north." He glanced at Jamie. "Ye, on the other hand, appear uncommonly fit, Drummond. It seems that the privations o' life in the open are preferable tae leisurely pursuits indoors."

Jamie spread his hands deprecatingly. "The work was unco difficult, wi' lang hours in the field and saddle, but the lads and I still found time fer swordplay and football."

Lockhart-Ross lifted an eyebrow. "Football?"

Jamie grinned. "Aye, it is nae a game common in the Highlands, but yer nephew Matthew brought a ball frae the Lowlands and taught us the rudiments o' the sport. I must admit that the lessons were harsh. The lads were quick wi' the ball, and I got a bluidy shin fer my pains. I limped aboot fer a week. Tae retaliate, I taught them fencing and exacted a measure o' revenge."

The sea captain-turned-lord's scowl turned slowly to a grin. "Mischievous rascal, Matthew. I spoke wi' him this morning. He admitted disliking ye fer yer harshness but confessed that he owes ye much."

Jamie shook his head. "I am honor bound, my lord. Rescuing someone in my charge is my duty."

John Lockhart-Ross cut in. "He is happy tae survive the storm and blames his own carelessness fer falling off his horse. But I was speaking o' his gratitude tae ye fer accepting him as part o' the surveying crew. He is also grateful fer ye nae sending him hame when he and the other lads arranged fer three lasses frae a neighboring village tae visit them in the dead o' night."

Jamie started. It had been a late summer's night with no moon. A small noise had awakened him, and he had risen to investigate without lighting a lantern. Creeping to the tent and bending down, he grasped the flap and yanked it high to discover the six youths in various stages of undress. The girls had screamed and covered themselves; the boys had shouted and tried to hide. Jamie grinned at the recollection, for he had been forced to use stern measures with the lads. The girls he had escorted home weeping to their parents. When he returned, he imposed the same punishment that he had used successfully in the military, hours of hard work for the malefactors, with a promise not to report their indiscretion. He had kept his end of the bargain, but someone had told of the incident.

He cleared his throat. "Milord, ye trusted me tae manage the crew as I saw fit. I discovered them in the act, sae tae speak, and imposed a fitting punishment. I saw nae reason tae report them since there were nae further incidents. It was a matter fer me tae handle."

A smile creased the laird's face. "Aye, it was a youthful indiscretion but could hae been serious. Crofters wilna oppose young bucks taking liberties, but the resentment runs deep."

Jamie said, "I dinna see that the lasses were coerced. I think it was an arrangement fer mutual pleasure. They were caught early in the act and received a thundering condemnation. Fright is a powerful disincentive tae romance."

The laird burst out laughing. "Captain Drummond, ye must hae been a terror descending on them unawares. I trust yer judgment in the matter and the punishment—nay, the instruction ye imposed. Hard work is an excellent curative fer misbehavior. We will nae speak o' it further, and Matthew wilna ken that I told ye. I forced the lad on ye, and ye took him in hand, treating him the same as those much older. He hae grown much in a few months' time. I see a new soberness in him, and I am grateful." He turned to gesture through the window at the bare trees blowing in the wind. "I expect that ye will resume the survey as soon as spring weather permits, but I also assume that ye are anxious tae return tae Abergeldie fer the holidays?"

Jamie said, "Aye, but that must wait fer a fortnight. I hae many notes tae review and details tae map. When the weather moderates, we will set oot, in spite o' snaw and cold. We are in the Highlands after all. It will take months to complete the survey, starting wi' the lowlands o' Easter Ross and then returning tae the western mountains."

Lord John returned to the table to study the map. "I will require yer utmost diligence. Commit all the resources ye need tae complete the work before the end o' next year."

Jamie said, "I wish tae retain the same crew and complement o' animals. The surveyors hae sufficient experience fer twa teams tae operate independently."

Lord John said, "I am curious aboot yer observations. I read some o' yer notes and would fain hear mair. Ye commented on the productivity o' crops in Wester Ross and the use o' kelp ash tae fertilize."

Jamie replied, "Ye hae expressed yer concerns aboot low productivity o' crops and impoverishment o' the soil. The crofters I spoke wi' in the east complain that they hae insufficient manure frae their ain stock tae meet their needs. There is nae sufficiency in the neighborhood, and they must buy frae elsewhere. Maist canna afford it. They pick kelp but find it sparse on this coast. In the west, crofters in their spare time easily pick vast quantities frae the shingle and sand and dry it on ricks before burning it tae ash, making it light and easy tae transport. Since they collect it themselves, they obtain it wi' little cost."

Lockhart-Ross warmed to the topic. "Transporting the ash frae west tae east should require little effort. It appears tae be a sound business venture fer some enterprising crofters and carters. I would be willing tae underwrite the initial cost against the gain frae better crops. I am also contemplating changing leases tae eliminate some o' the nonsensical planting in unprofitable rigs and relieving the exhaustion o' upland pasturage by changing breeds o' kine and sheep. I aim tae make Ross-shire a model o' improved agriculture and herding. I must rely on the factors and tacksmen tae help convince the crofters tae change auld habits."

Jamie said softly, "How will ye solve the problem o' excessive population on the land?"

Ross left the map and sat down heavily in a large chair. He looked out the window at the dark leafless trees flexing in the swirling wind. There was a faint sound of twigs drumming against the glass. He said, "Improvements in productivity will help, but some must leave. The survey will tell me which fields and pasturage are marginal."

Jamie persisted. "Aye, sir, but how will ye choose which families must leave and which may stay? Which people are marginal and which productive and resourceful? Will ye choose them, or will ye allow them tae choose fer themselves?"

Lord Ross frowned. "They hae been bound tae the land fer generations unmeasured, yet they are nae peasants, as in Poland or Russia. I would wish those wi' indolent habits tae leave while the industrious remain. Those wi' useful skills may find employment in Dingwall and other touns. Fer young men, the Royal Navy and Highland regiments still take recruits, even in this time o' peace. Those wi' strong backs but few skills can find work as navvies or laborers. Unfortunately, those trades benefit young men but take them awa' frae the land while leaving the elderly, women, and children behind as dependents."

Jamie studied his employer's face. He saw no duplicity. Lockhart-Ross was no tyrant, but had no practical sense of how to manage the dilemma. Jamie thought of Ian MacTaggart and his father's secret plans to take his tacksmen and crofter families to North Carolina. He knew that MacTaggart was an effective factor who coaxed good productivity from the crofters and herders. Jamie could not guess at the laird's reaction or what measures he might take to prevent them from departing.

At length, Jamie said, "Ye wish fer the best outcome fer yerself and yer house, my lord, and that is natural. Auld loyalties bind men mair than chains. It is also natural fer those wi' ambition tae choose the course that they think best benefits themselves and their families. The emigration experiences in England and Ulster show that principle tae be true. The ambitious are frequently those maist likely tae depart. Those transported fer criminal acts are another matter. I hae heard a prominent colonial denounce the practice o' the crown dumping them in the New World tae relieve the auld."

Lockhart-Ross's smile was rueful. "A wise observation. I am committed tae improving my ain patrimony and will do what I can tae help those in my charge. I hae nae godly powers, Mr. Drummond. We live in a world that is rapidly changing. We dinna hae the Sight and canna foretell what will happen. I only ken that we must do something tae save our way o' life. Many lives depend upon it."

The surveying crew's hasty departure from the camp at Loch Maree in a raving storm meant that notes, calculations, and sketches were in disarray. It would not do to leave them unsorted until survey work resumed in the spring. There were calculations to complete and verify, data to transfer to the master map, and planning required for the coming season. Jamie, with help from Archie, Ian, and Matthew, worked on these activities every day and far into the evening. One night, after he had dismissed his surveyors, Jamie sat hunched over the master map, inking in details around Loch Maree. At first, he was not aware of someone clearing his throat behind him. A discreet cough broke through his concentration. He turned to stare at the bulk of Hugh MacTaggart. The factor raised a massive fist to knuckle his forelock. "Beggin' yer pardon, Mr. Drummond. 'Tis late, but I must speak wi' ye before ye depart. I trust that ye ken the reason."

Jamie set down the quill in its stand and flexed his cramped fingers. "I do. I reassured yer son that I would nae speak o' the matter tae the laird. If ye doubt me—"

The factor shook his head vehemently. "Nae! I hae nae fears on that matter. I ken that ye are a man o' integrity."

Jamie motioned to a chair. MacTaggart sat, clearly agitated. He looked around the darkened room, where the only light came from hanging lanterns above the map table. Jamie said, "Rest assured that we are here by ourselves. Everyone else hae retired tae bed lang since."

MacTaggart sighed, clearly relieved. "The matter indiscreetly revealed by my son is very much unsettled. We live in uncertain times, sir, and our plans are little mair than dreams."

Jamie asked, "How so?"

MacTaggart gripped the arms of the chair tightly. "The crops this season were puir in quality and quantity. The money we received and shared among the crofters was less than we expected. I dinna think that next summer's cattle and shearings will make up the loss, nor the fall's crops, though the laird is promising help wi' obtaining kelp ash frae the west."

Jamie said, "Ye are telling me that yer plans may fail. If so, what will ye do?"

MacTaggart's shaggy head came up. "We still intend tae leave. Some may be forced tae remain behind or indenture themselves and their families. Our hope is that we can arrange credit wi' some banker or investor wha will advance funds until we can repay. I will travel tae Edinburgh after the holidays tae seek it."

Jamie said, "How much are ye lacking, Hugh?"

MacTaggart grimaced. "Perhaps five thousand pounds."

Jamie whistled tunelessly. "'Tis a considerable sum. Bankers and investors insist on collateral, Hugh. What will ye offer them?"

MacTaggart's face fell. "We need tae preserve our cash tae purchase land in North Carolina, which we canna mortgage until we receive title. I hae title tae my ain lands, crops, and herds here in Ross-shire but hae committed the entirety tae purchasing transportation fer my people. Wi' puir prices, what we hae is nae sufficient and that is why we need a loan. We hae nae collateral tae offer, excepting our ain labor."

MacTaggart fell silent. Jamie mused on the dilemma. "I can think o' nae laird in the Highlands wha will undertake tae make such a loan against the interest o' a peer, though I will mention it tae my uncle and cousins. Very discreetly, ye may be sure."

MacTaggart rose. "Ye hae my thanks, Mr. Drummond, fer yer help and yer silence. Somehow, I will find a way tae bring this people tae a new land."

Jamie grinned. "Aye, I believe ye can. Ye will be a veritable Moses tae this people."

o———o

Every member of the crew had volunteered to be ready for the new season's mapping expedition, and Jamie was glad of their enthusiasm. He praised them all in the presence of the laird and presented each of them a Christmas bonus before departing.

A winter storm had swept in that morning from the west, bringing a downpour with brief periods of sleet. Wind churned the Cromarty Firth. Few travelers ventured on the muddy coastal road that connected the intervening villages and settlements to Tain northward and Dingwall to the south. Jamie pulled his hat lower and rode hunched over his horse's withers. He had grown very fond of the mare. He had never named her, but his surveying crew had taken to calling her Stormshadow, claiming that her dark gray coloring made the name a perfect fit.

Rain worked its way into his coat and trickled down his back. He regretted having delayed his departure from Balnagown castle to five days before Christmas, but he had had little choice. After departing Dingwall, he crossed the Black Isle. The wind was fierce when he reached the Kessock ferry. There was only a single boat making the crossing of the Beauly Firth, and he had to wait nearly an hour for it to make the half-mile trip back to the north shore. The two ferrymen were reluctant to make another crossing in the strong chop, but the promise of a double fare for a man and horse was persuasive. The ferrymen were fearful that the mare would be spooked by the rough water, but Jamie refused to blinker her. It took another fare to persuade the men to make the trip. The patient mare eyed the surging waves fearfully, but Jamie's grip on the reins and soothing voice in her ear were enough to calm her.

The ferry nosed into the smoother water in the inlet of the River Ness before tying up at a town pier. Remounted, Jamie guided the horse along Harbor road from the landing. He stopped at a public house on the outskirts of Inverness and provided the horse the luxury of a rubdown, a bag of oats, and an hour in a warm stable out of the downpour.

Homecoming to the castle at Abergeldie was joyous. All the old traditions were honored, and the holidays sped by. At his mother's urging, Jamie accepted invitations to several balls held at nearby castles. He found the entertainment amusing and the local lasses winsome, pleasant, and more than willing to engage in coquetry and flirtatious small talk. Jamie cooperated but found none of the girls who could compare to Sarah, his lost love, and he became disinterested. His military experiences and attitudes distanced him from the youthful crowd. He found himself sitting by himself, listening to conversations and speaking little. Jamie was grateful that his Uncle Charles had refrained from bringing up the topic of arranged marriage with the eligible Gordon heiress. He had one encounter with his mother in her apartment when she broached the subject of marriage. It was an awkward discussion, with Euphemia questioning and Jamie providing increasingly reluctant and circumferential answers. At length, she threw up her hands and exclaimed, "Jamie Drummond! Ye are turning into an irascible and disagreeable auld bachelor! I see that ye will do naething tae advance yer prospects. Perhaps I must alter my approach tae the subject and find ye a match, a young lady o' quality determined tae land ye hersel', like the great fish ye are, wi' a strang hook and line." Jamie gazed at his mother in astonishment. She burst out laughing. "Ye are a delightful laddie, my Jamie, sitting there wi' yer mouth open, ready tae receive the bait and feel the tug o' the line!" Her smile softened and grew pensive. "I wish the best fer ye. There hae been much sorrow and trial in yer life, and ye deserve much happiness, success in a profession, restoration o' yer inheritance, a guid wife, and bairns. I ken that I must bide a wee fer these things, but I am restless."

Jamie's smile was mischievous. "Patience, Mama. Ye hate that word as much as I. Perhaps the prophecy will bring fulfillment sooner rather than later. Seventeen sixty-five is a new year that may bring many surprises. We hear naething frae the government aboot restoration, but I hae come tae expect naething and must make my ain way. I am nae langer afraid o' pursuing my ain fortune."

Euphemia's dark eyebrows rose. "Ye hae heard something frae Peter or Hugh? I was disappointed that they dinna return frae London fer Hogmanay, but I understand the press o' their obligations."

Jamie said, "Aye, we communicate in the modern way—through letters, Mama."

His mother's eyes flashed a warning that stifled Jamie's jest. "Ye are indeed a cantie and cheeky lad. I will hae ye tae understand that unlike England, much mair than half o' Scotland's population can read, and the Highlands are nae exception. Your uncle Charles subscribes tae the *Edinburgh Evening Courant* and the *Caledonian Mercury*. I read every article when they arrive. The London papers come much later, and it is interesting tae me tae see the differences in viewpoints expressed."

Jamie said soothingly, "Aye, Mama. 'Tis useful tae read the printed news, but nae every event is reported, and many journalists are hesitant tae offend the government. That is why letters, preserved frae censorship, permit mair honesty."

His mother, piqued by the conversation, pressed him. "And wha hae ye learned frae letters?"

Jamie shifted uncomfortably. "The ministers and Parliament are obsessed wi' the colonies. The colonies are prohibited frae issuing paper currency. They passed a Sugar Act in April. These measures are already encountering outright resistance in Boston, and Peter thinks that other colonies will soon follow."

Euphemia sniffed. "Highlanders are nae the only people feeling the sting o' government oppression. I pity the colonists, but I am glad tae hear that they hae spirit."

Jamie continued, "Hugh is mair than usually gloomy. According tae his contacts, King George and his closest advisors still imagine a Jacobite spy peeping frae behind a bush in every Highland glen and French agents paying clansmen tae stir up trouble. I hae it on guid report frae Jock McRae that naval patrols continue among the islands. But I rode past Fort George. The sentries were lax. He claims that they are vigilant in the west around Fort William and still patrol often. It hae been nearly twenty years since the rising. Except fer Papa, King James, and the Bonnie Prince, nearly all the banished leaders hae passed on. Hugh dinna think that there ever will be a restoration or a lifting o' the attainder. I agree wi' him, Mama." He clenched his fist and pounded the arm of the chair emphatically. "Fer yer sake, I will nae think on it further."

That winter's weather was not harsh, and the young men of the family found plentiful opportunities to ride, exercise the dogs, chase foxes, and hunt. Every day, Jamie worked on his notes and surveying plans for the new year, but late every afternoon he and David Gordon fenced. In spite of work, Jamie succumbed to the urging of his sisters and wee Jock to sled and play in the snow. Abergeldie lacked the extensive formal gardens of Strathallan, his childhood home, but the children worked out schemes for playing all the old games.

Winter inactivity chafed Jamie, and he was almost glad to pack when the first day of March arrived, cold and blustery. The road winding from the castle to the bridge over the Dee was muddy, frozen ruts making the going hazardous. However, for Jamie and Stormshadow, the beginning of the long ride back to Balnagown was welcome activity. Jamie stared at the bare branches of the trees lining the road and sighing in the wind, knowing that when he next saw Abergeldie, the trees would be bare once more and the same road would be dusty, strewn thickly with the gold and red leaves of late fall.

Spring came late in Ross-shire that year. The surveying crew was filled with enthusiasm, but buffeting wind, snow, fog, and freezing rain soon dampened it. They spent nearly half of the days working by lantern light in their tents on calculations, tables of data, and updates to the slowly growing map. Other days found them huddled inside bawns and sheds for hours, waiting for rain and sleet to stop. When the weather was too wet or windy to set up the plane tables and transits, the surveyors trekked to croft houses to collect data on crops, livestock, and families.

Jamie had begun the surveying on MacTaggart lands to ensure that survey data and maps on those lands would be available to Lord Lockhart-Ross when Hugh MacTaggart announced the departure of his people. The lands lay between Balnagown and Alness, rich farmland and groves of timber.

A month after the survey crews had started, they set up camp between Kincraig Castle and Newmore Wood, a convenient location that would support them as they surveyed all the fields and groves to the River Averon, which marked the southern boundary of Hugh MacTaggart's lands. The crews had worked hard for five days, taking advantage of the improving weather and every minute of daylight. On Saturday morning, he ordered the surveyors to stand down for the morning to enable them to do laundry, repair equipment, and enjoy a few hours off duty.

Jamie sat in a camp chair before his tent, absorbed in reviewing the notes compiled by the two survey team leads. He did not notice the lone rider approaching the camp until the young guard startled him with a loud hail. The rider yanked off his hat. Jamie looked up and recognized Alex MacCulley, one of the grooms at Balnagown Castle.

The groom approached, hat in hand. "Captain Drummond, sor. I was sent tae bring ye a message frae the Ross. He bids ye attend him immediately."

Jamie frowned. "Immediately?"

The groom nodded vigorously, "Aye. He said it was maist important, aboot a visitor tae the castle, one o' yer kinfolk."

Tension gripped Jamie's throat. Who was the visitor, and what message did he convey? He thought to query the groom, but realized that the man probably did not know. The camp lay less than six miles from Balnagown Castle. A ride of less than thirty minutes would resolve the mystery. He called for Ian MacTaggart and Archie Mitchell, his lead surveyors, and issued them instructions for the afternoon's work. That done, he mounted Stormshadow and rode for the castle, the groom trailing.

He swung off the mare and handed the reins to MacCulley, who slid to a stop beside him. A servant escorted him to the laird's study. Lockhart-Ross sat at his desk wearing a pair of spectacles. A man was seated before the fire and turned as Jamie entered. It was his cousin David Gordon, weary and mud-spattered.

John Lockhart-Ross said softly, "Please sit down, Jamie. Captain Gordon has brought news of great sadness."

Jamie pulled off his gloves and took a chair. He had had enough encounters with tragedy to know that he was about to receive bad news.

David Gordon took a letter from his jacket pocket. Before handing it to Jamie, he said, "Tae relieve yer mind, cousin, yer mama and the children are well. The news is frae France. I bid ye read the letter. It is dated a month past."

Jamie's fingers began to tremble as he tore open the envelope to extract several pages of thin foolscap.

The first page was written in French in a tightly precise script that Jamie recognized as the handwriting of Madame Hilbert. She had addressed the letter to his mother and him. Jamie looked up at David, tears blurring his vision. "Hae ye read this letter, cousin?"

David nodded grimly.

"Wha else hae read it? My mama? Uncle Charles?"

David said, "Aye and aye. Yer mama took it weel, fer she hae steeled herself o'er many years tae receive such news eventually. She sent word tae yer Uncle William, as well as tae his brothers."

Jamie bent to read Madame Hilbert's tiny handwriting. "She says that my papa was hale and hearty. He was planning a journey in disguise tae Peterhead tae visit my mama in their auld trysting place. He loved tae ride in the countryside. It was a fine spring day, and he set oot tae follow the river wi' twa companions. They startled a fox and began a chase that ended when my papa's horse broke its leg by stepping in a hole dug by some burrowing animal." Tears filled Jamie's eyes, and he brushed them away. "My papa was thrown. His friends called fer a farm cart to convey him unconscious back tae Madame Hilbert's. The physicians—the damnable charlatans—said that while he dinna hae any broken bones, he had massive swelling pressing on his brain. They bled him several times that night. He woke only once tae whisper:

'Strathallan! I will ne'er see ye again. Ah, my dear Euphemia! I am sae sorry I brought ye and the children such sorrow. Tell Jamie—' but he dinna finish." The paper fluttered to the floor as Jamie was overcome. He sat with his face in his hands, rocking slowly back and forth, his shoulders shaking. David silently retrieved the thin sheets of paper from the floor. He passed them to John Lockhart-Ross and bent to embrace his cousin.

Lockhart-Ross read the remainder of the letter. "He did not regain consciousness and the physicians left off bleeding him further. He declined rapidly, but dinna suffer, fer his face relaxed, and he appeared tae be smiling in his sleep. All we could accomplish fer him was tae make him comfortable and bathe his face wi' cold cloths. His spirit left the body aboot sunset.

"I must tell ye that yer husband and father was a man o' noble sentiments and gentle heart. We sat before the fire on many evenings while he consoled me on the loss o' my dear husband and I him on his grief at his isolation frae the family and hameland he held sae dear. Although he did not profess a belief in Catholic practices, Father LeCroix administered the last rites. After Lord Drummond died, the guid father said a mass fer his soul. We buried him in the crypt o' the Cathedrale Saint-Étienne de Sens. He lies wi' the other staunch heroes o' the cause wha hae already passed on in the little chapel close by the sacred relics o' John the Baptist."

David stood, still gripping Jamie's hands. He said quietly, "Yer mama hae instructed yer Uncle William tae petition the government tae permit yer papa's body tae return tae Scotland fer burial, but that may take many months and perhaps years. James Drummond, even in death, hae many enemies."

In the morning, Jamie was composed enough to undertake the long ride back to Abergeldie with David, for Lord Lockhart-Ross insisted that he take at least a week to be with his family. Jamie left Archie Mitchell and Ian MacTaggart in charge of the surveying crew. By the time they arrived two days later, Euphemia

Drummond was dry-eyed and dressed in black mourning garb, as was all the Gordon family. While Charles Gordon had never approved of the Jacobite rising and chafed at the danger to his own family, he had sheltered his sister and her children and continued to provide a home for them twenty years later. As Charles had often said, ties of kinship were strong in the Highlands.

○────────○

Patches of snow lay on the grass clothing the mound where Viscount William Drummond had been laid to rest after the disaster at Culloden. The spring day was cold but clear. The trees were still leafless, but some flowers peeked from the slush and cover of last year's brown leaves. Jamie set down Wee Jock, who marched stolidly to the graveside bearing a white lily in his chubby fist, just as he himself had done as a lad for their grandfather nineteen years before. Flanked by his mother and sisters and surrounded by the Gordons of Abergeldie and many neighbor folk, Jamie stood staring somberly at the scattering of spring flowers on the grassy mound with its simple granite pillar.

Euphemia murmured, "He should lie in his ain garden at Strathallan, but the feckless ministers fear William Drummond and his son in death as much as they did in life."

Jamie had no words of comfort, for he felt a great emptiness. He heard the tread of boots behind him. Pipers and drummers dressed in Huntley Gordon regalia took up positions on one side of the grave. A minute later, they heard the measured beat of drums and turned to see a startling sight. More pipers and drummers dressed in tartan and with the Drummond badge of holly pinned on their bonnets took up positions on the opposite side of the grave.

One of the pipers stepped forward, nodded, and stamped his foot twice. The drums began a slow ruffle as the pipers inflated their bags. The pipes droned and then skirled into a melody that

Jamie recognized as having been especially written years before to commemorate his grandfather's command of the army that confronted and defeated General Sir John Cope at Prestonpans in the heady early days of the Rising of '45. When the stirring tune ended, in accordance with custom, the musicians began a mournful pibroch, whose origin was lost in time. With a start, Jamie realized that these musicians were publicly defying the government's Act of Proscription by their dress, music, and gathering.

When the music ended, Jamie became aware of others who had joined the graveside service, including two aged men he did not know, both dressed in clerical garb—one Anglican, the other Catholic—and therefore proscribed by the government. In an act of mutual toleration, people of both faiths had gathered, and none would report the priest's unlawful participation.

Jamie's eyes brimmed as he embraced Maggie McRae. Her iron-gray hair was the only sign of her age, for she was as lithe as a girl. Jock embraced Jamie in his old gruff way. He was bent, and his gait had a noticeable limp, a product of his fall from a horse years before. His hair was white and sparse, but his leathery face cracked in a grin. "Ye are a braw lad, Jamie, sae like yer papa. I remember carrying ye frae this spot when we held the funeral fer yer grandpapa, the Viscount. Do ye remember that nicht?"

Jamie whispered, "Aye, as if it were today, and the horror o' watching the surgeon remove the balls frae Peter's body. I was terrified that nicht. It was unco difficult fer a wee lad tae pretend tae be brave, Jock."

The old man patted his arm. "Ye must continue tae pretend, fer the sake o' yer family, though yer heart is breaking. It is sometimes o'erwhelming tae be a leader, tae gie consolation tae others when ye grieve to receive it yerself. Ye can weep in solitude later, but fer now, ye canna."

Jamie's heart swelled with compassion for those who had come to honor his father, whose devotion to the cause of the

King o'er the Water and the Bonnie Prince had cost him so much. He had died young, not even fifty, far from wife, children, and country, bereft of titles, lands, and wealth. It was fitting that James Drummond be honored, and Jamie was grateful to all those who had defied government bans to do so.

A week later, sitting in the solar after Maggie and Jock McRae had departed for Portree, Jamie said, "Mama, I am o' a mind tae resign frae this assignment in Ross tae remain here wi' ye."

Euphemia fingered the high lace collar of her mourning dress and arched her eyebrows. "It dinna fash, my son. Ye made a commitment, and ye are honor bound tae fulfill it. I hae lived lang years wi'oot my husband and father o' my children. I will manage, fer I am made o' sterner stuff than ye ken. Unlike maist widows wha lose their husbands abruptly, I hae grieved fer near twenty years fer wha I hae lost. I rejoice that although I nae langer hae the love o' my heart, I hae his children tae cherish. Now, my son, I wilna hear mair o' yer well-meant proposal. Ye hae yer duty, and I hae mine, as do yer sisters and brother. I hae taught ye many principles which I expect ye tae remember and practice yerself. Chief among them is this: we canna change that which is done, but must make the maist o' wha we hae. Hie ye back tae Balnagown wi' our prayers. Return when the assignment is finished. We will celebrate yer success and a fine start in yer new business."

Jamie tried repeatedly to persuade his mother to change her mind, but she was obdurate. In a flash of insight, Jamie realized that it was not his father but his mother who had trained him to his high sense of duty and unquenchable drive to fulfill commitments. She had her way, and Jamie conceded. He composed a letter of gratitude to Madame Hilbert to add to that which his mother had written and posted it. He included a bank draft on his account to reimburse her for his father's funeral and crypt in the cathedral. Three days later, he bade farewell, swung into the saddle, and rode Stormshadow along the lane that crossed the River Dee to where it turned onto the old military road northward.

15

The survey crew had moved in Jamie's absence. He found them camped in a meadow on the outskirts of Strathpeffer. They had made excellent progress in his absence, and he congratulated Archie and Ian, the team leaders, for their fine work. Inspecting their notes and sketches that evening in the yellow lantern light revealed many errors in calculations that would require the crew to double back to repeat some of the surveying. He had no heart for chastising the young surveyors. He had left them in the lurch after all, and all of the errors were fixable. One was not.

Sixteen-year-old Matthew Davidson, he who had narrowly escaped freezing to death during their escape from Loch Maree, had learned little from his ordeal on that winter's day. In Jamie's absence, he had bought and smuggled in whiskey from locals. The night guard had discovered the liquor and confiscated it in spite of Matthew's threats of revenge. Three days later, Archie Mitchell was patrolling the camp boundary when he heard voices in the woods. Investigating, he had discovered Matthew engaged in a tryst with a fourteen-year-old crofter's daughter. He chased down the scantily clad girl, dragged her to his horse screaming vile oaths all the way, and flung her face down over the horse's withers. When he came back from returning her to her father's croft, young Davidson had packed his kit, saddled a horse, and vanished.

Jamie glared at Mitchell and MacTaggart. "Ye couldna stop him?"

MacTaggart shifted his feet and hung his head. "It is true that ye left me in charge, but ye must remember that he is nephew o' Lord Lockhart-Ross and I am only his factor's son."

Jamie said softly, "Nay, I dinna find fault wi' ye, Ian. Deference tae aristocratic authority is difficult tae o'ercome. I often saw it aboard ship. While some midshipmen were firked unmercifully fer minor infractions, the same behavior frae the son o' a laird or senior officer often received nae mair than a few hours at the masthead. Captains were loath tae administer deserved discipline. How lang hae young Davidson been missing?"

Archie Mitchell said, "The affair wi' the lass was nicht before last."

Jamie sighed. "I suspect that ye dinna send word tae Balnagown aboot his absence?"

The two young surveyors shook their heads glumly.

Jamie pushed to his feet. "I must leave ye in charge o' the team fer another day. I hae my responsibility tae report the matter tae his uncle. While I dinna think that Matthew hae met wi' an accident or fallen into the hands o' bandits, there must be an accounting."

Ian MacTaggart said hopefully, "Perhaps his uncle will send him hame. Although the lad's surveying skills are excellent, I would be pleased tae see him nae mair."

Jamie growled, "I doubt that we will be sae lucky. Expect that I will return wi' the young rogue before sundown tomorrow. While his aristocratic status may enable him tae escape corporal punishment, there are mair exquisite tortures that I intend tae inflict. It is my intention that he perfectly performs every mean and onerous task in this camp before I liberate him."

Mounted on Stormshadow, Jamie spent two hours composing a list of tasks for young Davidson. Before he finished the mental exercise on the outskirts of Dingwall, he caught sight of two figures on horseback cresting a low ridge, riding slowly in his direction. One was tall and bulky and the other of medium height and slender. He smiled inwardly, but kept a stern demeanor, for he recognized them. It was the factor, Hugh MacTaggart, riding upright and Matthew Davidson, slumped and dispirited. After perfunctory greetings, MacTaggart passed Jamie an envelope, after which he sat smoothing his red mustaches, his blue eyes expressionless.

Jamie removed his gloves and opened the letter. Lord John Lockhart-Ross was not only displeased with his nephew, he was furious. He had wormed the entire story from him and was returning him to the camp with strict instructions to obey Jamie's orders and accept his punishment without reservations under threat of dismissal from his house and disinheritance. In bold strokes, the retired naval captain admonished Jamie to choose for himself whether to accept his nephew or send him away. "If ye reject his service, he will return tae Dumfries in disgrace. I urge ye tae act as a father tae the lad, imposing the strictest measures fer his recovery, fer discipline and hard work are the means tae salvation." Jamie recognized the overtones of the Presbyterian ethic of the virtue of work and moral rectitude in the laird's instructions. He read the letter twice while the factor and Matthew waited. When he was finished, he sat musing for a moment. With the letter in one hand and the reins in the other, he gigged the mare. She moved obediently until Jamie faced Matthew Davidson, who had not looked up during the long wait.

Jamie held up the letter and stared at the boy, his face hard. "Hae ye read this letter penned by the laird concerning ye?" Matthew did not look up but nodded, then reached to swipe away tears with his hand. Jamie continued, "Ye ken that I am at liberty tae send ye awa'. Ye may stay on only the strictest conditions. Honest toil is the hallmark o' an honest man. I gie ye a chance tae demonstrate by wark rather than punishment that ye deserve my trust and that o' the rest o' the surveying team. Nae matter how mean the task, I expect prompt obedience and performance. Ye are unco intelligent, lad, but hae a streak o' willfulness and disregard fer guid order that canna be o'erlooked or tolerated further. I wilna thrash ye but intend tae impose my will fer the guid o' the team o'er yers. Do ye ken my words?"

The boy snuffled and mumbled a reply. Jamie rose in the saddle and towered over him. "Speak up! What is yer response?"

Matthew muttered, "Such measures are mair than should be inflicted by anyone except my father."

Jamie gritted his teeth to control his temper. He was perilously close to sending the defiant boy back to his family. "Hae ye nae pride? Nae heroes whose behavior ye wish tae emulate? Would a Wallace or Bruce snivel and make excuses? Being Anglican, I dinna share all beliefs wi' the Scottish kirk, which preaches endlessly on this subject. But it is a universal principle, common tae a' cultures which value honor. If ye e'er wish tae be a man wha is honor bound, ye will swallow yer boyish tears and learn through obedience and yer ain effort tae excel. I offer ye a choice betwixt childhood and manhood, indolence and effort, and rejoining the survey team or a shameful trip hameward tae Dumfries. The road forward may be painful and humiliating but leads tae attainments. The road back tae retreat and failure. I gie ye five minutes tae make a decision, but once the choice is made, I will tolerate nae turning back. Now choose!" Leaving the boy staring at his hands with the reins drooping, Jamie motioned to Hugh MacTaggart to join him. They trotted to a tree by the roadside, where they sat their mounts side by side, talking quietly.

In a low voice, Jamie confided, "As I promised before Christmas, I spoke tae several people aboot yer need fer borrowing money tae secure passage fer all yer people, but wi' nae success. There hae been many such efforts, and the frenzy tae emigrate tae America is growing in Argyll and other places in the Highlands. Soon it will match the fever in Ulster and the Lowlands. There is a concern that emigration may take awa' the industrious rather than the indolent, as feared by Lord Lockhart-Ross. Other lairds are worried o'er losing their best tenants. I heard nae voices willing tae extend credit."

Hugh nodded. "It is as I feared. Weel, the crops are growing favorably, and we hae seen a guidly number o' calves and lambs. We are still months frae harvest time and canna guess wha prices may be. I am hopefu' that they will be guid, but I hae nae illusions that we will hae enough tae transport a' families. My trip tae Edinburgh hae uncovered some willing moneylenders, but they offer usurious rates. I found nae lender wha would make a commitment."

Jamie rubbed his nose reflectively but said nothing, for Hugh MacTaggart raised his index finger. Matthew Davidson was approaching. The factor glanced at the boy's face, raised his hand to his hat, and moved away. Squirming in his saddle and in halting words, the laird's nephew accepted Jamie's terms, promising obedience and hard work in return for permission to stay.

The survey team ranged across Easter Ross favored by good weather. The young men shared equally in the hard work and long hours, with no mention of Matthew Davidson's humiliation and reconciliation. Jamie was under no illusions that a complete turnabout could be achieved by the sixteen-year-old and he did not expect it. He was only a decade removed from that age himself and had a bright memory of his own derelictions and punishments.

They encountered no trouble from lawless men in the countryside, for the size of the survey team deterred bandits. Spring stretched into summer, bringing lengthy days and short nights. While the surveyors were willing to work deep into the evenings, Jamie ordered work stopped so that the young men could enjoy daylight time for sports and other amusements.

While the matches were friendly, errant kicks and shoving by the enthusiastic players led to painful injuries. Even Jamie ended up nursing a purplish bruise under his right eye.

There was no time for home visits, but a rider from Balnagown brought letters to their encampment once a week. The summer had been pleasant and peaceful, but one letter from Peter Gordon brought jarring news. The previous year, John Wilkes had been expelled from Parliament for printing what the government called seditious libel, criticizing the new king. That act had stifled public expression of complaints against the government, but an angry opposition was growing. George Grenville's government continued their obsession with insisting that the American colonies shoulder some of the burden of paying for their defense. The Earl of Bute, his predecessor as prime minister had decided to leave a standing army of ten thousand men in the colonies to enforce order and put down raids on settlements and frontier forts by Chief Pontiac in the interior. To raise revenue to pay for this force, he and his ministers had pressured Parliament into passing an act the previous year imposing a tax on sugar and another restricting the colonies from printing their own currency. They also insisted on strictly enforcing the old tax on molasses, which had been largely ignored by the colonists, but cutting the rate in half to encourage compliance. By summer, Boston had erupted in rioting. In March of the new year, Parliament tightened the fiscal screws on the colonies by passing the Stamp Act, requiring the purchase of stamps for all official papers, and two days later, the Quartering Act forcing households to house and feed troops sent to the colonies.

Peter's letter ended by describing the fruitless appeals that he and Joseph Cotes had made to various ministers to grant restoration of Drummond lands and titles. All of their efforts had been met with smiling assurances that they would eventually succeed, but no one was willing to say when or under which circumstances that it might happen. The king and Parliament were too busy with more important and timely matters to consider it.

The letter brought on a gloomy mood, and he flung it across the tent. He was struck with a bizarre thought. His acquaintance with colonials in Canada and New York had been brief, but he had been impressed with their qualities and resourcefulness. A long evening of discussions with Benjamin Franklin reinforced those feelings. Cavalier treatment of loyal colonials by Parliament could bring on resentment and resistance. They had raised forces, paid for them, and fought loyally in the recent war, suffering privations and casualties alongside the regulars. He wondered what a king and Parliament intent on their own objectives and insisting on stifling dissent would make of such resolute men. A cold evening breeze blew through the tent opening, fluttering the candles.

The survey teams completed their work in the lowlands of Easter Ross in mid-August. Jamie had sent the drover and grooms to recover the cart and cache of equipment abandoned in the snowstorm that had driven them out of Wester Ross the preceding year. Except for some minor damage by rats, there were no losses. Jamie had feared that the cache would be discovered by one of the many gangs of landless men roaming the mountains, but they were lucky.

They moved into the treeless mountains of Wester Ross, mapping tiny settlements in the deep glens and along the convoluted rocky coastline. Luckily, he and several of the men in the team spoke passable Gaelic, which greatly eased their ability to interact with the farming, fishing, and herding communities. The folk were so isolated by the rough terrain of high bens, cold green lochs, and deep glens that they had little knowledge of conditions outside. Their world, if they would be allowed to control it, consisted of their livestock, boats, shielings, and meager fields around rock and thatch croft houses. Their loyalty was to local clan chiefs, only nominally to the laird in far-off Balnagown, and not at all to the king in London. Jamie marveled at the stones dangling from the thatched roofs, anchored with strong netting to resist the violent gusts that swept in from the nearby sea from carrying them away.

Jamie cantered Stormshadow down a steep swale into a settlement boasting five crofts, scattering clucking chickens. He halted in the hard-packed space that in a larger settlement might have qualified as the town square. Narrow rigs of cabbage, kale, potatoes, and turnips fringing the huts where scrawny children played were well-kept but invariably small and stony. Suspicious shawled women stood in the low doorways, holding leather curtains shut behind their bodies, concealing the dark interiors. One, bolder than the rest, advanced to confront Jamie, who sat his saddle with the reins drooping while he sketched a drawing of what he saw with a charcoal stick.

She recoiled in surprise when Jamie answered her question in Gaelic to identify himself and state his purpose in coming. She gave him a charming but toothless smile and adjusted her tartan shawl to reveal more of her face. Recognizing that the stranger was not threatening and was a Highlander but from far to the east and south, the children gathered swiftly to inspect him and his artwork.

The friendly crowd would not release him until he sketched more likenesses of their settlement and the families who lived there, who plied him with water and oatcakes. This pattern of initial suspicion overcome with friendliness and hospitality was repeated many times as the survey teams traversed the western coasts and the glens feeding off the lochs stretching inland for miles.

On a crisp day in early November, with hard frost decking the yellow broom clothing the hills, the survey was done. Fifteen months had elapsed since they had started, but every feature of the physical and human landscape of significance had been surveyed. Jamie ordered his team to pack up the equipment so that they could cross the mountains in safety, without a repeat of the race to escape the appalling snowstorm that had almost trapped them. The expedition would end for all but the surveyors, who faced another month of careful checking of all measurements, redrawing of maps, and compilations of information on people, lands, crops, and livestock. That work would be completed at Balnagown while the remainder of the crew scattered to their homes.

Bundled securely against the cold wind that swept up the loch, Jamie led the caravan eastward from their camp on the shores of Loch Inver and up the wide stream called Allt an Tiaghaich that grew steadily stonier as they climbed to where it entered miles-long Loch Assynt.

They camped in view of Castle Ardvreck, looming on its rocky promontory on the north shore. Ian MacTaggart had steered them along the more difficult southern shore of the loch, for as he explained to Jamie, the entire northern shore lay in Sutherland, where there was a smooth trail. He shook his head when Jamie wondered why they were taking the more difficult route. MacTaggart's young face creased in a scowl. "Because the laird o' Sutherland is greedy and nae on guid terms wi' Clan Ross. He hae imposed a strict toll on all travelers traversing *his* road." His voice emphasized the possessive. "Ye will pay dearly fer the privilege, but I will steer ye hame wi'oot such extortion."

They saw no riders on the Sutherland side of the loch and left at dawn. The road bent southward for many miles until they came out of the hills where Bonar Bridge crossed the Kyle of Sutherland and emptied into the Dornoch Firth and the North Sea beyond.

In the morning, a brief snow shower delayed them, although Jamie was anxious to reach Balnagown before darkness ended the day. Twelve miles of steady riding brought them to Tain, where they took up the muddy road southward. Two hours later, the tower of the castle loomed over the trees, and by three in the short afternoon, they reached the castle grounds. Grooms from the stables rushed to help the cavalcade dismount and tend to the horses. Jamie supervised unpacking of the surveying equipment and the precious maps, charts, and voluminous notes. Sometime after sundown, he was satisfied at last and led his team to the kitchens, where the cooks had prepared a welcoming meal. Jamie slipped the kitchen staff sufficient coins to assure that the famished team would not only be fed, but well fed. For himself, he was content to fill his belly once and carry a tankard to his room. He yearned for a good night's sleep in a comfortable bed, a soak in a tub, a shave, and clean clothes.

Lord Lockhart-Ross ensconced the survey team in his library. The tall windows provided the best lighting available in the venerable castle, augmented by numerous lanterns dangling from the tall ceiling, for the days of late autumn were short. They seldom saw blue sky, only a uniform gray. Rain sheeted down, and the wind whined incessantly, probing the window casings.

The team breakfasted together at dawn and worked until noon, took lunch in the solar, and then worked until well after dark. The exacting labor on maps, charts, and inventories taxed the mind and eyes. Jamie insisted that his assistants take exercise every day. The heavy rain precluded riding, so they resorted to their daily fencing as when they had camped in the hills.

After a week, John Lockhart-Ross returned from a trip to Edinburgh and promptly became a frequent visitor to the library, poring over the evolving great map of Ross-shire and the pile of inventories of crofts, fisheries, and villages. His curiosity about their work was pleasing at first, but his hovering presence made the young surveyors nervous. He was somewhat taken aback when Jamie asked him to leave the team to its work. He reddened but agreed, admitting that his enthusiasm for the project was akin to a schoolboy's on first learning a new subject. Jamie offered a compromise. He would brief the laird each evening after the team laid down its tools and papers.

It was Saturday afternoon. The rain had stopped after six days of continual downpour. Jamie canceled work for the week and strode to the stable. The two young grooms looked up from shoeing a black gelding and grinned for he was a frequent visitor to their lair. One dropped his hammer and took down Stormshadow's saddle from its place on the wall. Jamie had scarcely cinched it in place when the door opened. It was the factor, Ian MacTaggart, and the look on his face was enough for the grooms to hastily excuse themselves and lead the gelding outside.

Jamie waited expectantly while MacTaggart fumbled for words and then said gently, "I hear the distress in yer voice. Ye are trying tae find a way tae tell me that ye dinna hae enough money tae transport yer families and can raise nae mair."

MacTaggart nodded and said, "I must admit that I dinna anticipate the difficulties I hae encountered. The shipping masters drive unco hard bargains. The cost fer transportation fer adult passengers is twelve pounds sterling and nine fer children."

Jamie expostulated, "Robbery!"

MacTaggart nodded. "Ach, aye, but the people must hae money fer food tae eat and clothing sufficient fer a winter crossing. Ye yerself hae told me that the voyage can take far langer than planned if the winds are adverse. I hae discussed a contract wi' the master o' a ship called *The Duke o' Montrose*."

Jamie chuckled. "Weel, the Grahams are a great family, and there hae been many Dukes o' Montrose, but I recall that ane was hanged. Nae matter, is it a weel-founded ship?"

MacTaggart shrugged. "She seems clean enough, and the captain's reputation on the waterfront in Edinburgh seems adequate. The ship will hold three hundred and fifty passengers. I am short o' funds, sae I must leave some families behind.

Departure will be delayed, fer the shipping master must recruit mair passengers tae make up the difference."

Jamie held up a hand. "What is the extent o' yer shortage?"

MacTaggart looked uncomfortable. "I hae sufficient fer transportation, land purchases, and equipment, but the shortage is considerable and canna be bridged by borrowing. I could raise nae mair frae the lenders."

Jamie gripped his arm. "How much, Ian, tae transport a' those wha wish tae leave?"

MacTaggart mumbled heavily, "Twelve hundred pounds."

Jamie's face cleared. "Ye may need a leetle mair fer emergencies. I will gie ye a draft on Barclay's Bank fer twa thousand pounds, repayable in five years. Ye should be weel-established by that time."

MacTaggart's face crumpled as he sobbed in relief. "Ye would do that fer us wi'oot collateral?"

Jamie smiled. "Aye. I hae collateral, which is yer guid word, and that is sufficient fer me. Ye must leave, fer ye may ne'er get a better opportunity. Ye hae the ambition required tae succeed. The Highlands canna support ye further, man. I will gie ye the bank draft in the morning, but I insist that ye settle wi' the laird and make a clean admission o' yer intent tae depart. Ye canna leave wi'oot notice, skelping off in the middle o' the nicht like a thief." MacTaggart gave him his hand, and Jamie finished saddling Stormshadow.

In the morning, he put the signed bank draft into Ian MacTaggart's hand. The big factor said, "I wilna ferget this favor, Mr. Drummond, though ye may find yerself in muckle trouble fer aiding us. I ken the story o' yer family's attainting and loss o' titles. Ye are the finest and noblest laird that I e'er met. I wish ye every success."

Jamie nodded. "And ye as weel, MacTaggart. If I e'er reach North Carolina, I will rejoice tae see ye and a' yer families set up on fine farms." The factor departed, and Jamie rejoined his team in the library.

John Lockhart-Ross raged profanely while Jamie and Ian MacTaggart stood before his desk. The servants had hurriedly shut the doors in a vain attempt to contain their master's voice. The naval captain, who'd turned landowner and peer, had a vocabulary honed by years at sea and used it to great effect. At length, the gales of profanity lessened. Jamie marveled not only at his employer's vast command of language but at his own realization that he and the factor were not the sole targets for the laird's wrath. His rage had cooled, and his invective seemed aimed at the difficulties inflicted upon his efforts to improve his estates. It was as if he was coming around to agree with Ian MacTaggart's citing of reasons for departing for America with his family and taking so many of his tenants and subtenants with him. He raged on about his efforts to improve the terrible conditions under which they had struggled to eke a living from the poor soil and underfed livestock. Abruptly, he stopped, breathing hard, although the protruding veins in his neck were testimony to his wrath.

MacTaggart's gruff voice broke the sudden silence. "Ye must understand, milord, that we are sick at heart. It is a grief tae our spirits tae leave our native land tae venture a' on this voyage and a fresh start in a new land, but there is nae help fer it. We hae labored fer years wi'oot number tae improve the soil and reap a declining harvest that scarcely feeds the families. Rents continue tae rise, although we ken that ye dinna charge us at the rate that others inflict on their tenants. We hae raised scarcely enough tae leave. If we wait, prices fer land across the water will rise, and rents here will take wha we hae saved. We must do something tae ensure that the bairns hae bread and a chance tae obtain an inheritance on which they can live when we are gane. We dinna wish tae see our families reduced tae beggary." He raised a hand to forestall another outburst from Lockhart-Ross. "Ye hae done mair than maist, milord, but there is also trouble beyond yer power tae control. There are many broken men and bandits in the hills that prey on tenants, stealing awa' cattle and emptying bawns. There hae been murthers and violence aplenty. The high sheriff canna find and punish them a'. They are sae many. When nicht comes doon, crofters listen fer riders and sleep fitfully, wi' a blade or gun close by."

Lockhart-Ross asked, "Do ye think that the frontier in America is a safe district, wi' savages and renegades nearby?"

MacTaggart shrugged. "Perhaps, but it canna be worse than here."

The laird retorted, "But ye are taking the maist productive crofters wha hae ambition and resourcefulness."

Jamie spoke up. "Aye, they are, and that is the reason why they are prepared tae venture abroad. They hae ambition and sufficient funds tae acquire lands, clear them, and establish farms."

Lockhart-Ross said, "Leaving behind those wi' less ambition and ability."

Jamie responded in a soft voice, "Ye must understand human nature. Can ye offer them adequate fields and pasturages if they stay? Will ye provide an inheritance tae their children when they come o' age?"

The laird seemed shocked by the questions and shook his head. "I can alleviate some distress by reducing rents and providing manure, kelp and better tools fer the mair industrious husbandmen and their families."

Jamie pressed on, his voice conciliatory. "Ye ken that such solutions are merely temporary, milord. There is nae enough fer a'."

Lord Lockhart-Ross said nothing further, and the silence stretched, broken only by the loud ticking of the spring-wound naval chronometer on the laird's desk. At last, he stood up and extended his hand to Ian MacTaggart.

"I see that this affair is inevitable and that I canna offer sufficient reasons tae restrain yer leaving. Ye hae served me weel, and I wilna impose barriers tae yer departure, nor tae those wha wish tae join ye. As an experiment, I will reconstruct the tenancies ye occupy tae support a smaller number o' crofters. It was my intent tae do that on other lands, but yer leaving may be opportune. Ye realize the risks o' a winter departure?"

MacTaggart nodded and replied, "Aye, but the passage is less expensive than in spring, and Captain Forrester hae agreed tae anchor in the Dornoch Firth fer a week in early January tae take us aboard."

Lockhart-Ross nodded. "We will speak further soon tae arrange the transfer o' tenancies and final settlement o' accounts. And now I would speak wi' Mr. Drummond in privacy."

MacTaggart looked with alarm at Jamie, who smiled but said nothing. The factor departed, shutting the door behind himself.

The laird moved from behind the massive desk, waving Jamie to a table and two leather chairs by the fire that crackled behind a screen. A wolfhound lying next to the hearth raised its head, looked inquiringly at its master, yawned hugely, and settled back into a curled position.

Jamie accepted a glass of Madeira. He thought, in spite of Lockhart-Ross's earlier rage, that the drink implied that the remainder of their conversation was destined to be pleasant. He was wrong.

The laird sipped at the dark red wine, then placed the glass carefully on the oak table between them. "Before I invited ye tae join us, Ian MacTaggart told me that he approached ye some time past wi' a request tae help him obtain funding fer the voyage."

There was no point in denying his involvement. Jamie said, "Aye, he did, but I was nae successful in spite o' several attempts."

Lockhart-Ross regarded him steadily. "Why did ye nae inform me?"

Jamie put down his own glass. "Because he approached me in confidence. It was his responsibility tae inform ye at the appropriate time, milord, nae mine. I urged him tae lay oot his plans and intentions when he hae made a decision."

John Lockhart-Ross grimaced. "Weel, it probably made nae difference in the results, but I would hae been able tae counsel ye tae avoid involvement."

Jamie stiffened as the laird continued, "Ye may be surprised, but I hae been expecting at least some o' the tenants tae depart, but nae my principal factor. I can even understand yer ain sympathies fer their cause, but tae involve yerself enough tae lend them a considerable sum o' money, I consider unco unwise, an act o' great foolishness."

Jamie sat up. "Why do ye consider it foolish?"

Lockhart-Ross sighed. "I dinna doubt that MacTaggart's people will make guid on the loan. North Carolina offers great promise, and Ian MacTaggart is a man o' integrity. The foolishness lies in the act itself, which canna lang remain a secret. While the crofters and tenants may applaud yer generosity, yer name will become anathema tae the lairds o' the north. They will blame ye fer encouraging a large group tae flee the Highlands fer the colonies. While the land continues tae support mair people than is wise, the lairds are fearful o' losing the best tenants and their lucrative rents. The contract between us, which pleases me greatly, fer the work ye performed was excellent, will be the last ye will receive in the north. Ye will nae be hired again fer such work by any Highland laird."

Jamie reflected on his words. In truth, he had not considered the risk to himself. "Milord, I took pity on the plight o' the people. I hae seen the poverty o' the land, which ye intend tae enrich. Wiser land distribution, fertilization, and crop rotation will yield greater productivity, but the growing population will soon o'erwhelm all attempts at improvement. Many people must depart fer the rest tae gain a reasonable livelihood. I made the offer tae provide a determined group o' my countrymen hope—a better chance tae prosper."

His comment met a determined shake of the head. "I understand that sentiment. A pity that others wilna care a whit fer yer compassion, especially William Gordon, the eighteenth Earl of Sutherland. Ye ken that his father opposed the Jacobite cause and hae spent heavily tae expand the family holdings in Sutherland. He was most rapacious in his rack-renting practices, and his son continues that heinous tradition. He is weel-connected in Whitehall and is nae a man ye should openly offend."

Jamie sank back. "Will ye withhold my fee fer the work in retaliation?"

The laird shook his head. "Nae, ye hae earned it, and I look forward tae receiving the results. I hae seen enough tae trust the accuracy o' the maps. They will prove o' great value in improving my estates. When will they be finished?"

"In perhaps ten days."

"At that time, we will settle our accounts, and ye may depart. I trust that ye will return hame fer Christmas and Hogmanay?"

Jamie nodded.

Lockhart-Ross tapped the tabletop. "I will gie ye a guid recommendation, but I advise ye tae seek further employment in the south or return tae naval service if that option becomes available. Edinburgh and Glasgow hae better prospects than the north, and England than Scotland."

Jamie inquired, "What aboot Ireland? I hae a friend living there."

With derision evident in his voice, the laird said, "Ireland is a beautiful land full o' mystery, cruelty, and seething resentment by the native people. It is also a medieval backwater entirely controlled by rapacious English landlords. There is little industry, and few opportunities are available."

Jamie was correct in his prediction. Ten days later, the team delivered the master map of Ross-shire, inventories, sketches, and voluminous notes. Lord Lockhart-Ross staged a farewell party and gave generous gifts to the young men of the survey team—horses, weapons, and appointments to positions in his household. Jamie had secretly arranged for delivery of several fine Italian rapiers, which he presented to those young men who had spent untold hours fencing with him in their encampments.

The sky was a white overcast, with snow filtering down, coating the rooftops and lawns, when Jamie shook hands with Lord John Lockhart-Ross, accepted the reins from the groom, mounted Stormshadow, and turned the mare's head southward. He knew that he was taking a risk with the weather, but he philosophized that every day in winter was a risk in the Highlands. He was anxious to reach Abergeldie to enjoy the holidays and show his mother the large stipend he had received. However, his anticipation was mixed with foreboding, for he was uncertain how he was going to explain to her that he was once again unemployed, with no hope of work in the Highlands, no discernible prospects, and had lent out the same sum that he had received for a year and a half's work.

16

Charles Gordon shut his eyes and squeezed the bridge of his nose to alleviate the ache in his head. All his efforts to convince his stubborn nephew had been fruitless. For the better part of an hour, he had patiently explained the miserable state of Jamie's prospects and the myriad benefits to be gained from engaging to manage the estate of the wealthy Huntley Gordon, whose property would pass to his only child, a daughter nearing thirty. Jamie rose from his seat by the fireplace and paced his uncle's office distractedly.

"Uncle, we discussed each o' these points a year and a half ago. Naething hae changed."

Charles Gordon's temper flared. "We discussed them, and much hae changed. At that time, ye hae a fine position in the north, wi' prospects fer continued employment. Ye hae provided financial support fer crofter families and hae lost any hope o' further work wi' the northern lairds, wha follow the Sutherlands. Ye need employment. A position is open fer the taking. Ye need nae commit tae marry the lass."

Jamie growled. "Based upon yer ain statements, she is nae langer a lass. I daresay that she is some years my senior."

His uncle overrode him. "'Tis a foolish notion that there is only a single woman that a man can love. Romantic nonsense! Ye must be practical. She stands tae inherit a fine estate wi' a handsome income. While the Drummonds o' Strathallan are a great family wi' a legacy stretching back generations, ye hae nae lands, nae income, and nae title. Wi' such a marriage, ye would take the Gordon name but will hae all that the Drummonds lack."

Jamie stopped and faced his uncle. He was dangerously close to an outburst and bit his tongue. Charles Gordon had known him all his life and recognized the stubborn set of his nephew's jaw. At last, Jamie spoke, and his voice was husky. "I am grateful, Uncle Charles, I am. But ye must see that honor canna be sae easily cast aside. Before God, I canna will myself tae abandon my heritage, nae matter how faint the prospects. If the king and his ministers are obdurate and that door closes forever, I wish tae earn my ain way in life. Nae other recourse will satisfy me."

With asperity, Charles said, "I admonish ye tae reconsider, nephew. It appears that ye hae torched yer chances in the Highlands. What will ye do, and where will ye journey? I fear that it may be a far place tae escape the wrath o' the northern magnates."

Hesitantly, Jamie reached into his jacket for an envelope. He passed it to his uncle. "This letter came by courier the day before Christmas, three days past. It is nae the reason why again I must reject the notion o' managing the heiress's estates and wooing her tae my ain advantage, but it is a timely intervention. I am being recalled tae active service in the Royal Marines."

Charles read the two-page letter and then reread it. "Aye, it is framed as an order and nae a request. Hae ye been expecting such an action?"

"Before I left active service in '63, Lieutenant Colonel MacKenzie assured me that short o' a resumption o' war wi' the French or Spanish, there was little chance that I would be disturbed in my ha'-pay status. The orders are a surprise, particularly a command assignment and promise o' a promotion."

Charles folded the letter and replaced it in the envelope. "Did the colonel inform ye o' the location o' the assignment?"

Jamie shook his head.

His uncle said, "I still advise ye tae marry the heiress. Ye would sail as a baronet, certainly an advantageous title fer a newly promoted officer." He searched Jamie's face and then shook his head. "I see that ye are obdurate, fer I recognize the same look that sat on yer sonsie face when ye were five years auld. Weel, at least this letter gies me a pretext tae excuse yer refusal o' the position tae manage the Huntley estates. Since I hae heard naething frae yer mama, I ken that she hae nae heard this news. I suggest that ye carefully prepare yer speech fer her ears. She will be less than pleased tae hear it. She was expecting ye tae tarry in Abergeldie until the spring thaw."

Peter and Rachel Gordon were delighted to welcome Jamie after his ten-day journey to London. He had regretfully left Stormshadow in David Gordon's care after wringing a promise from his cousin to ride the spirited mare as often as his duties allowed. After a romp with the Gordon children and a fine meal, Peter took Jamie to his study, where green- and gold-bound law books lined the walls and a servant had thoughtfully laid a fire.

Peter picked up his pipe and began filling the bowl with tobacco from a wooden box. He glanced at Jamie, recognized his look of disapproval, and laid the box aside. He said, "Ye are such a paragon that I feel guilt at enjoying my decadent pleasures. Ye would make a daunting but straitlaced vicar if ye were inclined tae that profession, cousin."

Jamie smiled. "It seems that I am nae inclined tae any profession except the military. I canna stand by wi'oot taking sides in matters pertaining tae my hameland."

Peter nodded, toying with the long stem of the white clay pipe. "The letter frae Lieutenant Colonel MacKenzie is troubling. The navy hae been decommissioning ships every month since the war ended. My friends assure me that there is nae naval buildup and nae threat frae the French. The kind dismissed Grenville as Prime Minister last July and promptly appointed the Marquess o' Rockingham tae replace him. He is young but a thorough Whig, whose first act was quite competent. He selected Edmund Burke as his private secretary."

Jamie's pulse quickened. "Then there is still hope fer restoration o' Drummond titles and lands."

Peter laid down the pipe and templed his fingers. "Alas, that is nae likely. Like Grenville before him, Rockingham is obsessed wi' colonial affairs. He wishes tae repeal the Stamp Act, which hae led tae considerable unrest in Boston and deep unpopularity wi' colonial merchants. Neither I nor Joseph Cotes hae the least success in influencing those close tae the Prime Minister. There is nae minister willing tae risk his position on such a delicate matter on which the king hae expressed his displeasure, although a great obstacle hae been removed. The king's uncle, the odious Duke o' Cumberland, died in October."

Jamie said, "Aye, it is puir manners tae celebrate anyone's untimely death, especially at a young age, but that man was a scourge wha killed and persecuted thousands. If there is truly a hell, he deserves a lang sojourn in its depths."

Peter continued, "Even wi'oot the duke's baleful influence, the king hae made remarks that indicate that he will ne'er forgive the Jacobite attempt tae remove his grandfather's crown. The death o' James, the Auld Pretender, in Rome on the first day of January is nae the end o' the Jacobite cause, but it is woefully moribund, wi' that drunken sot Charles Edward as the Stewart heir. I dinna think that resurrection o' the Jacobite hopes is possible, fer the king is stubborn."

Jamie scowled. "Then my options hae shrunk tae this." He flourished Lieutenant Colonel MacKenzie's letter.

Peter raised an admonitory finger. "There is a possibility mentioned by Joseph Cotes on his last visit. I wish that he were in

London tae discuss it personally, but he is detained in Cornwall attending his daughter's wedding."

Jamie sat up abruptly. "What? I dinna expect that Adele would marry. I expected she was resigned tae spinsterhood!"

Peter said, "I hae ne'er met her but understand that she is a formidable lass wi', shall we say, weel-formed and frequently expressed opinions."

Jamie laughed. "She is breathtaking, mair handsome than beautiful, but wi' as fine a mind as any Parliamentarian or barrister." He turned solemn. "Perhaps I should hae married her. But I am pleased fer her guid fortune."

Peter chuckled. "She is marrying Richard Hawkins of Trewith, second son of Thomas Hawkins. The family hae considerable wealth derived frae Cornish mining. Richard fancies himself a classical scholar wha hae traveled widely in the Mediterranean and Egypt studying ancient artifacts. He is already a member o' the Royal Society."

Jamie grinned. "A perfect match. He can carry Adele awa' frae politics tae the exciting world o' past civilizations." Then he turned sober. "What is the matter which Joseph Cotes wished ye tae address wi' me?"

Peter stared at the ceiling, and Jamie waited while his cousin collected his thoughts. "Hae ye met or heard o' Lord George Selwyn?" Jamie shook his head. Peter went on, "He hae been a member o' Parliament fer twelve years and hae the singular distinction o' ne'er making a speech in a' that time."

Jamie mused, "Perhaps he is wiser than most Parliamentarians. While maist hae naething important tae say, they persist in speaking. He seems tae possess the wisdom tae remain silent. Although I wonder how he maintains his seat wi' naething tae show his constituents."

Peter busied himself opening a leather portfolio. "He controls three seats and puts them at the disposal o' the king's ministers fer bribes, which he freely accepts tae lay off against his gambling debts and licentious lifestyle. He is also a friend o' Robert Walpole and a member o' the Hellfire Club."

"Fais Ce que tu voudras," breathed Jamie.

"Do what thou wilt," said Peter. "The members o' the Hellfire Club hae lang been recognized as at least mock pagan—blasphemous, licentious, and bawdy. While none o' these vices are illegal, they are certainly practices best kept in the dark. 'Tis said that they hold banquets where the men wear only a loose toga and the women frequently naething at a'."

Jamie said wryly, "I hae been tae many naval banquets where the drinking and debauchery are excessive, but there are nae women in attendance. I am surprised that the church and government allow them."

Peter said, "Dinna overestimate the virtues o' either churchmen or political figures, cousin. Many attend Hellfire Club gatherings, but in disguise. Even the acclaimed inventor, Dr. Benjamin Franklin, hae attended on occasion."

Jamie smiled. "I dare say he attends nae because o' the fine conversation and victuals but fer the privilege o' providing a lap fer scarcely dressed young ladies."

He and Peter laughed heartily.

Jamie stared at his cousin. "Hae ye attended, cousin?"

Peter flung up his hands in mock horror. "Wi' the risk o' my Rachel discovering the secret? Nay, my lass dinna carry a sgian-dubh but certainly is skilled in its use." The two laughed again.

Jamie asked, "Wha is the relevance o' Lord Selwyn tae me?"

Peter spread out papers that he had taken from the portfolio on his lap. "The Granville properties in North Carolina were originally granted in 1742 tae the great grandson o' the original Lord Proprietor, Sir George Carteret. That one-eighth share consists o' a sixty-mile-wide strip across the royal colony. It was originally surveyed by Samuel Warner. As the frontier moved westward, the crown extended the Granville grant several times. A large portion frae the Atlantic tae the region around Charlotte hae been sold off and settled, but there are disputes regarding property lines and much ill feeling by those wha paid fer the land and settled there. It seems that Lord Selwyn, reprobate and mildly corrupt parliamentarian, hae obtained the charter o' a large tract o' what was the estate after Lord Granville, George Carteret, died twa years past. His son, Robert is indifferent tae the problems involved in land management, which is undoubtedly how Selwyn got his hands on a portion. He hired an agent, Henry McCulloch, wha hae lived in the region fer years, tae commission a survey and dispose o' the land fer settlement. He hired a surveyor, John Frohock, wha arrived in the region and within a fortnight, being a meek man, took ship back to England claiming that he could nae perform the work due tae McCulloch's endless disputes wi' the local settlers, some o' which confronted him wi' loaded firearms. The land remains largely unsurveyed and the disputes unresolved."

Jamie asked, "And Lord Selwyn is looking tae hire a surveyor, competent wi' pistol and sword tae complete the work? Will the royal governor pardon him if he shoots a settler or twa?"

Peter ignored the question.

"It explains why Selwyn ended his employment o' McCulloch and is seeking a replacement agent tae send tae Charlotte. I dinna remember the prime candidate's name, but heard that he is a man wi' a reputation fer firmness and skill wi' weapons."

A thought began to grow in Jamie that Peter had far more knowledge of Lord Selwyn's plans than expected. He asked sharply, "Cousin, hae ye been retained tae find such a surveyor?"

Peter struggled to keep his face impassive. He said, "I dinna hae a financial interest in the effort. A partner in my law firm heard o' Lord Selwyn's interest at his club and told me. While Selwyn is dissolute and prone tae using bribery tae achieve his ends, he is nae mair corruptible than maist o' the peers o' the realm. His financial affairs are aboveboard. He is nae accused o' cheating either employees or contractors."

Jamie snorted. "Ye ken that Lieutenant Colonel MacKenzie's letter makes this entire discussion pointless? I am a king's officer, and if I hae been recalled, then I must report fer duty."

Peter spread his hands. "Do ye hae knowledge o' where and on which ship or station ye will serve?"

Jamie shook his head. "I will discover those facts tomorrow when I report at the Admiralty."

Peter said, "If the assignment is nae tae yer choosing, what will ye do?"

"I was avoiding the inevitable, I suppose, in accepting ha' pay and nae pressing fer acceptance o' my resignation. Even if I resign now, the Admiralty may nae accept it. They refused shortly after the war. If naething else comes my way, then I am truly stymied and must serve."

Peter allowed Jamie to read the papers and then put them back into the portfolio. He asked, "Will ye meet wi' Lord Selwyn before reporting at the Admiralty?"

Jamie said, "There is nae time. My meeting wi' Lieutenant Colonel MacKenzie is tomorrow at eleven. In the event that I find the assignment impossible tae accept and the Admiralty releases me, then I may agree tae meet wi' Lord Selwyn. I confess an uneasiness concerning this surveying task. I suspect that there is much aboot the assignment that remains tae be told."

Over two years had passed since Jamie had put on the white breeches, ruffled shirt, and red coat with white facings of a marine officer. He was shocked to realize that he had put on some weight during the winter and had to struggle with the lacings. He snapped the gorget in place around his neck, clapped the horsehair wig on his head, and carefully settled the tricorner black hat over it. His Andrea Ferrara rapier and dark blue boat cloak completed the ensemble.

The children were still at the breakfast table and clapped their hands at Jamie's appearance at the bottom of the landing. Rachel smiled broadly, saluted him, and then wrinkled her nose. "I detect a faint whiff o' naphtha."

Jamie laughed. "The uniform was sprinkled wi' the stuff when I laid it doon twa years past. I brushed the cloth thoroughly tae remove it, but it lingers. At least, the worms dinna eat holes in it. Perhaps a walk in this morning's brisk weather will eliminate the scent."

The morning was chill and the sky slate-colored and overcast. A westerly wind attacked Jamie exposed cheeks and blew away the smoke of his breath. He pulled on his gloves and set out on the short walk from Saint James's Square to the Admiralty offices.

He waited only a few minutes after handing his card to a chubby civil servant in dark green coat, brown breeches, and black shoes with silver buckles. The door burst open, and Lieutenant Colonel Raibert MacKenzie barreled out, seizing Jamie's hand and pumping it with vigor.

He led Jamie to his office, waving to a sideboard where a white china pot, a stack of cakes, pot of cream, and bowls of butter and jam waited. MacKenzie kept the conversation focused on providing an update on assignments and locations of marine officers of Jamie's acquaintance. When the stack of cakes had diminished and Jamie had poured a second cup of tea for each of them, the colonel shifted the conversation, punctuated with repeated clearings of the throat on his part and respectful silence by Jamie.

"I ken that ye are familiar wi' Vice Admiral Edward Hawke?"

Jamie nodded. "Aye, sir. He led the board o' inquiry that cleared my pressed status and approved my commission as a lieutenant. I fought under his command at Quiberon Bay."

MacKenzie said, "Weel, it seems that before he retired last year, he sent a request tae Admiral Augustus Keppel, wha chairs the Admiralty Board, concerning ye. I must admit that in getting yer name on the ha'-pay list, I overrode some contrary opinions that now put me in an unfavorable light."

Jamie realized that MacKenzie was anxious to reveal more, so he kept silence. "Weel, it seems that Admiral Keppel is anxious tae satisfy Hawke, wha is as close tae a national hero as we hae in these times. He is anxious tae correct wha he considers an error and restore ye tae active service. As a senior member o' the Admiralty Board, he is certainly in a position o' great power."

Jamie broke his silence. "I hae great admiration fer baith admirals, having served under them, and dinna wish tae offend them, except that I made my desires clear when I left active service. I resigned fer guid reasons, as ye may recall, sir, after serving fer seven years in fulfillment o' an oath I made under duress. I fought in mair engagements than many experience in an entire career at sea. I see nae compelling reason tae change my mind."

MacKenzie frowned. "Admiral Keppel understood that he must offer some incentives tae convince ye tae change yer mind. He hae authorized yer promotion tae the rank o' major, effective immediately, and a position commanding the marine detachment on a recently launched third rate. It is a choice position, being senior marine officer in a squadron and aboard a commodore's flagship."

Jamie asked, "Why select me fer such an assignment, and why now? Where is it?"

MacKenzie held up a hand to forestall further questions. "The position is now open and must be filled soon. Selecting ye dinna require us tae change any other assignments."

Jamie sensed that there was much that he was not being told. He pressed further. "There are mair experienced officers on the ha'-pay list. Again, I must ask, why me?"

MacKenzie leaned back and flexed his hands. His knuckles crackled in the silence. Jamie knew his former commander's temper and realized that his questions were pressing on the colonel's limit. "Ye yerself hae already stated the reason. Ye hae mair experience at sea and especially, in land combat than others, skills that are very needfu' fer this assignment."

Jamie asked, "We are nae at war, and I hae heard nae rumors o' war. What is this assignment?"

MacKenzie reached for the white porcelain pot and carefully refilled their cups. "Before I provide ye the details, allow me tae tell ye a story o' a great conspiracy we hae uncovered. People wha engage in the slave trade and colonists wha purchase and employ black Africans consider them all alike, but there are vast differences betwixt the various peoples. There is a people frae the Gold Coast o' Africa called the Coromantins. Fer o'er a hundred years, the kings ruling the Gold Coast hae provided thousands and thousands o' captives, which were transported tae Jamaica, other islands in the Caribbean, and the coast o' Guyana by British traders operating principally oot o' Bristol, as weel as ports in New England. Tis a legal and highly lucrative business. The merchants expect, and the crown provides the services o' the fleet tae protect their commercial interests, as weel as those o' merchants o' other commodities, such as cotton, palm oil, cocoa, and tobacco. Piracy hae been nearly stamped oot, but nae completely."

The colonel took a sip of tea and continued, "The Coromantin people sold by the Ashanti o' the Gold Coast tae British traders hae been principally prisoners o' war or taken in raids on their villages. It should hae been obvious tae the traders that such people were skilled at primitive arms and maistly shared Twi, a common language. These bonds allowed the slaves in Jamaica to organize under the noses of the planters."

"In 1760, the slaves hatched a conspiracy and rose against the whites. It was organized by Tacky, a Coromanti, presumed to be of chiefly descent. A prominent planter claimed that almost all Coromantin slaves on the island were involved without any suspicion from the whites. Their plan was to overthrow British rule and establish an African kingdom in Jamaica. Tacky and his forces were able to take over several plantations and kill the white owners. However, they were ultimately betrayed by a slave named Yankee, who ran to a neighboring estate and, with the help of another slave, alerted the rest of the plantation owners. The governor called up the militia tae augment the garrison o' the forts and enlisted the help of Jamaican Maroons, who were themselves descendants of runaways and rebels in the hills, to defeat the Coromantins. Eventually, Tacky was killed by a sharpshooter, and the rebellion collapsed."

"In '63, a slave rebellion occurred in Berbice in Guyana, led by a Coromantin named Cuffy and his deputy, Akra. Cuffy, like Tacky, was born into a chief's family on the Gold Coast before being captured. He led a revolt of more than 2,500 slaves. After acquiring firearms, the rebels attacked plantations. They gained an advantage after taking the house of the governor and capturing his family. They had told the whites that they could leave the house, but as soon as they did, the rebels killed many men and took the women prisoners."

"After several months, disputes between Cuffy and Akra led to a falling-oot between the leaders. Cuffy wrote to the English governor proposing a partition of the colony, with whites occupying the coastal areas and blacks the interior. Akra's faction won, and Cuffy killed himself. Coromanti slaves were also behind a conspiracy to revolt that began last year. The leaders of the rebellion sealed their pact with a blood oath. Coromantin leaders Blackwell and Quamin laid siege tae a fort near Port Maria, as well as ambushing other whites in the area. They intend on allying with the Maroons and splitting the island. The Coromantins plan tae gie the Maroons the forests while the Coromantins would control the cultivated land of the island. The conspiracy is growing and is beyond the capacity o' the garrisons tae control it. There is a risk that it will spread tae other islands."

MacKenzie fell silent while Jamie digested the information. "I see. The purpose o' the squadron is tae suppress the rebellion."

MacKenzie shook his head. "That is a principal purpose but nae the full strategy. As lang as the Coromantins remain organized, rebellion will flare repeatedly. The squadron will help wi' resettlement tae break up concentrations o' these people and move them tae other islands and tae other plantations in Guyana. Following that effort, the squadron will proceed tae the Gold Coast tae ensure that nae mair Coromantin captives contaminate the slave markets. There was an attempt tae pass a bill through Parliament last year tae prohibit importation o' any further Coromantins, but it failed. Such a bill, if passed into law, would have struck at the very root o' the evil. Nae mair Coromantins would have been brought tae infest British colonies, but instead o' their savage race, they would be supplied with blacks of a mair docile disposition and better inclined to peace and agriculture. Now it will be the duty o' the British navy tae fulfill wha the politicians refuse tae accomplish."

Jamie realized the danger of objecting to the assignment on ethical grounds, in spite of his aversion to the use of the navy for shoring up British mercantile interests and his deep-seated feelings against slavery. He wished his old friend Jock Armstrong were available, but he had sailed for North America in *Namur* a month before." Jamie jerked upright.

Lieutenant Colonel MacKenzie was scowling. "I will repeat myself since ye hae been woolgathering, Drummond. HMS *Monarch* is Ramillies-class, a purpose-built seventy-four completed at Deptford and launched last July. She recently completed her sea trials and now lies at the Dockyard in Portsmouth being fitted fer sailing tae join the Caribbean squadron.

"Jeremiah Blackstone is her captain, but the commodore wha will command the squadron hae yet tae be named. Fer the next three weeks, I wish tae retain ye in this headquarters tae assist me in several matters. When those assignments are completed, ye will be promoted and report tae Captain Blackstone. I expect that the squadron will sail fer Jamaica by the first week o' March."

Jamie drew a deep breath. Having made a decision, he decided to risk the colonel's wrath. "I am indebted tae the admirals fer holding me in such high regard and the efforts ye hae made tae return me tae active service and obtain a promotion. Sir, I hae great misgivings aboot accepting this assignment. If possible, I request that ye recruit another officer in my stead. I prefer serving elsewhere, foregoing promotion."

MacKenzie bristled, and his voice rose. "Captain Drummond, if the king or his duly appointed authorities o' the Admiralty Board command ye, it is yer duty tae perform wi'oot reservations. Wha cause could compel a man tae refuse?"

Jamie said softly, "Honor, sir. I hae been shackled in chains in Carlisle and Newgate before I served and again in Havana in the dungeon o' El Morro. I would hae great difficulty bearing arms against men and women wha rise up tae claim that which we cherish maist highly—freedom. I served gladly in many battles against the king's sworn enemies, but this assignment galls my soul. Ye ken that many prominent people in this nation and its colonies hae spoken oot against wha they pronounce the great evil o' slavery?"

MacKenzie thumped the table. "It is legal commerce. It is the Royal Navy's duty tae offer it protection!"

Jamie murmured, "Twill nae be legal forever. It is a blot on the nation. While it is just that those wha commit great crimes be apprehended and justly punished, I hae strong feelings o' support fer those wha fight fer freedom. Can ye no recall the stirring words o' the Declaration o' Arbroath? It declares 'It is in truth nae fer glory, nor riches, nor honours that we are fighting, but fer freedom—fer that alain, which nae honest man gives up but wi' life itself.' How can I lead troops tae round up and reconfine men and women wha struggle tae make themselves free?"

Lieutenant Colonel MacKenzie was implacable. "We serve the king, sir, wha issues lawfu' orders which we are bound tae obey."

The argument went on for more than two hours. They discussed every aspect of the assignment and every possible way for it to be fulfilled within the constraints laid down by the Admiralty. When the pair realized that compromise was impossible, Jamie penned and signed his resignation. The deed was done. Lieutenant Colonel MacKenzie folded the letter, and the two stiffly shook hands.

Jamie said, "I dinna fault ye, sir. I hae the utmost admiration fer ye and consider having served under yer command a great privilege."

MacKenzie said, "Ye hae changed in many ways, lad, and I am sorry tae part company under these circumstances. Ye may be the bravest man I hae been privileged tae command in my years o' service. Ye realize that while I am accepting yer resignation, the Admiralty may nae be sae tolerant."

Jamie nodded, finding it hard to speak. "I follow the same code o' honor as ever, sir. However, my experiences wi' those wha lay in the same shackles as I and crofters o' my hameland wha exhibited as great a dignity in their poverty as any peer o' the realm make me realize that they share the same devotion tae integrity and honor as those born tae the aristocracy. I feel compelled tae follow a new path in life. I canna say whether it will lead tae success and happiness or ostracism frae my ain nation and class. When can I expect a final decision frae the Admiralty?"

MacKenzie said, "I hae perhaps a fortnight tae find a replacement in order tae meet the squadron's sailing date. I admonish ye tae remain in London until this matter is resolved."

17

Sir George Selwyn's house stood in the middle of the magnificence of Cleveland Row in Saint James. The house was set well back from the street behind a high brick wall pierced by ornate black wrought-iron gates. Jamie stepped down from a hansom and paid the driver. A liveried servant stood watch inside a narrow wooden kiosk just inside the gate. At mention of Jamie's name, he unlocked and pulled open the narrow pedestrian gate that stood next to the wider opening used to admit horse-drawn carriages.

The day was intensely cold, and Jamie was glad to shed his heavy cloak, cap, and gloves in the vestibule. A servant left him in a brightly lit room with a cheery fire that exuded comforting heat. After thirty minutes of studying the prints and watercolors that covered much of the walls, Jamie grew irritated. While it was usual for gentry to be mildly late to appointments, thirty minutes bordered on effrontery. He had nearly decided to reclaim his outerwear and depart when the door opened and George Augustus Selwyn strode into the middle of the room, right hand extended in greeting.

He was a handsome man of just over middle height, in his midfifties, of ruddy complexion. He wore no wig, and his auburn hair was touched with silver over the temples. His mouth and chin were firm, but his eyes were dark with drooping lids, as if he were perpetually half-asleep. However, his vigorous manners belied that impression.

They sat with tea for another half an hour while Jamie answered probing questions about his surveying experience. While Peter Gordon had described Selwyn as a bit of a fop, his mind was agile and his questions insightful. At length, he appeared satisfied with Jamie's qualifications. He unrolled a map of the colony of North Carolina on the low table. His long index finger traced the outline of the Granville grant and tapped the area that constituted his own property.

"Four hundred thousand acres, Drummond. I have specified that the land be surveyed, staked, and sold off by my agent in the town of Charlotte in tracts of no less than two hundred acres. The man I hired to do that work has left the colony, threatened, as he says, by some of the powerful locals in the town of Charlotte. He came well recommended, but I have seen evidence of shoddy work, which underlies the disputes that he stirred up with those who have already begun to build on their tracts. These conflicts must be set right by resurveying or repricing of tracts, with results that will convince the settlers of the honesty of the survey. I must admit that they can be a contentious and stubborn lot. With one exception, a Dr. Brevard, a French Huguenot, they are all Ulster Scots and Presbyterian. They are also mostly interrelated and immigrated into the area from Maryland or Pennsylvania when this country was first opened for settlement. Governor Tryon has publically stated that he is on the brink of invalidating my ownership of the tracts, but private correspondence to me shows that he would be satisfied with a professional survey and a gift of three hundred and sixty acres arranged in town lots. The governor is not the moral icon that he professes himself. In a further attempt to placate the locals, I intend to replace my agent, Henry Eustace McCulloch. Until our contract is consummated, I am not yet at liberty to divulge the identity of his replacement. Let me say that being of Scottish Lowland heritage and skilled in management of men and stock, I have no doubt of his ability. I expect that he will be in place before you arrive. If not, please do not divulge this plan to McCulloch. Sacking him is my responsibility."

Selwyn looked sharply at Jamie. "Are you also Presbyterian?"

"Nae, my lord. Although I am modestly austere in my personal habits, as are many o' that dour folk, I was raised an Anglican. Being o' another faith and Highland tae boot, the settlers may be loath tae extend a hearty welcome. Having a Lowlander like themselves as the land agent seems a wise choice."

Selwyn smiled. "We are different men, Drummond. I was planning to invite you to partake of some pleasant entertainment, but I will refrain. I enjoy experiences that enhance pleasure. You seem content to cultivate the intellect and not engage in, shall we say, physical pleasures."

Jamie said, "On the contrary. I continue tae cultivate the martial arts, as do maist gentlemen. I greatly enjoy riding, reading, and scientific inquiry, but hae scant taste fer dancing, the theater, and social affairs."

Selwyn smiled blandly. "Truly a pity, but I will desist. You are a young man of obvious qualities and I desire to recruit you for my American endeavors. You bring leadership and a commanding presence, along with consummate skill with weapons. Your predecessor had none of those qualities, which made him vulnerable." He rose, poured, and extended Jamie a glass of Madeira. He sat and sipped from his own.

"I do not wish you to underestimate the magnitude of this assignment. Four hundred thousand acres must be formed into two thousand tracts. Most of the surveys already completed must be corrected. Additionally, there are numerous town lots to be surveyed. Two years, Drummond. This assignment may consume two years to complete, even with a good team, similar to that which you employed in the Highlands. Contrary to that arduous experience, the Carolina Piedmont has mild winter weather, with only occasional snowstorms. You should be able to survey most of the year."

Jamie injected, "I suggest that I hire the survey team locally. It will create a bond with the settlers."

Selwyn nodded approval. As the conversation unfolded, it became clear to Jamie that his enthusiasm and Selwyn's desire to hire him was growing. What cemented the budding arrangement was Selwyn's offer of a bonus of two acres of land for every hundred surveyed, in addition to a generous salary. Jamie closed his eyes to envision eight thousand acres deeded over to him, in addition to several town lots selected from those which Selwyn's agent had not yet sold off or gifted to the governor. Selwyn assured him that he would have little trouble selling off tracts to the crowds of settlers arriving yearly down the trail through the Shenandoah Valley of Virginia. While some of these settlers were fresh off the ships bringing them from Ulster and Scotland, many were the sons of those who had come to Pennsylvania over the previous fifty years. They had cash, stock, farm implements, and many children and were hungry for land.

When they shook hands at the end of their meeting, Jamie was elated. Not only did he have an offer of employment, but the chance to make a fortune from land sales. They agreed to meet two weeks later to consummate their agreement and sign a contract if Jamie was free of his military obligation. The delay was necessary because the Admiralty had not yet sent a notification of their decision.

In a corner bedroom in Peter Gordon's townhouse, Jamie worked every available daylight hour and frequently far into the night, busying himself with a multitude of planning tasks, including drawing up lists of equipment and supplies he would need. He knew that horses and cattle regularly crossed the Atlantic. He was so bonded with Stormshadow that he could not bear to think of leaving the faithful mare behind. He knew many of the other horses in Charles Gordon's stable and planned to make a generous offer to his uncle buy two or three other riding horses to accompany him. Winter weather would make it difficult to transport the horses south to the dock on the Thames, but he was determined to have them. Late one night, immersed in scribbling lengthy notes to himself, Jamie's head sank onto his chest, and he drifted into a restless sleep. An hour passed, the lamp guttered out, and the room was suddenly pitch-dark.

Another hour passed. Jamie stirred but did not awaken. A golden light grew, pushing back the darkness into the corners. The door opened with a creak, and three squat figures waddled into the bedroom. They bounded onto the desk. Jamie jerked awake at the noise and peered warily at the three standing before him. "Nae!" he shouted, clutching at the inkstand to keep it from tipping over. Now fully awake, he sat back to appraise his nocturnal visitors. He groaned. "Peallaidh an Spùit, the king and his companions."

A grin split the massive gray beard, revealing the stumps of yellowish teeth. The little man nodded, evidently pleased to be so easily recognized. The one to his left bowed. "Stochdail at yer service." The third little figure also bowed low. "Brùnaidh an Easain," he croaked.

Jamie ran his hands through his hair, which had fallen around his shoulders. "I dinna believe that ye would return tae bedevil my sleep! Why are ye here?"

In a coarse voice, the king grated out, "The signs and portents are favorable. Ye are on the right track, laddie. But ye must beware, fer there be dangerous foes wha will beset ye on yer path."

Jamie blurted, "Where? In London, Scotland, or North Carolina?"

The gruagach king raised a restraining hand. "Nae, in other places ye hae ne'er seen. If ye are wary, ye will evade their traps. There will be a day when ye will prevent a deadly deed on a battlefield and save him wha will greatly advance the cause o' liberty fer yer people and many others."

"Who and when?" Jamie pleaded. The three gruagach began fading from sight. He clutched for Peallaidh's arm but felt nothing. He grabbed for the others with no more success. The apparition, for it was clearly one, was gone, and the room was black, except for the crescent moon glowing through the window.

After ten days, a young naval officer arrived at the townhouse, asking for Captain Drummond.

Jamie raced down the stairs to the foyer, where Ensign Edward Bartlett handed him a packet from Lieutenant Colonel Raibert MacKenzie. As soon as the courier was gone, Jamie tore it open. Two letters fell out. The first was from the Admiralty accepting Jamie's resignation. The second was a short note from the colonel offering him congratulations and best wishes in his new life. Dazed at this turn of events, Jamie leaned against a doorframe, breathing heavily in relief. Giddy, he almost skipped up the stairs to the bedroom, where he hastily penned a note to Lord George Selwyn requesting a meeting and another to his mother.

With Peter's help, Jamie concluded the agreement to survey the two enormous Selwyn tracts. With the lord's commission in his pocket and a sizeable advance against expenses, he was anxious to return to far-off Abergeldie to collect his belongings and equipment and strike a deal with Uncle Charles for the horses he would need. To sit idly for ten days on the long carriage ride north was torture.

Euphemia Drummond took the news well, for she had realized for many months that Jamie would only find his fortune in a place distant from the Highlands. She had discovered her brother's plan to marry him to a Huntley Gordon heiress and secretly applauded her son's rejection of the arrangement. She had confronted Charles one morning. "God forbid that my son would be a sniveling opportunist, clinging tae a woman's skirts, embezzling her fortune fer his ain. It would be an ignoble fate fer a young man o' honor and integrity. He was correct tae reject the suggestion." She did not give her brother a chance to reply to her withering criticism, stalking from the room, her face pale with rage. Charles did not mention the arrangement again.

She had prepared her other children for the disappointment of the long absence of their elder brother. They greeted Jamie with glad cries, excited by his opportunity of a voyage to America. Jamie spent most of the two weeks at Abergeldie with them. Charles had been generous, selling two mares and gifting a fine young stallion to Jamie.

He observed reasonably, "Ye may want them strictly fer riding, but ye hae the makings o' a stable, in the event that ye must tarry fer mair than the agreed-upon time. The offspring o' sech fine horses will fetch ye a guid price fer a wee inconvenience."

At last, the day for departure came. Jamie had arranged for a freight wagon to convey the horses, along with the bulk of his books and personal belongings. He had elected to bring the delicate irreplaceable surveying equipment with him by carriage, stopping at Portree on Skye to visit Jock and Maggie. With their advancing age and his two-year absence, he was concerned that he might never see them again. From Portree, he would proceed southward via Oban, Dumbarton, Glasgow, Carlisle, and the English midlands to London.

A light snow had filtered down since midnight, coating the outbuildings, drives, and lawns of Abergeldie Castle. The sky was cloudy and the air cold, but this was winter in the Highlands and no obstacle to travel. The family gathered at the base of the steps leading down from the great front doors.

Euphemia broke the solemn atmosphere by observing that in the dozen or more departures of Jamie from his home, it always seemed to be in a light snowfall. Everyone laughed, for it was true.

Jamie embraced her tightly. Impulsively, he whispered, "Mama, bring the children and join me in the New World. Twill be a grand adventure."

She pushed him to arm's length, her eyes brimming. "Ach, laddie, ye ken that I would dearly love tae accompany ye, but wi' yer sisters and wee brother, I hae great obligations that nae sensible mother can ignore. Ye must make this voyage, and I must stay. I understood that frae the time that Maggie pronounced her prophecy. I also ken that ye will return wi' honor, having gained a legacy tae replace that which hae been lost. I dinna hae the Sight, but my heart tells me that ye will yet be master o' Strathallan, and I will live tae see it. Now, the carriage is coming. Kiss yer sisters and Wee Jock."

In spite of heartfelt good wishes from everyone, Jamie was unable to maintain a forced cheerfulness. He fought back tears as he made his way around the circle of the family. At last, it was time to depart.

The footman signaled that the luggage was loaded. Jamie swung into the door held open by the footman and took his seat. The carriage jerked forward. He leaned out the window to wave to his family. Abergeldie Castle dwindled in the distance. A bend in the road took them out of view just before the carriage rattled across the stone bridge above the frozen River Dee and out onto the road leading south.

A month later, with equipment, supplies, and the horses safely loaded, Jamie boarded the *Duke of Bedford*. She was not a sleek warship bristling with cannon but a fat-bellied merchant craft with a commodious hold, a reasonably clean bottom, and dry bilge. Her captain and master seemed competent. Her sails, rigging, and hardware were in good repair, and they were well stocked with food and water. Jamie's long experience afloat living in the hold and then in a junior officer's cramped quarters did not prepare him for the comparative splendor of a paying passenger's cabin. Situated aft on the main deck, it featured the luxuries of a single bed, desk, small settee, and a porthole admitting sunlight.

Their early spring departure meant that they had perhaps a month of adverse winds and seas on the westward crossing to the port of Chester, on the outskirts of Philadelphia, the largest city in North America. Jamie would have preferred a landfall further down the coast, at Alexandria or Annapolis, since those ports would have meant a shorter journey to the Great Wagon Road through the Shenandoah Valley to Charlotte. The detour to Chester could not be helped since there were no ships leaving for those ports for another month. Docking in Hampton Roads in southern Virginia or along the estuaries of tidewater North Carolina would have required a tedious journey across the sparsely settled Piedmont, where no east-west roads or trails led to Charlotte and the Catawba River settlements.

Nae matter, thought Jamie. *I will hae an opportunity to see more of the country.* He would join a group of settlers headed for Charlotte and hire a drover to help him with the wagon and horses.

Captain Nathaniel Spurlock announced that *Duke of Bedford* would depart on the early morning tide and proceed down the Thames past Gravesend and Sheerness to the North Sea. Jamie enjoyed a final dinner ashore with Peter and Rachel Gordon and returned to the ship past midnight. He kicked off his shoes and began undressing. There was a sharp knock on the cabin door. Captain Spurlock's orderly passed him a letter.

It was from Lord George Selwyn, wishing him a good voyage and informing him that he had hired a new land agent, who was sailing from Glasgow for Chester, where he would join Jamie for the journey south. Jamie read the agent's name and struggled for breath. In clearly printed letters, he read *Alexander Moffett*. Impossible! How could an escaped reiver with a price on his head who had shared a cell with Jamie in Carlisle Prison ten years ago become Lord George Selwyn's new land agent? He shrugged, folded the letter, and replaced it in the envelope. Moffett was a numerous clan, and there must be many Alexanders. Surely, it was a coincidence. Or was it?

NOTES

Chapter 1. The dungeon of Castillo de los Tres Reyes Magos del *Morro*, guarding the harbor entrance at Havana, Cuba, was notorious even by eighteenth century standards. Prisoners were routinely beaten, starved, and subject to disease and nighttime attacks by the huge Cuban rats. Standing high on a promontory, the fortress was a daunting enterprise to attack from the seaward side. After the failed attempt to destroy the seaward-facing guns, the British fleet was content to bottle up the Spanish fleet inside the harbor while the army battered it with over forty thousand artillery shells, bombs, and sapper attacks.

Lieutenant Javier Molina is imaginary, but the comandante of the fortress, Captain Luis Vicente de Velasco was real. He is memorialized in Cuban history for chivalry and his valiant but futile defense of the citadel, which cost him his life. Pepe Antonio, the physician and councilman of the district of Guanabacoa, led a counterattack and later organized the futile defense of the city after the Spanish military failed to provide even a rudimentary defense. He died during the battle and is fondly remembered as a hero of the Cuban people. After the fall of El Morro, the defenders who could escape crossed the channel to the companion fortress of La Punta.

Chapter 2. San Salvador de la Punta, like El Morro, was designed to protect the entrance to Havana Bay. The British cannonading of the fortress was devastating, once the guns were emplaced. The safety curtains and bastions of La Punta were destroyed during the bombardment.

Bastinado was a form of corporal punishment commonly used in prisons in many nations, in which the soles of a person's bare feet were beaten. Bastinado was mostly done with a device such as a cane, rod, leather whip, flexible rubber bat, leather strap, or electric cable. The prisoner was usually immobilized with restraints for the punishment. The strokes aimed at the longitudinal arch of the foot, which is a highly pain-susceptible area due to the clustering of nerve endings. The sensations are described as stinging or lightning, the aftereffect as searing or burning while the pain experienced on impact is intense and spreads through the body.

Chapter 3. Post-traumatic stress disorder is not a modern phenomenon. For thousands of years, those involved in military campaigns suffered its effects to some extent. Few were willing to admit the affliction, for it implied a lack of fortitude and might cost the victim his career and reputation. Most suffered alone, ashamed of their weakness and bedeviled by the symptoms.

Chapter 4. Superstition was rife among most people of the eighteenth century, in spite of the growing enlightenment. The gruagach, as they were known in the Scottish Highlands, were known by the term *brownie* in England, a variety of wee folk of legend and ancient beyond remembrance. Brownies seldom spoke with humans, but some could hear their frequent and affectionate conversations with each another. In parts of the Highlands, Peallaidh an Spùit (Peallaidh o' the Spout), Stochdail a' Chùirt, and Brùnaidh an Easain (brownie of the little waterfall) were names of note and deserving of great respect. According to Scottish legend, every stream in the north had a gruagach once, and their king was Peallaidh.

The lengthy discussions in Cuba and Martinique about the overbearing and condescending behavior of the aristocracy and military authorities toward colonials seem oddly prescient of the coming American Revolution. It is important to remember that the colonials of the Caribbean, Central America, and South America had similar grievances and aspirations for liberty. Their revolutions took generations longer than in the thirteen colonies, but they eventually took place.

Chapter 5. European discovery of the Gulf Stream dates to the 1512 expedition of Juan Ponce de León, after which it became widely used by Spanish ships sailing from the Caribbean to Spain. Ponce de León's voyage log noted, "A current such that, although they had great wind, they could not proceed forward, but backward and it seems that they were proceeding well; at the end it was known that the current was more powerful than the wind." Although many wise British, French, and Dutch mariners were aware of this powerful current, it was not until the 1770s that such knowledge was universal.

HMS *Marlborough* was an old ship, rebuilt twice, and had been badly damaged in the fruitless attack on the seaward side of El Morro. She was the old HMS *St. Michael*, a ninety-gun second-rate ship of the line launched in 1669. She was rebuilt at Blackwall Yard in 1706, at which time she was renamed *Marlborough*. In 1725, she was taken to pieces, rebuilt at Chatham Yard, and relaunched in 1732. *Marlborough* was reduced to a sixty-eight-gun ship in 1752. While making her way back to Great Britain after participating in the conquest of Havana in 1762, *Marlborough* was caught in very heavy weather. On 29 November, her captain decided to abandon the ship, which was sinking. Mercifully, HMS *Antelope* happened by. All of *Marlborough's* crew were saved. Sinking was a constant dread of seafarers, for no ships had enough boats to save all. There was no assurance that small boats could survive a major storm and make it to shore. Once there, the wind, cold, crashing waves, rocks, and shoals were further obstacles to a crew's slim chances for survival.

Chapter 6. The Treaty of Paris of 1763 ended the Seven Years' War between Great Britain and France, as well as their respective allies. In the terms of the treaty, France gave up all territories in mainland North America, effectively ending any foreign military threat to the British colonies. During the war, British forces had scored important victories against France. Not only had the British conquered French Canada, they had decimated the French fleet, won victories in India, and captured the French islands in the Caribbean. In March 1762, King Louis XV issued a formal call for peace talks.

The British were also interested in ending the war. It had been enormously expensive, and the government financed the war with debt. Creditors began to doubt Great Britain's ability to pay back the loans. In addition, King George II had died in 1760, and his successor and grandson George III was more amenable to ending the war.

Initial attempts at negotiating a peace settlement failed, and instead French and Spanish diplomats signed a treaty that brought Spain into the war against Great Britain. British Prime Minister Lord Bute continued secret talks with French diplomat Étienne François, the duc de Choiseul, and they came to an unofficial agreement in June 1762. Bute promised generous terms, and the two countries agreed to an exchange of ambassadors.

By the time the formal negotiations began, the situation had changed. News reached Europe of the British capture of Havana and with it all of Cuba. Spanish King Charles III refused to agree to a treaty that would require Spain to give up Cuba, but the British Parliament would never ratify a treaty that did not reflect British territorial gains made during the war.

Facing this dilemma, French negotiator Choiseul proposed a solution that redistributed American territory between France, Spain, and Great Britain. Under his plan, Great Britain would gain all French territory east of the Mississippi while Spain would retain Cuba in exchange for handing Florida over to Great Britain. French territories west of the Mississippi would become Spanish, along with the port of New Orleans. In return, while losing territory in India, Africa, and the Mediterranean island of Minorca, France would regain the Caribbean islands that British forces had captured during the war. The British also promised to allow French Canadians to practice Catholicism and provided France fishing rights off Newfoundland.

Choiseul wanted the Caribbean islands of Martinique, Guadeloupe, and Santa Lucia rather than the vast territory stretching from Louisiana to Canada. This decision was because the islands' sugar industry was enormously profitable. In contrast, Canada had been a drain on the French treasury. The loss of Canada, while a blow to French pride, made sense from a financial perspective.

Diplomats signed the preliminary Treaty of Paris on November 3, 1762. Spanish and French negotiators also signed the Treaty of San Ildefonso, confirming the cession of French Louisiana to Spain. Although King George III and his ministers were in favor of the treaty, it was unpopular with the British public. However, the treaty contained just enough concessions to war hawks that Parliament ratified the Treaty of Paris by a majority of 319 to 64, and it went into effect on February 10, 1763.

James Boswell is principally known as the diarist and traveling companion of the great Samuel Johnson. Before he formed that association, he was as he described himself to Jamie, the son of a prominent barrister and judge in Edinburgh. As the eldest son, he was heir to his family's estate of Auchinleck in Ayrshire. On turning nineteen, he was sent to the University of Glasgow. While there, he decided to convert to Catholicism and become a monk. On learning of this, his father ordered him home. Instead of obeying, Boswell ran away to London, where he spent three months, living the life of a libertine before he was taken back to Scotland by his father. Upon returning, he was reenrolled at Edinburgh University and forced by his father to sign away most of his inheritance in return for an allowance of £100 a year.

In July of 1762, Boswell took his law exam, which he passed with some skill. With this success, Lord Auchinleck decided to raise his son's allowance to £200 a year and allowed him to return to London. It was during his second spell there that Boswell wrote his *London Journal* and, on 16 May 1763, met Johnson for the first time. Boswell recorded their first conversation, which consisted of this witticism:

"Mr. Johnson, I do indeed come from Scotland, but I cannot help it."

To which the great man replied with acid wit, "That, sir, I find, is what a very great many of your countrymen cannot help."

Chapter 7. Philip Stanhope, fourth Earl of Chesterfield, was a British statesman and prominent man of letters, with many friends in government, as well as influential people across the political spectrum. While he was not particularly eloquent or supportive of causes, he surrounded himself with those who had those qualities. His sumptuous home at Chesterfield Square was the scene of many meetings of his influential circle of friends.

The defection of John Anthony to the East India Company is an example of a frequent occurrence among young officers and civil service administrators at the close of the Seven Years' War. Smelling great wealth to be won in the company's lucrative trade, they flocked to India in droves.

Vice Admiral of the Red Thomas Cotes is most famous today for the fine portrait painted by Sir Joshua Reynolds. He was relieved of his duties in Jamaica by Rear Admiral Charles Holmes. He retired from the Royal Navy and took the seat in Parliament arranged for him by powerful friends. His short political career was undistinguished, and he died soon after returning to his native Cornwall. It was not unusual for the landed gentry to arrange marriages for their children, particularly if the child was the heir, in order to enhance the prestige and holdings of the family.

The outflow of people from the north that is today called the Highland Clearances (in Gaelic *Fuadach nan Gàidheal*) actually began in 1763, although it did not become a flood tide until the nineteenth century. By the twentieth century, this movement (both forced and unforced but driven by economic necessity) had so depopulated the Highlands, following the earlier flight of transplanted Lowland Scots from Northern Ireland that there were far more Scottish people living in other countries than in Scotland.

The decompression of the military forces of Great Britain at the close of the Seven Years' War was astonishingly abrupt due to the perilous state of the nation's finances. Scores of ships were decommissioned and broken up, soldiers and sailors discharged by the tens of thousands, and installations closed. While the Peace of Paris left Great Britain the most powerful force on the planet, the nation did not feel that it could afford the honor. Its attempt to wring some tax money from the colonies that had just been saved brought on the unrest that led to American independence and another war.

Chapter 8. Jamie Drummond's battle to resign his commission is reflective of my own difficulty in doing so in the closing years of the Vietnam War. Although I had honorably completed twelve years of service and an overseas tour in a combat zone, it was not enough, and my resignation was refused. Eighteen months of intensive effort were required before I was allowed to transition to reserve status, similar to Jamie's half-pay status.

James Boswell's obsession with pursuing women and hangings are well-documented in his *London Journal*. The Hyde Park carousel debuted to great acclaim in 1763.

Chapter 9. The description of smoky and odiferous Edinburgh is consistent with travelers' journals of the time. It was called Auld Reekie for a good reason.

John Robison served in the navy and was a prominent Scottish physicist and mathematician. He later became a professor of philosophy at the University of Edinburgh.

A member of the Edinburgh Philosophical Society, Robison invented the siren and also worked with James Watt on an early steam car.

The Cairngorm Mountains and other waste places in the Highlands became the refuge for those fleeing the law and debt, who formed bands to prey upon the people and stock of the country. Banditry and reiving had always been problems, but the volume and frequency of the losses grew alarmingly in the 1760s. Landlords and sheriffs authorized posses to hunt them down and bring them to justice. While some malefactors were hanged or imprisoned, the majority ended up transported to the colonies.

Chapter 10. While Jamie rejects his Uncle Charles's suggestion of an arranged marriage with an heiress, it was an not uncommon practice. Many young men of aristocratic pedigree but without wealth engaged in the practice, in England as well as in Scotland.

The fear of republicanism among the aristocracy and landed gentry was strong. This was the era of John Wilkes, who was ejected from Parliament for preaching such ideals. The fear grew more pronounced as first the American and then the French revolution destabilized the old order.

John Anderson of the University of Glasgow was a major supporter of the early research and inventions of James Watt. Descriptions of his workshops on the campus of the university are taken from journals of the time.

Chapter 11. A major obstacle faced by James Watt in his early work on steam power was that which face many modern inventors and entrepreneurs: the fickleness of his supporters, who wanted far more progress faster than it was possible to create.

The strange tale of the Biddick Drummonds' relationship to the Drummonds of Strathallan may never be solved, but I enjoyed injecting its mystery into the story. South Biddick had an evil reputation for smuggling and other forms of lawlessness. The presence of the exiled James Drummond in such a place rather than on the continent does not square with other historical evidence, which is why I brought in the possibility of fraud.

Chapter 12. Well-documented in the journals of numerous tourists, travel in the eighteenth century was arduous and slow, with scanty accommodations. The city of Sens in Burgundy was the major place of refuge for expatriate Scottish Jacobites. It was there they found affordable living and camaraderie with old companions and sympathetic French citizens. Many of them never returned home and are buried in the vaults and grounds of Saint-Étienne cathedral.

Bloodletting was based on an ancient system of medicine in which blood and other bodily fluids were regarded as humors that had to be in proper balance to maintain health. It was the most common medical practice performed by surgeons from antiquity until the late nineteenth century, a span of two thousand years. In Europe, the practice was common until the end of the eighteenth century. The practice was abandoned by modern medicine for all except a few conditions. In the absence of other treatments for hypertension, bloodletting may have had a beneficial effect in temporarily reducing blood pressure and volume. In the overwhelming majority of cases, bloodletting was universally harmful.

The Garde Écossaise was an elite Scottish military unit founded in 1418 by King Charles VII as personal bodyguards to the French monarchy. They were part of the royal household and later formed the first company of the Garde du Corps du Roi or Life Guards. They served the kings of France for over four hundred years and were finally disbanded in 1830.

Chapter 13. Sir John Lockhart-Ross, sixth Baronet, was known as John Lockhart for the first thirty-nine years of his life. He inherited his title and estates from his mother, who was the third daughter of William Ross, twelfth Lord Ross. He was a highly regarded officer of the Royal Navy who rose quickly to command warships. He saw service during the War of the

Austrian Succession, Seven Years' War, and later in the War for American Independence. He served for a time in Parliament.

After inheriting his title, he devoted himself principally to improving his estates and the condition of the peasantry, and became known as "the best farmer and the greatest planter in the country; his wheat and turnips showed the one, his plantation of a million pines the other." He recognized that the land could not sustain the pattern of small crofter holdings and initiated land tenure reform which would later evolve into the Highland Clearances.

Peter Dollond was an English-born maker of quality optical instruments. He is credited with the invention of the triple achromatic lens in 1763, still in wide use today. Dollond telescopes were among the most popular in Great Britain and abroad for over one and half centuries. Admiral Lord Nelson owned one. Another sailed with Captain Cook in 1769 to observe the transit of Venus, a voyage that led to discovery of New Zealand, Tahiti, and the Hawaiian Islands.

The Highland midge is a species of small flying insect, found especially in northern Scotland from late spring to late summer. Highland midges are well known for gathering in clouds and biting humans and are the smallest flies in Scotland to do so. The majority of the blood they get comes from cattle, sheep, and deer.

The Hilton of Cadboll Stone was discovered on the Tarbat Peninsula in Easter Ross. It is one of the most magnificent of all Pictish cross-slabs. On the seaward-facing side is a Christian cross, and on the landward side Pictish symbols and a hunting scene including a woman riding sidesaddle. It dates to about AD 800.

Chapter 14. Kelp gathering in Wester Ross was a traditional way for crofters to obtain cheap fertilizer for their impoverished soil. Later, it became an industry that employed up to fifty thousand people, for it produced an alkali useful in the manufacture of soap and other commodities.

The seaweed was gathered and laid out to dry before being burned in a kelp kiln. The kilns were shallow stone-lined pits about five feet in diameter. Once a good fire was burning in the pit, the seaweed was added. The resulting product was light, dry, and easy to transport and spread in the fields.

With no ability to forecast weather, the people of the western Highlands were particularly vulnerable to sudden and frequently devastating winter storms. While the North Atlantic Drift provides mild weather most of the time, storms barreling down from the Icelandic Low toward Great Britain could hit the exposed northwestern coast with high winds and snow, producing zero-visibility conditions and extreme cold for a short time. Being caught out in such storms could doom travelers.

Between 1485 and 1487, MacDonalds and their allies (about 1,000 men) meeting at Cunndainn on their way to a punitive raid against the Mackenzies of Kinellan discovered the church was filled with aged men, women, and children trusting to its sanctuary. Alexander Macdonald ordered the door shut and the building surrounded so that none could escape. He gave orders to set the church on fire, and hundreds were burned to death. Vengeance from MacKenzies and MacRaes was swift. After the battle at Pairc, less than 200 out of 1,800 to 2,000 Macdonalds and their followers were left to escape as they could.

Various games called football were played in Scotland in the Middle Ages. Despite bearing the same name, medieval football bore little resemblance to the modern game. The ball was often carried by hand, teams were large or unequal in number, and scrimmaging was sometimes involved. Some of these games are still played to this day. The earliest historical reference to "futeball" in Scotland was in 1424 when King James I outlawed the playing of it by decree because of its often violent nature and the disruption football was having on military training. An early writer recorded his impressions, which ring true today:

'Brissit, brawnis and broken banis, Stryf, discorde and waistie wanis, Cruikit in eild syn halt withall, Thir are the bewties of the fute ball', which translates as: 'Bruised muscles and broken bones. Discordant strife and futile blows. Lamed in old age, then crippled withal. These are the beauties of football.'

Chapter 15. While the large landowners in the Highlands realized that the land was overpopulated and improvements were only a temporary fix to a universal problem, they still feared uncontrolled emigration taking away their best factors, tacksmen, and crofters. This was before they discovered that running Cheviot sheep on the land would yield them greater profits than the crofters could ever provide.

Sutherland was notorious for some of the worst depredations of the Highland Clearances in the early years of the nineteenth century, when news of the horrors of the burnings, persecution, and outright murder at Strathnaver sickened the nation. However, the pattern of overbearing control and greed had its roots in the previous century, when this powerful family consolidated its control in the far north.

The cost of a voyage from Great Britain to the American colonies rose sharply from 5 to 6 English pounds per adult (somewhat less for a child) in 1720 to an average of 12 pounds by 1765. This was exclusive of food and drink, which passengers were expected to provide themselves, fuel for cooking and to keep themselves warm, and additional costs for transporting household goods and tools necessary to establishing a household in the New World. There were additional charges if they chose to transport livestock, horses, and mules.

Chapter 16. The Coromantee, also called Coromantins or Coromanti, was the designation for recent Caribbean and South American people enslaved and brought from the Gold Coast or modern-day Ghana. Coromantins were from several Akan ethnic groups—Ashanti, Fanti, Akyem, etc.—presumably taken as war captives. Owing to their militaristic background and common Akan language, Coromantins organized dozens of slave rebellions in Jamaica and the Caribbean. Their fierce, rebellious nature became so notorious among white plantation owners in the eighteenth century that an act was proposed to ban the importation of people from the Gold Coast despite their reputation as strong workers. The Coromantins and other Akans had the largest African cultural influence on Jamaica. Names of notable Coromantee leaders such as Cudjoe, Quamin, Cuffy, and Quamina correspond to Akan names Kojo, Kwame, Kofi, and Kwabena, respectively.

In the seventeenth and eighteenth century, captive Africans from the Gold Coast area, modern-day Ghana, were sent to British Caribbean colonies. Jamaica received a high percentage of people from this region because of Great Britain's control of the Gold Coast. Coromantee was defined as the country from where these people came since they shared a common language known as Twi, which formed a loosely structured organization of people who socialized and helped one another. Edward Long, an eighteenth century white Jamaican colonist who strongly advocated banning Coromantins noted that this unity played an important role in organizing plots and rebellions despite the geographical dispersion of Coromantins across different plantations. The organizational unity of Coromantins due to their common background also contributed to a mutual aid society, burial group, and places to enjoy social entertainment.

Most of the slave revolts in Jamaica were led by Coromantin slaves. Coromantin warriors captured in battle did not easily leave their leadership positions for servitude. A noteworthy example of such a Coromantin chief–led rebellion is Tacky's Rebellion on Jamaica in 1760. Tacky led slaves around the island to revolt, murdering a shopkeeper on Easter morning and stealing guns, gunpowder, and other supplies. They moved inland, taking over estates and killing the whites of the plantations, who were often still asleep in their beds. Though the militia and armed troops quickly captured and put down this first outbreak, the next several months on the island of Jamaica were filled with slave uprisings. In the end, sixty whites and between three hundred and four hundred blacks were killed.

Names like Tacky, Albert Sam, Quamina, Cudjoe and Adoe, documented as rebel slave leaders, have their roots in Ghana. The reference to British slaves as Coromantee Negroes is traced to the Ghanaian fishing community Koromantin, where the British built a fortified lodge to keep slaves brought from the hinterland. Presently, there are people in the Caribbean whose names and cultural traits bear close resemblance to the Ghanaian culture.

Chapter 17. George Augustus Selwyn was born on his family's estate near Maston in the Cotswold Hills overlooking the Severn Valley. His father, Colonel John Selwyn, was well known in the courts of the Georges; Selwyn also served as a member of Parliament for Gloucester as well as the treasurer of Queen Caroline's pensions. After his father and older brother died in 1751, George inherited large tracts of land in Piedmont North Carolina, that the Crown granted to his father in 1737.

As a member of Parliament for over forty years, Selwyn was indifferent and inattentive, showing no serious interest in affairs of state. The town of Charlotte was being established on a small part of Selwyn's land about the time he inherited it. The whole tract was known as the Selwyn Grant. Because the land was a grant from the king, there was a requirement to settle at least one person on every two hundred acres. In 1766, Selwyn had the four hundred thousand acres of his Carolina land surveyed. Though he never visited his vast possessions in America, Selwyn showed a great deal of interest, as reflected in his correspondence and his agent's activities.

Selwyn's reputation rested on his wit and humor. An early member of the leading London clubs, he was widely known and frequently quoted. He was on friendly terms with statesmen, politicians, and literary men, as well as with the court circle. His fascination and involvement with bawdy, licentious, and profane members of court society were legendary.

Song of Honor

In early spring of the year 1766, Western Europe and the Americas lay at peace, but the peace was unsettling. Seven years of worldwide war had exhausted the resources of losers and winners alike. The British reigned supreme on the seas. France's navy had been decimated and her armies humiliated. She had lost her American colonies and mercantile position in India. Although having won the long war, Great Britain inherited a crushing national debt, which forced the nation to raise taxes and dismantle much of the magnificent military that had been assembled to win the war. Ships were broken up, including those recently completed. Battle-experienced officers were retired or placed on half pay. Tens of thousands of soldiers and sailors were discharged and pushed on to a civilian workforce with too few jobs for those seeking employment.

British colonies in America were free from the oppressive threat of invasion by the French, but Parliament was intent on requiring the colonists to pay for the cost of quartering soldiers among them and raising funds to help pay for the war. Such measures aroused the hostility of colonial legislatures and the populace, who had long enjoyed a measure of independence from Parliamentary domination. Much of the hostility played itself out in debate, but especially in Boston, it was difficult to distinguish between protesting citizens and mobs. North Carolina, on the other hand, was a royal colony where the governor appointed by the king exercised considerable power, and there was relative peace, except in the hilly backcountry, settled principally by swarms of Ulster Scots migrating south from other colonies and some directly from Northern Ireland. These were a people with a long history of hardiness, self-reliance, and more than a little mistrust of royal authority.

Every year, hundreds of ships made the trans-Atlantic voyage to colonial ports from Boston, Massachusetts, southward to the new colony of Georgia at Savannah. These ships brought merchant goods mostly British products such as fine carriages, steel tools and cutlery, woolen and linen cloth, wine, rum, brandies, tea, and a myriad of other items that colonists could not manufacture on their own. Merchants bartered these items for American tobacco, cotton, indigo, furs, timber, meat, and fish. Ships also brought thousands of immigrants, both bond and free, as well as transporting merchants, military personnel, and families in both directions.

While ships sailed from many ports in England, Scotland, and Ireland, the queen of commercial enterprise was London. In addition to shipping to America, London served the merchant fleets sailing to and from the North Sea ports on the continent and along the Baltic. The capital was a vast emporium offering everything that ship captains and their employers chose to ship. Warehouses lined the docks surrounding the Pool of London, where the merchant ships tied up for loading and unloading. Teams of draft horses hauled wagons packed with crates, barrels, bales, and boxes onto the docks. Hundreds of stevedores pushed their way through the throngs to take their places booming cargo into holds and wrestling containers up the gangplanks where sweating crewmen took them below into cavernous holds to be lashed in place.

Crowds of emigrants with restless children, burdened with their pitiful possessions, squatted or sat waiting their turn to embark. Those condemned to transportation stood chained in long coffles, guarded by prison bailiffs. Voluntary indentures were allowed to sail without chains, but they too would be forced to mount a platform once they arrived to be inspected and have their indentures bought up by landowners and craftsmen for the years of service required to pay for their passage. Once aboard, passengers disappeared into compartments that had more in common with cattle pens than bedless staterooms, allowed to emerge only infrequently to blink in the sun after many days lying or sitting in near-total darkness and filth.

Passengers who could pay well for their accommodations fared better, although nearly everyone had to share the cramped spaces. It was not uncommon for two passengers or even three to share a bed, taking turns sleeping. Food, water, and fuel for the long voyage were carefully rationed because no one understood weather and how long a voyage might last. If forced to navigate through adverse winds, a voyage could take weeks longer than expected. While there was great risk that they would run short of food, it seemed that there was always a plentiful supply of spirits aboard. Many passengers claimed to survive a stormy voyage only because they were drunk for most of it.

Once a ship was loaded and a captain determined that all was in readiness to sail, crowding in the Pool of London meant that only a few ships at a time could be allowed to sail with the tide down the narrow Thames to Sheerness and the open waters of the North Sea beyond. The danger of collisions was great, particularly on those days and nights when heavy fog obscured vision. Delays were the rule, rather than the exception, and anyone attempting to predict a ship's actual sailing date and time would do better consulting a soothsayer than a port authority.

Jamie Drummond, a young Highland Scot and former military officer, a week short of his twenty-eighth birthday entered this maelstrom of activity shortly before dawn in early April. He brought a string of four fine horses—three mares and a young very skittish stallion—and three heavy trunks in a drover's wagon. Two contained his clothes, books, and writing materials. One was exceptionally heavy, for it bore the most precious cargo of all—two sets of precision surveying instruments. He was headed to the port of Chester in the colony of Pennsylvania, where he would begin an overland trek of six hundred miles southwestward to the Catawba and Yadkin River valleys of North Carolina to fulfill the surveying contract he had signed with Lord Sir George Selwyn. Would he find profit in fees and land from the venture sufficient to restore his family's fortunes and avoid deadly conflict with the restless settlers who disputed Lord Selwyn's claims to the land? Would Jamie find fulfillment of the prophecy pronounced by Highland bard and seer Maggie McRae long years before?

Bibliography

1. The book addresses so many events, areas, and people that it is difficult to cite all contributions. While there are many references, the following were particularly valuable in writing *Honor Bound*:
2. "Battle of Havana 1762." Library of Battles. Accessed April 7, 2015. http://libraryofbattles.com/Battle/10222.
3. "Sail–1719 to 1785–1st to 4th Rate." Sail–1719 to 1785–1st to 4th Rate. Accessed April 7, 2015. http://www.britainsnavy.co.uk/Sail/Sail–1719 to 1785–1st to 4th Rate.htm.
4. Anderson, Fred. *Crucible of War: The Seven Years' War and the Fate of Empire in British North America, 1754–1766.* New York State Historical Association, 2001.
5. Winfield, Rif. *British Warships in the Age of Sail.* Chatham Publishing, 2005.
6. Google.earth Products. Accessed April 7, 2015. http://www.google.com/earth/explore/products/earthview.html.
7. "Castles.nl–Home." El Morro Castle. Accessed April 7, 2015. http://www.castles.nl/el-morro-castle.
8. Campbell, John Gregorson. *Superstitions of the Highlands & Islands of Scotland.* Glasgow: JAMES MACLEHOSE AND SONS, GLASGOW, 1900.

9. Campbell, John Gregorson, and Ronald Black. *The Gaelic Otherworld: Rev. John Gregorson Campbell's 'Superstitions of the Highlands and Islands' and 'Witchcraft and Second Sight in the Highlands and Islands of Scotland'* Edinburgh, Midlothian: Birlinn, 2003.

10. Pottle, Frederick A. "A Candle on a Naughty World, Boswell's London Journal, 1762-1763." *Saturday Review*, November 4, 1950, 11.

11. McLeod, Donald. "Gloomy Memories, An Account of the Highland Clearances." electricscotland .com. Accessed April 7, 2015. http://www.electricscotland.com/hiStory/gloomy.htm.

12. Hill, Frederick. *The Pitman of Biddick and the Earldom of Perth. An Account of the Fate of James Drummond, Sixth Earl of Perth, after His Attainder in 1746, and of the Lives of His Descendants.* 1946.

13. Lewis, J. D. "Early History of Land Grants in North Carolina and the Roles of George Augustus Selwyn and Henry Eustace McCulloch." The Royal Colony of North Carolina Henry McCulloch, Esq.–A Man of Mystery Uncovered. January 1, 2007. Accessed April 7, 2015. http://www.carolana.com/NC/Royal_Colony/nc_royal_colony_henry_mcculloch.html.